I0612518

His Mate Series

Charli Mac

Winnipeg, Canada

Developmental editor: Sanford Larson
Proofreader: Margaret Larson

Published Nov 2022 by Deep Desires Press, an imprint of Story Perfect Inc.

Deep Desires Press
PO Box 51053 Tyndall Park
Winnipeg, Manitoba R2X 3B0
Canada

Visit http://www.deepdesirespress.com for more scorching hot erotica and erotic romance.

Subscribe to our email newsletter to get notified of all our hot new releases, sales, and giveaways! Visit deepdesirespress.com/newsletter to sign up today!

Contents

CHARLI MAC

HIS MATE SERIES

BOOK 1

HIS CURIOUS MATE

Chapter One

So, do you like to be spanked, baby? Tied up? Do you want to get down on your knees and take my cock all the way down your throat like a good whore?

I stared at my laptop screen, a flush running the length of my body. Jesus, that heated up fast. Playing with my tongue between my teeth—a nervous habit I'd never grown out of—I tapped out a reply.

I...don't know. This is my first time in this forum. I've never tried anything like this before.

Do you want to?

That was the million-dollar question, wasn't it? I'd read dozens of books where the heroine had gotten off on some dirty, kinky sex—and I'd gotten myself off to it thanks to my trusty vibrating friend. But reading about it was a lot different from doing it.

Anna, you there?

I'm here.

...I thought I'd scared you away.

No.

Not yet anyway. It had taken two glasses of wine to get up the courage to log on and create an account on the *Bound and Proud* forum, and another one before I'd dared to type a response to any of the men who'd sent private chat requests through to me. I'd picked this one, Alpha1980, which I doubted was his real name, because of his profile picture. It didn't show his whole face, only his eyes. They were emerald green and staring right out at me.

So, do you?

Do I? I frowned at the screen, confused.

You're cute, baby. Do you want to do all those bad girl things?

To hell with it, it was an online forum. If I couldn't even type the things I wanted, how was I ever going to try them in real life?

Yes.

Time crawled by in painful thumps of my heart as I waited for his response.

I thought so.

Something slipped free in me then, a reckless streak I didn't even know I had. What did they say? Admitting it was the first step in dealing with the problem. My problem was I was a lonely divorcee with a head full of dirty fantasies and no one to fulfill them.

I also had an empty wine glass.

When I got back to the computer, drink refilled, there was another message waiting for me.

Describe it to me.

I sat down slowly, gazing at the words. Describe one of my fantasies? Tell it to a total stranger? Embarrassment warred with excitement and won. Playing for time, I typed out a question mark and sent it back to him.

Don't be coy, baby. You know what I want. Describe it to me. If I was there, right now, what would you want me to do to you?

Oh God. My clit pulsed just thinking about it. Was I really going to do this?

If not now, when?

I'd want you to take charge, I wrote.

Go on.

You'd…you'd tell me to take my clothes off. Slowly. Then you'd tell me to get on my knees, head down, thighs spread, palms up, until you were ready for me.

Submissive's pose, that was called. I'd read all about that.

You'd get undressed, then you'd order me to crawl over to you and…

I paused, arousal making me wiggle on the chair. Was I really going to type this?

And…?

I liked what you said, about making me take you deep down my throat.

Have you done that before, baby?

No.

There's a first time for everything. What else?

What else? This guy was going to make me spontaneously combust. Taking a healthy slug of wine to cool myself down, I started typing again.

You wouldn't let me get you off. You'd get close, then tell me to stop. You'd take a grip on my hair and lead me to the kitchen.

Are you still on your knees? I'm picturing it.

If you like. You'd tell me to get up and lean over the island, legs spread. You'd make me reach around and part my ass cheeks so you can see my arousal.

And are you? Aroused?

Oh, yes. So aroused I was thinking about trying to type with one hand.

I want to touch myself.

Don't. Not yet. I like to think about you, squirming.

Jesus, this was hot. I was more turned on right now than I'd ever been with my husband, and I hadn't even heard his voice.

Are you touching yourself, Anna?

No.

Good girl. What next?

The counter's cold, and I complain about it. You smack my ass, tell me to be quiet.

Just the once?

Three times, until my skin is hot and pink.

I think it would take more than three, but if this is your first spanking, maybe I'll be nice.

It is, I typed. The walloping I'd got from my father after crashing my first car into a tree didn't count.

I thought so. For a nice girl, you're being a good whore. I think you've been thinking about this for a while.

I laughed. He had no idea. It had been eighteen months since I divorced, and the marriage had been sexless for three years before that. Dirty daydreams had been the only thing sustaining me.

Do I fuck you now?

No, I licked my lips, getting into the fantasy. *You go down on your haunches and lick me from behind. You tongue my clit and slip two fingers inside me. Once you've got them wet, you start circling my asshole.*

Butt play, Anna?

Yeah, butt play. Hidden in a drawer, in the deepest recesses of my bathroom, I had a little butt plug. I'd only ever played with it by myself, but it turned me on, the feeling of having something there, in my asshole. I wanted to try going out with it in one day, walking down the street, surrounded by people, none of them knowing my naughty little secret.

Another thing I was still trying to work up the courage to do.

Maybe, I replied. A smile slid across my face, the rush of endorphins from my own daring making me feel giddy.

He took a while to reply, so long I wondered if he'd gotten bored with the fantasy and left. Eventually I saw the little message box pop up on the screen. *Alpha1980 is typing...*

What are you doing right now, Anna? Are you home?

What? I stared at his words, my heart starting to thump for a different reason this time.

Yes.

I'm close by. Why don't we do this for real?

Thrown, I glanced out the darkened windows of my condo. There was a street light just down the road, but there were plenty of shadows for someone to hide in. Unnerved, I jumped up and closed the blinds.

How do you know where I am?

It's in your profile, baby. Along with your full name. That's not smart. We can talk about that when I'm spanking you. What do you say?

What did I say? Hell no, was the first thing. But underneath that…my body was singing. I'd never felt like this, and I wanted to know what it would be like to do all the things I'd imagined, with a partner who would take control, bend me to his pleasure. Make me submit to him in a way no other man had been able to.

It's late, I hedged. And I was also in my pajamas, hair in a messy bun, not a scrap of make up on my face.

It's 8.30 p.m. The night is young. We can meet in a public place, get to know each other. Then, when you've decided I'm not a psycho killer, I'll take you home and make you come so hard you see stars.

Sensible Anna told me to shut the laptop off, go to bed early with the last of the wine and spend the rest of the evening using the chat to bring myself to orgasm. It wouldn't be hard, I was already ready to detonate. But Sensible Anna had married a boring man, got me a boring job, and left me mid-thirties and dissatisfied.

Sensible Anna could go fuck herself.

All right, I typed. *Where do you want to meet?*

Chapter Two

Callum glanced around as he shouldered his way into the bar, leaving the cold and the rain outside. It was quiet, at 9 p.m. on a Wednesday night. The bar was propped up by a handful of regulars, three young boys were playing pool on the far side of the room and a couple of older ladies playing checkers at a small table in the corner. She wasn't here yet.

He ordered a beer and took a seat in a booth along the wall where he could watch the front door, his phone on the table in front of him. He'd given her his number before he logged off, giving her a way to contact him if she chickened out, but he had a feeling she wouldn't. Her need to be fucked, and fucked right, had practically screamed at him through the screen.

Hopefully, a night introducing a sweet little thing to the pleasures of Dominance and submission would be enough to settle his wolf, because the thing was driving him stir crazy, whining and restless and lashing out at his packmates. He'd always been fairly level headed, for a shifter, but right now he felt like killing someone or screwing someone, and option b came with a lot less hassle.

The door swung open and his gaze immediately went there to see a couple falling in, their arms wrapped around each other, faces chapped with cold but mouths smiling widely.

"Christ sake, Tommy," the barman growled. "I thought you'd gone home. The back alley is not for a quickie fuck."

"It's sheltered. We'd have gotten wet in the truck bed," Tommy replied, taking the two bottles of beer the barman laid on the counter for him and slapping down a note. "Don't you remember when you were young?"

"When I was young, old Hanson would have filled my ass with buckshot if I'd taken a girl out back for sex."

"Then maybe you need to get yourself a gun."

"Maybe I will!"

Callum smiled at the banter. The girlfriend, satisfaction writ all over her face, saw him watching as she headed to a table with the indomitable Tommy and winked. That made Callum grin, the expression still on his face as he turned back to the door and saw a woman standing there, pale faced and staring at him. Anna.

She was clutching her phone in her hand, and as he stood up to greet her, his phone lit up on the table, started to vibrate.

"It's you, then," she said, walking over shyly.

"It's me."

She was exactly like her picture, a candid shot of her outside in a park somewhere. A little on the short side, a little on the round side, her hair was dark brown and hung in waves around her face. She'd put some make-up on, but not much. Just enough to magnify already large brown eyes and add a little color to lips she was currently gnawing down on. She was obviously shy, but she'd come. He was impressed with that.

"Well, aren't you fucking adorable," he said.

She blushed, looking down and away from him. He eased out of the booth and took the final two steps to reach her.

"Let me get you a drink, yeah?" He leaned down to murmur the words in her ear, getting a blast of her scent as he did so. She'd sprayed on some perfume, something floral, but it was the dark, musky scent beneath that had everything in him sitting up and paying attention. She smelled fucking mouth-watering.

"Wine, please," she replied, voice low and sweet.

"You don't want to drink the wine here, baby. How about a beer? Something light?"

"Sure." She lifted her eyes to his long enough to flash a smile and he realized they weren't just brown, they had golden flecks in them that made them come alive. And if that wasn't some poetic shit, he didn't know what was.

He was on his way to the bar when he realized what was going on. The gut punch of her scent, the draw of her eyes that on any other woman would just be fucking eyes. His wolf, who'd been a cantankerous bastard for weeks, was practically rolling over in delight, tail wagging and tongue lolling. Mate, it said. Mine.

Mate.

Mine.

Fuck. Claim.

Christ. He took a moment at the bar to get himself together, ordering her beer and another one for him, and when he returned to the booth, she had her head down, fingers dancing across the screen of her cell phone.

"Letting your in-case-of-emergency contact know where you are?" he asked, smiling wryly as he slid in opposite her. He wanted to take the seat next to her, cuddle up to her on the narrow bench, but she'd deliberately perched herself on the end, leaving him no option but to sit on the other side of the table. She was going to take some wooing, his mate. Callum figured he was all right with that.

"No, sorry." She shrugged apologetically. "My husband wanted to know something about the insurance for the truck."

"Husband?" he asked, everything inside him going cold.

"Ex-husband," she corrected. "It's his truck, but it's still in my name. We need to get the title changed over."

Good. Callum wouldn't have to kill him then, providing his texting Anna was an unfortunate coincidence and not a regular thing.

"How long ago did you separate?"

"Eighteen months. I know we should have sorted everything by now, but it's...you know. There are a lot of threads to untangle when you end a relationship like that."

"I wouldn't know," Callum replied. The only time he got tangled was in between the sheets. He fucked women, he didn't get involved with them. Till now.

"Oh." She clearly didn't know what to say to that, her gaze going across the bar to the boys playing pool, hiding from him again.

"See that couple over by the jukebox?" he asked. She glanced in that direction and nodded. "They were just outside, fucking in the alleyway." He paused, licked his lips. "If I asked you to come out there, would you?"

He wasn't serious—though if she said yes, he'd be out the door like a shot—he was just testing her. Pushing.

She took a deep breath, shuddering slightly, then turned to him and held his gaze.

"It's raining," she said.

Fuck him if that wasn't a challenge in her stare. His shy little mate wasn't as submissive as he'd thought. Inexperienced, yes. Nervous, definitely. But there was a core of steel in there that Callum was going to have a lot of fun bending to his will.

"According to our friend Tommy over there, it's sheltered. We won't get wet."

She frowned, confused, then that little flame lit up inside her again. Callum could practically see it happen.

"Well then, what's the point if I'm not even going to get wet?"

She arched a brow and Callum burst out laughing.

"I am going to enjoy taming you," he said, the words coming out a growl.

She liked that. Red crept over her cheeks and she shifted slightly in her seat. Callum inhaled deeply and there it was, the scent of her arousal. His dick went from semi-hard to throbbing stone in the space of a heartbeat.

"What do you say, Anna? Are you going to let me take you home and do bad, bad things to you? Are you going to let me redden your ass, bend you over and fuck you? I don't have a kitchen island, but I'm sure we can work something out."

She took her time to think about it. Callum's wolf paced in his chest, impatient, but he wouldn't push her. If it wasn't this night, it would be the next. Or the one after that. One way or another, he'd have her. Mark her. Fuck her until she understood that she was his now. But he really, really wanted it to be tonight.

"All right then," she said, her head tucked down low, her eyes peeking at him from under thick lashes. "But I want to see stars. You promised."

Chapter Three

My heart was going a mile a minute as I climbed into Callum's truck and snapped my seatbelt on. The bar he'd suggested was close enough to my place that I'd walked over, despite the rain, but now we were going back to his.

I was going home with a man I barely knew, with the intention of having hot, nasty, dirty, sweaty sex. It was everything I'd ever fantasized about, but I still couldn't quite believe I was doing it.

This is a bad idea, a little voice whispered at the back of my head. *You don't know anything about this guy. Go home with him and you could wind up dead.*

I wasn't worried about that, though. Call me crazy, but I trusted him. There was something about him that said he'd keep me safe even as he was making me beg for mercy.

The sound of the door opening made me jump, then Callum slid into the driver's seat. I hadn't been able to see his picture on the forum, but he wasn't a disappointment. Tall and lean, he had dark brown hair and tanned skin, a tattoo winding up one arm all the way from his wrist until it disappeared beneath the sleeve of his T-shirt.

"All right?" he asked, firing up the engine.

I nodded.

"Having second thoughts?" There was a gentle smile on his face, though his eyes were intense as he stared at me. They were the same eyes as in his picture, and if I'd thought they were striking on the screen, it was nothing compared to the impact they had on me now. They almost glowed in the dim light of the truck cab and there was something raw and primal about them. It was hard to hold his gaze, but I found myself returning to it time and again.

"Anna?" he prompted. "If you don't want to do this, I can take you home."

"No," I said, my reaction to the idea of him leaving me almost visceral. "I want to come back with you. I'm just…nervous."

"I know," he grinned, "you're a good girl. By the end of the night, you're going to be my bad girl."

Yes, please, I thought.

It wasn't a long drive to his place. He'd been right, he was close. He lived just outside the town, on a five-acre lot with an older style ranch house. When I slipped out of the truck, I could still see the lights of civilization but the night was quiet, insects chirping, the only sound other than the crunching of gravel as Callum came round the vehicle toward me.

"Come on," he said, taking my hand and leading me toward the house, "let's get inside."

The front door opened directly onto the living room and when Callum open it and gestured for her to enter, I saw it was nicely decorated, if a little impersonal. The floors were a gleaming wood and there was a large fireplace with a big oak mantle. An aging sofa took up most of the floor space and faced a gigantic television, which took up a whole wall and was incongruous with the rustic look.

"I like my sports," Callum admitted, seeing me raise an eyebrow at it.

"I don't have a TV," I told him. "My ex-husband took the one we had and I've just never bothered to replace it. I stream shows on my laptop sometimes, but mostly I just read books."

And if that didn't make me sound like a pathetic wretch, I didn't know what did. Callum was smiling at me, though, one cheek tugged up in amusement.

"Of course you do," he said. "The next thing you'll be telling me you're a librarian."

"I am a librarian," I said. "I work in the Special Collections department at the university."

It wasn't what I wanted to do, I wanted to be a writer, but it was safe and secure, and it paid the bills. To Sensible Anna, it had been a good choice.

Callum dropped his head and shook it, and for a heart-stopping moment I thought he was going to say he'd changed his mind. That he'd take me home and find some other, more exciting woman to screw. When he lifted his head, though, his eyes were blazing.

"I just got a bucketload of new fantasies," he said. "And I can't wait to try them out. I want you to dress up in your librarian's gear, put your hair up. Do you have glasses?" I nodded. I'd put my contacts in because my eyes were my best feature, but normally I wore thick-framed specs. "Wear them next time."

"We'll see after tonight if there's going to be a next time," I replied.

It took all of my courage to make that snarky reply, but it was worth it to see the spark of heat that lit up Callum's eyes.

"There will be," he assured me. "Now, how did we start again. That's right," he lounged back on the armrest of his sofa, folding his arms across his chest. "Take off your clothes. Slowly."

I froze, staring at him. This was it. This was the moment I either went for it, or ran. If I ran, I'd regret it, I knew that. Still, it took a lot of courage to reach for the tie belted around the waist of my jacket. I tugged it free then worked on the buttons one by one, feeling naked as I slipped the garment off my shoulders even though I was wearing a perfectly respectable blouse and my good jeans, the ones that shaped my butt, underneath. Once the jacket was off, I toed off my shoes. Callum watched all the while, showing no impatience with my hesitance to get to the good stuff.

Blouse or jeans? I deliberated for a heartbeat then popped free my jeans button and pulled down the zip. I was no seductress, but with Callum watching my every move, I rolled my hips as I slid the denim down and off. I hadn't bothered with socks, so I didn't have to go through the indignity of bending down to remove them. Instead, I went to the placket of my blouse and worked the buttons free one by one. It wasn't a figure-hugging garment— I'd chosen it because it was a deep blue that I fancied brought out my eyes— and so it hung closed until I reached the bottom. Hands slipping up to grasp the lapels, I hesitated. Callum's gaze was riveted on my breasts, waiting for them to be revealed.

You've come this far, I told herself, don't back out now.

The blouse hit the floor with a soft splat and I stood before Callum in my underwear, heart galloping, hands in fists against my sides as I fought against the urge to cover myself.

"You're fucking gorgeous," he murmured, appreciation in his eyes. "Now the rest, Anna."

My fingers shook, but I got my bra unclasped and it joined the blouse on the floor, my underwear following a moment later.

"You know what to do now," he said, voice low.

I did. Slowly, one leg at a time, I got down on my knees. I dropped my head to stare at the floor and placed my hands palm up on my thighs.

The floorboards creaked with each step as Callum crossed the space toward me. His boots came into view and he tutted.

"Anna," he said reproachfully.

I fought with myself for a moment before I opened my thighs, an inch at first, then wider, until my pussy was fully visible, nestled beneath a small patch of trimmed hair.

Callum crouched down in front of me, and it was hard not to raise my head and look at him, but I managed.

"Good girl," he crooned, then he reached out and ran two fingers right up the center of me, dipping into the heat where I was already slick with need and sliding up until his fingers lightly brushed my clit.

I cried out, my whole body bucking, pleasure flaring like a streak of lightning, but I held my position.

Callum chuckled then stood up. I heard the sound of his belt buckle unfastening and the quieter rasp of his zip drawing down. A moment later, his hand touched my hair.

"Look at me," he said.

I lifted my head and saw him towering over me, his jeans pulled down to reveal his cock. It was already erect, thick and long, the tip glistening slightly. It was beautiful, like the rest of him.

"Hands behind your back," he ordered, and I complied. "Now suck me."

He was tall, I had to lift up on my knees to reach him, and it was awkward, without my hands to steady me, but I closed my mouth around him, taking in the head and sucking lightly, then drawing back and licking down his shaft, tracing a vein that ran all the way to the base of his cock.

I worked my way back up with open mouth kisses, then licked around his slit, taking in the musky taste of his precum.

"You're a tease," he growled, as I wrapped my lips around him once more, bobbing lightly, taking him to the back of my mouth but no further. "You know what I want, Anna."

I wanted it, too. But I'd never taken a cock that deep before, wasn't sure how to go about it.

"Will you help me?" I whispered, staring up into his intense gaze.

"Fuck yeah," he whispered. He took a handful of my hair, held it tightly. I tugged experimentally, but I couldn't dislodge his grip. He grabbed my chin and tilted it up, expression stern. "Pay attention. The first lesson is breathing, baby. Take a deep breath beforehand, then open wide."

I did as he said, and he took his cock and guided it into my mouth. He pushed in deep, right the way to the back, retreating slightly when I gagged.

"Lesson two, is swallowing. When you feel me there, swallow, baby."

He pushed forward again, and I panicked and gagged. He backed off, murmuring encouragement, and the second time I swallowed, felt him slip beyond, into my throat.

He groaned. "That's good, baby. That's really fucking good. Now for lesson three: hold on for the ride."

He slipped his cock back out until he was able to paint my lips with my saliva, giving me a moment to breath, then he surged in again, this time sliding back and forth in a sawing motion. I lost control of my hands, reaching out to grab at my thighs to steady myself, but he didn't rebuke me, snapping, "Look at me!"

I dragged my eyes up to meet his and saw they were mesmerized, watching me take his cock all the way until his pubic hair brushed my nose. It was uncomfortable, my jaw stretched wide and my lungs burning for air, but the satisfied, utterly male look on his face had me so turned on I could feel my arousal weeping onto the tops of my thighs.

He sped up, his thrusts reduced to short bursts accompanied by snarling grunts, then he pulled back, his hand jerking at his cock as it spewed jets of cum over my mouth and chin. I lapped at it, chasing the streams of pearly white, consumed to take him into me in this small way.

Afterward, he stood panting, his hand still wrapped firmly in my hair. He collected the remaining cum smeared across my face and fed it to me, his fingers mimicking the movements of his cock, encouraging me to lick up every last drop.

"That's what a good whore does," he murmured approvingly. "And do you know what good whores get?" I shook my head. "Rewarded."

Chapter Four

Callum was still reeling from the force of his orgasm when he led Anna through to his bedroom. The dirty little fantasy she'd spelled out to him in the BDSM forum had involved the kitchen counter, but after pushing her boundaries with the blow job, he wanted to reward her with the softness of his silk sheets. And the wolf wanted her in his bed, wanted to make sure her scent was marked there.

The way her pussy was weeping, her scent was going to be permanently ingrained into the fabric of the whole house, and Callum didn't mind that idea at all.

He'd made his bed that morning, thankfully. It was a monstrosity of a thing, a rustic wood frame put together by Callum himself. He'd only ever slept it in alone, but he liked room to play when he brought a female back. He couldn't claim that Anna would be the first woman to get fucked in his bed, but she'd be the first—and only—woman to spend the night in it. And every night after this one.

"On the bed, baby," he ordered.

She went, as sweetly submissive as she'd been since he told her to strip, but he knew that little defiant streak was still there, waiting to come out and sass him. He hoped she did it soon; the palm of his hand was itching to pinken her pretty ass like he'd promised.

"On your back," he told her.

She rolled over, propping herself up on her elbows, the arch of her back offering those tantalizing breasts up to him. They were more than a handful, her nipples stiffening under his gaze. She was all curves, and his eyes followed the sweeping line of her hips as she pinned her legs together and brought them up and to the side. It was a protective position, and it hid her pussy from his view. Callum wasn't having that. Leaning forward, he grasped her ankles and rearranged her, legs spread, knees bent and feet flat on the covers.

"Stay just like that," he warned.

Her thighs twitched, her teeth back to chewing on her lower lip and betraying her nervousness about lying there, fully exposed, but she held still, eyes riveted to him as he pulled his T-shirt over his head and kicked off his boots. His cock was already hard again and ready to go, thrusting outwards as he shoved his jeans down and off his legs.

"Are you ready to come, Anna?" he asked.

He knew she was, he could smell her heat, couldn't wait to taste it on his tongue. He wanted to hear it from her, though.

She nodded, eyes wide, breath coming in little pants.

"Not good enough, baby. I want to hear you say it."

"I want to come," she replied immediately. A flush was spreading over her cheeks and working its way down her throat. She was desperately shy, and he was pushing her hard, but he'd make it up when he had his tongue in her pussy and she was coming around his fingers.

"Lean back, baby. I want you to grab your knees and pull them up to your chest. That's it, just like that. Spread your legs a little wider. Good girl."

He moved forward toward the bed, went to his knees in front of her. She was wide open like this, her pussy gleaming with wetness, her clit peeking out from beneath its little hood. Just below, her asshole, a little rosette of delicate pink. Callum had been surprised when she'd thrown butt play into her little fantasy. No, not surprised. Fucking delighted.

He glanced up from his perusal of her sex and saw her watching him. She was apprehensive, maybe even a little scared.

"Don't be nervous," he murmured, running a soothing hand up and down the back of her thigh. "I'm going to make you feel good." He licked his lips, his mouth watering. "I want you to stay just like this, open and ready for me, all right?" He grinned wickedly, "If you can't hold still, I'll have to tie you down and make you."

She made a little whimper at that, but she wasn't scared. He saw the muscles in her core contract, her asshole clench. Oh yeah, she liked the idea of being bound and helpless. Next time.

Tired of making them both wait, he dipped two fingers into her wetness and slid up to circle her clit. He kept the touch feather-light, but she jerked like he'd electrocuted her. His little mate was sensitive.

Eyes on hers, making sure she was watching, he dropped his fingers back down to her core and worked them inside. Pumping slowly in and out, he stiffened his tongue and flicked it over her clit, a quick swipe that had her crying out. She dropped her hold on one of her knees, was halfway to trying to close her pussy off to him before she remembered herself.

"I'm going to let you get away with that one," he said, "but you try to close your legs to me again and there's going to be punishment."

She flexed on the word 'punishment', and he could see the curiosity in her eyes. She wanted to know what he was going to do. Callum had a whole arsenal of ways to punish a naughty sub, but he wasn't going to tell her what they were. Let her wonder.

"It's too much," she whined.

"No, it isn't. We're only just starting, baby." He leaned forward and just blew over her pussy. She was so wound up she almost came then and there, pulsing around his invading fingers.

"Not yet," he scolded, pulling them free. "I'm not done with you yet."

Giving her a chance to settle down, he ran his fingertips around her outer lips, teasing her, making her squirm as she sought to get his touch on her hungry little clit where she wanted it. He smiled as he lifted his fingers to his mouth, made sure she was watching as he sucked her essence off them. Fuck, she tasted good. He reached down and palmed his cock, which was throbbing, desperate to get inside her.

"Tell me what you want, Anna."

"I want to come," she pleaded.

He grinned. Words were hard for her, made her squirm and whimper, made her needy—which was exactly how Callum liked her.

"And how should I make you come, hmmm?"

"With…with your tongue."

"Just my tongue?"

She gasped, shaking her head. He licked at her, once, from her asshole all the way to her clit and she gave a little wail.

"Come on, Anna. Just my tongue?"

"Your fingers, too."

"Now we're talking." He paused, grinning, knowing he was taking her outside her comfort zone. She loved it, though. "Where should I put my fingers, baby?"

He started stroking her as he spoke, rubbing either side of her clit, his fingers spread just enough to deny her the contact she needed.

"Oh God," she panted. "I…*everywhere*."

"You got it."

Giving in to the wolf's need to taste more of her, he replaced his fingers with his mouth, lapping at her clit with the flat of his tongue in slow, steady strokes. His fingers he dipped down to press into her channel, going in deep and crooking them to rub against that little rough spot on her front wall. After being teased so much, held taut on a bow, the double stimulation was too much for Anna and she thrashed. Wanting to draw it out a little longer, Callum backed off, nuzzling at her thigh while he fucked her with his fingers.

She was a greedy little thing, though. As soon as she'd come away from the immediate edge, she started flexing her hips at him. "More," she pleaded.

He pulled his fingers all the way out and she whined. That whine turned into an eager little groan when he started circling her clit again with the tip of his tongue, the movements light and fast, rushing her to the brink of orgasm but not allowing her to slip over the edge. He took his fingers, slick with her arousal, and dropped down to her rosebud. He circled that, too, matching the motion of his tongue.

Anna had been writhing against him, chasing her orgasm, but now she stilled entirely.

"Callum?" she whispered.

"Butt play, Anna," he reminded her. "That's what was in your fantasy. Let's see how you like my finger, then we'll see about my cock."

It wouldn't be tonight, though. He pressed in lightly with the tip of one finger and groaned at the pressure. She was tight, would need to be slowly introduced to the pleasures of anal sex. Her sphincter pulsed as he pushed into the first knuckle then retreated. Moved a little deeper, then slid back. He lifted his head to watch her. She wasn't staring down at him anymore. She'd dropped her head back to the cover and was whipping it from side to side, her grip on her knees white-knuckled. Knowing he was being cruel, he blew on her clit again.

Her whole pussy spasmed, her rear muscles clamping down against his finger. She arched her back, pushing her pussy up into his face.

"Please, Callum. Please!"

"All right baby, since you asked so nicely."

He shoved his thumb into her core, pumping it in tandem with his finger in her asshole and dropped his head to her clit. Pressing tight against that hard little nub with his tongue, he rubbed and sucked simultaneously.

Anna screamed. Her entire body clenched for an endless moment, then she was jerking and bucking, coming hard. Callum held her still with one arm wrapped around her thigh, keeping up the pressure on her clit and fucking her with his thumb and fingers, making her ride out the wave. He didn't stop until her hands started patting at his head, his shoulders, chasing him away.

"No more, please. I can't take it." Then she said the magic words. "I need you in me."

Chapter Five

Callum gave an honest to God growl when I said that. He crawled up my body, which felt limp as a noodle after an orgasm that made me wonder if I'd ever actually come before in my life, running kisses up over my stomach. He stopped to nip at my breasts, which had never been particularly sensitive but were aching now, upset at having missed out on all the fun. I held my breath, hoping he'd play awhile, draw my nipple into his mouth, rub it with his tongue, maybe even bite at it a little bit with his teeth, pinch it with his fingers, but he moved on, licking my throat then coming up over me, those intense eyes staring down into mine.

Next time, I promised my breasts.

Because as far as I was concerned, there was definitely going to be a next time.

I tilted my chin up, expecting him to kiss me, but instead he nuzzled at my nose with his. It was surprisingly sweet.

When he spoke, though, his voice was rough and commanding. Dominant.

"Roll over. On your hands and knees."

I hesitated, because my legs were spread wide around his hips and I could feel the hard length of his cock against my soaked pussy. All he had to do was shift his hips a little bit and he'd be *in me*, easing the ache that my mind-blowing orgasm had only exacerbated.

He growled again, the sound making my heart flutter in my chest, torn between panic and excitement. "Now, Anna."

He didn't shift back to give me any room, lifting his hips only enough for me to slide my leg out, the heat of his body crowding me, letting me know exactly who I was in the bed with. Exactly who was in charge. When I made it onto my front, he slid an arm under my stomach and pulled me up on my knees, the heat of his front plastered to my back, then he pushed down on my shoulders until I dropped onto my elbows.

My back was arched in this position, my pelvis tilted to give Callum access to my clit, my pussy and my asshole. I held my breath, waiting for him to penetrate me, my core clenching in readiness.

"Mmmm," he said, running a warm hand up and down the length of my spine. "I like this. Look at you, all ready to be fucked. *Are* you ready, Anna?"

"Yes." Though I'd come—and come hard—I could feel the excitement building in me again. Every time Callum spoke, whispering filthy things to me in that rasping, sexy voice, my arousal soared to new limits. He was so male, so dominant.

He was exactly what I'd always fantasized about.

"Good." He gathered some of my slickness with his thumb and pressed against my asshole again, making me feel the pressure but circling slowly, not pushing inside.

I tensed. He wasn't thinking about fucking me *there*, was he?

"Callum—"

"We've got something to discuss before I take this hot pussy of yours, though."

My relief that he wasn't planning to try and initiate me into anal sex was short lived as I frowned at his words. We did?

"What?" I asked, the word coming out in a little gasp as I pushed back slightly, searching for his cock, hoping he might stop teasing me with his thumb and slide it a little deeper inside.

"Mmhmm." He stopped stroking my back and moved his palm to rub over my flank. "I believe I said we needed to talk about your profile. About what you were putting up there."

"I changed it," I panted. "I updated my privacy settings so all you can see now is my first name."

"Good girl," he crooned. "But what about all those men who could've seen it before? You know how many perverts there are looking to take advantage of naive women on these things?"

"You were there," I pointed out.

I tried to lift up, not wanting to have this conversation while I was bent over, like a mare about to be seasoned, but Callum put his hand between my shoulder blades and pushed me back down.

"You're lucky I was there," he said. "You're lucky you picked me to chat to." He paused. "I think you need a little lesson to remind you not to be so trusting in the future. You're going to count to five, Anna."

He anticipated my attempt to rise this time, his hand in the middle of my back holding me in position.

"Callum—"

"Five, Anna. I think that'll be enough to turn you a beautiful pink color."

I quivered, wanting him to do it and not. Afraid to feel the sting, but at the same time intrigued.

Feeling cheeky, I turned my head so I could look at him out of the corner of my eye, one eyebrow raised.

"I thought you said you'd make it three, since it's my first time?"

Crack!

The first smack came even as his face was unfurling into an amused smile. All the breath blew out of me in a rush as I registered first the sound, then the sharp sting. It bloomed across my ass cheek, a hot throb.

"Count, Anna," he reminded me, "or I keep going."

"One!" I squeaked hastily.

He gave me a little nod of approval, then spanked me again.

I gasped, the sting much more intense this time, the throb going deeper.

"Two," I choked out, wondering why all those women in those books actually liked this. It hurt! It—

Callum rubbed a couple of soothing circles into my skin then drew back slightly. I braced, waiting for the next smack and thinking I really didn't want it, but he slid inside me instead.

"Ahhhh!" The noise I made was half surprise, half moan as he penetrated me deeply, forcing swollen tissue to accept his thick, hard cock. I had a moment to wonder at the incredible fullness before he pulled out and pushed forward, pulled out and pushed forward.

Oh God, that felt good.

He'd angled his hips just right so that every forward motion rubbed against my g-spot, sending a rolling wave of pleasure rippling through my lower body.

"Yes!" I cried. "I…oh fuck, Callum. Yes!"

He thrust twice more, the pleasure building until I started to anticipate another orgasm, then pulled free.

Smack!

His open hand landed on the other cheek this time, startling me. I'd barely wheezed out, "Three!" before he was back inside me, thrusting hard, a hand reaching around to press against my pubic bone, fingertips nudging my clit every time his hips pushed me forward.

I made a strangled sound as pleasure returned with a surge. It coalesced with the burn from his handprints until it was all one big hot, throbbing rush of sensation.

Slap!

He didn't withdraw this time, barely pausing in his thrusting as he skated his palm across my cheek, whipping up the sting. My clit pulsed hard, making my eyes roll back in my head and I barely heard his warning, "Anna!"

"Four," I got out. Then, "Oh fuck, Callum. I'm going to come!"

"Not yet," he grunted. "I said five."

I didn't know how he expected me to hold off, not when he was thrusting inside me like a battering ram, fucking me with deep strokes that set fire to that glorious spot inside I'd never even found on my own explorations. I lost control of my body, barely able to remember to keep breathing as I waited for the next strike, anticipated it desperately.

"Now, Anna," he commanded, punctuating his words with a final smack then grabbing my hips with both hands and plunging deeper and faster. I cried out at the loss of his fingers on my clit, but this new rhythm hit my g-spot over and over in quick rapid pulses. My orgasm came barreling over me, flushing the length of my body, rolling on and on as Callum fucked me.

Suddenly he stuttered in his movements, hips jerking out of rhythm. He was coming, spilling his seed inside me. It almost seemed like I could feel it, a wicked heat shooting deep inside. He leaned forward and latched onto my shoulder with his teeth, biting down as he lost himself in his own pleasure, the sharp spike of pain making me wince in my satiated haze.

He held on tight as he shuddered, then his weight dropped onto my back and we both collapsed into the softness of his bed. He was heavy, sprawled out on top of me, but I liked it. His cock was still buried deep inside me and I could feel the wetness of our mingled releases between my thighs.

"Wow," I murmured, arching against him, feeling the slight sweat from his body, the crispness of his sprinkling of chest hair against my back. Then, smiling wickedly, I murmured, "Five."

"Hmm?" I felt his pause, then a ripple against me as he chuckled. "Too late, Anna baby. We'll have to start again. You can remind me…next time."

So, he wanted there to be a next time, too? That was good. Really good.

He lifted off me slightly, still keeping me pinned beneath him with his lower body, and traced a finger over the spot on my shoulder where he'd got me with his teeth. It stung.

"You bit me," I said.

"I did." He didn't apologize, just licked at the wound.

"Is it bleeding?" I asked, reaching around to feel.

"A little bit. Don't worry about it." He batted my hand away and licked at it again.

"You a vampire?" I asked sleepily.

"Something like that," he murmured, still laving at the spot.

"I don't think that's hygienic." I yawned halfway through, the final word coming out a mush.

"Sleep, Anna," he whispered. "You need to rest so I can fuck you again."

I liked that idea, my inner muscles pulsing around Callum's cock, softening but still large inside me, but I was too tired to suggest we go for another round right then. I closed my eyes and let sleep claim me.

Chapter Six

My dreams were vivid. I was padding through a forest, the floor a carpet of crisp autumn leaves. Sunlight dappled down through the trees, sparkling on the surface of the fast-flowing stream I was following. It looked inviting, but I didn't have time to dip my toes into its coolness. I was looking for someone.

Lifting my head, I sniffed deeply. There it was, that wild, dangerous scent that belonged only to him. I followed it and found him lounging in a pool of bright sunshine. He lifted his head and looked at me, those piercing green eyes glowing brightly. It wasn't Callum's face, though, wasn't his sharp-angled jaw or his heavy, slashing brows. Those eyes were staring out of me from the face of a wolf.

Its body was lean and long-legged, its fur a thousand different shades of black and white and grey. It wasn't until it rolled to its feet and trotted over to me that I realized I was a wolf, too. It nuzzled at me, rubbing the side of its face against mine, then it yipped and turned away, running a few paces before looking over its shoulder at me, daring me to follow. I couldn't, though, my feet seemed pinned to the floor, holding me in place. The last thing I saw was its tail, raised high in the air, as it disappeared over a fallen tree trunk while I stood there, too afraid to follow.

I woke up with a heavy feeling of regret and a pressing need to pee. Callum's arm was flung over my stomach, his face tucked into the crook of my neck. Lifting my head, I saw the clock on the wall said 7am. Too early to get up, but I'd have to do something about my bladder before I could go back to sleep.

I slid out from under him as carefully as I could, but his eyes flashed open before I made it to the edge of the bed.

"Bathroom," I explained quietly.

He gave a little grunt and closed his eyes again. "Thought you were trying to skip out on me."

"Not yet," I replied, smiling. "I'm hoping you're going to make me breakfast."

There was no response to that—he was already snoring softly. Amused, I grabbed his T-shirt off the floor and pulled it on, breathing in the masculine scent of him, then tiptoed out of the bedroom. I found the bathroom just a couple of doors down, opposite a second bedroom that had been turned into an office. I did my business and washed my hands, taking in my appearance in the mirror above the sink.

I looked like a woman who had been well and truly fucked. I grinned at myself, barely recognizing Sensible Anna in my tousled hair and flushed cheeks. My eyes, too, looked brighter, the gold specks seeming to take over more of the brown than usual. I twisted my shoulder to look at the bite mark Callum had left on me, but it wasn't as bad as I'd thought. There was no blood and hardly any bruising, it was really just a pink mark in the shape of his teeth. I'd have to wear high collared tops until it went away.

Or maybe I wouldn't.

I quite liked the idea of people noticing, wondering what saucy things I might have gotten up to. No matter how lurid their imaginations were, they weren't likely to come close to what I'd actually done. My lower stomach clenched just remembering it. Never mind breakfast, perhaps Callum would be up for a little more fun before I had to go. I certainly had enough fantasies stored up that I wanted to try.

Body humming with anticipation, I left the bathroom, thinking about waking him up with my mouth, showing how well I'd learned last night's lessons. I stopped dead in the doorway, though, because there was a man in the hallway.

He was tall and rangy, with features so similar to Callum's I guessed he must be a brother or a cousin. He was dressed in workman's gear, cargo pants with a dark blue hoodie and a bright orange safety vest over the top. He looked as surprised to see me as I was him, but that quickly gave way to a slow, knowing grin.

"Hey, there," he said. "I'm going to guess you're the reason Callum forgot he was supposed to meet me at the site at six thirty."

"Uh, maybe," I replied.

I was uncomfortably aware that I was standing there in nothing but a T-shirt, although it was long enough to hit me mid-thigh so at least it covered all my important bits. I felt a lot more naked than I was, though, when the man made a show of looking me up and down. I wanted to run back to bed, to Callum, and hide, but he was standing between me and the bedroom.

"I'm Gregor, Callum's cousin." So, I'd been right, they were related. "I wish he'd called me," he said ruefully, eyes dropping to my breasts. "We could have shared."

I must have looked as shocked as I felt because he laughed.

"Have I offended you? I'm sorry. You look a little classier than Callum's usual conquests. Though," he grinned, "you don't look any less fucked."

My face threatened to go up in flames. Giving a tight smile, I muttered a polite, "Excuse me." I took a step to the side, hoping he'd get the message and move out of my way, but instead he came toward me.

"You know, there's nothing so urgent it can't wait at the site. How about you and I go and wake Callum up and we'll have some fun? We could—" He stopped two feet away, his gaze fixed on the mark on my neck. I lifted my hand up to cover it, unnerved by the astonishment that slid over his face.

"Fuck me," he muttered.

He took another step closer still, ignoring the way I backed up into the wall to get away from him, leaning down to sniff at me.

"No fucking way. He's mated you. Where the hell did he even find you?" He backed up a step, frowning slightly. "What pack are you from?"

"I...what?" I asked. "I don't understand. Look, why don't I go and tell Callum you're here and—"

"You're not from a pack, you're human. Or you were." His eyes widened. "You don't even know, do you?" he whispered. "He didn't tell you."

"Tell me what? I don't know what you're—"

A loud snarl ripped through the air and we both froze. The next moment, Callum had shoved his way in between the two of us and was up in Gregor's face. He was completely naked, I noticed. He hadn't even taken the time to pull on boxers.

"What the fuck are you doing here?" he demanded.

Gregor retreated a step but he didn't back down from Callum's anger.

"What do you think? We were meant to be meeting at the site an hour ago. You didn't show, so I came here." He flashed a glance over Callum's shoulder at me, eyes amused. "Now I see why."

The snarling sound came again and I realized it was coming from Callum. It was an inhuman sound. It gave me tingles, my body frightened by it and drawn to it at the same time.

"You better not have touched her."

"I didn't," Gregor protested, "I was just saying hello." He looked to me. "Right sweetheart?"

He'd said a bit more than hello, but given how furious Callum was, I didn't think it was smart to mention that Gregor had suggested we go wake him up for a three-way.

"Sure," I said.

Callum whipped his head round toward me, his eyes running up and down my body as if he was searching for some sign of injury. Satisfied that I was unharmed, he swung back to Gregor and advanced another step. "I don't want you near my mate."

His...mate? What? I shuffled back a step, taking refuge in the safety of the bathroom. Callum had seemed normal enough last night—okay, he'd seemed incredible—but now he was starting to freak me out.

See, Sensible Anna grumbled, *this is why we don't go home with strange men. I told you so.*

I really hated that she was right.

"Okay, Callum, okay. Chill. You're starting to freak her out. Look at her, she's scared."

Callum spun around to stare at me, and I saw his canines, which had been perfectly normal last night, were now elongated, razor sharp in his mouth. His eyes were burning, the pupils pin pricks and the irises a startling shade of green that was just not normal. He took a step toward me and I made a split-second decision. I stepped back and slammed the door, twisting the lock.

"Anna?" The pounding started as soon as Callum rattled the handle and realized it wouldn't give. "Anna, open the door."

I shook my head, even though he couldn't see. When he did it again, hitting the door so hard it rattled in its hinges, I scuttled back until I hit the toilet, sitting down on it and clutching at the lid beneath me.

"Anna, baby, come on. Open the door and just let me explain. You're safe, all right? I promise you're safe. I just...I need you to trust me a little bit, can you do that."

I bit my lip to hold in a frightened sob. I wanted to go home. I looked to the window, the only other way out of the room, but I was wearing nothing but a T-shirt and I'd come here in Callum's car.

I was thinking about trying it anyway when I heard him speaking to Gregor. "Go around the house, would you? Make sure she doesn't try to climb out the window."

"Callum, seriously. Take a moment to think here, all right? You just need to give her a moment to calm down. She'll—"

"Just fucking do it, Gregor. It's your fault I'm in this mess!"

"My fault? I'm not the one who mated her, turned her, without telling her a God damned thing."

I heard the sound of a scuffle and drew my legs up onto the toilet, curling into a ball and hugging my knees. There was a muffled, "Oof!" then Callum repeated. "Outside."

It was quiet then, but I didn't trust it. I kept my eyes on the door, waiting for Callum to start trying to break his way in again.

When his voice came, it sounded tired and a little sad. "Anna, sweetheart, please. Can you just open the door? We need to talk about this, face to face."

I didn't answer him. I was too busy staring at my hands, which I'd lifted up to burrow into my hair. Something odd had caught my eye as I'd raised them past my face and I paused, examining them with dawning horror.

I'd painted my nails a pretty lavender for my date with Callum. I could still see remnants of it, clinging to the surface, but my short, sensible nails had thickened and lengthened, the ends tapering to wicked sharp points. I had claws.

Chapter Seven

Last night had been the best night of Callum's life, but his morning was going to shit. His mate had locked herself in the bathroom and was refusing to come out, was refusing to even talk to him. He sighed, banging his head back against the wall. Gregor was right, it was his fucking fault. When he'd realized what Anna was to him, he should have explained everything to her. Told her what he was, what would happen when they mated.

Instead, he'd thought with his dick and now look at the mess he was in.

His stomach rumbled, but he ignored it. He'd intended to make Anna pancakes, feed her them by hand and then talk to her about things. After that, if things had gone according to the plan he'd constructed in his head last night, he'd been going to tumble her back into bed and see if he could convince her to ride him. His cock stiffened at the image, still hopeful, but Callum knew he'd be lucky if she didn't call the cops before she high-tailed out of there.

She'd be back—she'd have no option, selfish bastard that he was, he'd made sure of that—but it wasn't exactly the best start to a mating he'd ever heard of.

He was just deliberating whether he should go and hang out in the living room, give her the space to get to the bedroom and at least put her own clothes on before she had to face him, when he heard the scraping of the lock turning. He wanted to jump up, reach for her as soon as she opened the door, but he held his position on the floor. He needed to tread carefully, he didn't want to scare her into running and hiding from him again.

When she opened the door, her face was pale, her eyes wide with fright. She held her hands up in front of her, showing Callum evidence of the mini shift he'd forced her into when he frightened her so badly.

"Callum," she whispered, "what's happening to me?"

He couldn't help it then, he had to go to her. Lifting up slowly so she wouldn't spook, he ignored her outstretched hands and put his hands on her shoulders, gathering her in to him. She was so scared, she went, head tucking into his chest.

"It's all right," he said. "It's normal."

She hiccupped a slightly hysterical laugh. "It is *not* normal, Callum."

"Not for a human," he agreed, "but it is for a shifter."

"*I'm* a human," she protested.

Not anymore, Callum thought.

It was wrong, he knew, but he couldn't help the surge of pride seeing his mate come into herself. Shifters were almost always born, not made. Most humans couldn't make the change, and if he'd screwed and bitten any other female, nothing would have happened except she'd have had a good time. A really good time. There were a few, though, who had the ability. Callum didn't know why, he wasn't some smart-arse scientist. Maybe they had a shifter descendent, or maybe they had some mutant gene, who the fuck knew. The important thing was that Anna was one of them—and now she was a shifter. Just like him.

"Come and get some breakfast," he suggested. "I'll explain everything."

He led her into the kitchen and pulled together some toast and slightly stale cereal. She was so on edge he didn't think she would sit still long enough for him to whip up some pancakes. Which was a shame, because if there was one thing Callum was good at—other than fucking—it was making pancakes.

"Do you have coffee?" she asked.

"Only decaf," he said apologetically. "The real stuff makes me jittery."

The wolf was already restless, constantly on edge. Give it caffeine and it became crazed.

She waited until she had her coffee in front of her, both hands wrapped around its heat, her breakfast beside her untouched, before she hit him with her gaze. He felt it wallop him right in the chest. He should have known when she'd challenged him in the bar, made those saucy, snarky little comments when they were having sex, that she wasn't a natural submissive. Oh, she wanted to submit, but she needed a hell of a strong male to do it, because she had a dominant streak a mile wide. Now that she was a shifter, it was easy to see. She was scared right now, uncertain, so it was bottled up tight inside, but when she grew into herself he was going to have a feisty female on his hands. Callum couldn't fucking wait.

"All right," she said. "You wanted a chance to explain. So, explain."

"I'm not human." She raised an eyebrow at that, but said nothing, encouraging him to go on. "I'm a shifter. I can…transform into a wolf. What you did back there, with your claws? That was a mini-shift. You probably did it unconsciously, in the stress of the moment, but you can learn to control it."

"Like you did, in the hallway, with Gregor," she commented. Callum frowned. *In the hallway?* "Your teeth?"

Oh. He grimaced. "That wasn't on purpose. I was stressed too."

"So, you infected me."

"Infected? I...no. It isn't a disease, Anna. It's a gift. I gave it to you."

"Well, don't you think you should have fucking asked if I wanted it?"

He started, thrown by the vehemence of her words. "That's the first time I've heard you swear," he commented.

She blushed. She fucking blushed. God damn, but she was adorable.

"I swear a lot," she said. He raised his eyebrows and she made a face. "Mostly in my head." She sighed, looking as exhausted as Callum felt. "What does this all mean, Callum?"

It means your life has changed.

It means you just inherited a pack, a bunch of nosey bastards who'll want to poke and prod into every aspect of your life.

It means you're mine.

Right. He could just imagine her reaction if he told her that.

"On the face of it, not that much. You'll still go out to work, you'll still have friends. I mean, you'll want to take a leave of absence until you understand your wolf, until you're sure you have her under control, but after that," he shrugged. "Not that much has to change."

"You said I was your mate."

"You are my mate." The words were out before he could call them back, but he wouldn't have anyway.

"Why? Because we spent last night together? According to Gregor, I'm far from the first female you've had in your bed. Do you have mates all over the city?"

"I only have one mate," he growled, "and it's you. I knew the moment I scented you, what you were to me. You wouldn't have become changed otherwise."

"Don't you think that's something you should have shared with me?" The confrontation was gone from her tone, and the question was harder to answer because of that.

"I should have," he admitted. "I just...fuck Anna. I'm an asshole, okay? You were there, all sweet and excited and just about trembling with the need to jump on my cock, and I couldn't help myself."

"You should have given me a choice," she said quietly.

"Should I have?" He glanced up at her, his heart on his fucking sleeve. "I didn't get one. Shifters don't pick their mates, their wolf does."

That hurt her. He saw it, though she wiped the expression off her face between one heartbeat and the next, taking a slug of her coffee, picking up a piece of toast.

"Well, maybe we can just…not be mates. I mean, if you don't want me—"

"I didn't say I don't want you," he told her quickly. "The wolf chose you, but I'm not complaining." He paused. "You had a good time last night, didn't you?"

She sighed and he thought she was going to deny it, but the tell-tale flush started to creep up her neck. "Last night was incredible. But—"

"But?"

"It was sex, Callum."

"It was a connection."

"A *physical* connection."

"No." He shook his head. "Don't lie. I touched your soul last night." He reached for her, fingers wrapping around her hand. "You touched mine."

She pulled in a deep, shuddering breath, her eyes shining.

"I'm scared, Callum. I don't know who I am anymore. I don't know what's happening to me." She looked away. "I wish I could turn back the clock and ignore your message."

She was tearing his heart out.

"I don't," he said. "I never expected to find my mate, but now that you're here, I feel…" he shrugged, embarrassed, "…blessed. I feel blessed, Anna."

She stared at him, eyebrows pulled together, lost and confused and scared and so fucking cute.

"What now?" she asked.

Now you move in with me and love me and screw me and have my babies and we live happily ever after.

Even Callum wasn't stupid enough to say that.

"You'll need to meet the pack," he said. "Be introduced to the Alpha. We'll help you understand the wolf, teach you how to shift."

"I'll be able to do that?" she asked. "Shift?"

He nodded.

She licked her lips slightly, smiled. "I had a dream last night, you know.

You were in it, as a wolf. I guess it was a premonition." She blew out a breath. "And what about me and you?"

"We're mates, Anna. You're mine and I'm yours. But I understand that it's, well, it's a hell of a fucking shock."

She snorted a laugh then covered her mouth with her hand, horrified. A-dor-able.

"The stronger your wolf becomes in you, the harder you'll find it to fight the connection between us. She'll want to be with me."

"She has good taste."

He was about to plough on with the little speech he'd prepared when her words registered.

"She...does?" When Anna raised an amused eyebrow, he rolled his eyes. "That wasn't supposed to be a question."

"If it was up to you, what would happen next?" she asked.

If it was up to him? They'd go to her place right now and collect all her stuff. Then he'd take her to bed and not leave it for the next month.

"It's not up to me," he said instead. "We're a partnership, you and me."

He was quite impressed with that answer, but a frown creased Anna's forehead.

"If it *was* up to you, though?"

"You'd move in."

"What?"

"You'd move in with me. Let me guide you through all this shit." He took a deep breath. "Let me love you."

"You mean sex."

"I mean love."

She snorted, rolled her eyes. "People don't fall in love overnight."

"Shifters do. When it's their mate."

"Then it isn't real," she threw back.

"It feels real," he told her. "It feels like I'll die if you walk out of here."

She took a deep breath, then another. When she looked away from him, Callum felt his heart plummet.

"All right," she said.

He blinked, confused, convinced he'd misheard.

"What?"

"All right. We'll...try. I mean, God knows I'll need someone's hand to hold. And I trust you."

"You do?"

She laughed, the sound sweet music to Callum's ears.

"I shouldn't?"

"I haven't really given you reason to," he admitted.

"I know. Still, I feel safe with you."

"That's the mate bond," he told her. "It pushes you toward me."

"Maybe," she said, "but I was drawn to you when you were just *Alpha1980*, a stranger on my computer screen."

"That is not a cool username," he replied, wincing. "I'm amazed you even bothered to reply to me."

"I thought it was pretty cool," she admitted, smiling impishly, "and I'm glad I did."

She smiled at him and he felt his heart soar, hope for the future finally daring to take hold.

They were interrupted by the front door banging open, Gregor standing there red-cheeked with the cold, his hands tucked into his armpits.

"So, I assume she's not escaping out the bathroom window," he commented sarcastically. "Can I come in now? It's fucking freezing." He eyed Anna's toast and cereal with a distinct lack of enthusiasm and turned to Callum optimistically. "Are you making pancakes."

Anna, too, looked down at her untouched toast and now soggy cereal. She gave Callum a hopeful little smile. "I like pancakes."

He stood up, his wolf wagging its tail in happiness. "Pancakes it is!"

Chapter Eight

I stood in my bedroom and listened to the sound of Callum downstairs, talking on the phone and clearing his schedule for the rest of the week. It was crazy, totally insane. Sensible Anna was shaking her head at me in utter disdain, but I didn't care. For once in my life, I was going to do the stupid thing and enjoy it.

If I got my heart broken, well, I'd rather live with memories than regret.

A restless, uneasy feeling wriggled inside me. Go back to Callum, it said. Cuddle up to him, smell him. Fuck him.

The wolf, or so Callum said. It was a strange sensation. I felt like I was sharing my body. It didn't have thoughts, exactly, but it had no problem conveying what it wanted. Right now, it was blasting me with an image of me, on the kitchen counter, legs spread, Callum thrusting his cock inside me. A flush of arousal rolled over me, because along with the image came a cramping at my core, my nipples beading. The wolf was right, that would feel good.

"Concentrate," I told myself, "pack. Then you can go downstairs and do the nasty with him."

I was trying to be pragmatic, just taking things for a few days. If it didn't work out, it would be no big deal to stuff my things back in my duffel bag and come home. I had a feeling that wasn't going to happen, though. I'd dated Colin, my moronic ex-husband, for three years before we got married, and I'd never felt about him the way I did for Callum. Infatuation, I told myself, that was probably what it was. Well, maybe so, but I was going to wring every drop from it either way. And maybe, just maybe, it was something more. Maybe we were mates, as Callum said.

Someone had to live happily ever after or there wouldn't be so many stories, right?

I'd already called my work and begged for an impromptu week's holiday, so I didn't bother packing any work clothes, though, as my gaze landed on my tortoiseshell glasses, sitting discarded on my dresser, an idea sparked into my head.

I want you to dress up in your librarian's gear, put your hair up. Do you have glasses?

Playing with my tongue between my teeth, I picked them up and rolled them around in my hands. Did I dare?

"Baby? You just about there?" Callum's shout from downstairs made me jump. I put the glasses back on the dresser and continued stuffing clothes and bathroom necessities into my bag. Pajamas, Anna. And underpants. Nice ones.

"Almost," I called back.

A minute later, I was finished. My gaze went back to those glasses. My heart started thumping in my chest as I realized I was going to do it.

"Seize the day, Anna," I told myself.

I started yanking at my clothes, shimmying out of my jeans and pulling the T-shirt I'd changed into back over my head. I tugged a severe white blouse from its hanger, one that I'd retired because I'd put on ten pounds since my divorce and it was now snug across my bust, and shrugged my way into it, pairing it with a pencil skirt that I never wore to the library because it was a shade too tight, the slit running a little too high. And, also, because I dressed like someone's Great Aunt Mildred at the library, in beige slacks and brown loafers.

I rooted around in my underwear drawer until I unearthed the single pair of stockings I owned, fancy ones with a line up the back. When I slipped them on, I noticed the lace toppers flashed every time I took a step. Perfect. My hair I wound up into a severe bun and then I fished out my contacts—which took a couple of attempts because I was severely out of practice—and jammed my glasses on my face.

I looked in the mirror and a different woman stared back. She had curves and attitude, the prim and proper outfit sexed up with a lacy, push up bra and the hint of lace at my thigh. And then, of course, there was the look on my face. Hiding behind those thick glasses, the woman in the mirror had shining gold eyes that said she wanted to get fucked, and fucked nasty.

I picked up my bag and grabbed a couple more things before I made my way out of my bedroom. I had to stop for a moment on the landing, blowing out a breath, trying not to lose my nerve. When I got downstairs, the hallway was empty but I could hear Callum, opening cupboards in my kitchen. I dropped the bag down and slipped my feet into my work shoes. The nice ones with the small heel and little silver buckle. Then I sashayed into the kitchen with all the confidence I could muster.

"Hey," Callum said, his head in the fridge as I entered from the dining room. "I thought I'd make lunch. What do you think about..." He glanced over at me and trailed off. I watched his eyes start at my glasses and work their way down to the pointy toes of my pumps. Without looking away from me, he shoved the fridge door closed. "Never mind."

"Do you like it?" I asked. My voice came out lower, huskier than usual. I couldn't tell if it was because of my nervousness or the...changes I'd undergone recently, but I liked the way it made me sound. Sexy. Wanton.

"I think it would be an understatement to say I liked it, baby," he replied, prowling across the room toward me.

I pulled in a deep breath and reached down to the deepest depths of my courage.

"I thought we could play." I held up the things in my hand, the things I'd grabbed from the furthest recesses of my deepest bathroom drawer before coming down the stairs. My fingers were trembling.

"Oh Anna," Callum breathed, taking the butt plug and the small bottle of lube from me. "You bad, bad girl."

I felt like a bad girl. I licked my lips and turned around, bending over the kitchen counter. The granite was cold beneath me, I could feel it against my tight nipples, beneath my slightly sweating palms. Callum put the butt plug and lube on the counter beside my head, right in my line of sight, then gently placed a hand between my shoulder blades, a silent command to stay. My stomach clenched when he reached down and grabbed the hem of my skirt, began inching it up my thighs. It was skin-tight, and I heard a few threads snap loose as he worked it over my hips. A moment later, he snagged the sides of my lace panties and slid them down, his movements slow and unhurried, a contrast to my frantically pounding pulse.

When he stood up, he ran his fingertips up the line at the back of my stockings, from my ankles all the way up to the lacy tops. He stopped short of touching my core, though.

"Spread them for me, Anna," he said.

I hesitated briefly, suddenly shy even though this was my fantasy, spelled out to Callum in explicit detail on the online forum, and got a sharp swat on my backside in punishment.

"I said spread them."

Swallowing hard, I slid my arms back and reached for my ass cheeks. I cupped them, shielding myself from further spanking while I played for time.

"Disobedient girls don't get to come," Callum murmured. "You want to come, don't you, baby?"

I did want to come. I was already halfway there, my pussy slick with arousal and my clit throbbing. Closing my eyes, I reached a little further, took a grip on each cheek and pulled them apart, exposing myself to Callum's gaze. He dropped down on his haunches and I felt his mouth there, hot and hungry as he licked at me, his tongue sliding into my channel and flicking at my clit.

I cried out, pleasure crashing down on me, but before the orgasm could gather, he'd pulled back. He stood up and my eyes opened just in time to see him pick the lube and the butt plug off the counter.

"This is an adorable little thing," he said, referring to the plug which was bubble-gum pink with a little heart at the end. It was only two inches long, the widest part just big enough to stretch me and no more. Still, it took me a while to work it in. Callum was much less hesitant. He poured a dollop of the lube into my crack, letting the cool liquid seep down until he gathered it at my rosette, spreading it around before sliding some just inside with his fingertip. A moment later, I felt the tip of the butt plug nosing in and out, slick enough that he must have smeared lube on it, too.

"We can start with this," he said conversationally, rotating the plug in little circles so it stretched me and stimulated all my nerve endings at the same time, "but I plan to have you taking my cock in your ass before long, so we're going to have to upgrade you to something a little more...challenging." He paused. "Maybe one that vibrates."

I liked the sound of that, so much so that I pushed back on the plug, wanting to feel it fill me. I couldn't imagine taking Callum's cock—it was so much bigger than the plug, it was laughable—but I was game to try.

"Push back a little more, baby," he murmured. I did as he said and he slid it easily all the way inside. "Mmm." He ran his fingers around the edge of it, making my sphincter pulse. "That is just too fucking cute."

He pulled me upright, holding me tight against his body and nuzzling at my neck, grazing his teeth over the place where he'd bitten me, leaving what I now knew was a mating mark. It tingled, the area suddenly hyper sensitive.

"Are you ready to get fucked?" he whispered in my ear.

"Yes," I panted.

He turned me round and lifted me up onto the island countertop, spreading my legs with firm hands, the movement ripping my skirt even further. I didn't care, especially not when he tore my blouse right open, buttons scattering everywhere. He left it hanging from my shoulders and slid a hand round my throat. He held me there, just for a moment, his touch light but his eyes burning vibrant green into mine, before gliding down my sternum to my breasts. His second hand joined in the fun then, shaping them and squeezing gently.

My blouse was in the way for him to take my bra off me but he tugged at the cups, pulling the bra down and forcing my breasts to spill out over the top. He swooped down onto my right breast, sucking my whole areola into his mouth and rolling his tongue around it while his fingers went to my left nipple and pinched and rolled it. I moaned, dropping my head back and pushing my chest out, loving the dual sensation of pleasure and slight pain, feelings that became mixed up even further as he swapped sides and continued his cruelty.

"I can't wait to get you in clamps," he said, lifting his head and flicking at my nipples with his thumbs, making me jerk and gasp. "Jeweled ones, with a little chain in between them. Now, lean back. Onto your elbows."

"I want to feel you," I complained, reaching for his jeans.

He batted my fingers away, a hand on my sternum pushing me back into the position he wanted.

"You're going to feel me," he said, ripping open his jeans and shoving them and his boxers low enough for his cock to spring free, hard and ready.

He stepped closer to the counter and tugged me forward until I was in danger of toppling off the edge, his hold the only thing keeping me balanced. He took a moment to line himself up with my core, then surged forward in one powerful thrust. I hauled in a deep breath, caught off guard by how much more aware I was of everything down there, the plug shifting slightly inside me as he moved in and out, nudging it, sensitizing my asshole. He wasn't touching my clit at all, but it didn't matter. I came, and came fast, the orgasm starting deeper inside me and rolling through me in a heavy wave. My asshole contracted hard against the butt plug, my toes curling at the added sensation.

"Fuck, Anna. Fuck me, I'm going to come."

Callum pounded against me, jerking his hips in quick, hard strokes, pulling me onto his cock with every thrust. It was rough and fast and dirty, and when he licked his thumb and pushed it hard against my clit, growled, "Come again, Anna. Now," I couldn't do anything but obey, squeezing him tight with my thighs and arching my back until my head connected with the countertop.

"Yes," Callum grunted, "yes." He snapped his hips forward one more time, burying deep as he emptied himself inside me. He was panting hard, and when I sat up, he pulled me into him, wrapping his arms around me and dropping his head onto my shoulder.

"You are just perfect, baby," he murmured. "I can't believe I am such a lucky bastard."

"I think I'm pretty lucky," I replied quietly. "I picked the perfect man to confess my fantasies to."

I felt his smile against my skin. He pulled back and placed both hands on my face, drawing me to him as he pressed a soft, lingering kiss on my lips. It was our first kiss, and after the hot, dirty way he'd fucked me, it was incredibly sweet.

"You can tell me all your fantasies, baby," he said. "I'll do them all."

I looked at him shyly from under my lashes, a coy smile on my lips. "What do you know about ropes and bondage?" I asked.

His eyes widened and I felt his cock pulse inside me.

"Let's get back to my place and I'll show you," he promised.

Epilogue

"Take your time, baby," Callum murmured to me. "She's there, and she's ready to come out. She just needs you to give up the reins."

"I like the reins," I babbled nervously. "I'm not sure I want to give them up."

He chuckled, stroking a comforting hand over my hair.

"You give the reins over to me all the time."

"That's different," I shot back, anxiety making me snappish. "You make me come."

He grinned, sliding his hand from my hair to my shoulder, rubbing his thumb over my mating mark.

"She's going to make you happy, too," he told me. "She's going to give you a freedom you've never dreamed of."

I met his eyes, frightened. He stared back at me, warm and reassuring. I might not trust myself—or the wolf inside me—right now, but I trusted him.

"Okay," I said. "Okay."

Taking a deep breath, I reached down into myself and felt that Otherness that was the wolf. She was there, waiting impatiently. I let go of the tight control I'd been holding over her and let her unfurl inside me, through me. It was overwhelming, the rush of sensation blinding and deafening.

When I came back to myself, my hands were paws, the loamy forest floor cool beneath my pads. Callum was there beside me still, already a wolf. He yipped in approval, then rubbed his face against mine, fur against fur. He smelled incredible, the masculine musk of him multiplied tenfold thanks to my enhanced shifter senses.

I watched him dance away, pausing in a patch of sunlight, his body powerful but lithe, his coat dappled in white and grey. It was so like my dream that I froze, staring at him in astonishment. He gave me a toothy grin then turned and ran off, jumping lightly over a fallen tree branch. I whined, scared to follow, then heard a sharp bark from just out of sight, encouraging me to chase him, find him.

I knew I'd be rewarded if I did.

Taking one hesitant step forward, then another, I discovered the wolf knew how to move on four legs even if I didn't. I moved forward, cautiously at first, experimenting with the odd sensation of walking on four feet. If I thought about it, I stumbled, my center of gravity too different, my front feet still half-convinced they were hands, but if I let go, if I let the wolf take the lead…moving fluidly, she took me across the clearing, her desire to follow Callum palpable. He gave another bark, calling for me, and she, we, barked back, the sound odd and natural in my throat at the same time.

Mate, she whispered to me. *Hunt. Find.* Then, with a depth of feeling that came from both of us, *fuck*.

And for once in her life, Sensible Anna said not a damn word.

Delighted, I started forward, bounding over the tree branch, the scent of my mate in my nose, running to my future.

CHARLI MAC

HIS
MATE
SERIES

BOOK 2

HIS
CAUTIOUS
MATE

Chapter One

Gregor pulled the truck over to the side of the road, killing the lights as he stared across the street to the construction site. Everything looked quiet and calm, but the perimeter alarm he'd installed last week after two successive break-ins told him otherwise. The thief was in there, and Gregor was going to get the bastard.

Under normal circumstances he'd just have called the police, but they wouldn't be any use this time. After the second burglary, he'd shifted and cased the site from end to end. The thief had been careful, but at the back corner of the site, where a broken streetlight left a deeper pool of shadows, he'd caught the scent. It was icy, burning his nose. As improbable as it seemed, Gregor knew what that meant: vampire.

Why a vampire would need to stoop to stealing supplies and equipment from a construction site was a question he'd be asking the blood-sucker…provided he could catch him.

Stuffing the last piece of garlic bread into his mouth—which was mostly dinner but also a precaution because the myths had to come from *somewhere*—he eased open the truck door and slid out.

It was quiet, the row of shops Gregor had parked in front of all closed, their lights off. There were one or two lights on in the apartment block across the way but he didn't see any faces peering down at him. He crossed the road, hands in his pocket, head down. Vampires had super senses—even better than shifters—so he doubted his arrival had been missed. Hopefully the vamp would just think he was heading into the apartment block, on his way to a late-night assignation. Gregor bloody wished. Since his cousin had found a mate, his wolf had lost all interest in meaningless, casual sex. He'd tried to convince it that a little bit of fun was good for them, but the beast was refusing to play ball—literally.

He passed by the front entrance to the apartment block and circled the building. It was dark and silent, the only sound the rustle of a garbage can as a rat hunted for a late-night snack. When he reached the fence that ringed the construction site, he smelled it straight away, that sharp, acrid stink of the undead. Gotcha.

Vaulting the fence in one smooth movement, he landed in a crouch, listening. The thief had targeted the office cabin on his first trip, stealing two laptops and emptying the safe, which, thankfully, had only had the petty cash tin inside. The second time he'd gone for the equipment, stealing a generator. How he'd got it over the fence Gregor had no idea because the thing weighed half a ton. Vampires were strong—as strong as shifters, if he was being honest, and faster too—but the generator was big and unwieldy, it didn't exactly make for easy lifting.

What would it be this time?

He heard a rattle coming from the direction of the storage container. It was locked, a thick padlock holding the clasps in place, but that wouldn't deter a determined blood-sucker.

Moving quietly, he ghosted across the yard, hunkering down behind a back hoe. Peeking round the enormous tire, he saw the container door was propped open. There was no flashlight beam darting around inside but then, vampires had pretty good night vision. He heard the sound of something crashing to the ground, the tinkle of broken glass, then a voice muttered, "Junk, this is all junk. There has to be *something* decent here."

Well, that just pissed Gregor off on every level possible. First of all, the asshole blood-sucker was breaking his shit. Second of all, there was a *lot* of expensive gear in the container. The vampire didn't know what he was talking about.

Determined to apprehend the uneducated leech before he broke anything else, Gregor shifted his nails into claws, elongated his canines (hey, the blood sucker had pointers!) and sprinted across the open ground in a crouch. As soon as he reached the container, he yanked the door open wide and shined his cell phone torch inside.

"Hey, asshole!"

The thief froze in the sudden flood of cold white light. He was definitely a vamp, his skin deathly pale and his eyes an eerie blood red. Beyond that, though, he was unimpressive. He was a weedy little thing, several inches shorter than Gregor and at least fifty pounds lighter, with black hair falling in limp curtains around his face. In fairness, his clothes were the height of fashion…in the nineties.

Despite his earlier words, he'd actually managed to pick out the most valuable thing in the container: a thick coil of copper wiring that he'd hefted up onto one shoulder. He held tightly onto his prize as he turned to Gregor, hunkered low and hissed, lips drawn back to reveal the trademark vamp teeth.

"You're not taking that with you," Gregor told him, eyes narrowing. "You've already taken more than enough from us."

"Get out of the way," the vampire demanded.

"Not a fucking chance."

He grinned, the expression creepy as hell on his death mask face. "You've no idea what you're dealing with."

"You're a vampire," Gregor snarled. "How's that for a guess?" He shifted position, covering more of the exit. "Maybe you don't know what *you're* dealing with."

The vampire frowned then, eyebrows drawing together over those freaky eyes. He sniffed, nose wrinkling.

"Dog," he spat.

"That's shifter to you," Gregor shot back, insulted. "You're not leaving here with that," he said, nodding at the copper coil. "Put it down."

The vampire hoisted it higher on his shoulder, giving Gregor an implacable glower. "I need it."

"Tough shit, it's mine."

"You can write it off on the insurance."

Was this asshole for real? Though he hadn't lessened his aggressive stance, his voice was almost pleading.

"I'm not going to have to," Gregor told him, "because you're not taking it."

The vampire hissed at him, frustrated, and Gregor responded with a low growl. They were coming to it now, violence only a whisper away. Gregor had never killed a vampire before, but he'd seen every episode of *Buffy*. He reached into his back pocket and drew out the sharpened stake he'd made.

The vampire locked onto the thing and his eyes widened in fear. A minute later he'd covered the slip, but it was too late, he'd given himself away. The stake thing was real. Gregor tightened his grip and prepared to poof him out of existence. Or, more likely, kill him and then have to wait for the sun to rise so he'd turn into dust.

And if that didn't work, well, there were plenty of machines on site that could dig a big hole.

He was deliberating between the back hoe and the excavator when the vampire got the jump on him, exploding forward in an astonishing burst of speed and leaping over Gregor. He still had the coil of copper slung over his shoulder.

"Shit!"

Gregor spun on the spot and took off after him. The vamp bolted across the yard toward the front gate, ignoring his discreet entry point in favor of easy access to the road and the warren of streets that branched off it. Gritting his teeth, Gregor put on a burst of speed, but he still couldn't reach his quarry before he jumped, easily clearing the gate. Unable to match the height the blood-sucker achieved, Gregor vaulted over the thing, cursing as his jacket caught in the barbed wire strung across the top.

When he hit the road, he dropped down onto his haunches, eyes scanning. He thought he'd lost the fucker, but he caught the gleam of a street light bouncing off the copper coil as the vampire sprinted down a side street. Gregor launched himself after him, teeth gritted as he pushed his body faster. Vampires were much faster than shifters, but the copper coil was heavy and awkward. Gregor was also intimately familiar with this area, something he hoped the blood-sucker couldn't claim.

Gambling that the vampire was heading for Main Street, where there was enough traffic to disappear into, even at this late hour, he cut through an alleyway. It was filthy, his sneakers slapping down into stagnant puddles that stank of things Gregor didn't want to think about, but he exited onto the street at the exact same time as the vampire, slamming into him.

Unable to get a firm grip on the slippery bastard, he grabbed the coil. His stake clattered to the ground as he and the leech played tug of war over it.

"Give it to me, you thieving blood sucker."

"I can't," the vampire replied, almost desperately. "I *need* it!"

Who the hell needed a coil of copper wire? Well, Gregor did, because it was expensive and his big cousin would kick his ass if he let it get away. He hung on with all his might but the vampire must have fed. He was stronger than seemed possible, given his weedy stature, and he swung Gregor, launching him out into the road—just as a truck was barreling down the street.

It hit Gregor in the side, the PIT bar slamming into his hip. He rolled with it and landed hard on the tarmac, his hands taking the brunt of the impact. The truck squealed to a stop and the driver's door opened almost immediately.

"Hey, man, are you okay?" a man's voice shouted.

Gregor ignored him. The vamp, the God-damned vamp was getting away. He went after him, but all he could manage was a stumbling limp. By the time he'd reached the other side of the road and got himself over the low fence he'd seen the vampire leap—Gregor's fucking copper coil in hand—he knew it was hopeless. He stopped, dropping his head and panting. Pain was rioting up his left side, pulsing with every beat of his heart. His head was swimming, too, the distant street lights multiplying as he squinted through the dark.

"I just need to rest a minute," he murmured. "Just a minute."

Then he'd get back in his truck and call Callum, tell him what had happened. His cousin was going to lose his shit, he hated vamps and he hated losing money. Exhausted, pissed and not sure he didn't have some broken bones, Gregor dropped down onto a lounge chair on the decking of the garden. He hit it off-center, though, and the thing collapsed, making a loud bang as it dropped him onto the ground. Gregor didn't care. Shutting his eyes, he let darkness claim him.

Chapter Two

A loud noise outside pulled me out of a dream about a hot man, grinning at me as he stroked wicked, wicked hands all over my body. Since that was the closest I got to hot men, I was unimpressed as I rolled out of bed and shoved my curtains aside, preparing to glare down at the street and whatever noisy asshole woke me up. There was a bar down the street with late night opening hours and I frequently had to put up with drunken idiots singing and falling over things as they stumbled their way home.

The street was empty, though. I even went so far as to slide open the window and glance left and right, but there was no one hurrying away after accidentally smashing up a flowerpot.

My heart stopped beating in my chest then. The noise had been loud, definitely close by. If there was no one outside, did that mean there was someone *in* the house? Had the bang been them forcing my back door open? Breaking a window?

Shit!

Trying not to panic, I got down on my hands and knees and tugged the baseball bat out from under my bed. My dad gave to me it after I refused his first present of a shotgun. A woman on her own had to have some protections, he told me. My charming baby brother replied that my face was ugly enough to be a deterrent, and he was coincidentally the first person I tried the bat out on. It worked.

Holding it tight in my hands, I crossed toward the door as quietly as I could. It was already ajar, allowing me to peer out onto the landing, but it was pitch dark. I suffered frequently from insomnia and I couldn't sleep unless there was total darkness, so I had blackout curtains on every window. Helpful most nights, not so much right now.

As I made my way over to the top of the stairs, bare feet avoiding the squeaking floorboards as best I could, I cursed myself for not having a dog. A big one, with a deep growl and sharp teeth. I'd wanted one, had even gone so far as to visit the rescue center and walk down the long line of cages, my heart bleeding for every hopeful face that gazed back out at me, but I had to travel quite often for my job, doing health and safety evaluations for a big restaurant chain, and I didn't want to do that to an animal.

I paused, one foot on the first downward step, listening hard. Everything was quiet, there was no sound of anyone rooting about in my house. Maybe I'd imagined it, or maybe it had just been a truck backfiring or some yahoo firing off late night shots after too many beers. I wasn't going to be able to go back to sleep until I'd checked, though.

Trying to keep my breathing quiet, I crept down the stairs. There was no one in the living room or the dining nook, and my kitchen was empty. That was it for the downstairs except for the powder room. Heart in my mouth, I approached it silently, reached out for the doorknob…and wrenched it open.

Nothing.

My house was empty, except for one idiot with a baseball bat.

"You're getting paranoid, Bea," I muttered to myself.

Deciding I'd get a glass of water before I went back to bed, I headed for the kitchen and threw on the light. It blinded me, and then I knocked myself in the nose with my stupid bat, trying to cover my eyes. I chucked the slugger onto the table and grabbed a tumbler from the drying rack. Filling it over the sink, I looked out of the window. The light from the kitchen was bright enough to illuminate my brand-new decking with built in flower beds that I'd filled with daisies and geraniums which were flowering beautifully and not instantly dying like I'd assumed they would. I'd gone to the garden center last weekend and bought a gorgeous reclining chaise so I could lie out there and bask in my green-fingered success.

A chaise which was currently occupied.

"What the—"

There was a drunk taking a snooze on my brand-new chaise on my brand-new decking among my beautiful flowers. Filled with an outrage that overrode my common sense, I snatched up the baseball bat and stormed out the back door.

"Hey! Hey you! Get off that!"

I slapped the back light on as I marched outside and saw that it was worse. He wasn't just lying on my chaise, he'd *broken* it.

"Oh, you are kidding me!" I saw red, poking him with the end of the bat. "Get off that right now! I hope you didn't spend all your money at the bar, because you're going to pay for that!"

He didn't get up, he didn't even open his eyes. He groaned and tried to roll away from me, and that was when I saw the bloodied handprints on the cream linen cushions.

I gasped, backing up a step. "Please tell me that's yours," I muttered.

Leaning forward to get a better look—but prepared to swing and smash his brains in if he so much as sneezed—I saw he had a gash at his temple and the little I could see of his hands, suggested he'd landed hard on them at some point. So, his blood, probably.

"Are…are you all right? Should I call an ambulance?"

He managed to rouse himself then, shaking his head and mumbling something incoherent.

"Are you sure? You look—" He looked like he'd been run over by a truck. Whoever he'd been in a fight with had kicked his ass. "You look like you could use some help."

His eyes fluttered open briefly, giving me a glimpse of pale green irises. "No. No ambulance."

Okaaaaay.

"Should I call the police? Did someone hurt you?"

He snorted. "Police can't help."

I bit my lip, not sure what to do. I wanted him gone, but now that I was looking more closely, he didn't seem to be the drunk I'd taken him for. He was a couple of years younger than me, I thought, still on the good side of thirty, and he was well-dressed save for a few tears in his jacket that looked new. He had razor sharp features and stubble decorating his jaw. Okay, fine, he was gorgeous, and I didn't want to get him into trouble with the cops for no reason.

"I don't know what to do with you," I confessed.

"Just let me rest here a little bit," he pleaded. "I just need a minute to rest."

I stared at him uncertainly, rubbing at my arms in the chilly night air. I wasn't getting any sense of threat from him, I could just go back inside and hope he was gone by the morning. But it was cold, and I was loathe to leave him here like this.

"Come on," I said, making a snap decision. "You can rest inside, then in the morning maybe we can call someone to come get you."

I dropped the baseball bat down onto the deck and took a firm grip on one of his arms. He groaned heavily, back to mumbling, his eyes staying closed, but once he realized what I was doing he made an effort to help me.

He couldn't put his weight on one leg, so I had to throw his arm around my shoulder and support him as we wobbled inside.

My corner sofa was new and cream and very much not long enough to fit him comfortably—I was a healthy five foot seven and he towered easily half a foot over me, even hunched over—so I made for the stairs. It took some work to get him up them. He was clearly in a lot of pain, his breath coming out in little pants.

"Are you sure you don't need an ambulance?" I asked. "Or I could drive you—"

"No," he ground out between gritted teeth. "No ambulance, no hospitals."

I sighed. "All right."

We made it to the landing and I steered him toward the spare bedroom. The bed there was enormous with a chunky wood frame. I let him go briefly, intending to pull the covers back, but he pitched forward and fell face first onto the mattress.

Stretching the tension out of my shoulders—he was heavier than he looked—I turned on the bedside lamp and got a proper look at him for the first time. My first impression had been right, he was extremely handsome. He was also more injured than I'd realized. The side of his face was black and blue, and I knew there were more injuries under his clothes. His leg, in particular.

Figuring I should try and make him as comfortable as I could, I tugged off his boots, heavy, steel toe-capped ones that were splattered with muck I was probably going to have to scrub off my carpets in the morning. His jacket was a little harder, but he was conscious enough to roll and help me get his arms out of the sleeves. He wore a T-shirt underneath, and it rode up enough to reveal a tattoo across his stomach and a collage of bruises on his hip.

I wasn't a nurse, but I'd done an unholy amount of First Aid and Health and Safety training for work, I thought I'd be able to tell if he actually had any broken bones—and if he did, I was going to call an ambulance no matter what he said—so I unbuckled his belt and started tugging off his jeans, wanting to get a look at his leg. I tried very hard not to ogle his tattoo or his defined stomach muscles, the little happy trail that wound down into his boxers, but I was only human.

"Figures the only way I can get a hot man into my bed is when he's unconscious," I griped.

"You wanna play, baby?" I heard mumbled above my head, but when I looked up, startled, he was snoring softly.

I managed to get his jeans off his body then gave a low whistle. The bruising continued all the way down what I had to admit was a delicious thigh to his knee. It didn't seem to be broken, just hot and tender. I was starting to think he *had* been run over by a truck.

"You're going to be stiff in the morning," I told him. I absolutely did not look at his cock, outlined in his tight-fit boxers when I said it. And if I did, I definitely didn't notice that it was long and thick looking even in repose. Disgusted with myself—I needed to get laid, like, a year ago—I took the throw blanket I'd crocheted during my many hours of not having sex and threw it over him. He stirred in his sleep, burying his nose into it and sniffing deeply. I guess he liked what he smelled because he was tenting it before my very eyes.

"You get off on crocheting," I joked quietly. "That's not weird at all."

Jesting aside, it did worry me. Not the strange crochet fetish—everybody had their kinks, right?—but the fact he was here at all. It was still only 2 a.m. and I had hopes of going back to sleep, though the sexy dream was likely long gone. The thought of a strange man in the house while I was so vulnerable unnerved me.

I picked up his jeans again and pulled the phone I'd felt there out of his pocket. It had survived whatever accident had left him a patchwork of bruises, maybe I could call one of his friends, have them come get him. I'd lose an hour's sleep, but I also wouldn't have to worry about waking up to a man preparing to use my own baseball bat against me. Or not waking up at all.

The phone was fingerprint locked, though, and he was out cold. I tried shaking him gently by the shoulder—the least damaged bit of him I could find—but he didn't stir.

Okay, then. My choices were to call the cops and have them haul him out of here, or trust he was as harmless as he seemed. Or…

I looked at the big oak bed frame, at the reason I slept in the front room even though this was really the master and was quieter, looking out onto the row of gardens. It was a rented townhouse and it had come with all the furniture, beds included. Whoever had lived here before had…*decorated* the frame with metal rings. The kind of rings you use to tie up a horse in the stable yard, or a partner in the bed. So, I'd read. The little sexual experience I had, had all been strictly vanilla.

The rings had been enough to scare me into sleeping in the front room, which was smaller but bright and sunny and lacking any BDSM accoutrements, but they might be useful now.

"No," I muttered, "you can't."

Yes, you can, a little voice replied. *After all, you're helping him, aren't you? If you called the cops, he'd be arrested. He should be grateful.*

Right. I wasn't sure he'd be grateful to wake up tied to a bed. I wasn't even sure I had anything to restrain him with.

Even as I thought it, though, I was running ideas through my head. I didn't have ropes or chains or anything like that (because, the previous townhouse renter aside, who did?) but my robe had a tie long enough that I was able to wrap it twice around my middle—and I didn't have a particularly narrow waist.

You really can't, Bea, I thought, but I was already in my room, tugging it free and measuring the length. It would definitely do the job. I'd cut it in half with a pair of scissors and was back in the room before I'd actually decided whether I was going to do it or not, but there was no way I was going to get any sleep unless I knew he couldn't repay me for my kindness by murdering me in my own bed.

"I'm really sorry," I whispered to his sleeping face as I tied the robe belt around his wrist and connected it to the metal ring. "I'll make it up to you; I won't make you pay for the chaise, and it was expensive."

I did the same on his other side until both his hands were up by his head, the ties short enough that he wouldn't be able to put them together and untie himself. He looked comfortable enough, but I still hesitated as I reached for the light, ready to switch it off.

"Please don't call the cops on me," I murmured, then I plunged the room into darkness and scurried out.

Chapter Three

Gregor felt like he'd been run over by a truck. Which, he supposed was only to be expected. He groaned and rolled over, but was brought up short when his hand refused to follow the rest of his body.

What the hell?

Opening his eyes, he saw a length of purple satin tied around his wrist, the other end connected to a heavy-duty metal ring drilled into the bedframe—which was not his bedframe.

To be fair, this was not the most compromising position he'd ever woken up in, but it was close. More worrying was that he didn't remember where he was or how he got here. He'd chased the vamp, lost the tussle over the copper wiring—which stung—and then…bam! Afterward he'd barely made it off the road before collapsing into someone's garden.

Now he was here, apparently a prisoner—although a tug at the restraints proved they'd snap easily enough. Gregor didn't, though, because there was another mystery to be solved. His wolf was completely okay with the strange turn of events. The beast, who went nuts if it was caged or restrained in any way, was relaxed and happy. It was waiting for something, or someone, but with anticipation rather than the urge to rip their head off for daring to try and shackle him like this.

What the fuck was that about?

Trying to pull memories out of the pain-filled blur of the night before, Gregor shifted position on the bed and discovered two things. One, his left hip and thigh hurt like hell and two, whoever had tied him had removed his boots and jeans. Huh. He was still wearing his T-shirt and, according to the tightness against his slowly dissipating morning wood, his underpants. He grinned, imagining he'd been "rescued" by some Florence Nightingale in disguise who wanted to stroke him and pet his boo boos when the bedroom door opened and in she walked. Florence fucking Nightingale.

She was on the taller side of average, her curves outlined by the soft yoga pants and long-sleeved tee she wore. Her hair was a glossy chestnut pulled back into one of those claw hairclips and she had not a scrap of adornment— no make-up, no jewelry, nothing. Before his wolf decided he was tired of having fun, Gregor had fucked a lot of hot, sexy women. He wouldn't put this one on the list and yet…as she squeezed in the door, a breakfast tray he hoped was for him in her hands, he couldn't take his eyes off her.

Really? he asked his wolf. *Her?*

Her, the wolf replied in no uncertain terms.

"You're awake," she commented shyly. Okay, maybe the wolf was on to something. Her voice was low and soft, stroking over him.

"Hey," he replied. He kept his own voice deliberately quiet, trying not to spook her because she already looked nervous, her body language stiff and her eyes darting about the room.

She approached the bed and put the tray down, then skittered backward until she was against the wall. It took her a moment to settle enough to focus her gaze on him, but eventually she offered a small smile.

"How are you feeling?" she asked.

A hint of wickedness hit him, and he struggled to keep the smirk off his face.

"Stiff," he offered. If he hadn't been watching so closely, he might have missed it, but her eyes flickered to his cock for a brief moment before she realized what she was doing and fastened them deliberately on his face.

"What happened to you?"

A vampire threw me into traffic. Right, that would help convince her he wasn't crazy.

"I was run over."

She bit her lip. "I…I checked you for injuries, you don't seem to have any broken bones. But I'm not a doctor, I still think you should go to a hospital."

Yeah, no. That wasn't happening. Shifters and hospitals went together about as well as vampires and cops. One look at his accelerated healing, his superior senses, and they'd have him locked up in some government laboratory before he could blink.

"I don't feel that bad. It's just bruising." He gestured down to the tray with his head, where she'd brought him a bagel and, God bless her, a steaming mug of coffee. Gregor stayed away from the stuff as a rule, but today he definitely needed the pick-me-up. "Is that for me?"

"What? Oh, yes!" She made a little face. "I hope that's okay. It's what I have for breakfast and I didn't have anything else in. I really need to run to the store, but work has been so busy and—" She was babbling and he saw the moment she realized it. She blushed, those rounded cheeks flaming fire-engine red, and trailed off.

"It's fine," he assured her. When she still didn't move from her defensive position against the wall, he waved his hands in their restraints. "You'll need to untie me, though."

Her eyes widened as she realized her mistake. She hurried over to him, then put the brakes on just a foot from the side of the bed.

"I, uh...I'm sorry about that. It's just, well, I didn't know you and I was nervous about going to sleep with you—Well, I don't mean...I didn't think you were going to do anything, I just—"

"I understand," Gregor said. "You were being smart."

She gave him a grateful smile, then finally came close enough to untie him, her nimble fingers cool against his wrist as she fought with the knots. He leaned toward her slightly and drew in her scent. It had been a subtle hint in the flower-patterned blanket she'd slung over him, but now it blasted him, a double hit in his chest and his cock. It was warm, like sunlight and lemons, a hint of the flowers she'd crocheted.

See? The wolf rumbled. *Smells good. Ours.*

She did smell good, and from the way she kept giving little glances at his arms, his body, his cock, he could tell she was interested, but she was the most skittish female he'd ever met. As soon as she had one wrist untied, she jumped back, leaving him to reach across and untie his other arm.

He was free now. He could get up out of the bed, stick his face into the crook of her neck and pull that mouth-watering scent into his lungs until he was dizzy with it, get his hands on those tantalizing curves, but instead he reached down—suppressing his groan, because *fuck him*, he hurt—and grabbed the breakfast tray. Looking as unthreatening as possible, he started to butter the bagel.

"What's your name?" he asked her.

"Huh?" She dragged her gaze away from where she'd been apparently mesmerized by his fingers, wielding the blunted knife—or, perhaps, his cock, which was lifting the crochet blanket in the optimistic hope that his mate might whip the thing back and jump on it. Unlikely, he thought, but possible.

"Your name, baby," he repeated, grinning at her.

"It's Bea," she told him.

"Bee? Like—" He buzzed, the sound rolling off his tongue. "Like honey and shit?"

"Bea, short for Beatrice," she corrected. She rolled her eyes. "It was my grandmother's name. Shortening was the best I could do since my mom's feelings would have been hurt if I'd changed it. My grandmother died really early and—" she shrugged.

"I think it's cute," he offered. Quirky, but cute. And he was starting to think that maybe it suited her. "I'm Gregor."

She quirked her lips into a soft smile. "Hi Gregor."

Yeah, and if her scent had rocked his world, hearing her say his name in that sultry voice of hers had his balls drawing up tight to his body, ready to explode.

He concentrated on his food so she wouldn't see the hotly possessive look in his eyes and run from him. He didn't think he was in any fit shape to catch her.

Though, it'd likely be easier than the damn vamp. He was going to have to tell Callum about that. His cousin was probably already at the site, staring at the container which—fuck!—he'd left wide open, and the missing coil of copper wiring which was going to be ridiculously expensive to replace.

He saw Bea shifting out of the corner of his eye and when he turned to her, she'd approached, hand outstretched. His phone was nestled in her palm.

"Do you want to call someone, let them know where you are? I've got a car, well, it's a company car and I'm not supposed to use it for personal things, but I could drop you off somewhere?" Her last few words rose in uncertainty as he scowled at her, an automatic reaction. She was trying to get rid of him? Didn't she feel it?

No, of course she didn't. She wasn't a shifter. Yet. Callum's little mate had taken to it like a duck to water, though; there was no reason Bea couldn't do the same.

"I don't have anyone I need to call." Liar. "But I—" he grimaced. "I don't quite feel up to travelling just yet. Maybe I could stay here, just a little bit? Work the stiffness out?" Of his cock. With her mouth, or other delectable parts of her body.

"Oh. Uhm. Well, yes, I suppose so. It's just—" she grimaced.

"What is it?" he asked.

"I need to go out, run a few errands."

"That's all right, I don't mind staying here."

She bit her lip, staring up at him doubtfully. "By yourself?"

Absolutely. A chance to snoop around and find out a little more about his mate? Find some ammunition to help him win her over? Sign him up.

"Sure." He glanced down at the bed, saw the satin purple belt she'd tied him up with and an idea slipped into his head. "You can always tie me up again, if it'd make you feel more comfortable."

"Oh, I couldn't," she said. But she was thinking about it.

"It's fine," he soothed. "I'll just nap. You'd be helping me out, there's no one at home to check on me, in case I have a concussion or something."

He was a lying motherfucker and he was going to go to hell, but it was worth it when compassion replaced concern and she gave a little nod.

"All right then. If...if you're sure you don't mind."

He held his hands out to her, grinning. "Tie me up, baby."

Chapter Four

There was a man in my bed. Oh, all right, not *my* bed because I never slept in it, but he was a man, and he was hot (smoking hot) and he was in *a* bed in *my* house.

Even better, he was *tied up* in a bed in my house.

I left the grocery store without half the things I needed because I couldn't stop thinking about it. When I'd left, he'd been reclined against the pillows, his hands up by his head, purple bindings round his wrist. The position had made the muscles in his arms pop, the T-shirt pulled tight across his chest and…oh my. That was an image I was going to hold deep in my heart and bring out the next time I wanted to play with my vibrator. Which was probably going to be about thirty seconds after he walked out the door.

I was excited and jittery when I hurried up the little path toward my front door, which was stupid because I still didn't know a thing about him and, let's face it, my grandmother could have got out of the bindings I'd left him in with enough effort, and she was dead. The house was just as I'd left it, though, and when I headed upstairs, Gregor was there, just like I'd left him, only this time his beautiful long eyelashes were resting against his cheeks. He was asleep.

I left him where he was while I rushed to put everything away and then, like the awkward nerd that I was, I brushed my hair and swapped out my plain, serviceable bra for the fancy one that dug in but lifted my breasts up to twenty-five-year-old Bea level. When I crept back into the room, his eyes were open and he was watching me.

"Hey," I murmured. "I got back a little while ago but I didn't want to wake you. How are you feeling now?"

"I'm getting there," he said. He did look remarkably better, though there was still dried blood on his temple and, I realized, the cuts on his hand had dirt encrusted into them. That wasn't good.

"Let me help you up," I offered. "Then you can take a shower."

Hot man, naked in my shower. Yes, please. I mean, obviously I wasn't going to be in there with him, but I could imagine.

He made a face, though. "My hip is still pretty sore," he said. A strange look came over his face, almost hopeful. "Maybe you could give me a bed bath?"

What? Was he for real? I almost laughed at the absurdity of the suggestion but I managed to hold it in. I eyed him for a moment, trying to decide if he was being serious. He seemed to be. All right, then. If he wanted to give me the chance to get my hands on a glorious, tanned and muscled body, who was I to say no?

"I'll just go and get some water," I said. "And a wash cloth."

The grin he gave me was beatific. "I'll just wait here, shall I?"

I was running the hot water in the bathroom when I realized I'd been so flustered that I'd left him tied up still. Oops. I hurried back as quickly as I could, and when I shouldered my way into the room, a basin of soapy water in my hands, he was still there, tied up against the headboard…with his T-shirt off.

I narrowed my eyes at him and he shrugged impishly. "It makes you feel more secure."

"Not if I know you can get out of them any time you like, it doesn't!" I replied.

His eyes sparkled. "I promise not to move. At least," a glance down at his groin, which I wasn't going to look at, I *wasn't*, "the parts of my body I can control."

"I'm sure you won't have a problem," I replied tartly, rolling my eyes, but it was an act. A man who looked like Gregor getting a hard on over me? In my dreams.

I sat on the edge of the bed and squeezed out the excess water in the washcloth, trying to look like I wasn't having heart palpitations. I started with the dried-in blood smeared across his temple, mindful of the gash which looked far too small to have caused that amount of bleeding, because I figured that was a safe, less intimate body part. Apparently not. Gregor watched me intently, eyes on my face and his breath hot on the underside of my forearm as I worked. I'd leaned forward to see what I was doing and when I glanced down at him and our eyes locked, there were only inches between our gazes. My breath stuttered, time stopping as we just…stared at each other. When I finally ripped my gaze away, my heart was pounding.

From his temple, I moved onto his cheek, stubble rough beneath my fingertips. The blood and dirt came away easily, but underneath the skin was unblemished. Confused, I ran my cheek over the spot but it was smooth and, well, perfect. There was no hint of a graze.

"Are you stroking me?" Gregor asked flirtatiously.

"No." I jerked my hand away so fast my fingertips burned from the friction against his stubble.

"That's a shame."

I didn't know what to do with that, not at all, so I dunked my washcloth back in the water and started cleaning one of his palms.

"I should untie you," I said, unable to keep my gaze away from the purple tie wrapped around his wrist.

"But then you might run away," he murmured.

I eyed him askance. "I could run away right now," I said. "You're the one tied up. Though," I huffed, "we've already established the ties aren't holding you."

"Mmmm." He smiled at me and I had to look away. He was devastatingly handsome, and I reminded myself not to take his sensual teasing seriously. It was just who he was, he didn't mean it. A man like Gregor could—and probably did—have any woman he wanted. And that didn't include Plain Jane's like me. "I do have to wonder, though," he purred, "why you have the rings? What sort of naughty things do you get up to in this bed?"

"I…this isn't my room," I spluttered. "It's a rental, the bed was here when I moved in."

"You've never taken advantage of them?"

"No!" I goggled my eyes at him.

"That's a pity." He gave me a wicked grin. "But it's not too late to change that."

I felt my breathing stutter and knew I was done. I dumped the washcloth back into the basin and closed my eyes.

"Please don't," I said.

"Don't what? Hey, What's wrong?" He paused. "Bea, look at me."

I obeyed, feeling beyond stupid as I felt tears prick my eyes.

"Please don't make fun of me," I said. "It's not fair."

His frown slid into a look of horror when he saw how upset I was. He reached for me, but the tie pulled him up short. I saw him flex his muscles, preparing to snap them, but then he checked himself. I was glad because he was right, I would be off like a shot if he freed himself.

"What do you mean, don't make fun of you? I thought we were having fun."

"Come on, Gregor," I said quietly.

He shook his head at me, frustration lending a hard edge to his tone. "No, Bea. Talk to me. What's wrong."

"The flirting," I spat out.

"You don't like it?" he asked.

I did like it, way too much. That was the problem.

"It's too much," I told him. God, this was excruciating. "We both know you'd never really touch a girl like me."

"I can't touch you," he joked, tugging at his restraints. I didn't laugh. He tilted his head to the side, eyes searching my face. "A girl like you? What's that supposed to mean?"

"You know." I shrugged, squirming uncomfortably. "I'm just...completely ordinary. And you're—"

Beautiful. In a ruggedly masculine away that was every girl's fantasy.

"You really believe that?" he asked.

"It's true."

"Is it?" he threw back, that hard edge back again.

I bit my lip, suddenly uncertain. He seemed angry at me, hurt even. Had I totally misjudged the situation?

"Yes?" I offered tentatively.

He stared at me for a long, uncomfortable moment.

"Put the basin on the table," he ordered suddenly.

What? Thrown, I did as he said.

"Now get over here." He jerked his head, indicating that I should join him on the bed. I did, getting on my knees beside him, eyeing him warily, but that still wasn't close enough. He jerked his chin again and I hesitated before sliding my leg over him. I was straddling him and the first thing I felt was the enormous erection he was sporting, pushing against my pelvis through the softness of my yoga pants. He let me feel that for a moment, eyes holding a wealth of meaning, then shifted his knees up until I toppled forward, off balance, my palms landing hard against the heat of his chest.

And what a chest. It was hard with muscle and as tanned as the rest of him, a soft pelt of hair spreading out across his pectorals before narrowing to a thin trail down to his stomach.

"Kiss me," he demanded.

"What?" I gaped at him.

"Right now. Kiss me."

I hesitated, torn between the self-preservation of my heart and the perfection of his lips. To hell with it, I thought. You only live once.

I leaned forward and pressed my mouth to his. Even though he was the one tied up, he directed the kiss from the moment my mouth touched his, playing with my lips, encouraging me to open my mouth so that he could lick at my tongue. It was such a fragile connection, just our mouths and nothing more, but it was glorious. When I drew back, I was breathless.

Gregor's eyes were glowing as they stared into mine.

"If you disparage yourself like that again, I'll snap these ties and spank you, do you understand?" His voice was a rough growl, and it made my core clench. He felt it, I saw the flare of heat in his gaze. "Do you, Bea?"

"I...yes." I tried to sound like I meant it, but I was still reeling, first of all, from the kiss and, secondly, that this was actually happening. It was like my dream from last night, only way, way better. The heat of his skin beneath my hands, the tingle on my lips from his kiss. I even had the scent of him in my nose, masculine and sexy.

"You're wearing too many clothes," he told me. "Take them off."

Take off my clothes? In broad daylight, where Gregor could see me? Gregor with his perfect muscles and his flawless skin and his—

"Bea!" My name came out like a whip crack. I jerked, staring at Gregor wide-eyed. "I was not joking about that spanking. I see you disappearing into your head." He softened his mouth, eyes warming. "Stay here, with me." It wasn't a question but I nodded anyway, and received a smile of approval. "Good. Now take off your clothes."

I slipped off him to divest himself of my pants and my underwear, then returned to straddling him. I felt a weird need to be touching him that I didn't want to examine too closely, but it also helped that it was harder to see the cellulite on my thighs this close up. Especially when his gaze was pinned to my breasts as I slid my T-shirt up over my head. I was grateful I'd taken the time to slip into my least comfy, most sexy bra when he gave a little groan of appreciation.

"Your tits are gorgeous, baby," he murmured, "but I can't get my mouth on them like that. Take it off."

It took a little more courage to do that—my breasts were bigger than I'd like—but I'd come this far. I wasn't leaving this room without my first orgasm given to me by another person. I hoped. I reached back and unsnapped the clasp, sliding the straps off my shoulder and dropping the bra to the floor.

Gregor growled. He actually growled.

"Feed them to me," he demanded.

Feed them to him? That sounded a lot raunchier than I was capable of. I eyed his bindings uncertainly.

"Why don't I just—"

I was reaching for one wrist when he snapped his teeth at me, making me jerk my hand back.

"Feed them to me," he repeated.

Trembling slightly, my skin rising up into goose bumps, I shifted forward on my knees until my breasts were level with his face. He held my gaze the whole time, clutching me to him with his eyes. I cupped my left breast and lifted it for him, offering it to his mouth, and he watched me watch him as he stuck his tongue out and flicked it lightly over the tip of my nipple.

I gasped, sensation streaking through me like lightning, and then he did it again, repeating the motion, lashing at me until my nipple was tight and tingling. Then he nuzzled his way to the other breast and gave it the same treatment.

"Fuck yeah," he murmured. "These are incredible. I can't wait to get my hands on them. Next time."

There was going to be a next time? Yippee. My inhibitions were slowly seeping away and as I fed Gregor my breasts I started to grind down onto his cock. I'd have slid right onto it if his boxer shorts hadn't been in the way. I was feeling breathless and wanton. I was going to fuck a virtual stranger on the previous renter's kinky bed, and if the way my clit was pulsing was any indication, I was going to come hard doing it.

"Fuck, Bea," Gregor moaned, pulling away from me. "You gotta stop that or I'm going to come."

"That's okay," I breathed. I was weirdly turned on by the thought.

"No, it's not," he grouched. "I want to be in you when I come." He grinned. "And I want to feel you coming all over my cock first."

I wanted that, too. My core was already clenching disappointingly on air, causing a sharp ache.

"Take my underwear off," he said, and I scrambled to obey.

They were tight, and when I pulled them free his cock sprang up, thick and erect, the head a deep plum color. I wanted it in my mouth, and I leaned forward and licked him before I could think better of it. He made a harsh, urgent sound, his cock jerking, so I did it again, running my tongue around the tip before taking all of him in my mouth and sucking.

"Baby," he panted, a sheen of sweat breaking out on that beautiful chest. "Baby that feels amazing, but stop. I want—" He flexed, thrusting his hips up, almost choking me. "I want to come inside you."

I didn't want to stop. I wanted him to come like this, paint my face with it, but like he said, there was going to be a next time. I released him with a gentle plop and crawled back up his body.

"Ride me," he commanded. "Now."

He hadn't touched me anywhere except his mouth on my breasts, but I could feel myself hot and slippery between my legs. I knew he'd slide right inside.

Settling myself on his lap, I lifted up enough to take him in hand and guide him inside me. His hands were still held by the ties and he opened and closed his fingers into frustrated fists. I thought about freeing him but…I kind of liked that all his strength, all his masculinity, was held in check. He was a dominant man, I could tell. Even though I was the one free to move, to touch, he was still in control. The fact that he was holding himself back for me, letting me feel my way into our pleasure, it meant a lot.

"Ride me, Bea," he growled. "Fuck me. Hard."

I held his eyes, slid him in an inch, and held there. It was a challenge, and my heart gave a heavy thump against my rib cage.

He grinned. "Oh sweetheart, you are storing up trouble for yourself. Next time, I'm not going to have my hands tied. You tease me now, I'll make you beg to come later. I can hold you on the edge for hours."

I felt a rush run through my body, coalescing in my clit. I was coming, I thought, astonished. Gregor was making me come with nothing more than a few dirty words. Feeling it flood over me, I slammed down onto his cock and cried out. Pleasure spiked, my breath leaving me in a rush. I hauled in a breath and did it again, lifting up and dropping down. Hard.

"Jesus. Jesus, Bea. Faster."

I did as he said, feeding the orgasm with every slide down Gregor's cock. It filled me, stretching me, and Gregor's piercing eyes watched every movement, drinking me in. I felt desired, beautiful, and when his cock pulsed as he emptied his seed inside me, I felt pretty fucking satisfied.

My legs jelly, sweat beading on my skin, I slumped against him, reaching for his mouth, kissing him frantically. Fumblingly. Gregor didn't seem to mind. There was a snap as he pulled free of the ties and wrapped his arms around me, devouring me with his mouth.

"Fuck, Bea," he panted. "That was the hottest thing I've ever fucking done. I think you've emptied my balls!"

"Wow." I smiled, then I raised an eyebrow. "How quickly do they refill?"

He blinked at me, astounded, then he laughed and hugged me.

"For you, I have a feeling it won't take long." He punctuated the end of the sentence with an ear-splitting yawn.

"Maybe you should nap first?" I suggested, amused.

"Nap with me," he murmured. "You had a disturbed night's sleep last night."

"I did," I agreed. "Some obnoxious man destroyed my new chaise."

He drew his eyebrows together. "That would be me?"

"That would be you."

"I'll buy you another one," he promised. "Later."

"After we nap?"

"After we nap, then fuck."

"We might need another nap then," I suggested.

Gregor nodded seriously, though his eyes were dancing with amusement. "Nap, fuck, nap…then shop."

"That sounds like a plan," I agreed.

Chapter Five

I woke up before Gregor and spent several long minutes just looking at him. It was still hard to believe that someone as handsome as him would desire me, but I'd felt his arousal, seen it in his eyes. As improbable—impossible—as it might seem, it was real.

I was hungry and thirsty, so I slipped out of bed, dressed and headed downstairs—via a quick trip to the bathroom to clean myself up. I was a little sore (it had been a *long* time), but I didn't care. It was totally worth it.

When I got into the kitchen, I grabbed a tumbler and went to fill it at the sink. Looking out the window at my new garden—and my broken chaise—I experienced a serious case of déjà vu. There was a man out there, only this one wasn't collapsed on my patio furniture, he was hunkered down beside it, gazing at the bloody handprints patterning the cream-colored cushions.

My tumbler clattered down into the sink and the man whipped his head toward me. We locked gazes for a heartbeat, his eyes blazing into mine before I had to rip them away. My pulse was thundering, my legs shaky. I had the distinct urge to run and hide. Whoever the man was, he was seriously scary.

The back door was unlocked. I had that thought as the man unfolded his body and started heading for my house. I tried to dart across the room to hit the latch, but I was too slow. He had the door open before I could reach it. Frightened by his height, his stare and the sheer aggression that seemed to radiate from him, I backed up until I felt the coolness of the fridge door down the line of my back.

"What have you done to him?" he demanded.

"What?"

"Where is he?"

"Gregor?"

"Yes, Gregor." He advanced on me and I tried to back up further, but the fridge refused to move. "What the fuck have you done to him? That's his blood out there."

"I haven't done anything to him!"

"Liar!"

He closed the distance faster than should have been possible, a hand wrapping around my throat. I whimpered, more terrified than I'd ever been in my life, but it didn't move him. He loomed over me, his lips pulled back to reveal sharpened teeth. The hand around my throat squeezed to the point of pain and then relaxed. A warning.

"Where the fuck is he?"

"He's upstairs," I got out.

"And why is his blood outside?"

"I don't know." I was shaking now. If he hadn't had me by the throat, I would have dropped down and curled up into a ball.

He leaned down into me, ignoring me when I tried to cringe away, and sniffed.

"You fucked him?" he asked, confusion bleeding into his expression.

"What?" How could he possibly know that?

I didn't get a chance to ask. The next moment I heard Gregor clattering down the stairs at breakneck speed.

"Bea!" He burst into the kitchen, eyes taking in the two of us, pressed up against the fridge, the man's hand gripping my neck. "No!"

He crossed the room in a heartbeat, snatching me away from the man and wrapping his arms around me.

"Fuck, Logan!" he spat. He lifted my chin and examined my neck, gentle fingers running across the red marks there. "Are you okay, Bea, baby? Did he hurt you?"

I opened my mouth but no sound came out. The rapid shift from fear to relief was shooting adrenaline into my system and overwhelming me. I burst into tears.

"It's okay, I've got you." He pulled me against the heat of his body, resting his chin on the top of my head. He glowered at the man he'd called Logan. "What the hell did you have to scare her like that for?" he demanded.

"I hardly touched her," Logan replied. I peeked out of the corner of my eye and saw him folding his arms across his chest and scowling at me.

"You shouldn't have touched her at all!"

"What was I supposed to do? You disappear, you don't answer your phone. I finally track you here and I find your blood smeared across her garden. Tell me that doesn't look suspicious!"

"Stop yelling."

"I'm not yelling!"

"You're frightening her!"

Logan threw his hands up in frustration. "What is she, a fucking mouse?"

The sound that ripped out of Gregor's throat was like nothing I'd ever heard before. It was an inhuman sound, a vicious snarl. If I hadn't felt it vibrate in his chest, I'd have been looking around for a wild animal.

"Watch yourself," Logan replied darkly, and though he kept his voice deliberately low, there was a wealth of threat in those two words.

"She's my mate," Gregor replied. He was still staring hard at Logan, but the heat was gone from his voice. He almost sounded like he was apologizing.

I was so focused on measuring the aggression between the two men, my mind almost skipped over what he said. I was his...what?

His friend? That stung. It also didn't explain the astonishment that flooded Logan's face.

"She can't be," he said. "She's human."

"Anna was human."

"Yeah, and she made the change the first time Callum mated her. You've done that, I can smell it. You didn't mark her?"

"I did," Gregor admitted. He swept my hair over my shoulder, ran his fingers over a spot that made me wince. "I did it while she was sleeping."

"So why didn't she transform then? You must be wrong."

"I'm not wrong!" The aggression was back, and in spades. "She is my mate. I just...I don't know. I guess the change didn't take."

The conversation was getting weirder and weirder, and it was starting to freak me out. I wiggled out of Gregor's grip. He didn't want to let me go, but I was determined. When I tried to step away from him, however, to get some space, he reached out and snagged my hand.

"What's going on?" I demanded. "What are you talking about?"

Gregor turned to me, and the expression on his face could only be described as sheepish.

"You didn't tell her what you were?" Logan guessed. Gregor winced, looking even more uncomfortable. "You didn't tell her *anything*?" There was a brief pause and then he said, "I seem to remember you giving Callum a lot of shit for doing that."

"There wasn't time!" Gregor complained. "I was going to, I just—"

"Yeah," Logan cut in, voice hard. "Callum said that too."

"I was injured!" Gregor complained. "I got run over by a truck chasing the damn vampire."

"Vampire?" Logan and I spoke at the same time, he sounded furious, though, whereas I was just confused. And worried. And starting to wish the two of them would just get out of my house.

"You should go," I told Gregor.

"What?" He turned away from Logan, giving me his full attention. "No, Bea, baby—"

"Your friend is here," I pointed out. "He can take you home." I gestured to his hip, which seemed to be working perfectly given how crippled he'd been last night. "You're fine now. You don't need me."

Those last few words were the hardest to say. I'd just had the most erotic experience of my life. I'd felt sexy and desired—desirable—for the first time, but like Gregor said, we were just friends. Not even that. I didn't know him at all, and the crazy conversation he was having with his friend—vampires?— was making me uncomfortable.

"Please," I added. "Just go, Gregor."

His eyebrows drew forward into a scowl and he set his jaw mutinously. "No."

"No?"

"No. I'm not leaving."

I was flabbergasted and, honestly, getting a little bit scared. "You can't just refuse to leave! This is my house! Get out. Get out or," I drew in a shaky breath, "or I'll call the police!"

Logan smiled at me, the expression condescending. "I don't think you want to make that threat, honey."

Honey?

I was about to tell him exactly where he could stick his patronizing bullshit when Gregor stepped in between us, cutting Logan off from my line of sight. "I'll handle this," he growled over his shoulder.

Oh, he was going to handle me, was he? I folded my arms over my chest, my fear dissipating beneath feminist anger.

"Look, Gregor—"

"No baby, listen to me—"

"I'm not your baby!"

"Yes, you are." He grinned at me, looking delighted about it, and I felt my anger thaw a little. He really was that charming. "I know this seems crazy fast, but you and me, we're meant to be together."

"It is crazy," I agreed. "*You're* crazy."

Logan snorted in the background. Gregor ignored him, stepping closer, staring down at me with those beautiful, beautiful eyes and I couldn't look away.

"I need to explain some things to you, but it's easier to show you rather than tell you. Will you come home with me?"

"Show me here," I said.

"I can't." He grimaced. "Please, baby. It's not far. You can come with us or take your own car." He winked at me. "I'll even give you the address so you can call your mom and tell her where you're going."

God, I was such an idiot. I was going to go, because even though I'd just ordered Gregor out of my house, the thought of him actually doing it, or him walking out the door and never coming back...was like a physical pain.

"I am going to call her," I warned him. "And I'm taking my own car."

His smile was blinding. "Absolutely, baby. Whatever you want."

Chapter Six

"You should probably have ridden with your little human," Logan told Gregor. "Otherwise, I think she's going to get cold feet and turn around."

"She won't," Gregor assured him. "She's tougher than she looks."

"If you say so."

"She is," Gregor insisted. "Besides, she needs to make the decision to come to me. I won't force her."

"And if she doesn't come."

Well, then maybe Gregor would have to force her. Gently. With lots of kisses. Maybe on that sweet little pussy of hers. He hadn't had a chance to taste her there yet, and he was dying to.

Logan was right. He should have ridden with Bea. Then he could have convinced her to pull over into a layby and he could be between those thighs right now. He could be—

"Tell me about these vampires." Logan's command cut through the fantasy he was building where Bea rode his fingers, let him tongue her clit while cars whizzed by, totally oblivious to what they were up to.

"I smelled the vamp after the second break-in. I installed a perimeter alarm, so when it tripped, I went to confront him."

"And knowing it was a vampire, you didn't think you should have called in reinforcements?" Logan's tone dripped ice. Gregor's hackles rose at the implication he couldn't handle a single bloodsucker by himself—but then, he hadn't handled it, had he?

He wasn't upset about the outcome—he wouldn't have met Bea if he'd been able to contain the vampire at the site—but he'd still fucked up.

"I thought I could sort it."

"Obviously not."

Gregor shrank down in his seat, his alpha's clear displeasure making his wolf cringe.

"Did you recognize the vampire?"

"No. He was young looking, though, that doesn't mean anything. I didn't get the feeling he was old, though. He was still pretty weak, kind of nervous looking. And who lives for centuries and is still penniless enough to need to steal a coil of copper wire?"

"That's what he took?"

"Yeah, but the last time it was a generator, the time before that, the petty cash tin. I got the feeling he was just going after whatever he could flog, he must need cash."

"If you'd called me—or your cousin—to help, we could have asked him."

"I know," Gregor muttered. "I'm sorry."

He glanced in the side mirror, like he'd done every twenty seconds since they pulled away from the sidewalk outside Bea's house.

"She's still there," Logan commented, amused. He took a long look at her in the rear-view mirror and gave a shake of his head, his lips twitching. Gregor knew what he must see. Bea was driving a sedan in a sensible shade of beige, though she'd said it was a work car. She was holding her hands precisely at the two o'clock and ten o'clock position, teeth gnawing on her bottom lip as she followed them at precisely the correct distance. She looked fucking adorable to Gregor, but she wasn't exactly his usual type—and Logan had met quite a few of Gregor's exes.

"I don't understand why she didn't transform," he said. The words were mostly for himself, because it was weighing on him, even though he was one hundred percent sure that she *was* his mate, but if anyone would know, it would be Logan.

Unhelpfully, his alpha gave a casual shrug.

"If you're sure she is your mate—"

"I'm sure."

"Then maybe she just doesn't have the gene. It's rare, but I've heard of couplings before where the female doesn't make the change." He glanced at Gregor as he spoke. "You'll need to watch out for her. She'll be more vulnerable. There are a few in the pack who'll give her a hard time."

"Let them try," Gregor growled. He grimaced. "You think she'll still be able to have offspring?"

Logan rolled his eyes. "Why do you think I keep chucking condoms at you idiots? Humans can get pregnant even without the mate bond. The babies are always able to shift, can you imagine how much of a shock that would be to a woman if she wasn't still with the father? What she might do to the child?"

They turned off the highway toward the pack lands. Some shifters, like Callum, preferred to live apart, but Gregor liked being surrounded by his pack, his family. Even Callum had started talking about moving back once his mate Anna got pregnant. It was safer, grouping together. The outside world was not usually friendly to anything that stood out as different.

Logan wound up the road through the trees and parked in front of the main house—his house—and killed the engine. Gregor watched as Bea carefully maneuvered her car alongside. He grinned at her through the window and her returning smile was brittle.

Several pack members wandered over to see what was going on. There was a small, sarcastic cheer when Gregor emerged from the car. He shot them the bird and there was a smattering of laughter.

"You're not dead!" the alpha's second, Kenny, hollered. "Pity, I was measuring up your cabin for my furniture."

More laughter.

The mood changed abruptly when Bea opened her door and slid cautiously out of the sedan, though. It became tense, watchful. Non-shifters were rarely brought onto the pack lands, and never people who hadn't been carefully vetted first. Bea was a stranger, an unknown. Gregor felt the weight of accusatory eyes on him as he rounded the car and got up close and personal to her. He wound an arm around her waist before he met those stares, letting them know that she was his. He vouched for her, and he'd protect her.

Of course, it helped that they'd arrived with Logan. If the alpha sanctioned her presence here, there wasn't a damn thing anyone else in the pack could do about it. Though that didn't mean they wouldn't bitch—and it definitely didn't mean they wouldn't all be up in his face, asking a million questions.

"Where are we?" Bea asked. "Who are all these people and why are they glaring at me?"

Gregor winced. Bea spoke in little more than a whisper, but that didn't mean anything here. He needed to warn her about that.

"Come on," he said. "Let's go to my place and I'll explain everything."

She let him lead her away from the small crowd, down a path that wound through a thick copse of pine trees, though he could feel her reluctance.

"I still don't see why you had to drag me all the way here," she complained. "Why couldn't you have just explained at my house?"

Because Gregor needed to shift to do that properly, and he wasn't going to go wolf in the middle of a residential street. Especially not if Bea freaked out and started screaming. At least here he could contain her until she calmed down.

"You'll see," he told her.

They rounded a corner and Gregor's house came into view. It was a single-wide trailer, not a log cabin he'd built with his own hands or some shit, but he had dragged it onto the site himself and he'd clad it in pine so it kind of *looked* like a log cabin. Only with insulation and a lot more outlet sockets. And he hadn't had to get callouses cutting and sawing and hammering and drilling, so Gregor counted that as a win.

"This is me," he said. "Come on in."

He led her up onto the small front porch—which he *had* built himself, thank you very much—and opened the door. It was neat and tidy inside, the dishes done and the bookshelves dusted, which meant his mom or aunts had paid a visit. That also meant there would be food in the fridge and clean sheets on the bed, if the "discussion" with Bea went well. There were some benefits to overly obtrusive relatives.

"Okay," she said, moving into the middle of the living room space and facing him, arms folded across her chest. "I'm here. Explain."

Actions spoke better than words, Gregor figured. He tugged off his jacket then whipped his T-shirt up and over his head. When his hands went to his belt buckle, Bea took a small step backward.

"What are you doing?" she asked nervously.

"Explaining."

"And you have to do that naked?"

He grinned and pulled his jeans and boxers off in one smooth motion. Bea's eyes immediately went to his cock, which sprang free and then jutted out proudly, reaching for her. She licked her lips unconsciously and Gregor bit back a groan.

Explain now, fuck later, he told his wolf.

Closing his eyes, he let the beast spring free. His hands morphed into paws and claws, and fur burst through his skin. He felt his center of gravity change, heard the small gasp Bea made as his hearing sharpened. When he opened his eyes again as the wolf, she hadn't moved a muscle and she hadn't screamed, but she was deathly pale, her eyes wide with shock and, yeah, maybe a little fear.

He canted his head and wagged his tail, doing his best impression of a cute puppy—albeit a puppy that weighed over two hundred pounds and had a mouth full of razor-sharp teeth. When she exhaled the breath she'd been holding, he figured it was safe enough to move forward. She twitched when he took the first step, but then held still and let him approach. Pleased, he butted her hand with his nose and she raised it automatically and stroked him.

"Jesus, Gregor," she gasped. "I thought I was hallucinating, but you're real. How…I don't understand. Can you still hear me like this? Can you speak to me?"

No, and that was a problem. Though his wolf wasn't finished saying hello to their mate, he pulled it back in, feeling his body morph back into the one with a voice box capable of speech. Bea stayed where she was, so when he stood tall as a man again, he was able to draw her into his arms. She was trembling.

"You okay?" he murmured into her hair.

"I'm not sure." She made a strangled little noise. "I'm having a rapid rethink about everything I thought I knew about the world. And wondering if I might be having a breakdown. So, you're a what, a werewolf?"

"You're not crazy," he assured her. "Shifter is the term. We're not werewolves, we don't go wild with bloodlust under the full moon or any of that shit."

She chuckled shakily. "Good to know. You mentioned vampires. Is everything in the horror stories real? Ghosts? Demons? Griffins?"

"Vampires, definitely. Demons too. I've never seen a ghost and I don't know what a griffin is."

"Okay." She took a deep breath and he could practically feel her pull herself together. She stepped back and though he didn't want to let her go, he knew he needed to give her space to assimilate. Just a step, though. His wolf didn't want her any further away than that. "Why are you telling me this? I have to imagine you usually keep it a secret or the whole world would know and you'd probably all be locked up in some secret government facility. You only just met me, Gregor. Why are you trusting me like this?"

"You're my mate," he said simply.

She stared at him and wetted her lips again in a nervous gesture that made him want to kiss her. "I'm going to assume that you don't mean like friends."

"No," he replied, voice low and rough. "You're my mate, the other half of my soul. The one I'm going to spend the rest of my life with."

"Uhuh." She lifted her foot to take another pace backward and Gregor stepped with her this time. Then some thought passed behind her eyes and he felt a wave of fear and wonder wash through the room. "Am I going to be like you? Is that what Logan was talking about when he said I didn't transform?"

Gregor grimaced. "I don't think so, baby. If you were going to be like me, it would have happened when we mated and I marked you."

"Oh." She looked like she didn't know whether to be pleased or disappointed. "What does that mean?"

It meant he'd never be able to run as a wolf with his mate, which killed Gregor, but he wouldn't swap. Bea was his, and it didn't matter to him that she couldn't shift.

"It doesn't mean anything." He paused when someone thumped at the door. It was Logan. He recognized the heavy force of the knocks, but, also, he felt the pull of his alpha, the dominance he exuded.

Logan didn't wait to be invited in. He stuck his head in the door, obviously curious. The alpha was as nosey and interfering as the rest of them.

"Hey," he said. "Fran's made dinner. She wanted you to bring Bea over, introduce her to everyone. Make sure they know who she is."

Gregor had been all set to say no to Logan—something that was best done sparingly—but he changed his mind as his alpha's words sunk in. The pack needed to meet Bea, get acquainted with her scent. As a non-shifter, she'd be weaker, more vulnerable. He didn't want there to be any accidents of misunderstandings.

"Fran's made meatloaf," Logan added, as an extra incentive.

"We'll be there," Gregor replied. "Give us five minutes."

Logan nodded his head, satisfied, then disappeared as quickly as he'd come. Gregor turned back to Bea, who'd said not a word during the whole conversation.

"Dinner?" he asked.

She gave a jerky nod. "Sure. I could eat."

"I'll be with you the whole time," he promised, and she smiled gratefully.

Unfortunately, Gregor broke his promise within five minutes of stepping inside the alpha's house—which *was* a log cabin that the older man *had* built from scratch with his bare hands...and a lot of heavy equipment. They did run a construction company, after all.

"Gregor," Logan jerked at him with his head, pulling him over toward where he was standing with Callum and Kenny, and Fran, his mate. Bea came over with him, her fingers wrapped tightly round his hand. "We need to talk about the thefts at the site."

The thefts, and the vampires. Right.

"Why don't I take Bea—it is Bea, isn't it?—into the kitchen while you guys talk?" Fran suggested, smiling sweetly. "Anna's there, too, knocking together a dessert. She's a new mate as well, so you two can compare notes."

Gregor frowned. It was a good suggestion, and he'd intended to introduce Bea to Anna as soon as possible, but Fran was being just a bit too nice, a bit too accommodating. That wasn't like her. She wasn't a total bitch or anything—most of the time, anyway—but she rarely went out of her way to be this welcoming, especially to non-shifters. She'd given Anna a hell of a time until Callum had stepped in and asked Logan to intercede. Callum's mate was still terrified of her.

Bea was looking at her appreciatively, though, and she'd already released her death-grip on Gregor's hand.

"Sure," she said. "I can help with the food."

"Excellent."

Something twisted inside Gregor as Bea walked away, his wolf whining unhappily, but Logan commanded his attention almost immediately.

"I told Callum and Kenny what you told me," he said. "I know you said it seemed like the vampire was just looking for things to sell, but it seems suspicious to me that he'd target us three times. I think we need to consider that this is more personal. You said you thought he was just a lackey vamp?"

Gregor nodded distractedly, his gaze still across the room on the kitchen door.

"I think we need to try and find out who the master is, then. I've got a few ideas how we can do that…"

For the next ten minutes Gregor listened to Logan outline ways to try and identify the bloodsucker, but almost none of it went in. He was increasingly restless, his wolf urging him to go and check on Bea. Just in case. Because—

"Gregor?" Logan's voice was sharp and unhappy. "Are you listening to me?"

"He's thinking about his mate," Kenny commented, grinning wryly. "I remember what that was like. My dick was red raw for weeks from too much sex." He winked. "It didn't stop me, though."

"Hell, mine's like that right now," Callum drawled, and the trio laughed. Gregor didn't, though. Anna had emerged from the kitchen looking pale, and her gaze darted around the room, not settling until it landed on Gregor. He was in motion a heartbeat later.

"Gregor!" Logan called.

For the first time in his life, Gregor ignored his alpha.

"What is it? What's wrong?" he demanded, meeting Anna in the middle of the room.

Anna bit her lip. "Gregor, it's Fran. She's upset Bea. She started making all these comments about a proper mate and what a shame it was that Bea would never be able to shift, be a real partner to you. And then she started talking about Janna—" Janna was Fran and Logan's daughter. "She said that Janna had been meant to mate you and how disappointed she was going to be."

Fuck. Gregor shouldn't have ignored his instincts, he'd known Fran was up to something.

"Where's Bea?"

"That's just it," Anna said. "She's gone."

Chapter Seven

Of course, what every male really wants is a female who can run beside him—as a wolf…it's such a shame you'll never truly be one of us dear…Janna and Gregor were made for each other, but, you know, these things are meant to try us…He was all set to mate her before you came along.

I wiped my eyes as I guided the sedan down the rutted dirt road. My boss would have a conniption if I damaged the vehicle. And how would I explain it? Oh, well, you see, I had to go with the stranger I found in my garden and took into my house to fuck, so that he could show me how he turns into a wolf. But don't worry, it won't happen again.

No, it wouldn't happen again. The acid had practically dripped from Fran's words as she used them to stab at me, even as she smiled. God, I felt so stupid. I'd wanted to run back to the living area, to Gregor, but that would have been even more humiliating, so I'd just fled. I got in my car and I drove away. It was cowardly maybe—okay, definitely—but I didn't care. I just wanted to go back home to my ordered little life and live in my safe and ordinary world. And if I said it enough, maybe I'd start to believe it.

The trees thinned as I reached the end of the long and winding drive. I could see the road to freedom, helpfully tarmacked so that I could accelerate hard and get the hell out of here. I was just putting my blinker on, even though there was no one around, because I was sensible to my core and I needed to remember that, when a speeding blur darted out in front of my car. I braked hard, skidding to a stop just in time to avoid running over what I could now see was a wolf. A moment later, it became Gregor.

A very naked, angry looking Gregor.

He stormed around to my side of the car and yanked the car door open. He was breathing hard, a sheen of sweat breaking out over his skin despite the chilliness of the day.

"You can get out or I can climb in there with you," he warned when I didn't move.

The thought of what my boss would say if she knew that Gregor's naked ass—even if it was a glorious ass—had been in contact with the work vehicle's leather seats had me clambering out of the car with a squeak.

"Where were you going?" he demanded, closing the door behind me as soon as I was clear of the car and then pushing forward so I was pinned between it and him. Naked him. Very, very naked him. I could feel his erection pressing into my stomach, and I pressed my hands against the side of the vehicle so I wouldn't do something stupid like clutch at him and beg him to fuck things better.

"I…home?"

"This is home." His eyes glared down at me and I swore I saw the wolf there. It wasn't happy with me either, it seemed. It was also hurt that I'd run out on them. I didn't know how I knew, but I did.

I softened my voice, lifting my hands to rest them on his chest. "It isn't," I said gently. "I don't belong here."

Fran had been very clear about that.

"What did that bitch say to you?"

I didn't ask who he was talking about, or how he knew what had happened. Anna, Callum's mate—who was lovely and sweet and who had made the change the night they met—had watched Fran cut me down with wide, worried eyes.

"Nothing that wasn't true."

"Bullshit!" He snarled the word. He was furious, but I wasn't afraid of him. His anger wasn't directed at me, and besides, though we'd only known each other for a couple of days, I knew him. Gregor would never hurt me. "You belong here, with me."

"I'm not a shifter, and I'm never going to be."

"You don't know that."

"I do." I felt it, an instinct. "I can't be like you."

"I don't care, you're mine."

"You don't care now," I said quietly. "But you will. Janna is—"

"Janna is a bitch like her mother." I winced, although I couldn't argue with his assessment of Fran's character. "I wouldn't touch her even if I'd never met you. You can't leave me, Bea."

I could. I could get in my car and get on with my boring little life, doing my boring little job. But I really, really didn't want to. Looking up into Gregor's piercing eyes, seeing the naked emotion there (I seemed to have naked on the brain, it couldn't have anything to do with the huge cock currently stabbing at me), my heart twisted.

"They don't want me there," I reminded him.

"Fran is one person," he replied shortly. "You can avoid her. I do."

I giggled, dropping my head to rest my forehead against his pectoral, right over his heart. I breathed him, felt his arms come around me, one around my shoulders, the other sliding through my hair to cup the back of my head. Nothing had ever felt so right.

A car whizzed by on the main road, reminding me that civilization was *right there*.

"You should put on some clothes," I told Gregor. "You could get arrested."

"I'm on pack lands," he told me, smiling smugly.

"Uhuh. I'd like to see you explain that to the nice police officer."

"You're going to have to take me back, then," he told me, "Because I don't have any clothes. But first—"

He dipped his head down and captured my mouth in a kiss. It wasn't a gentle kiss. It was hard and demanding, his tongue plunging into my mouth. His hand tightened in my hair, telling me to hold still and take it, take him.

I didn't protest, my hands sliding from his chest to grab at his muscular biceps. One hand was sliding down toward his elbow, thinking of moving even further south to grab onto a tight buttock when he abruptly pulled away from me and dropped to his knees.

"Gregor?" I asked.

He went right to the waistband on my yoga pants, yanking them and my panties down to my ankles.

"I have to taste you," he said.

I repeat, the road was *right there*. Granted, the car was shielding me, but any curious passer-by who stopped was going to very quickly get more than an eyeful.

"Gregor, the road," I panted, lifting my feet as he tugged on them, allowing him to slip my clothes off my body. "People might see."

"Don't worry about them, baby," he told me. "Just concentrate on me."

Then he lifted my leg and placed it on his shoulder, opening me up for him. He shoved at my T-shirt until it rested just beneath my breasts and I felt his hot breath on my stomach a moment before he nuzzled me. It was surprisingly sweet, and he followed it up with fingers, stroking at my core. I gasped, feeling the stretch as he slid two fingers inside me but they were gone a moment later, riding up to circle my clit.

"I've been looking forward to this," he murmured.

I stood there, just feet from the public highway, leaning back against my work car as Gregor knelt between my legs and tongued my pussy. He didn't rush, either, licking around my labia and flicking at my clit, teasing me with shallow thrusts that just made me ache for the thickness of his cock.

"Please," I gasped. "Fuck me."

"I am fucking you," he mumbled.

I whimpered as he flattened his tongue against my clit and rubbed, giving me just enough pressure that I was going to—

He took his mouth away just as I felt the orgasm threaten to wash over me and I cried out, smacking a hand against his shoulder.

"Gregor!"

"Not yet, baby."

"Now!" I pleaded as he kissed at my spread open thighs, leaving me pulsing on air. "You're torturing me!"

"You deserve this," he replied cruelly. "You ran from me."

He licked at my clit once, twice. The orgasm came rushing back. One more and I'd fall over the edge.

Instead, Gregor shifted lower and thrust his tongue inside me, lapping at my juices.

"God!" I whined. "If I say I'm sorry, will you let me come?"

He shifted back to grin up at me, wetting a fingertip and tapping against my swollen bud. I jolted with every contact, it was *just* not enough.

"Maybe. If you mean it. And you agree to come back with me."

"All right," I said, all but mindless with the need to come already, the cool autumn breeze against my pussy a sharp contrast to the heat of Gregor's mouth. "I'll do it. Just...oh God. Just lick me. *Please*, Gregor!"

"You got it baby."

He thrust two fingers into my sheath, fucking me with them, going all the way to the knuckle, at the same time as he set his mouth over my clit and sucked, tongue lashing at the little bundle of nerves.

I screamed, coming immediately, my head thumping back against the car roof, eyes closing in ecstasy. It ripped through me, almost painful in its intensity, leaving me deaf and dumb and blind for an endless moment. I didn't notice Gregor standing up, didn't register when he grabbed my legs and wrapped them around his narrow hips.

I felt it, though, when he slid home in one long, firm glide.

"Yes," I panted, opening my eyes and watching him watch my pussy take his cock. "Fuck me, Gregor."

There were no little jokes or quips this time. His gaze was fire on me as he started to move, hard and deep, each thrust lifting me up against the car. I held on to one wide shoulder, my other hand dropping to my breast and squeezing through my clothes, fingers finding my nipple and pinching hard.

"That's right, Bea," he breathed, "Touch yourself."

He was hitting my g-spot with every thrust, lighting me up. Trusting in his strength, I let go of him and slid my other hand down until I reached my clit. I rubbed at it, timing my circles with each of his thrusts.

"You ready?" he asked, grunting as he drove home a little harder, a little faster. "You ready to come with me?"

"Yes," I panted, so turned on I was ready to explode again already. I felt it wash over me, singing through my nerves. Gregor jerked his hips against me as he found his own release, his head tipping back as he poured it into me. He was so beautiful. My heart clenched as I realized that he was mine. It was crazy, but it was real too.

"Fuck baby," he growled. "That was amazing."

I smiled, not even caring that a truck was driving by, the driver probably able to see us from his elevated position. Let him look. Let him see.

"It was," I agreed.

He grinned at me and pulled out, letting me drop slowly back down to earth. Warm hands tugged my T-shirt back into position, and he paused to run a hand over my stomach. "I can't wait to see you swollen with my babies," he murmured.

Wow. That was taking things a bit too fast. Even as I thought that, though, my mind conjured up an image of Gregor, kids climbing all over him. He'd be a good dad, I reckoned.

Then a horrible thought struck me.

"Gregor," I said slowly. "If…if we do stay together—"

"We are together," he growled.

All right, then.

"What if we can't have kids?" I asked. "Because I can't become like you."

He grinned. "Don't worry baby. We'll still be able to have pups."

I smiled back at him, reassured, then my brain froze.

"Pups?"

CHARLI MAC

HIS
MATE
SERIES

BOOK 3

HIS
CAPRICIOUS
MATE

Chapter One

Her hands were tied high above her head, her weight on her tiptoes. The spreader bar cuffed to both ankles prevented her from closing her legs as he glided closer.

"Do you want to come, little one?" he purred.

Yes fucking please. I buzzed the bullet vibrator lightly over my clit as I turned the page.

The flogger stung as he whipped it across her stomach and her breasts. She cried out, arching into the pain.

"More?" he asked.

"Please. More."

This time he concentrated on her inner thighs, pinkening the skin, making it burn. Her clit pulsed, desperate for his touch. She tilted her pelvis in silent plea, too lost in sensation to be embarrassed any more.

I closed my eyes briefly, trying to imagine it. The freedom of surrender. My hips flexed, my clit searching for harder pressure from the vibe, but I deliberately pulled away. I'd been edging for the last twenty minutes, ever since the heroine stepped inside the dungeon. My orgasm was *right there*, just a decent press with the buzzing little vibrator away, but I didn't let myself fall over the edge.

God, how I wanted to find a man who could handle me like that. Who could turn me into a quivering pile of jelly. Unfortunately, that seemed to be the effect I had on most men.

His fingers slid right up her centre, her desire glistening on his fingertips. Holding her gaze, he put them into his mouth and sucked.

"You taste delicious," he told her.

He ran the flogger up between her legs, a gentle stroke, teasing her. She whimpered, tried to grind against it, but he pulled it away with a laugh.

The next strike was harder, a lash across her right breast, catching the nipple. She screamed, writhing in her restraints, but a moment later she was arching forward again, begging for more.

"Brave girl," he whispered. He lifted the flogger again.

"Fuck!" I lost the fight against my orgasm, yanking in a gasp as it hit me. Pleasure pulsed over me in waves, the book dropping out of my hand. I rode out the aftershocks as my pelvis contracted and spasmed, revelling in the almost painful sensitivity of my clit.

I was just thinking about going for round two, buzzing the little vibe in gentle circles to reawaken my nerve endings, when the shattering of glass smashed through my post-orgasmic haze.

I was on my feet in a heartbeat, listening hard. My flat was above a store, *my* store, and the breaking glass had sounded like it was coming from directly beneath me. I heard a scrape and a muffled thump, the sounds of things shifting about. Someone was breaking in! They were stealing my stuff!

Fury overriding common sense, I hauled my sneakers onto my feet and grabbed the store keys from the kitchen counter. I didn't own a gun, hadn't touched one since I handed in my badge three years ago, but I grabbed a rolling pin from the kitchen drawer and stuffed the handcuffs that I'd, um, kept for personal reasons into my pocket before I jogged quietly down the back stairs.

It was almost midnight. Nothing moved in the alleyway, even the rats seeming to hold their breath. My hands shook slightly as I inserted the key into the lock, anger and fear coalescing into one big adrenaline rush. I opened the door silently, noticing that the alarm wasn't even blinking. Someone was smart enough to disable it before they busted in.

The scent of paint overwhelmed me as I tiptoed into my workshop. Half-finished canvasses watched me silently from their positions on easels around the room. As I passed by my workbench, I grabbed one of the scalpels I used to do tile-printing, the blade glinting dully in the soft light filtering down from the back alley.

The door to the shop itself was fully closed and I knew the handle was sticky, the hinges never giving way without a loud, resounding squeak. I'd have to move fast. I took a moment to ready myself, trying to calm my racing heart and push back the fears that would cloud my thinking, make me hesitate.

An instant later, I erupted into the room, smacking the switch and flooding the space with light. I already had my eyes half closed in preparation, but whoever was in there gave a squawk as they were instantly blinded. Squinting, I saw a man, whippet thin with greasy dark hair cut in unfashionable curtains, look around in terror, his hands wrapped around a large landscape that had been hanging in pride of place on the wall. That was my best piece, with a price tag of over a thousand dollars, and he had his thieving hands all over it!

"Not a chance!" I spat.

I rushed across the room, rolling pin held high. He didn't put it down to defend himself. Instead, he turned his shoulder to me, taking the blow across his back. I put everything I had into it, expecting him to drop, but he was stronger than he looked. My blow bounced off him, sending shockwaves up my arm.

He twisted away from me, trying to dart toward the broken window and freedom, my painting still in his hands, but I cut him off. He could have ploughed right through me, but he pulled up, avoiding contact. Weird.

"Put the painting down!" I ordered. I'd put hundreds of hours of work into that thing, and I had a customer coming tomorrow to look at it. It took a lot more than I realized to keep a shop afloat, even when I only employed an assistant part time, and I *needed* that sale.

"I can't," he stammered. "I need it! Please, get out of the way!"

"Not a fucking chance!"

"I don't want to hurt you!"

He darted to my left, trying to squeeze through the opening. God, he was fast, and I was out of shape. If I didn't avoid all of my old colleagues like the plague, they'd be horrified to see me wheezing, my ass wobbling as I lunged to cut him off. He drew up again, knocking over a glass vase I'd hand painted. It hit the ground and exploded, taking the two hundred dollars I'd hoped to sell it for with it.

"Dammit!"

"I'm sorry! I'm sorry! I'll pay for it!"

"How? You're stealing my painting *for money*, you're clearly cash strapped!" Because there was no other reason to pinch one of my pictures.

And he obviously really needed it, because he could have gotten away from me easily if he'd just put the damn thing down.

"I'll get money, okay? Just, please, let me take it."

He held the painting away from me, attempting to spin away, but the big counter I'd had installed in the centre of the floor space made everything just a bit too tight and there wasn't quite room. Reaching back, I yanked out the handcuffs then struck, slapping one of the circles around his wrist. Unfortunately, there wasn't anything to handcuff him to, and although I tugged with all my strength, I couldn't pull his arm back, had no chance of getting it behind his back. Out of other options, I locked the other side around my own wrist.

"Oh no!" he moaned. "No, no, no!"

"Yes," I replied grimly. "Put the painting down."

Admitting defeat, he lowered it gently to the floor. I eyed it carefully, but it seemed to have survived its brush with death.

"What are you going to do now?" he asked mournfully.

I eyed him askance. "What do you think? I'm calling the cops."

He was incredibly pale anyway, but at my words, he went bleach white, his eyes darkening with fear.

"Please, no. You can't. They'll arrest me and take me away."

"Well, yeah." That was kind of what cops did.

"No, you don't understand. I'll die!"

That was a bit dramatic. "Look, it's okay. You didn't actually steal anything. It'll just be breaking and entering, and criminal damage." I thought of my lovely vase with a pang of regret. "It's not that big a deal. You'll get a record, probably a suspended sentence, but they're not going to call for your execution."

He shook his head, those awful curtains flicking across his face.

"I can't. I can't let them take me away. The sun will come up and I'll—" He cut off abruptly, strangled sounds coming out of his throat like he was choking. "Please!"

The sun will come up and what? He'd go poof? Did he think he was a vampire or something? I looked down at the handcuffs, suddenly having serious doubts about cuffing myself to this guy. I'd left the keys upstairs—because the handcuffs were no good if they could be used against me—and I definitely didn't want to take him into my home.

"Maybe I could call you an ambulance instead," I offered gently. "There are places you can go if you're having—" I winced. "If you need to talk to someone and..." I trailed off because he was shaking his head with dark amusement.

"I'm not crazy," he said.

"I didn't say you were," I assured him, though I was starting to think it. "Let's just call the police and you can explain things to them."

His whole demeanor changed then. It had been verging on desperate, now he was grimly resolute. I didn't think that boded well for me.

"I can't let you call the cops," he said, all pleading gone from his voice.

"I've tried very hard not to hurt you, but if you try to put me in danger, I will have to stop you."

Yup, I was right. Not good.

"Don't do anything you can't take back." I warned him.

The look he gave me was grave. "You need to listen to that advice yourself. Let me go. I won't come back, and I'll find a way to pay you back for the window." He winced. "And the vase."

"Not good enough," I said. "You broke in here to steal from me, I'm not just going to let you get away with it."

He snorted. "If you want to punish me, it's not the cops you need to call."

"Oh, who is it then, your mom?" Always snark in the face of danger. That attitude had got me through years of policing.

He threw me a look, unimpressed. "It is my master."

Master? The breath stalled in my lungs. That was just a little too close to the very dog-eared paperback I'd dropped on the floor in my rush to get down here.

"Your…Master?"

He nodded, not at all embarrassed to be throwing a word like that about. "Trust me, if he finds out what I have done, I will be punished."

"And will he pay for the stuff you damaged?"

He nodded.

"All right, then." I felt a rush of something like destiny coursing through me. "Let's call your Master."

Chapter Two

Tobias Hunter was a bastard. In both senses of the word. His mother had been a whore who couldn't have picked his father out of her long line of customers if her life depended on it. He'd been born a gutter rat, and he'd learned to cheat and lie and steal while most children were playing with dolls and spinning tops. He might not wear rags anymore, and his accent was smooth and carefully cultured, but he never forgot his early education. He was cold, ruthless and cruel, and he knew it.

If he had an ounce of decency, he'd feel bad about it, but he didn't. In fact, he was quite proud of it.

He looked down at the plaything currently mewling at his feet. Like a junkie hungry for her fix, she knew he was going to hurt her, but she wanted it anyway.

"Look at me," he commanded, and her head snapped up at once. Her face was beautiful, her eyes a dark blue and shining with the need to please. She'd do absolutely anything he asked her to, and that was the problem. There was no spark of defiance there, no pride or sense of self. She was nothing but a puppet ready to dance to whatever tune he wanted to play.

"Get out," he said softly.

Her eyebrows drew together in confusion. "Master?" she warbled.

Irritation surged. "Get out before I kill you."

She got her feet beneath her and stood, but then she hesitated, as if he was a magnet, drawing her irresistibly.

"Out!" He grabbed a pewter goblet from his desk and launched it at her. He missed, deliberately, but red wine sloshed up and spattered her skin, dripping like the blood that was going to flow if he had to tell her again.

She got the message this time—or maybe she read her death in his eyes—because she scuttled out, running on bare feet, her naked buttocks jiggling with every step. Tobias watched her go with something like regret. She was a beautiful creature, but that wasn't enough. Not anymore.

His phone rang, a welcome distraction because he was thinking about calling her back and playing with her anyway, and he knew that in the mood he was in, he'd be crueller than even he liked to be.

"What?" Not the politest of greetings, but only his children had this number.

He knew from the sharp intake of breath that it was not one of his children.

"Who is this? How did you get this number?"

Whoever they were, they took a moment to respond.

"I think I have something of yours." A woman, her voice was nervous but there was a core of steel underneath. "He says his name is Kevin."

Of course, it would be Kevin. If it weren't for the fact that Tobias never made mistakes, he might have admitted a certain…regret in adding him to his ranks.

"May I speak to Kevin?"

"No, I don't think so. You can come and get him, though. And bring your wallet."

Tobias blinked, astonished. No one had talked to him like that in a hundred years.

"Are you attempting to blackmail me? I feel obliged to tell you that would be unwise."

"He's damaged my property and broken some of my work. He tells me you're good for it." She paused. "Are you going to come and get him or not?"

Tobias smiled. He had a dozen people he could send to sort out this little mess, but he was intrigued to meet the little spitfire who spoke to him so disrespectfully.

"Give me your address and I will be there momentarily."

She rattled off an address in the old town and then, without even waiting for confirmation, hung up on him. Oh yes, Tobias was looking forward to meeting her.

Standing up, he closed his eyes and felt for his connection to Kevin. It was weaker than the bond he had with all of his other children but then, Kevin was weak. He had his uses, occasionally, and this night he'd done better than usual. He had provided entertainment.

Allowing himself a small chuckle of anticipation, Tobias dematerialized. A moment later, he rematerialized in a small boutique gallery. It was modern art, he realized with a hint of distaste, though there was something joyous in the vibrance of the colors. There was evidence of a struggle, fragments of glass scattered across the floor, a breeze flowing through the space from a broken window.

And there was Kevin, sitting against the wall, hand-cuffed, of all things, to a dark-haired, dark-eyed woman. She blinked twice, as if she couldn't believe her eyes, and Tobias braced himself for the screaming. He had very sensitive hearing.

She didn't scream, though. She scrambled to get up, forgetting she was attached to Kevin, who was very wisely cringing into his bent knees and trying to make himself as small as possible. The handcuffs jerked her to a stop and she half fell back down, landing on top of Kevin. She gave a little pained cry, muffled quickly, and Tobias felt an unreasonable anger explode through him.

Get up, fool! he threw at Kevin.

The younger vampire hurried to obey, knocking into the woman as he did so, wrenching at her arm with his superior strength.

"Idiot!" Tobias hissed. He stormed forward and grabbed at the handcuffs, squeezing until the metal links disintegrated.

Separated, and feeling his Master's fury, Kevin prostrated himself on the floor. The woman looked down at him, surprised, then eyed Tobias warily.

"How did you get here so fast?" she asked.

"I can do that." He gave her a smile, deliberately flashing his teeth.

"What were you outside, waiting in a car?" She narrowed her eyes at him. "Did you send him in here to steal from me?"

Tobias drew himself up, affronted. "I assure you I did not. I was at home when I received your phone call."

"I don't see how that's possible," she shot back.

Unable to decide whether he was amused or insulted by her blatant distrust, Tobias dematerialized and rematerialized again, moving across the shop floor.

"Jesus Christ!"

The astonishment on her face and in her voice was gratifying. As was the fact that, though fear widened her eyes, she still didn't scream.

"What the hell are you?" She glanced down at Kevin, who hadn't moved a muscle, then back up at Tobias. "Are you a vampire?"

He raised an imperious eyebrow. "What led you to that conclusion?"

What did you say?

Kevin whimpered apologetically. "Nothing, Master. She...she said she was going to call the police and I—The sun!"

The woman glanced back and forth between the two of them, clearly confused.

"Are you talking to him?" She frowned, almost embarrassed. "Mind to mind."

"Very astute," he complimented her.

She snorted. "It wasn't that much of a guess. He's answering a question I didn't hear." She pierced him with her gaze again. She was very direct, and very, very brave. "Are you a vampire?"

He liked this woman. It was a shame he was going to have to wipe her mind of this entire conversation.

"I am." He bowed. "Tobias Hunter, at your service."

She gave him a polite smile, and that irked him. He wanted a real one. "I'm Cat Jenkins."

"Short for Catherine?" he guessed.

"Catriona."

"A beautiful name."

She ignored the compliment, inclining her head toward Kevin. "He said you were his master."

Tobias gave a small nod. "I created him."

"Are you responsible for him?"

"For my sins." Tobias heaved an unhappy sigh and Kevin cringed, trying to worm his way into the flooring.

"Well, he broke into my shop and smashed a two-hundred-dollar vase. He was going to steal a painting worth a thousand dollars."

"I will replace the window," he assured her, "and pay for the vase. The painting is undamaged?"

"It seems to be."

"Nonetheless, I will pay for it." He curled his lip at Kevin, though the younger vampire was studiously avoiding his gaze and couldn't see it. "This one will pay for it with his hide."

Kevin knew better than to make a sound, but fear radiated off him in waves. Perhaps Tobias wouldn't punish him too harshly. He was very much enjoying this unexpected little interlude.

"Why does a vampire need to steal art for cash, anyway? I thought you guys were all loaded, living in creepy mansions and shit?"

Tobias laughed, he actually laughed. It had been so long since he'd heard the sound, he barely recognized it. "My mansion is very much not creepy, I assure you. But as to why Kevin should need money so badly, I should very much like to hear the answer to that myself."

Mind to mind, to Kevin, he added, *Explain yourself.*

The truth should have fallen from Kevin's lips like rain at that command, but he shuddered silently instead, trying to defy the order. Tobias eyebrows twitched, whatever his recalcitrant child had been up to, it must be very bad indeed.

"Speak, Kevin." He put every ounce of his dominance into the words, shoving down on Kevin's will with his considerable might. Kevin cried out helplessly.

"What are you doing to him?" Cat demanded.

"Showing him who is the master here," Tobias replied darkly.

He expected Cat to wilt then, too. Instead, her breathing quickened and her pupils dilated, cheeks turning pink. Interesting.

"I'm sorry, Master," Kevin wailed, squirming, trying to escape the pressure Tobias was pushing down on him. Instead of letting up, he increased it. "I've lost the ring."

"You've...what?" It took a lot to instil panic in Tobias. Kevin had managed it in just four little words.

"Forgive me. I beg you."

Hot on the heels of panic came apoplectic rage. "How the *fuck* did you manage to lose it? All you had to do was take it back to the vault?"

He never swore. It was coarse and vulgar, and it reminded him of the gutter rat he used to be. It was a sign that he had lost control. Tobias knew it, and yet still he couldn't rein himself in.

He didn't realize what he was doing to Kevin until Cat stepped over to him and got right up into his face, shouting, "Stop it! Stop it!"

She shoved at him, and the physical contact was enough to shock him back into reality. Glancing down at Kevin, he saw blood pouring out of his nose, his hands clawing at his hair.

Taking a deep breath—yes, vampires breathed—he let him go and Kevin slumped onto the ground, panting.

"I apologize for my behavior," he told Cat, meticulously polite. Inside he was a riot of emotions. The ring he had entrusted Kevin to return to his secure vault was almost six hundred years old, had belonged to Vlad the Impaler. It was a powerful magical object, and being its keeper ensured Tobias reigned supreme across his territory. Without it—

He'd be vulnerable to every strong vampire with ambitions.

"How did you lose it?" he demanded.

"I—It was stolen from me."

"You were set upon?" No. Kevin looked shifty. Guilty. "What were you doing when it was taken, Kevin?"

"I was feeding," the vampire admitted in a whisper. "They took me by surprise."

"I hope you enjoyed it," Tobias replied, anger seeping back into his carefully even tone. "Because you won't be tasting blood again for a long time."

Vampires could go a long time in between feeds. It quickly became uncomfortable, then painful, then agonising, but they wouldn't actually die. Kevin was about to discover just how uncomfortable a starving vampire could get.

"This still doesn't explain why you were trying to steal my painting," Cat cut in.

Kevin hung his head, shame-faced. "They have been blackmailing me. They demanded money, and I paid it. But then instead of returning the ring, they asked for more, and more."

"Extortion," Cat said flatly. She glanced at Tobias. "I used to be a cop."

"You did?" That explained the bravery. A woman police officer would have to develop a thick shield to deal with such unpleasantness. "Excellent. You will retrieve the object for me."

The idea came to Tobias as the words came out of his mouth, but even thinking it over, he was pleased with it. Cat intrigued him, drew him, and he liked the idea of extending their acquaintance.

"Wait," she said, holding her hands up. "I said I used to be a cop. I'm not one anymore, and I'm not a private investigator either. I'm an artist."

"I'll pay you, of course," Tobias answered smoothly. "Handsomely."

That gave her pause. She looked around her store, at the artwork hanging on the walls, unsold. This area had been a slum in Tobias' youth, but now it was up and coming. Trendy, even. Rents were expensive, he'd presume.

She licked her lips, considering, and he knew he had her.

"How much?" she asked.

Chapter Three

I crouched in the bushes and stared across the street. It had taken me four days to find the petty gang of thieves who were extorting the *vampires*—my brain still stuttered over the word—from the information Kevin had given me, but I had them now. Their base was an old, abandoned church. It didn't look very secure, there were three entrances and plenty of windows that could be used as access points too. There was always someone there on guard but still, I'd expected more from crooks who had the balls to steal from vampires.

I probably could have gone to Tobias with the information and taken the healthy pay packet, congratulated myself on a job well done, but I wanted to be able to hand him the ring, too. I wanted…Oh, all right. I wanted him to be impressed with me. He was pretty fucking scary, but he was also the hottest man I'd ever seen. It wasn't handsomeness per se, though he was very good looking. It was the aura he exuded. He was just…more than any man I'd ever met. He was powerful and controlled and commanding.

If he wanted to tie me up in his dungeon and have me call him Master, I just might do it.

"Focus, Cat," I hissed to myself.

I'd been hiding in the bushes for the past hour, watching the light leech out of the sky. The guard at the church had changed twenty minutes ago, and I wanted to give him the chance to get good and bored before I snuck in and surprised him. I was unarmed, because I wasn't a police officer anymore, and if things went tits up, without a knife in my back pocket or a gun strapped to my thigh, I'd have an easier time worming my way out of trouble if the cops showed up. Not that I owned a gun. There were plenty of things I could employ as a weapon if need be, but I was hoping to get away with simple stealth. The thing about tracking thieves for a decade was you learned lots of tricks of the trade.

I was just about to inch around the back of the church, find an entrance on the side of the building away from the street, when I heard a rustle nearby. I froze, doing nothing to give myself away, ears listening and eyes searching even as my heart threatened to thump out of my chest. I spied a flash of pale skin and reached out for the thick branch I'd grabbed on my way into the thicket, planning to bludgeon whoever was trying to sneak up on me, when Kevin came scuttling from his patch of cover, running in a crouch to my side.

"You!" I exclaimed. "What the hell are you doing here? Are you spying on me?"

"Master told me to," Kevin replied, without any hint of apology. "He told me to make sure you stayed safe, help you if I could."

"Scaring me to death is not helping me!" I complained.

He shrugged and turned to look at the church building. "Is that where the ring is?"

"Yeah," I replied. Now that I'd got over my shock, I was starting to notice that he looked different from when I'd last seen him just a few days ago. He seemed to have shrunk, his cheeks hollowed over sharp cheekbones, the bones of his shoulder blades visible through his thin T-shirt. "Are you all right?" I asked.

He cocked his head at me, confused.

"You look...different." I gestured at him, and grimaced.

Understanding slid into his eyes, along with regret. "I am being punished," he reminded me.

"Right." I decided not to ask further. I nodded toward the church. "It's just one guard. It seems a bit too easy, but I scoped it out the last two nights; I can't see any traps."

Keven gave a grim smile. "Easy for you, maybe," he said.

"What do you mean?"

"I can't go in there."

"Why not?" I frowned at him.

"It's a church," he said, as if that explained everything. Maybe it did.

"What, because it's consecrated ground?" He nodded. "But it's closed down. It isn't a church anymore."

"Doesn't matter," he said. "I still couldn't cross the threshold. Not even on pain of death."

"Can you die?" The question was out before I could stop it.

He shrugged ruefully. "I can cease to exist. That's pretty much the same thing, isn't it?"

"Fair enough." I sighed, looking over at the church again. "I guess it's me that's going in there and facing the guard, then?"

Typical.

"Draw him out," Kevin suggested. "If it's only one of them, I can handle it." He saw the uncertain look I gave him and made a face. "I have not equipped myself well in this whole fiasco, but I am not entirely useless. I can deal with one human man."

"All right, then."

Drawing the guard out proved incredibly easy. I picked up a few stones and started lobbing them at the building. I wasn't a great shot and most of my efforts fell short, but Kevin saw what I was about. He picked up a good-sized pebble and launched it at the church, shattering a window. I heard a muffled exclamation and then a moment later the guard emerged, creeping cautiously out of the front door, gun drawn.

I turned to Kevin.

"Can you dodge bullets, too?" I whispered, but I was talking to the empty air. He was gone.

I'd barely turned back to eye the armed guard who was now going to be coming for me and me alone, when Kevin stepped out of the shadows behind him. He must have moved blindingly fast. I saw him reach for the gun and pull it from the man's hands, then he reached for his neck and made a quick, jerking gesture and the guard dropped.

"Shit!" Not sure what the hell had just happened, I abandoned my cover and ran toward the two of them. It was as I feared—the guard was motionless, his head twisted at an angle that was just wrong. "You killed him!" I yelped.

Kevin gave me a strange look. "He stole from Master. Now that you have identified the group, they are all going to die. This one should be very thankful that it was quick and painless. Any my master gets his hands on are going to suffer endlessly before he grants them the mercy of death."

Fuck me. It hadn't occurred to me what Tobias would do about the group of extortionists, but having met him, I probably should have guessed. And I was the one responsible for finding them.

"If he's going to murder them, I won't tell him who they are," I said.

Kevin shot me an alarmed look. "I would advise against that," he cautioned. "He will have the information from you one way or another." Great. He looked toward the church. "You will go inside and get the ring now, yes?" He paused. "If you refuse, I will have to inform my master. You've seen how quickly he could be here to...persuade you."

I shivered at his words, and not entirely in a bad way. I was starting to think maybe I might need some therapy.

"Okay," I said. "I'm going in."

I'd intended to sneak in the small rear door, but given that the guard had been so helpful as to open the front door for me, it seemed silly not to go in that way. The church had a tiny lobby and then opened up into a huge room. Most of the pews remained, though they were no longer organized in rows, some of them toppled over and others skewed to create little pockets of space. At the front was the alter, a monstrosity of gold leaf two stories high. The plinths for the statues to perch on were all empty and a couple of the decorative finials carved along the top had been snapped off.

I glided down the central aisle, vaulting a couple of pews, and glanced around, looking for possible hiding places. In the end, I didn't really have to hunt at all. They'd put the ring in the font, of all places. It was full of water and I wondered for a moment if they'd gone so far as to get their hands on holy water as an extra layer of protection.

Holy or not, the water wasn't a deterrent to me. I stuck my hand in it, shuddering at its icy cold grip, and plucked the ring from the bottom.

It was ugly, as rings go. A tarnished silver, it had a huge cabochon ruby that was cracked, right down the centre. Surely that made the thing essentially worthless? I didn't quite see why Tobias had made such a fuss about it, but maybe it had sentimental value or something. Shrugging, I tucked it into my jeans pocket and made my way outside.

Kevin was waiting for me, and the dead body was nowhere in sight.

"You have it?" he asked.

"I have it. What did you do with the body?" Then I held my hands up. "You know what? I don't want to know."

Plausible deniability. I did not want to go to jail.

I'd left my car some distance away, wanting to make sure nobody clocked it and related it to my theft of a theft, and came looking for me later. I figured it didn't matter if Kevin followed me there, given that he knew where I lived anyway.

"So should I give the ring to you or what?" I asked.

Kevin actually backed away from me, shaking his head rapidly.

"Master said I am not to touch it," he confessed. "You are to deliver it to him personally."

"Great." I huffed out a sigh, but I was being *really* well paid for this. I could do a personal delivery. And then, I'd get to see him again, bask one more time in that forbidding aura that was going to feature in my fantasies for some time to come. "So, shall I follow you or what? Where's your ride?"

"I don't have one." He looked at me pitifully.

"All right." I rolled my eyes. "Get in."

It was awkward, driving with Kevin. He didn't say much, and he wasn't a fidgeter, not moving a muscle and staring straight out of the windscreen beside me, but there was a whole barrage of questions I wanted to fling at him, and keeping my mouth shut and my nose out of vampire business was killing me.

"Why is Tobias so desperate to get the ring back?" I blurted. "I mean, it's broken." A horrible thought occurred to me. "It was broken before, right?"

Kevin gave me a small smile. "Yes, it was already broken. As to why it's important, you'll have to ask my master."

"Maybe I'll do that," I muttered, and Kevin's smile widened. I eyed him askance. Since I'd started with my questions… "How did you become a vampire, anyway?"

"The process, I'm forbidden to tell you. Why me? Master saw me and wanted me. I'm not sure he intended to make me one of his children but—" He gave a little shrug. "It happened, and now I'm his."

"He wanted you? For like food, or…" I tailed off indelicately.

"Both," he said. Then grinned. "Have I shocked you?"

"No," I said honestly. "I used to be a cop, I'm harder to shock than that."

"I believe I could, though," he teased. "Vampires are renowned for their hedonism. There are no taboos between consenting adults."

"I see." I kept my voice deliberately mild, although fuck, was I curious. "Do I turn here?"

"Yes." Kevin directed me into the posh part of the city, where the houses were spaced far apart and encircled by big brick walls that meant you couldn't see their extravagance from the road. When he finally instructed me to turn onto one of the sweeping drives, a gate barred our way.

"Is there a code?" I asked.

"Wait," Kevin instructed me. Sure enough, the thing opened a moment later and I was able to proceed up toward a house.

It looked exactly as a master vampire's house should look. Made of grey stone, it was enormous and creepy looking. There was even a turret, for fuck's sake. I parked in the wide, empty forecourt and followed Kevin up several steps toward an enormous oak door. Kevin flung it wide and then turned to me.

"Do you enter of your own free will?"

I stared at him uneasily. "Are you fucking with me?"

He gave me a devilish look. "Yes."

When we made our way inside, Kevin's playful attitude slipped away. There was a huge entrance foyer and a woman standing there, waiting for us. She had a definite Morticia Adams look going for her and a very severe expression. The glower she fixed Kevin with should have had him dying on the spot.

"You were successful?" she asked.

Kevin nodded.

"Thank you, Kevin," she said, not sounding thankful at all. "I will take her to the master."

Oh goodie. I would much rather go to see Tobias with Kevin, but when I turned to look at him, he was already backing away, his head bowed low. I guessed there was a pecking order, and he was at the bottom of it.

I was probably the thing being pecked.

Chapter Four

The cupboard door thumped again, rattling the whole thing on its hinges, and the woman screamed once more. Tobias ignored the ruckus, focusing on the voice coming through the phone receiver.

"There have been three thefts from my construction site, all by your fucking vampires. I don't know what the hell your problem with me and my wolves is, Hunter. I don't want to fight with you, but if it happens again, I will burn you out."

Logan Murray was coarse and vulgar, all brute strength and violent aggression—he and Tobias had a lot in common, actually, not that he was going to tell the alpha wolf that—but he was a good leader who kept his pack in check. And it was a large pack; Tobias had no intention of fighting with him, either.

"I assure you it was unsanctioned," he soothed. "The vampire responsible has been identified and is being punished. It will not happen again."

There was a pause on the other end of the phone, and Tobias gave a small smile. The wolf wanted to know what he did to punish his children, but he was smart enough not to ask. Tobias would never give away information on how to hurt any of his kind, even if most of the methods were not effective on someone as old and powerful as him.

"All right, then," Logan growled. "And the items that were stolen?"

"You'll be compensated for them," Tobias assured him. "And for the inconvenience. Send an invoice and I will take care of it."

He heard the sound of approaching footsteps, one the whispering grace of Evangeline, the other an inelegant thump of boots on marble floor. Cat. He grinned just thinking of her stomping along in his eldest child's wake.

"I'm afraid I must go," he told the wolf. "I appreciate your understanding in this matter."

He hung up before Logan could reply, watching the door. Cat had the ring, he could feel it pulsing, ready to return to his side, but that wasn't why anticipation was stirring inside him.

The cupboard door thumped again, harder this time, but he ignored it.

"Come in," he called, before Evangeline could even lift her hand to request entry.

The door opened smoothly and the beautiful vampire bowed respectfully.

"The police woman is here to see you."

"Former police woman," Cat muttered from behind her.

"Thank you, Evangeline. I'll see her."

Tobias stood up as Evangeline glided out of the way and Cat stomped forward. He glanced down and had to work to stop himself from grinning. She wore stout walking boots, spattered in mud.

"I have your ring," she declared, pulling it out of her pocket and dropping it onto the shining surface of his antique mahogany desk. "Kevin assures me it was already broken."

Even though he'd felt its presence, Tobias felt the tightness in his gut loosen seeing it there, unharmed and his once more.

"It was," he agreed. "And the names of those involved?"

Cat's lips flattened. "I already gave the details to Morticia out there."

Morticia? He frowned then gave a small chuckle of understanding. "Evangeline," he corrected her.

"Whatever."

Giving in to the need to be closer to her, he rounded the desk, not stopping until less than a hand's breath separated them.

"Thank you for returning the ring. It means a great deal to me."

She shrugged uncomfortably. "You're welcome. I mean, I'm getting paid for it, so…" She glanced at him suspiciously. "I am still getting paid, right?"

"Of course."

"Well, then." She shifted her foot back, as if she was going to take a step away, but instead of moving back, her body swayed forward, eyelids fluttering. Vampires had an intoxicating scent, it was one of the ways they lured their prey to them. Some humans were immune, Tobias was glad to see that Cat was not. In fact, she seemed more susceptible than normal. "It was a pleasure doing business with you."

"There hasn't been any pleasure yet," he contradicted her. "But there could be."

Her breath paused, everything in her going still. She liked that idea. He lifted a hand, intending to run it down the smoothness of her cheek, when the banging from his cupboard door started up again. The space was soundproofed, but it could not entirely contain the screams of, "Help! Heeeeeeeelp!"

Cat stumbled back then, staring at him wide-eyed. "What was that? Who do you have in there?"

"No one you need to trouble yourself with." He made his voice a seductive purr, put some power into it, but she shook it off with a jerk of her head. The spell he'd been weaving over her was broken.

"I should go," she said.

A shame, but for the best really, because the little female had been weaving her own spell on Tobias, and that was dangerous.

"I'll have Evangeline see you out."

The vampire in question opened the door silently as if she'd been waiting for her master's command—which, of course, she had.

Cat didn't want to go, he could see that, and it cheered the sudden despondency within him, but after giving the cupboard door one more dubious glance, she left without a word of farewell. Tobias exchanged a look with Evangeline and she nodded. She knew what to do.

Sighing, and more annoyed than was probably wise, Tobias strode to the cupboard door and hauled it open. A short, squat, auburn-haired witch tumbled out, her curvaceous figure having been pressed to the door, likely trying to listen in.

"Ow!" she complained, rubbing at a bruised elbow. She threw him an annoyed look, but it was no match for his and he had the pleasure of watching the blood drain from her face.

"Up," he ordered.

She scrambled to obey, getting her feet beneath her and darting across the office until her back was pressed to the door. She was smart enough not to try and go through it, though. There were any number of Tobias' vampires roaming the mansion tonight, any of whom would be delighted to have a midnight snack fall into their lap. Though he was undoubtedly the most dangerous vampire in the building, she was also safest with him. He had a need for her that went beyond her blood.

"You should let me go," she told him, her brave words belied by the wobble in her voice. "I could curse you. I know all sorts of spells to hurt vampires."

"You would be wise not to threaten me," he said mildly. "There is something I need from you. Do it, and I'll let you go. Unharmed." He smiled, letting her see his teeth. "Refuse, and I'll find myself another witch. You, however, won't be in any fit state to curse anyone."

She shifted on her feet, thinking. "What do you want me to do?" she asked eventually.

Smart girl.

"A protection spell. That's simple enough, yes?"

She nodded warily. "Yeah, I can do that." She frowned at him. "You didn't have to kidnap me for that, you could have just asked."

"Perhaps I could have." Honestly, the thought hadn't even occurred to him. "I wanted to ensure you were here at my convenience."

"Right," she muttered, looking away from him so she could roll her eyes. "What do you want the protection spell on?"

"This?" he gestured to the ring on the desk. "I want it so that none other but me and my children can touch it."

"Your children all have a blood connection to you?"

"They would not be my children otherwise."

"All right, I can do that." She hesitated. "What do you want to happen to anyone else who touches it?"

"They die." His power crackled through the room as he said the words and the witch shivered.

"You got it."

He took a seat in a Victorian wing-backed chair beside the window, wanting to give her space to work. Now that she had agreed to help him, he had no need to intimidate her, and he didn't want any mistakes made because of nervous, clumsy hands. She began to chant, her hands hovering over the ring emitting a muted glow, and he let his thoughts drift.

Evangeline would be escorting Cat to her home right now, they might even be there already. Then she'd wipe the human's mind of all interactions with Tobias, Kevin and Evangeline herself. It was tricky, meddling with the mind like that, especially when the memories connected different people and events, and, he liked to think, strong emotions, but Evangeline was his best and brightest. He had faith in her abilities.

He wouldn't be able to see her again, though. Not without undoing Evangeline's hard work. It was possible to perform a second wipe, but the results were...inconsistent. It might not work, and it might leave her a drooling vegetable. Neither outcome was acceptable.

What also wasn't acceptable was how unhappy that made him. Cat had been a blazing beacon of light in the dreariness of endless monotony. She was a fleeting flame, a morsel of forbidden fruit, he tried to tell himself that was the only reason that he wanted her. A quick fuck, or, more enjoyably, a long, slow session in his playroom, and he'd be as bored of her as he was all the others. He repeated the words to himself and tried to make himself believe it. It was too late now, anyhow.

Of course, he could call on Evangeline, mind to mind, stop her if she hadn't already performed the wipe. He could, but he shouldn't. He was a cat to her mouse, and he needed to let this one go.

Chapter Five

It was dark outside when I turned the *Open* sign to *Closed*. I twisted the lock and sighed, stretching the tightness out of my shoulders. I'd had to close the store for three days while I waited for the replacement window—which Tobias had kept his word and paid for—so I'd thrown a little *Hey, we're back in business* party with punch and nibbles to try and draw customers back in.

It worked, too. I'd sold four pieces, one of them a five-hundred-dollar diptych, and I was smiling as I shut down the computer and tidied up my sales counter.

"I like this one."

"I'm sorry, we're closed." A polite smile was on my face as I turned to shoo out the errant customer—the sign said *Closed*, people...and hadn't I just locked that door?—but I froze when I saw who was actually in my shop. "Tobias!"

He stilled, too, when I said his name, and my eyes went nervously to the delicate crystal figurine he held in his hand.

"You remember me," he said.

What? He sounded surprised and my eyebrows crept up my forehead.

"Well, yeah. It's not every day you have dealings with master vampires." Or any vampires at all, really. "I'm not likely to forget."

He stared at me for a moment longer, then shouted, "Evangeline!"

My heart had time to thud three times before she popped into existence in the middle of my shop floor. She took one look at Tobias and dropped to her knees, bowing her head to the floor.

"Master?" she quivered.

I blinked, utterly lost by the turn of events. I'd no idea what Evangeline was doing here or why she was cowering. I'd kind of gotten the impression that she was one of Tobias' higher up vamps, she'd certainly been haughty enough. Not right now, though. Her fingers were shaking as she pressed them against my laminate flooring.

"You left her memories intact?" he asked quietly.

Evangeline glanced at me, wide-eyed. "No! I was careful, Master. I swear it. I wiped her clean and then left her sleeping."

"You tried to wipe my memory?" I asked, catching up with lightning quickness and getting mad just as fast. "What the hell?"

I mean, it clearly hadn't worked, because I remembered everything just fine...except, okay, the moments between when we parked in the alley at the back of the shop and waking up the next morning with a blinding headache.

"It is standard practice," Tobias told me. He wasn't angry with me, but I still felt the heat of his displeasure roll over me, had to lock my knees to stop myself dropping like Evangeline. He wasn't *my* master. "We cannot have humans running around with the knowledge of our existence. Our best protection is our secrecy."

I thought their best protection was their strength, speed and the whole poofing in and out of existence thing, but whatever.

"How would that even work?" I asked. "Don't you think I might wonder what happened to my window? Where the last few days went?"

"Evangeline." Tobias prodded her with his foot. It was a gentle nudge, but she flinched like he'd electrocuted her.

"I planted false seeds," she whispered. "I made you think it had been nothing but vandals, and you'd spent the last few days tidying your store, organizing things."

"Clearly not," I said. "Because I remember what really happened."

"You shouldn't," she replied. She lifted her head to Tobias, stared at him beseechingly. "I swear to you, Master. I was careful. She must have some sort of...mental protection against us."

"Perhaps," Tobias muttered, looking at me. He glanced down at Evangeline and curled his lip. "Return to the mansion. I'll deal with you later."

Sheer terror crossed Evangeline's face before she vanished.

I was very aware suddenly that it was just the two of us in my dimly lit shop. There was no one else in the building, no one passing on the street outside. We were alone. I watched as Tobias put the crystal figurine down with deliberate gentleness then turned to me.

"You tried to steal my memories," I blurted.

"I told you," he smiled conciliatorily, "it's standard practice."

"I don't care," I told him. It still stung. Like he'd just tried to delete me or something. As if I was nothing, a nuisance fly waved out the window, never to return. "What are you doing here, anyway? Did you come to check it had worked?" I paused. "If you were trying to pretend to be a stranger, it would have been a lot less suspicious if you'd walked in the door rather than poofing into a locked-up shop."

"Poofing?" he asked, amused. "It's called rematerializing."

"Poofing," I repeated, just to annoy him. "Why are you here?"

"I shouldn't be," he admitted. "Even if the mind-wipe had worked, seeing me might have undone it."

"So, why are you?"

The look he gave me was impish, almost shy. "I wanted to see you," he admitted.

"You did?"

That earned me a grin, complete with pointed incisors. "Why are you surprised?"

"You're a master vampire," I pointed out. "Don't you have important things you should be doing?"

He shrugged. "I have people. You may not have seen the best of them, but they can generally be trusted to see to things in my stead."

"I see," I said, though I didn't. Not really. I scowled at him, an expression that was hard to hold on to when he was being charming like this. "Are you going to try to wipe my mind again before you leave?"

"No." He shook his head at me. "Evangeline is extremely proficient at altering memories. If she says she did it properly—"

"If she's telling the truth," I added.

"She cannot lie to me," Tobias corrected. "I am her master. If she says she did it properly, she did. Were I to push any harder, I risk destroying your mind completely."

It should have freaked me out, the things he was saying. It did, only…every time he said *master* like that, in that silky, self-assured voice, it gave me shivers. The good kind.

"So, what now?" I asked. "I know about you, and you can't make me not know, so what do we do?"

"Ordinarily, I would not tolerate such a threat."

"Ordinarily?" I squeaked, latching on to that because the rest of the sentence was frighteningly ominous.

"Are you a danger to me, Cat?" he asked.

"No," I said. "But that's taking a lot on trust. I'm not one of your children, I can lie to you if I want."

"You are welcome to try," he suggested, eyes darkly amused. "I am adept at reading people, I've had centuries of practise. You wear your honesty in your face, Cat." He breathed deeply. "And other places."

What? What the fuck did that mean? My panties were damp—I couldn't help it, his *voice*—but he couldn't smell that, could he? Did vampires have super noses along with strength and speed? Christ, I hoped not.

"So where does that leave us?" I asked.

He took a moment to answer, winding his way toward me in a way that was sinuous and sensual. Jesus, I even found his walk sexy.

"I have a…proposition for you," he said. He was close enough now that I could breathe him in with my ordinary, human nose. There was an icy bite to his scent, like he'd been sucking on a breath mint. It was clean and fresh, and it left me feeling a little light-headed.

Focus, Cat.

"Go on," I prompted. "I'm listening."

He lifted a hand and tucked an errant strand of hair behind my ear, deliberately stroking the backs of his fingers across my cheek as he did so. The contact was fleeting, but it burned—a good burn, like velvet-covered dry ice. That eucalyptus scent was in my nostrils and my thoughts scattered.

"I'd like to get to know you better, Cat," he murmured.

"Like a date?" I asked stupidly. I couldn't imagine Tobias sitting opposite me at Old Chicago's, ordering pizza. Did vampires even eat, anyway?

Blood, Cat. They eat blood. You know, that stuff that's flowing through your veins?

Eek!

I couldn't seem to find my fear, though. I was too entranced, too turned on by his nearness and his quiet, compelling voice.

"Not quite," he replied softly. "Though we can dine, if you wish. Beforehand."

"Beforehand?" I echoed.

He smiled. "I have a playroom, in my mansion. I'd like to invite you there."

"To play?" I sounded like an idiot but he was stealing my braincells one slow, seductive smile at a time.

"Very adult play," he assured me. He leaned down to murmur his next words into my ear. "I can show you such pleasure that you will scream with the agony of it, and then you will beg me for more."

Oh boy!

Yes, fucking please.

Still, I wasn't going to make it easy for him. I shifted back so I could look him in the eyes.

"I don't beg," I told him.

The grin he gave me was devastating. "You will."

Chapter Six

I looked at myself in the mirror, still undecided. It wasn't the sheer, cap-sleeved black top I had on, my best bra clearly visible underneath it, that was giving me second thoughts. It was the whole fucking thing.

Was I really going to do this?

I was under no illusions exactly what it was I was signing up for. Sex. Kink. Dominance and submission. Possibly a little (I hoped) bloodletting.

I wasn't some blushing virgin. I'd had sex, plenty of it. Though not recently, and never mind-blowing. That was the lure, if I was honest with myself. I had the distinct impression that Tobias could make me see stars. I had the feeling he could reach through the walls I'd built and pull out my soul, give me that elusive thing none of my other partners had ever been able to.

I'd never gone to meet someone just for the purposes of having sex, though. I'd never had a one-night stand. I wasn't a third date kind of woman; I was a six weeks and lots of careful thought type. This wasn't just pushing my boundaries, it was changing the entire way I viewed sex.

But the idea that I could finally find what I'd been searching for? That I could experience the things I'd fantasized about, read about in book after book? It was a potent one.

I wasn't a girl, I was a woman. It was time to find out exactly who I was. What I liked…and what I needed.

"Fuck it," I told my reflection.

It was the perfect night for an illicit liaison. As I drove through the city toward Tobias' mansion, lightning lit up the sky and rain lashed against my windscreen. The storm was fierce and wild, a perfect match to my mood.

When I arrived at the gate, it was closed against me. I put the car into park and eyed the discreet panel on the wall. Before I could open the car door and step out into the rain, however, the gate started to open. It felt a bit like I was passing through the point of no return as I started forward up the long sweeping driveway. I was committing to whatever Tobias had in store for me.

I was excited, so excited I could already feel that my panties were damp, but I was nervous too.

I parked my car in the large forecourt. This time there were two other vehicles parked there, a fancy Audi and a large pickup truck; my slightly dinged Subaru looked very out of place. I expected Evangeline to greet me at the door, or maybe Kevin, but it was Tobias himself who came out on the top step to welcome me.

"Catriona," he purred. There was no smile on his face but his eyes were warm. "You came."

Not yet, I thought. But I'm hoping to. I was attempting to be ladylike, however, so I tried to keep that off my face as I did my best to get up the steps in high heeled shoes without going flying.

A helpful overhang kept most of the rain off us as we entered the grand foyer. Tobias held his hands out for my jacket and I fumbled with the zip with slightly shaking hands. I was dressed far more sexily than I was used to, and I wanted him to like my outfit. It was also tight and sheer and revealing in quite a few places, so you could see more of me than usual…and I wanted him to like that too.

He didn't say anything, just took the damp jacket from me and hung it in a small closet. His eyes raked hotly over my body, though, and maybe that was better than a compliment.

"Have you eaten?" he asked. "I could have a meal prepared?"

"I ate." At lunch. I'd been too jittery to have any dinner and if I tried to put food in my mouth right now, I thought I might puke it right back up.

"A drink, then."

"That would be lovely."

"What is your preference?"

Ordinarily? Beer. I wasn't going to admit to that, though.

"A glass of wine would be great."

"Red or white?"

"White." I gave a small grin. "Don't bother asking me what kind, because I've no idea. When I'm in a restaurant I always just choose the second least expensive."

He didn't bother to hide how appalled he was. "I shall teach you," he said, as if that settled the matter.

"You are welcome to try," I replied, echoing his words to me from the other night.

It took him a moment to connect the dots, but then he laughed, the sound rich and full and beautiful.

The room he led me to wasn't his playroom. It was an intimate drawing room in shades of deep red and emerald green, the furniture all dark leather and the wood rich mahogany. He opened the door of what I thought was an antique cabinet to reveal a built-in wine fridge, a variety of bottles stashed inside. Tobias perused the contents for a moment before pulling one free.

"We'll start you on this," he said, pouring out two glasses.

So, vampires drank alcohol as well as blood, then.

He poured wine differently than I did, allowing the liquid to reach about a third of the way up the goblet before stopping rather than filling it almost to the brim like normal people. He handed it to me and then waited expectantly as I took a sip. It was tart and refreshing and colder than I could ever get my fridge to chill things. I could see he was watching me, waiting for my reaction, so I did my best to keep my face totally blank.

"Tastes like wine," I offered.

His eyes narrowed in mock annoyance.

"It would behoove you not to test my patience at this point," he told me. "You will regret it later."

"That warning might have more impact if I knew what behoove meant."

"You'll find out," he said.

Well, that was ominous.

I stared around the room as I searched for something to say. Tobias seemed perfectly okay with the silence, but I was too on edge to relax into it. I took another sip of my wine. Yeah, all right, it was much nicer than anything I'd ever bought. I shuddered to think how much it cost.

"So," I began. "I hesitate to ask, but did you track down the rest of the thieves? Have they been…dealt with?"

"They have," he confirmed. "I'll spare you the details, because this is not a night for such unpleasantness, but they were made to regret stealing from me before the end."

"What did you do with the bodies?" Not my business, really, but I'd had a hand in the whole thing, and I was very eager they never came to light.

"A little trust, Cat," Tobias murmured. Then he tilted his head, looked at me with those penetrating, self-assured eyes. "Tonight, I wish to concentrate on you."

Right, we were getting down to it, then. Good, because I hated waiting for things that made me nervous.

"Are you going to take me to your dungeon, now?" I asked, raising an amused eyebrow.

"I fear you're going to be disappointed," he said. "No dungeon."

"What, no hanging from chains by my ankles?"

"I did not say that there wouldn't be chains. Though, it's unlikely I'll hang you from your ankles on your first experience."

"Just my wrists, then," I said breathlessly.

"We'll see."

We'll see? What the fuck did that mean? What else was there to hang me from?

He smiled, clearly amused at having unnerved me so easily, then strode across the room. The place was full of surprises; what I'd taken to be a cupboard door instead opened onto a dimly lit tunnel.

"Do you come with me of your own free will?" he asked, standing by the door.

I rolled my eyes. "Kevin already pulled that one on me the first time I came in the house."

I walked toward him, intending to sweep past and head straight down the tunnel, prove I wasn't scared, but he stopped me with a gentle hand on my arm.

"I am serious, Catriona. I wish to know that you understand what you are agreeing to. I will give you pleasure beyond anything you've ever known, but I will also show you pain. Fear. I'll expect you to submit to me, and I will punish you if you do not please me. I will push your limits, perhaps beyond what you think you can bear. So, I need to know that you understand and accept what is about to happen."

Fuck. That turned me on like a lightbulb—and also made me feel like tucking tail and getting the hell out of there.

"Do I—" I had to lick my lips to continue, my mouth suddenly bone dry. "Do I get a safe word?"

"No," he said. He waited a beat. "Do you still wish to enter?"

Fuck!

I stood there like a startled deer, not moving a muscle, my breathing came in little pants. I was scared of Tobias, and scared of myself.

"You won't hurt me?" I asked. I sounded like a little girl.

"I will," he said. "But it will be momentary pain, the kind that becomes excruciating pleasure." Uhuh. Pain was pain in my book, but that was just it. All those books, all those fantasies. They made me feel alive, they touched my soul. This was my chance to live it for myself. "You will not leave my presence damaged," he promised.

Do it, Cat, I told myself. *You'll regret it forever if you don't.*

I made to move forward, decided, but he stopped me again.

"I would hear you say it," he repeated. "Of your own free will."

I looked in his eyes and saw desire and need, but also safety and protection. I will take care of you, they seemed to say. Trust me.

"Of my own free will," I whispered.

Chapter Seven

I almost changed my mind when I got my first look at Tobias' playroom. It was a large space, the walls clothed in dark red fabric to soften the squareness of the room. The floor was polished concrete, the ceiling painted black. Spotlights created a soft, ambient glow.

The main piece of furniture was, of course, a bed. It was a giant four-poster, swathes of fabric allowing me to catch only glimpses of the satin sheets and scattered pillows. There were other…things, though. Pieces of equipment that looked like they might be more at home in a gymnasium, if it weren't for the straps and chains that dangled from them. There was an X-cross attached to the wall, what looked like a gymnastics vaulting horse, and a bona fide stockade dangling from chains bolted to the ceiling. A handsome red leather armchair sat in the corner in front of a coffee table which was actually—I had to peer into the shadows to double check—a cage. The cages didn't end there, though. There was a bigger one hanging from the ceiling in front of the bed, so that someone could lie comfortably and watch whatever wretched soul was in there helplessly dangling.

If this wasn't a dungeon, I didn't know what was.

"Having second thoughts?" Tobias murmured from behind me.

"No." I stiffened my spine, tried to still the trembling in my hands. When he crossed the room and drew back one of the curtains, though, revealing a wall fully stocked with cuffs, whips, floggers, dildos and a whole host of other things I couldn't put a name to, my knees felt so weak I thought I might fall over.

"It's all right Cat," he said, coming back to me and taking the wineglass out of my numb fingers. "Just relax. Breathe. All you have to do in this room is listen to me, obey my commands, and feel. You can do that, can't you?"

I nodded, the moment feeling oddly uncoordinated.

"Let's start simply. When we're in this room, I am your master. If I ask you a question, I expect you to call me that. Do you understand?"

"Yes." My voice was a breath of sound.

"Yes, what, Catriona? Focus, please. Mistakes are punished."

"Yes, Master." I shivered all over. Just that word; just saying it here, in this room, to him. It sparked something inside of me.

"Very good." He smiled at me, pleased, and a warm rush flooded my system. "Take off your clothes."

I didn't let myself think about it. I went straight to the buttons on my skin-tight pants and started jerking at them with clumsy fingers. Tobias halted me with a series of little tuts, his head shaking. I froze, eyes on him.

"I gave you an instruction. I expect a verbal acknowledgement."

"I—" I swallowed. "Yes, Master. I'm sorry, Master."

"One more mistake, and you'll earn your first stripes. I'm particular to the cane, Catriona."

The cane? My eyes went helplessly to the wall of terror and oh yes, there it was. It was a long, thin strip of rattan with a black handle. It looked delicate, but I had enough knowledge from reading my little library of erotica to know it really fucking hurt.

"Your clothes," he prompted me, when I stayed there frozen for several long, drawn out seconds.

"Yes, Master."

My respectful response earned me a quiet, "Good girl." He watched with patient eyes as I fumbled through the task of unveiling myself. I tried to let go of the thoughts wishing I was thinner, more toned, more tanned. Tobias had seen enough of me to know he was getting a woman with curves, and he'd still invited me to play.

When I was fully naked, my clothes in a puddle at my feet, I made myself meet his gaze. He hadn't moved during my entire unrobing, was still standing, fully (and impeccably) dressed.

"Aren't you going to, you know—" My voice faltered when he raised an eyebrow. Sensing trouble, I dropped my gaze to the floor.

"Did you just question me?"

The "No, Master," leapt to my tongue, but I swallowed it back. I didn't think denial was going to help the situation.

"Yes, Master."

He sighed, and there was a wealth of meaning behind that non-verbal little sound.

"Time for your first lesson in punishment, Catriona."

No, it really fucking wasn't, but I didn't say that, either. I just let him take me gently by the hand and lead me over to a rope dangling from the ceiling, two cuffs swinging gently on the end, about level with my chest. I hadn't noticed it before—it seemed tame in comparison to some of the other things in the room—but now that I was stood in front of it, I was beginning to rethink that opinion. I looked up and saw that it ran through a pulley, the other end tied to a ring on the wall. It was a strappado, I realized belatedly.

"Five strikes," Tobias said quietly. "Turn around, Cat."

I did, and he chuckled.

"Five just became seven."

What? I stared stupidly at the X-cross nailed to the opposite wall, not understanding.

"Eight," he murmured.

Fuck!

"Yes, Master. I'm sorry, Master. I keep forgetting."

"Don't worry." His voice was right in my ear as he moved up behind me and started buckling the cuffs round first one wrist, then the other. "You'll learn. Spread your legs."

I did as he said, widening them, then squeaking out, "Yes, Master," just a few seconds too late.

His huff of laughter stirred the hair at the nape of my neck.

"I'm going to let you have that one," he murmured, "because you're being so brave."

Was I? I didn't feel brave. I felt scared, adrenaline spiking round my system. It was a heady feeling, making my every nerve come alive. I could feel goose bumps along my arms from the slightly chill air in the room, the smoothness of the polished floor beneath my bare feet. When Tobias stepped away and did something to the rope, lifting my arms away from my body, hands tied together behind my back, I felt the stretch and pull of my shoulder muscles, and had to go up on my tiptoes to relieve some of the pressure.

"Legs," Tobias snapped, and I realized I'd brought them together instinctively.

"Sorry, Master." I spread them once more, lifting high on my toes.

"If you do that again, I'll put a spreader bar there, understand?"

"Yes, Master."

A hand in the middle of my back urged me to bend forward. I went, but then Tobias pushed me past the point of balance. I gave a little yelp as I found myself dangling, all of my weight held by the cuffs around my wrist. I felt very vulnerable all of a sudden. I couldn't get back up unless he permitted it, unless he helped me.

"I—Master!"

"It's all right," he soothed. His hand slid from the centre of my back to curve around my buttocks. "Once your punishment has been meted out, I'll release you."

Oh God, the punishment. I'd almost forgotten about it in the excitement of being restrained.

He walked over to the wall and picked up the cane. In the eight paces it took him to return to me, my breathing escalated from quiet little gasps to panting. I wanted to cover my rear end with my hands, but they were tied up high above.

"Do you know what I'm going to ask you to do?"

"Count, Master?" I guessed.

"Very good." He toyed with the cane, rolling it between his fingers, drawing the moment out. A trickle of sweat started to slide down the middle of my back, the skin on my ass already feeling sensitized and he hadn't even touched me yet. I tried to follow him with my eyes as he walked slowly round to my exposed, soon to be an angry shade of red, butt cheeks.

The cane made a quiet whistle as it flew through the air. It took a moment for my body to register the connection, then I felt the sting. It was sharp, cutting, but then it bloomed into something bigger and warmer.

My conscious thoughts seemed a long way away from my body. I barely remembered to choke out, "One!"

Stroke two came too quickly. I hadn't even gotten my head around how it felt—how *I* felt—before that whistle pre-empted a sharp cut through the burn. I was writhing by the third hit, trying to get away though I was pinned in place. By the fourth, I was close to bursting into tears, my ass on fire. I'd stopped counting after the first number, was wondering if there would be any point in begging Tobias to stop.

I thought not.

He surprised me, then, when he dropped the cane on the floor, right in my line of sight, after the fifth stroke and started soothing me, rubbing his hands over my blistered flesh, murmuring gently.

"It's all right," I heard dimly. "You did very well."

Cool fingers went to my wrist and he unbuckled me, catching me when I almost dropped to the floor. I was free of the restraints, could have run for the door, but instead I clung to him, leaning on his strength.

He picked me up, one arm behind my shoulders and the other under my knees, and carried me toward the big bed. He lay me down on it, then rolled me over onto my front. The satin was cool against my overheated skin, it felt good. The cold air on my ravaged butt cheeks, however, was painful enough to bring tears to my eyes.

"Lift your head," he told me. "Just a little."

I did as he said and he slipped a blindfold over my eyes, fastened it behind my head. I held very still, thrown by the instant darkness. I could feel the pressure of his hand on my leg, though, and that grounded me.

"This will help with the sting," he said, a moment before I felt a cool liquid dribble across my skin. He rubbed it in with smooth confident strokes—maybe a little harder than I would have liked, given how tender I was—but he was right, the burn dimmed until it was a gentle throb.

"I don't think I like the cane," I mumbled. Then, hurriedly, "Master."

He chuckled. "That's the point of it. It's a lesson; you're supposed to learn from it."

I made a small noise, settled more fully down into the mattress. His massage was soothing, and with the blindness imposed by the blindfold, I felt almost like I was floating. I tilted my hips, hoping to shift his touch to my pussy. I got a little smack for my daring—a light tap that had the sting flaring anew and made me squeak—but then he shifted to stroke the very tops of my thighs, sliding down between them. I didn't hesitate, opening my legs to give him room, and when he finally ran his fingers right up the centre of me, I could feel how wet I was.

My breath left my body in a rush, my own arousal turning me on even further. Tobias was pleased too, making a soft noise in the back of his throat and lingering there, rubbing his fingertips up and down, up and down.

"Perhaps you deserve a little reward, for taking your punishment like a big girl. Would you like to be rewarded, Catriona?"

Yes. Definitely. My core clenched on the word *punishment*; even though I hadn't liked the pain, pleasing Tobias set something alight in me that made it somehow worth it.

"Yes, Master," I whispered.

"A little wider, then."

I did as he asked, remembering to murmur, "Yes, Master."

This wider position opened up my clit to his questing fingers and I held my breath, waiting for it. He avoided it entirely, though, teasing me with circles around and around my opening, sliding my slickness around, reminding me how turned on I was by him.

"I want you to count backward from ten, Cat. Slowly. By the time you reach one, I will have returned to you."

What? Where was he going? I mean, most people couldn't leave the room in that time, but Tobias had the ability to go to Vegas and back. I tensed, one of my hands already sliding up to yank at the blindfold, hating the idea of being blind and alone, but he stopped me with a gentle grip on my wrist.

"Stay here," he warned quietly, "just like this. I am not leaving you."

"Yes, Master," I whispered. I felt him draw away from me, the mattress shifting slightly as he rolled off it, and started my counting. "Ten, nine, eight…"

He'd said slowly, but even matching each number to every third beat of my heart, I was going too fast. I couldn't help it, I wanted to get down to one so he'd be with me again, trusted instinctively that he'd keep his promise.

"Six, five, four—"

"Good girl, Cat." A cool hand between my shoulder blades, stroking softly. He ran it all the way down my spine until he reached the cleft of my ass. Then he kept going, until one of his fingers reached my rosebud and circled it softly. Everything in me stilled at that ticklish touch.

"Cold," he murmured, an instant before cool liquid drizzled right where he'd had his fingers. He smoothed it around my rear opening then dipped a finger lightly inside. "This is going to look so pretty," he said, "and I think you'll like how it feels."

Pretty? I'd no idea what that meant, but at least it seemed to imply he wasn't going to try and stick his cock in there. Although, I'd never seen it, maybe it was pretty. A bubble of hilarity welled up in me, but it came out in a gasp as Tobias replaced his fingers with something smooth and hard. A metal plug? He eased it in and out, teasing me, making me lift my hips for more, but then there was a sharp pinch and I tried to retreat away from it. How big was it? I'd no idea, because I couldn't *see*!

"Relax," he said. "It isn't large, and you're almost there."

I tried to do as he said, gritting my teeth as he pushed past the point of comfort, but a moment later the widest point of the plug passed through the tight ring of muscle and I felt myself contract around it again. I flexed, cautiously examining how it felt.

Nice…I thought. I could feel it, but it didn't hurt. It just made me aware of myself, down there.

"Oh yes," he said. "That does look pretty. I think I'll leave that in when I fuck you. But first, your reward."

A low buzz started up. It was a vibe, I realized, an instant before he dipped it inside me, letting my inner walls feel the vibrations for a moment before pulling it out and down to roll lightly round my clit.

Ooooh, that felt good. I tilted my hips automatically, offering myself to him, hoping for a harder, deeper contact.

"You like that, don't you Cat?"

"Mmmhmmm." My face was pressed into the smooth satin of the bed coverings as I writhed happily—right up until the buzzing stopped. "Wha-?"

"I asked you if you liked it," he repeated.

"I do, I did. I—" I wriggled hopefully. "Please."

A moment's pause, then, "What are you forgetting, Cat?"

What? I—Oh, damn.

"I like it, Master. I like it a lot. *Please*, Master."

He chuckled, amused, but he switched the vibe back on, brought it back to my clit, which pulsed happily, ready to get back on the orgasm train. "You're lucky I'm in a good mood, Cat, and that I'm looking forward to being inside you." He punctuated his words with two fingers, thrust inside me hard and fast.

I gave a small, "Oof!" of surprise, the plug making the penetration fuller somehow, but when he started moving his fingers in a steady rhythm, that quickly turned into a series of pitiful moans and whimpers.

"You ask permission to come," he murmured, right when I was on the edge of what I was absolutely certain was going to be my first ever seeing-stars orgasm.

"Can I come, Master?" I asked immediately.

"Not yet."

Not yet? I yowled and tried to draw away from the pleasure, but Tobias moved with me, not letting up on the vibe.

"Please!" I gasped, knowing I was going to lose the battle in about three seconds. "Please, Master! Please, can I come?"

"Disappointing, Cat. We're going to have to work on this. All right, come for me."

I didn't make it to the final word, my body detonating without my permission. Bursts of color exploded behind the blindfold and my fingers clawed at the bedding, my toes curling up. I rode it out, my every muscle tensed, then twitched and writhed as Tobias made me suffer through the aftershocks, his fingers fighting against my rippling core.

"Good girl, Cat. Breathe, breathe." His words confused me until I realized I wasn't breathing, my lungs compressed and burning for air. I hauled in oxygen, blinking against the sudden brightness of the dimly lit room as Tobias removed my blindfold. Limp as a ragdoll, I let him roll me onto by back and then lift me up until I was cradled on his lap, the slightly awkward manoeuvre carried out as if I weighed no more than a child.

Vampire super-strength, I remembered dimly.

I rested my head against his chest as he lifted one hand to softly stroke my hair. I'd nestled into the hollow of his shoulder, his muscles firm over skin that was cool to the touch, before I realized that he no longer wore his shirt and the legs beneath me were similarly naked. In fact, all of him was.

"When did you get undressed?" I asked, too astonished to remember to add Master on the end. He didn't seem bothered, giving a shrug and a small smile.

"You counted to ten. How long do you think it took me to get to the wall and back?"

"I only made it to four," I reminded him.

The grin widened slightly. "I am very fast. Especially when I do not have to be concerned with being seen."

"I'd like to see that," I told him honestly.

A troubled look crossed his eyes briefly before he shrugged it off. "Perhaps you will." He dropped his eyes from my face down to my breasts, lifting a hand to play with them. He cupped me, then used his thumb to swipe over my nipple in a move that made me gasp.

"I had many, many ideas of what to do with these pretty breasts, but I think I have pushed you enough for your first time. They will have to wait until next time."

"Next time?" I asked, lifting an eyebrow at the presumption.

"Next time." His voice was firm, final. Normally I'd have rebelled against the arrogance in it, but there was no way I wanted this to be a one-time deal. And I hadn't even got my hands on his cock yet, though I could feel it, pressing against my hip.

I was thinking about slipping off his lap, going to my knees in front of him and showing him what I could do with my mouth—which might be a little rusty but I'd never had any complaints—when he rolled us both in one lightning quick move. Before I knew it, my head was on the pillow and Tobias' body was pressed the length of mine, my legs tight against either side of his hips.

"It has been a long, long time since I've taken a woman like this," he said. "Face to face, unrestrained. Like a man bedding his virgin wife for the first time. I tired of the simple pleasure of it centuries ago and yet, it's how I wish to take you."

He slid a hand under my buttocks and lifted me so that he could fit himself against me, slide inside. I gasped, feeling the unyielding length of him force its way past swollen tissue. The angle he held me at made his cock roll over my g-spot and I gasped, that gasp turning to moans as he moved in a slow, controlled rhythm that hit it again and again.

It was soft and quiet and tender, and absolutely not how I'd expected to get fucked given everything that had happened so far, but I revelled in it, holding him to me and giving myself over entirely. He kissed me, lips parting my mouth and then his tongue dipping in and tangling with mine. It felt…it felt like he was loving me, and though that sounded crazy I didn't question it, just held on and let myself feel.

His tongue flicked against mine in one last caress and then he pressed a tiny kiss to the side of my mouth, my check. The line of my jaw and then that tender spot underneath. A moment later, he placed his mouth over my neck, licked at the skin there.

"A taste. Just a taste, little Cat." His lips moved against my throat as he spoke, the ticklish sensation sending streaks of pleasure running across my skin. I moaned and arched my neck, wanting more, the meaning of his words lost.

When his teeth broke through the skin, it was with a burning rush that centred my awareness on that spot before everything spiralled outwards. Heat and ecstasy, rippling in waves that was like an orgasm but somehow *more*. I panted and whined, clutching at his shoulders, lifting my neck up into his bite, spreading my thighs wider so his cock could slide just a little deeper. If you'd asked me beforehand how I'd have felt about him feeding on me, my response would have been somewhere between *ick* and *hell no*. In that moment, though, all I felt was connected to him, everywhere. I even fancied I could feel his thoughts, his satisfaction. His pleasure in my blood, my body. My surrender.

"Oh God," I moaned. "Oh God, I—*Please!*"

It was incredible. Overwhelming. He drank, and he fucked me, and I took it and took it and took it until finally a cresting wave swept me over and into the dark.

Chapter Eight

Tobias looked down at her a moment longer, her skin pale, slight purple shadows under her eyes. Her breathing was deep and even, though. She was simply sleeping.

It was warm enough in the room, and he'd already covered her with the light satin covering, but he fetched a warmer fur and draped it over her, tucking it around her naked shoulders.

Kevin, he thought. The young vampire appeared immediately and dropped to his knees, head low enough to touch the floor. He was nothing but skin and bones, and as he waited to hear his Master's bidding, he shook slightly. Enough, then.

"Your punishment ends tomorrow," Tobias told him. Kevin made no response but Tobias felt his relief through their mental connection, weak as it was. "Tonight, your task is to watch over Cat. I want to be informed the second she begins to stir. The *second*, Kevin."

"Yes, Master."

Tobias nodded, satisfied, but still, he couldn't make himself step away. A glance down at Cat confirmed what his ears had told him: she was still sleeping. She would be for a good long while, and he had things to attend to.

Still, it rankled, having to trust another to watch over her in his stead.

"You will remain in the shadows, and you will not look at her. Kevin—" he paused, made sure he had the younger vampire's full attention. "Should any harm befall her under your care, should she feel even a moment's fear, the punishment you have just endured will be like the caress of a feather. Do you understand?"

"Yes, Master." Kevin was shaking so hard he could barely get the words out. Tobias jerked his head in a short, sharp nod, satisfied.

Kevin had already melted unobtrusively to the corner of the room when he exited, closing the door carefully to ensure Cat didn't wake.

Evangeline was waiting in the hallway outside.

"What is it?" he asked, strangely irked by her presence.

She flinched, then steeled herself. Whatever she had to say was important and he forced himself to pay attention, though his thoughts wanted to drift back to the woman sleeping in his bed in his playroom. The only woman who'd ever been allowed to do so.

"Is she to become one of us?" she asked.

"No." his response was swift and immediate. And it felt right. Cat was vibrant and alive, to take her and turn her into what they were—eternal, but cold and somehow less—was wrong.

"But she'll stay here. You'll keep her as your concubine?"

His concubine. He grinned at the idea, the expression spreading even wider at the thought of informing Cat that was what she was, that she'd be staying here with him, warming his bed, satisfying his hungers and desires. It would be worth it just to watch the explosion.

"No," he repeated, more gently this time. "I don't intend to cage her."

"You're going to let her leave?" Evangeline frowned, clearly confused.

She was right to be confused, what Tobias was doing went against every rule he'd ever instilled in his children.

"I am," he said. He had to, he knew. It was the only way she'd ever come to him again.

As he walked toward his office, a thousand important things on his mind, he had to wonder who was the more ensnared.

He didn't have an answer, and that fucking delighted him.

CHARLI
MAC

HIS
MATE
SERIES

BOOK 4

HIS
CALAMITOUS
MATE

Chapter One

My hands shook so badly I dropped the first match I tried to light and burned my fingers on the second. My basement was my safe space, my sanctuary, but right now I was jumping at every little noise, peering into every shadow. Spooked wasn't the word. I was fucking terrified. Eventually, though, I got the candles lit on their sconces and moved into the centre, trying to breathe, trying to centre myself.

The walls were hung with heavy fabrics. They deadened sound and gave the room a nice ambience, but mostly they hid the ugly concrete walls. The same concrete covered the floor, but I'd painted so many power symbols all over, you could barely see it. It wasn't a large basement, just twenty feet by twenty feet, but other than a small armoire—a gorgeous antique with ornately carved doors—standing against one wall, there was nothing to impede the floor space other than my free-standing candle-holders, far enough away from the walls that they wouldn't set the curtains on fire when power releases from my spells made the tiny flames flare.

I looked down at the centre of the pentagon I stood in, and breathed in, blew out. Breathed in, blew out. My feet were bare, but instead of feeling the tingle from the energy I'd imbued in layer after layer into the floor, all I felt was the chill of the concrete.

"Come on Daisy, get it together."

Daisy was a horrendous name for a witch, especially the kind of witch who was always cash-strapped and therefore performed a lot more dubious spells than her mother would approve of, but it was mine, and names were a powerful thing, so I was stuck with it.

I felt sick, a cold sweat making my thin T-shirt stick to my back. With shaking hand, I reached into my back pocket and pulled out the thick sheaf of creamy vellum, unfolded it so I could see the neatly penned words one more time.

> *Ms. Bennett,*
> *I would be grateful if you would join me at my residence to discuss a topic of some delicacy. I find myself in need or your skills once more. It is a matter of some urgency and I would appreciate*

your swift response. If you call the number below, one of my
children will arrange a meeting at your earliest convenience.
    Regards,
    Tobias Hunter

Beneath that was a phone number. The whole thing was in red ink. No, not red ink. I was a witch and I knew blood when I saw it.

Tobias Hunter. Vampire, scary man and fucking kidnapper. He'd had one of his "children"—his goons—haul me off the street in the dark and then locked me in a cupboard in his damn creepy mansion for days just so that he could have me perform a simple protection spell that I'd have done without a qualm if he'd asked. Or, you know, *paid me.*

And now he was sending me letters.

Asking me to go back up there.

Not bloody likely.

Realizing I wasn't going to get any more centred—and certainly not while I stood there reading the words over and over again like they might change and become a simple thank you note...which I'd also never received— I folded the letter back up and took it over to the stairs, putting it on the highest tread I could reach. I'd learned a long time ago not to have anything that might bring negative energy into my spellcasting space, and with the spell I was about to attempt, that was doubly important.

Trying to leave the fear and panic that the invitation inspired on the stairs with it, I grabbed a few things from my armoire and moved back to the central spot of my pentagram, where I sank into a cross-legged position. I winced as my jeans dug into my middle, thinking of the jog I'd skipped this morning (again), and the slab of chocolate cake I'd just finished polishing off when the vampire letter had dropped mysteriously through my letter box—in the middle of the day. I'd checked my security camera footage and no one had approached my front door either. If Hunter had someone capable of that kind of fancy magic, I'd no idea what he might need me for...and no intention of finding out.

Which led me to this.

I placed an incense bowl down on the floor in front of me and scattered the lavender and thyme petals across the bottom of the shallow disk. I had to shimmy to the side to get my matches back out of my pocket—I'd run tomorrow, I promised myself—then set one alight with a smooth flick of my wrist, dropping it into the bowl.

Closing my eyes, I drew in deeply through my nose, the calming notes of lavender already wafting up, and pressed the fingertips of each hand to the ground on either side of me.

There it was. The zap of power, the jolt of awareness I was looking for. More relieved than I wanted to admit, I pushed down into it at the same time as I drew it up into me, creating a flow, a circle, that magnified until I was all but pulsing with it.

God, it felt good. Like floating and flying. Like a shot of really good whisky. Or an orgasm that rolls on and on and on. I tilted my head back and revelled in it.

When I felt I had control of it, when I felt like the pulses were surging or retreating at my command, I started to chant. The words weren't English. I didn't actually know what language they were and, more worryingly, I didn't really know what they meant, but I did know they worked, and I'd been taught them by rote until I could repeat them over and over again, like right now.

I felt it the moment the basement became more than just a basement. When the concrete floor and walls became a liquid that would keep out nosey neighbors and (hopefully) vampires, but not other things. I didn't dare open my eyes. My mentor, Agnetha, who was long dead but had been a smart lady, as well as a mean old bitch, had told me never to look.

"There are things you don't want to know about," she'd said. "And then there are the things you *can't* know about. It's best if you just keep your eyes firmly closed."

She'd told me, on multiple occasions, that it would be best if I kept my mouth closed, too. I'd ignored that bit of advice, but I'd never, ever peeked when I performed a summoning. The creatures who lived in the other realm made Tobias Hunter looked like a bunny rabbit—that was why I was calling on one of them, after all.

"Orphon," I said, my voice lifting up until I was calling into the swirling void I imagined in my mind. "Orphon, answer my call."

I felt it when he arrived. I knew he was there, though he didn't make a sound, my straining ears not even picking up the grunts of harsh breathing. Coming through could be a brutal experience and Orphon was often grumpy, snarling and spitting at me until we settled the terms of our bargain. This time there was none of that but still, I could feel his presence, the heat of his aura pulsing at me. Keeping my eyes firmly shut, I released my power slowly, letting the other realm fade back and the laws of physics return to mine.

When my basement was back to being just a basement, a room with four walls and no gateways to hell dimensions, I freed my fingertips from their groundings and opened my eyes.

There was a demon, sprawled in a reclined half-sit on the floor directly opposite me.

That wasn't really a surprise, to be fair. It was a demon I'd been trying to summon. However, I'd been going for a lower-level demon, little more than an imp, really. Big, muscly, not overly bright. A bit like the hulk, but red. Good for short term protective detail like, say, keeping me out of the clutches of vampires.

I'd been looking for Orphon.

This was not Orphon.

I didn't know who the fuck he was. He was small for a demon, though he'd still have towered over most humans, and he had dark golden skin with thick, glossy black hair. I let my gaze dart across his square jaw, studiously avoiding those dark, dark eyes, before dropping down to look at the body on display. Oh my. It was clad in some very nice muscles and displayed to impress as he leaned back on one elbow, a single knee cocked while the other leg stretched out toward me. If I shifted in my seat just a tiny bit, I'd be able to see his, uh, bits.

I didn't move so much as a muscle.

"Who are you?" I blurted, then winced. I knew better than to ask such blunt questions, especially of a demon of unknown powers and unknown temperament. He'd come in response to my summoning, but that could just as easily be because he fancied draining all my blood and wearing my skin as a suit. Or maybe just a shirt. Even rounded as I was, there definitely wasn't enough of me to cover that long, lean body.

Focus, Daisy!

Thankfully he didn't take offense to my rudeness. He just smiled slightly, giving a long slow blink of those liquid eyes. Oh boy.

"I…uh, was expecting Orphon."

You know, since that was who I asked for.

"Orphon is busy." Oh God, the voice matched the look, all smooth and deep and delicious. Had I summoned an incubus? I hoped not. I wasn't going to get rid of Tobias Hunter by flirting with him.

"He…is?" Something about the way the demon said that had my inner alarm pinging. "Is he all right?"

"He's being punished."

Okay then. I wasn't opening that can of worms.

"I see. And who are…I mean, may I ask your name?"

"You can ask." A twitch of his lips. Oh, he was a tease, this one. I was not equipped to deal with a tease, especially one who could rip my head off with his bare hands if I made a misstep.

"All right." Deep breath. "What's your name?"

"Abigor." He said it quietly, letting the sound of it roll off his tongue, but it struck me with the force of a gong. Abigor? Abigor the warrior demon who commanded sixty legions? The one colloquially referred to as the Grand Duke of Hell?

Oh, no. Oh no, no, no. Not in my basement. I could not handle that.

He could blow the whole damn place up with a flick of his finger. He could probably take out the entire street if he wanted to. Or summon a squadron of minions to flatten my subdivision. I mean, he could also take out Hunter and his children without breaking a sweat, but one did not ask a higher-level demon to perform guard dog duty.

I had to send him back, now.

"I…oh. I mean, I'm so sorry." Wince. There was another mistake. Don't apologise to demons, it puts you in their debt. Wait, was that demons or fae? I was so panicky, my thoughts were a mess. Agnetha would box my ears.

Fae, that was definitely fae.

Breathe, Daisy. Calm.

"I didn't mean to disturb you. I was looking for Orphon, but clearly he's not available. If you give me a moment, I'll just send you back."

Every muscle in my body protested at the thought of wielding the spell again. It wasn't easy, and it wiped me out for days afterward. Doing it twice in one night, I'd be bedridden, easy prey for the vampires. I had wards, protective symbols painted all around my house and yard, designed to stop unwelcome otherworldly visitors from setting foot on my property, but those same wards should have prevented a letter from dropping into my lap, and that hadn't happened, had it? Still, I'd made a mistake and I had to fix it. I did not want to upset a demon like Abigor.

"Why did you summon him?" A quiet murmur.

"Huh?" I barked out my inelegant response as I prepared to hoist myself up for fresh incense to reopen the gate.

"Orphon." He pitched his voice a little louder this time, head tilted slightly to the side as he watched me. "Why did you summon him."

"Oh. I...well. I needed him to help me. With a problem. But it's fine." I smiled as brightly as I could manage. "I'll find another way to sort it. Let me just—"

"Sit." My ass banged back down onto the concrete at the quietly spoken command. He hadn't used any of his power to force me—though I was sure he could—he was just that...intimidating. Authoritative. "Explain this problem to me."

"Oh, it's nothing." I waved breezily, that same smile still stretched almost painfully across my face.

"You summon my demons for nothing?" There was no menace in his tone, but just the tiniest lifting of his chin had my heart freezing in my chest. *Fuck!* Dumb move, Daisy.

"No. I mean...it's not nothing. But, well, it's not something that I want to bother you with. So, if you'll just give me a moment, I can get you back home and stop interrupting your evening."

"No."

"No?" I blinked at him, confused.

"I want to hear about your problem."

"You really don't."

"I just said I did, didn't I?" He moved then, shifting sinuously until he was sitting just three feet opposite me, mirroring my cross-legged position. All I had to do was glance down and...

I kept my eyes fixed on his face, even if that meant gazing into those inhuman eyes.

"Vampires," I stuttered. He raised a single eyebrow in indication that I should go on. "They kidnapped me and made me perform a protection spell, and now they've sent me a letter saying they want me to go back."

"A letter?"

"Yes!"

"Well, that's an improvement on kidnapping you again."

"I—" His words slowly sunk in. "The point is that they kidnapped me in the first place! Who know what they might do this time!"

"Were you hurt during your last encounter?" A darkness entered the room, the candles flickering ever so slightly. Since I'd no idea what that meant, I decided to ignore it.

"They locked me up!"

"But you weren't hurt."

"No," I admitted, my annoyance at the fact the demon wasn't seeing my side making my fear of him abate a little. A very little. "But they didn't pay me, either!"

Ok, that sounded lame even to me. One did not summon a demon for debt collection.

"You wished Orphan to kill these vampires for you?"

"No!" My answer came out as a squeak. "Just…hang around and look intimidating for a little while until they went away."

The look Abigor gave me left me in no uncertainty how shit he thought my plan was. To be fair, now that I'd laid it out for another person, it was hard not to agree with him. Which was why I was so shocked when he gave a little nod.

"I accept."

I blinked. Stared at him. Blinked again.

"What?"

"I accept. I will stay here and act as your protector from these vampires."

I gaped at him, sure my ears must be broken or something.

"You'll…stay?"

"Yes."

"I'm, um, sure that won't be necessary. You must have other, much more important things to do."

Like killing, maiming, torturing. Thinking up evil plans. Demon stuff.

"I do, but I have decided. I will stay." Ok, then. I bit my tongue against protesting further, though any comments I might have made died in my throat as he gave a slow, wicked smile. "We have, of course, still to agree upon my payment."

Oh shit.

Chapter Two

Abigor grinned as the plump little witch paled and swayed. She was trembling with fear and her desperate need to have him gone was beating at him in pulsing waves. It was delightful.

She was right, he did have a million other things he could—should—be doing, but what was the point of being a higher-level demon if you couldn't have a little fun now and then? He had minions enough to handle things in his absence and, if they fucked up, he'd have the pleasure of punishing them.

It was a win-win situation as far as he could see.

"Payment?" she squeaked.

"You did not plan to offer Orphon payment?"

"Well, I did." She swallowed hard, the movement drawing attention to her creamy throat. It looked biteable, quite frankly, and he wasn't at all surprised that she'd caught the attention of the local vampire seethe. "But, uh…"

"But?"

She looked around the tiny, suffocating little room as if someone might pop out of the shadows and save her. Since Abigor knew there wasn't another living creature larger than an insect within the building, he waited.

"Orphan usually just likes, you know, pizza and stuff. Some chocolate. I cast a glamour on him and take him to the movies."

"I see." He gave a little shrug. "I'm afraid that won't work for me."

"It won't?" finely arched eyebrows drew together over big green eyes.

"No, it will not. I can get human fripperies any time I desire. And I'd think carefully before you offer to dispatch me back to hell again, little one," he added as she opened her mouth, the thought writ clear on her face, "else I shall start to think you don't desire my company."

Her mouth snapped shut with an audible click.

He had to smile. She had such an expressive face. It was clear to see that she didn't desire his company at all, though that, he was certain, was because the smart little witch knew exactly who she was playing with. Desire him? Well, that was a little different. She was being scrupulously polite, her gaze not deviating an inch from his face except for the little moments where she glanced about the room, hunting for an escape from her predicament. That in itself was telling. But even more so, to Abigor's amusement, every now and then, her stare would drop from his eyes, to his nose, to his chin, almost helplessly, before she caught herself and dragged it back up.

Yes, she was interested. Which gave him an idea…

"The payment I require is something more personal."

"Personal?"

He forced his lips not to twitch. "That is what I said."

Long seconds passed in heady silence as she fought not to ask. Abigor settled in, enjoying her discomfort and waiting for the inevitable.

"What sort of personal?"

"The personal sort of personal." He laughed, he couldn't help it. She looked so aghast, and yet at the same time insanely curious. "For however long I remain as your protector, you shall allow me to pleasure you."

"Pleasure…me?"

"You." He gave a wicked little grin. "You will allow me to stroke you, lick you, nibble on you, and bring you to ecstasy again and again and again." He gazed hard into her eyes and watched her pupils dilate, heard her pulse begin to race. "Those are the terms I offer, do you accept."

She took a moment to respond, then shook her head like she was chasing a cobweb off of a dream. Her expression was mostly bemused now, some of her fear having slunk away during their exchange.

"But why would you want to? You're not an incubus."

"I am not," he agreed.

"Then I don't understand—"

"You don't need to understand, you simply need to accept. Do you?"

She watched him with uncertain eyes for a long moment, and Abigor fought the urge to give her a little push. He wanted the bargain, more badly than he really understood, but he wanted it given freely.

"I accept," she whispered.

"Excellent." Knowing exactly what he was doing, he rolled to his feet, putting his impressive manhood directly in her vision. She squawked and hurried to join him, though even at her full height she barely reached the middle of his chest. He liked that. Size was no indication of power, but most demons were taller—all right, larger all over—than Abigor, and it rankled, even though he could blast the majority of them to pieces with one concentrated shove of power. Having a delicate, delicious little creature before him who had to tilt her head far back so she could gaze up at him with those big eyes, well, it pleased him.

And Abigor did what he pleased.

"Your name?" he asked her.

"Daisy."

Daisy? His mind stuttered for a moment before it brought forth an image of a small white flower with a yellow centre. Common, unremarkable, it suited his witch not at all. There was no changing a name, though. "I would see the rest of your dwelling."

"I…oh. Yes." She scuttled ahead of him, leading the way to a narrow flight of stairs. "And, uh—" Her eyes raked quickly up and down his form. "We should get you some clothes."

Clothes would get in the way, make it more difficult to pleasure her—which Abigor intended to get to right away, vampires be damned—but as she glanced uncertainly at his chest and arms, then wrenched her gaze away again, he decided a little wooing might be in order first.

He was surprised how much that idea pleased him, too.

As Daisy scrambled up the steps in front of him, her bottom jiggling deliciously in skin-tight jeans, he caught a glimpse of her snatching something off one of the stairs. A piece of paper, he thought, from the low crinkle of sound as she stuffed it into her pocket. And from the tinge of menthol sting in his nose, it was from her vampires.

Well, they'd get to that.

He strolled naked around her home as she scrambled to find articles for him to wear, the attire she'd been intending to offer Orphon swiped from the kitchen as she ran from him. It was a small place, but bright, late evening sun spilling in through the windows. There was only one bedroom, he was pleased to see, so she couldn't attempt to fob him off with a guest room, and neither of them would be sleeping on the ageing couch that was too short for his form and whose tired cushions wouldn't be comfortable for either of them. He wasn't sure he even wanted to sit on it.

The kitchen was small but clean, a frozen pizza waiting on the counter, along with an unopened pack of cookies. Fancy ones too, ginger and dark chocolate. He'd enjoy telling Orphon that when he returned, imagined that missing out on human treats might be more of a punishment for the demon than his current predicament, hanging by his ankles over the flames.

"Why is Orphon being punished?" Daisy asked, appearing quietly in the doorway behind him, a bundle of clothes in her hand.

"He displeased me," Abigor answered, holding his hands out for the garments.

She passed them over, but the uncertain look didn't leave her face.

"What did he do?"

"I have told you."

"No, you didn't, you just said he displeased you. That's not an answer."

He paused, a T-shirt in his grip that he could already tell was going to be too small, would pull over his muscles. Perhaps Daisy would enjoy that.

"Is it not?"

It took a moment for the tiniest edge in his voice to bleed through her thoughts. When it did, though, she blanched and dropped her gaze to the floor.

"I'm sorry," she mumbled.

Regret speared through Abigor, an emotion he was very unfamiliar with.

"He fought with another demon and damaged him. Badly. I had to make recompense to the demon's lord."

And hadn't that fucking stung. Nicon was a smug bastard who'd delighted in wringing words of apology out of Abigor—along with a very valuable relic.

"Is he all right?"

Abigor's eyebrows rose up his forehead. Was she actually worried about the clumsy oaf?

"He's a demon, he'll be fine. And, perhaps, more careful in future."

Though that wasn't bloody likely.

He pulled on the T-shirt and then a pair of jogging trousers, tossing the restrictive underwear she'd given him aside. It wasn't as comfortable as remaining bared, but he noticed she felt more free to look at him now, clear appreciation in her eyes as a little pink tongue darted out to lick her lips.

Good.

Let her stew on that for a little while.

"The vampires," he said.

She started at the abrupt change of subject. "What about them?"

"They sent you a letter." He held out a hand. "I would see it."

She seemed a little reluctant, but this was why she'd summoned a demon, after all. Abigor was utterly certain he could deal with whatever the issue was, but he needed to know the specifics first.

All right, he didn't really. Truth be told, he could wipe out the entire seethe in about five minutes, but then his time with the little witch would end abruptly—after he'd exacted payment, of course—and he found he didn't like that idea.

Perhaps a subtler approach could be employed.

"The letter," he prompted.

She handed it over, crinkled and a little warm from its snug home in the back pocket of her jeans. Abigor unfolded it and scanned the words briefly. It was impeccably polite, the words writing in a flowing elegant hand. Taking a moment to memorize the name signed beneath the note—*Tobias Hunter*—and the accompanying telephone number, he summoned a small surge of energy and the thick, creamy velum burst into flames.

"What are you doing?" Daisy shrieked. She scurried forward to try and snatch the letter back from him, but he held it aloft, easily fending off her efforts with one hand, until it was no more, a smattering of ash on the linoleum floor the only evidence of its existence. "Why would you do that?" she asked, eyes wide.

"To send a message."

"A…message." He saw the moment she understood what he'd just done. "They'll *know* that you burned the letter?"

"They will."

"*Why would you do that?*" she repeated. He thought he'd heard her panicked before, but her voice reached another stratosphere now.

"They need to know that I am here, and that I am dealing with this issue now. I don't intend to go to them." That would send completely the wrong message.

She stared at him, aghast. "They're going to come here?"

"I would," he answered, "if it was me."

"*I don't want vampires in my house!*"

He smiled patiently and dropped both hands on her shoulders. The muscles there were tight and tense.

"Your plan was terrible. It did not sort the problem, merely delayed it. If we do things my way, you will never have to worry about the vampires leaning on you ever again. You summoned me to handle this, so let me handle it. Trust, Daisy, please."

He was well aware that he was asking her to trust a near stranger who was a higher-level demon, with enough blood on his hands to stain the ground of the entire continent, but that didn't matter. He wanted her trust, demanded it, and when she blew out a breath and her shoulders dropped a fraction, he knew he had it.

Or, at least the beginnings of it.

"When…when do you think they'll come?" she asked, glancing dubiously out the window, where the sun had set and dusk was quickly gathering.

"They will not bother us tonight," he assured her.

"You think?" she asked. "If they know you burned the letter…"

"Hunter will send some of his children to investigate, but they will not get through the wards."

"They got through them easily enough to play postman," she reminded him ruefully.

"Your wards," he told her, grinning confidently. "I assure you they shall not make it through mine."

"And what'll happen then?" More trust. She was seeking his opinion, accepting his answers. Abigor pulled in a deeper breath to ease the odd tightness in his chest.

"They will report back to their master, and Hunter will know he is dealing with something more than a defenceless witch."

"I'm not defenceless," she muttered.

"He will take a moment to reconsider, and his next approach will be much more careful."

"You think so?" There was hope in that hazel gaze as it looked beseechingly up at him.

"I know so."

Chapter Three

Steam billowed out as I opened the oven door and peeked at the pizza to see if it was done. I could have peered through the door if I'd cleaned it once in the last two years, but it was coated with so much grime that I now couldn't get it off—I mean, I had *tried*—and it hid what was happening inside.

Since the most culinary thing to be made in the oven was ready meals and pizzas a lot like this one, I just lived with it.

The cheese was sufficiently browned and the crust not yet burned, so I yanked it out and cut it up into slices. My stomach was in absolute knots and I doubted I'd be able to eat anything, but my mother had drummed into me a long list of polite manners—some of which I'd since realized she'd completely made up—and one of them was that you ate when the guests ate. I slid a small slice onto my plate and then dumped most of the rest on Abigor's. If his appetite was anything like Orphon's, he'd eat the lot and be looking for more.

"Sorry," I mumbled as I placed the meal down in front of him at the kitchen table. "If I'd known...I mean, I'd have got something a little better in but—"

But Orphon loved all things cheese and grease, and that had been who I was expecting, not a demon who, even dressed in a simple T-shirt and jogging bottoms, had a poised, cultured look about him that said he was accustomed to the very finest of dining.

"This will suffice," he said. "Thank you."

I gave a small smile and took the seat opposite, digging into my stingy portion without enthusiasm while he inhaled slice after slice. I kept glancing out of the kitchen window at the dark outside, expecting to see malignant shadows lingering under the streetlight. Not that I'd see them if they didn't want to be seen, they might just wait until I was sleeping in my bed and then sneak in and—

"When do you think they'll turn up?" I asked, desperate to interrupt my nightmarish thoughts.

"Who?" Abigor asked, a hunk of pizza halfway to his mouth.

Who? Really?

"The vampires," I said carefully.

"Oh." He waved a dismissive hand and jammed the food into his mouth. "They're already here."

"What?" I screeched. I jumped up and hurried to the window, peering out into the night. I didn't see anything except next door's cat, stalking along the fence that ran between our properties so it could shit in my yard again. "Where?"

"Come and sit down."

I ignored the instruction, too unnerved by the thought of vampires wandering around my house. I had motion detectors angled to cover almost every square inch of the garden, but if Frank, the yard-befouling ginger tomcat, could get around them, I doubted vampires would be outsmarted. I'd had more confidence in my wards, until the damned letter.

I dimly heard the sound of the chair squeaking on the linoleum as I strained my eyes, trying to detect even a hint of movement in the shadows, but I didn't realize Abigor had crossed the room to me until he wrapped around me from behind, hands going to cover mine and releasing the death grip I had on my kitchen counter. He crossed my arms over my stomach, enfolding me in a hug at the same time and dropping his chin down to rest against the side of my head.

"I told you," he said. "They cannot get through my wards. They cannot get to you. You are completely safe."

I snorted. Somehow, I didn't think housing a higher-level demon as a guest constituted safe behavior.

"What about you?" I asked.

"What about me?"

"You're not exactly safe."

"You have nothing to fear from me," he promised, amusement in his voice. "We struck a bargain, remember."

We had. And so long as I held up my side of the bargain, Abigor would abide by his word. He'd sworn to protect me which, I reasoned, meant he couldn't harm me either.

Of course, that meant I had to hold up my side of the bargain. I gulped as I thought about what I'd agreed to. He wanted to…pleasure me. Ooooh boy. My face threatened to go up in flames as I thought about it. Not sex, he'd been clear on that—though, he'd also been clear that it was on the table if I wanted to—he just wanted to, uh, pleasure me.

You will allow me to stroke you, lick you, nibble on you, and bring you to ecstasy again and again and again.

Jesus.

I mean, I didn't understand why he would want to. Even though he scared the pants off me (ha ha), the man was sexy as sin. The face, the body…and now that he was wrapped around me, I could smell him and it was intoxicating. He smelled smoky and spicey, like a really good bourbon and oh yeah, my girl parts were definitely on board with that if—

My naughty thoughts ground to a halt as a growl rumbled through his chest.

"What? What is it?" I gasped. "Do you see them, are they coming in?"

"I gave you my word," he said. "They can't." He bent down and sniffed at my neck, his nose tickling me and sending little tingles over the sensitive skin there. "You smell delicious."

"I…do?"

"You do. You smell like need."

Like need? My eyes refocused on the dim reflection of us I could see in the glass as I processed those words, and so I got a good view of my face as it slid from confusion into mortification. He could smell my need, my arousal. If that wasn't embarrassing, I didn't know what was. I tried to wriggle away, to put some space between us, but he tightened his grip and nuzzled at the curve between my neck and shoulder, nipped at it lightly with his teeth.

I made a strangled noise because wow, that felt amazing, and he chuckled.

"I think it is time for me to begin collecting payment on our bargain."

"You're sure you can't just accept the pizza?" I asked desperately. "I have cheesecake, too. Really good cheesecake."

Actually, it was amazing cheesecake, made by old Mrs. Wilkins down the street who paid me in baked goods to scry her layabout son once a month and check that he was still alive and not in jail. Her cheesecake was the best thing I'd ever eaten—and I'd sampled a fair few sweet delicacies in my time—and I usually guarded it like a dragon over its hoard, but desperate times called for desperate measures.

"Cheesecake will be welcome," he purred in my ear. "After."

After?

"Life is uncertain," I babbled. "Eat dessert first."

He huffed a gentle laugh and unravelled from me, keeping hold of one of my hands so that he could tug me after him.

"Come, little witch."

We exited the kitchen and he ignored my attempts to guide him toward my living room, heading instead for my bedroom. I grimaced as we stepped through the doorway. It wasn't a big room and I was an untidy person with a lot of stuff. Clothes lay strewn across the barrel armchair in the corner and my closet door lay half open—because the hinge was loose and I hadn't bothered to fix it—revealing the disorganized jumble inside. My vanity was littered with toiletries and make up and, worse, a dirty cup and plate from last night's midnight snack. By some small mercy my bed was at least made, the pretty flowered bedspread pulled up over my collection of fluffy pillows.

"Not daisies?" Abigor asked, a hand going down to trail over the stem of a pink rose.

"No." I scowled automatically. The only daisy in this whole damn house was me. "I like my plants with thorns."

He laughed, throwing his head back, and my brain stopped working. He was just utterly stunning, and I had no idea what on earth he was doing in my bedroom.

Then his head snapped down and his eyes fixed on mine.

"Take off your clothes."

It was such an abrupt change of tone, from uproarious laughter to dark intensity, that my hands obeyed automatically, going down to grip at the hem of my T-shirt before my thoughts caught up with them. I froze, wondering if I'd been compelled, but I didn't feel anything other than some serious apprehension and a growing spark of excitement. I'd been compelled before, by a warlock and a couple of other nasty creatures of the night, I knew what it felt like.

This, this was nothing more than the arrogant dominance of an extremely powerful demon. And who was I to argue?

Moving a little more slowly, I tugged my T-shirt over my head, gathering it into a ball and holding it in front of my slightly-more-than-slightly-rounded stomach like a shield. I eyed him, standing there watching and still fully dressed.

"Aren't you…you're still wearing all your clothes."

"I am," he agreed. "The terms of our bargain were that you would let me pleasure you, nothing more."

I eyed him suspiciously. "Are you sure you're not an incubus."

"I am not," he assured me. Then he looked down to my hands, still clutching the shirt in a death grip. "Continue."

Continue. I blew out a breath and then made myself release the T-shirt. It fell to the floor with a soft plop. My hands fluttered up to my bra, but then I lost my nerve and went for the button of my jeans instead. They were tight—running, Daisy, running—and I had to work to wiggle them over my hips. I kicked them off, quickly divesting myself of my socks at the same time, then looked at him.

He looked back, waiting patiently.

Dammit.

Orphon, I hope you're hanging from your ankles somewhere, I thought viciously as I slid off my underwear and unclipped my bra, letting it slide down my arms until it dangled from my fingertips. With a flick, I dropped it down with the rest of my clothes.

"Mmmm," Abigor murmured. His mouth curled into a smile as his eyes raked up and down the length of my body. I kept my hands by my side, refusing to yield to the urge to shield myself. "Up on the bed," he said.

I obeyed, rounding it first so that I wouldn't be giving him an unflattering view of my backside as I scrambled up. Not really sure what to do, I paused on my knees in the middle of the mattress.

Abigor hadn't shifted, except for his eyes, which tracked my every movement. As I watched him, he brought his hands close together in front of him. Power coalesced there in a ball of light, and when it dimmed, he held several long, thin scraps of fabric dangling from his fists.

"You could have magicked your own clothes," I accused.

"I could have." He grinned at me, unrepentant. "Lie down for me, little witch."

I didn't move.

"What are you going to do with those?" I asked. Because the things in his hands looked nothing so much as restraints.

"I want to make sure you keep still."

"I can keep still," I said quickly. "You don't need to tie me up."

"You say that now. When you are in the throes of exquisite pleasure, you will not be able to stop yourself."

Well, now. That shut me up. I lay down on my back on the bed without further comment, staring up at the ceiling so that I wouldn't watch as he prowled toward me.

"You look like you are preparing for torture," he murmured as he picked up one of my hands and gently kissed the back of it. "Do you know how many women would sell their souls to be pleasured by me?"

"My soul is not for sale," I said quickly. Agnetha had been crystal clear on demons and souls, and all of it had come under the heading Don't Give Them It Ever.

"We'll see," Abigor murmured, so quietly I could ignore it. So, I did.

He wrapped the material—which was a soft, stretchy black—around my wrist then threaded it through the bars of my headboard before capturing my other wrist and tying the second end around it. When he was done, my hands were rested up above my head and though I could move them a bit, I couldn't bring them down any lower than my temples. Abigor wrapped warm fingers around my ankle and I expected him to tie another length of the fabric in it, but he didn't. He squeezed the delicate joint for a moment, then ran his fingertips up my skin, around the inside of my knee, then up my inner thigh.

I didn't even know I was doing it, but by the time he'd reached the soft skin just where my thigh met my centre, I'd shifted my leg to give him access to the very core of me, my eyes almost rolling back in my head with the tingling trail of pleasure he left in his wake.

Oh that…that was not normal.

Exquisite was right.

He didn't touch me there, even though my hips were tilted for him in open invitation. Instead, his hand skimmed over my stomach and breasts until he gently cupped my throat. Then he leaned forward and kissed me.

It was a sensual kiss, his lips toying with mine, his tongue slicking its way inside and teasing me with quick, darting strokes. I tried to bring my hands down, my fingers desperate to bury them in his luxurious hair, but the restraints brought me up short. I tugged on them, but they didn't give. Frustrated, I nipped at the tip of his tongue, making him jerk.

I realized what I'd done as soon as he pulled back and stared at me, surprised, and a tumble of apologies rose to my lips, but I swallowed them down, raising an eyebrow challengingly instead. My heart was thundering in my chest, my legs shifting restlessly.

"Oh, I was right about you," he said. Then he took a length of fabric and placed it over my eyes.

I gasped, unnerved by the sudden darkness. Of course, I was a witch. I didn't need my eyes to see. I ranged out my senses, and there he was, glowing like a beacon. Abigor. He looked bigger, his head slightly misshapen, and I realized I was seeing his true shape, the odd lumps on his head probably horns of some sort. I fought to bring the image into more focus, but it wasn't a skill I practised very often—all right, at all—and I was distracted by another kiss. This one was softer, no more than a press of his lips against mine, and then he trailed more down over my chin and along my neck.

He was a demon. An evil creature of Hell. He could rip out my throat with as much effort as it took me to rip off a new sheet of kitchen towel, but I found myself tilting my neck to give him better access rather than trying to protect my most vulnerable area. I was panting, I realized, panting and moaning as he licked and sucked and nipped his way all the way to my breast.

When he took my nipple in his mouth and drew on it, I arched right off the mattress. He released it with an audible pop and then blew on the wetted tip. I shuddered, feeling my whole breast tighten as goose bumps erupted over the skin.

"Mmm," he purred. "You have such sensitive skin."

There was a short, sharp flare of power, the light visible around the edges of the blindfold and the energy of it fizzing over my witch's senses. I tensed, having no idea what Abigor had summoned. My nose detected a slight hint of burning in the air. He'd lit a candle? I couldn't be sure.

He was still with me in the room, I knew that much at least.

A hand ran down my side, all the way from my underarm to my hip. I shifted into the touch, enjoying the warmth, the tickling of fingertips over sensitive nerve endings. A moment later, there was another touch, trailing along the top of my thigh to my hip. I gasped. This touch wasn't warm at all. It was sharply cold, leaving a wet trail.

Ice?

I tensed, waiting for the next touch, wondering if it would be the warmth of his hand or the chill of the ice cube.

Frigid cold ran down my left side, along the inner line of my right upper arm. Across my collar bones. Down my forehead and along the bridge of my nose. Faster and faster so that I was still feeling the trail of the previous touch when the next one hit. Streaks of cold raising goosebumps all over my body.

When the soft splat hit my belly, I thought for an instant that it was a drop of water from the ice cube, until my brain registered a bloom of scorching heat. Candle wax. I gasped, yanking my stomach muscles in, but was almost immediately distracted by ice down my left cheek. Over the curve of my hip, a droplet running down toward my centre. Splat. Molten fire on my left breast.

Ice up the centre of my palm. Blazing heat right on my pubic mound.

Chill across the top of my right foot, along all five of my toes. A droplet of burning wax on the delicate skin on the inside of my knee.

Two hands took told of my knees and eased my thighs apart. I felt the warmth of a body settle in there, hot breath on my core, at the same time as the ice cube ran down the chords of my neck.

What on earth?

How was he doing that? He only had two hands, and they were down there, spreading me wide, as another droplet of wax exploded on my belly, just underneath my right breast.

Demon, I told myself. His power far exceeded my own, getting an ice cube and a candle to obey his commands would be nothing.

Then I stopped thinking anything at all, because his tongue delved deep, lapping at me. Darting into my core, sliding round my clit. I didn't sense that he was using any power, but it was like little sparks of electricity each time he touched his tongue to me. It was better than any kind of vibrator, firing up my nerves.

"You taste delicious," he told me.

Hot wax hit my left nipple, the icy burn of the ice cube rolling round my right. Then his tongue was back there, flicking at me, shocking me with those sparks. Ooooh God, it was way better than any vibe. My stomach convulsed and I let out a strangled moan.

It was too much, my mind unable to keep up with the assault of cold and heat and sparks on my senses. I felt like I was going to explode out of my skin, my blinded eyes forgotten about, everything in me concentrated on my body.

"I...Oh God. Oh fuck, coming!"

"Come." He gave me the word in tandem with a trio of dots—my hip, my belly, and directly on my nipple—from the candle, and I screamed as an orgasm ripped through me at the same time the hot pain radiated across my torso. He made me ride it out, the ice cube dancing all over my body, his tongue pressed hard against my clit and rubbing as he sucked hard. I squirmed and writhed, my legs shifting useless on either side of his shoulders, my hands pulling hard on the restraints above me. I even bucked my hips, but I couldn't shift him, not until he'd wrung every drop of pleasure from me and my body lay limp across the sheets, little tremors wracking my frame.

When he finally took his mouth away it was to trail kisses up my torso until he reached my mouth. He parted my lips and delved in his tongue, making me taste myself, then slid the blindfold free. I blinked, my eyes tearing against the brightness, as his hands released my wrists. I let him manoeuvre me until I was on my side, my front plastered along the length of his body and my head resting on his chest. He had one arm underneath me, curled up so his fingers could play in my hair.

"Thank you," he said. "You honor me. Now, sleep little witch. The vampires will not get near you when I'm here."

The vampires. I'd forgotten all about the vampires. Still, I couldn't work up any energy to fret about them, not right now. As Abigor summoned a light blanket to cover us both, I closed my eyes and let sleep claim me.

Chapter Four

She didn't know what to do with him. Abigor smiled as the little witch scuttled around, fussing over breakfast. He felt refreshed and revitalized after drinking in her passion last night and then spending a night pretending to sleep like the humans did. Daisy, however had bags under her eyes and a lethargy beneath the manic energy she was exuding.

Oh, she'd lain there all night, not moving a muscle, allowing him to hold her, but after a brief nap brought on by the endorphin release of—he was one hundred percent certain—the best orgasm she'd ever had, she'd struggled to sleep. He'd liked to have thought that she had been, like he had been, simply enjoying the moment, but he suspected it had more to do with the vampires.

Which was fucking insulting.

Abigor had said he'd handle it, and he would.

Now that the sun was in the sky, she'd relaxed somewhat believing, falsely, that the threat could no longer reach her. The vampires might be trapped in their lightless vaults, but those who worked for them were not.

Daisy gave him a trembling smile as she dropped a plate of food in front of him.

"I, uh, I usually just have cereal in the mornings, so I hope this is ok."

A large bottle of syrup joined the plate of French toast on the table.

"It smells delicious," he told her.

The smile firmed up a bit as she sat opposite him, her breakfast a bowl of milk-smothered cardboard that she stirred unenthusiastically with a spoon while casting envious looks toward Abigor as he dug in. He'd eaten the world's finest delicacies, meals prepared by the most renowned chefs, and a stack of French toast could not compare. But she'd prepared it for him herself, in what was possibly the worst equipped kitchen he'd ever seen, so the simple fare rose above its humble origins.

"You should have made some for yourself," he commented, as she thrust a spoonful of the sodden mulch in her mouth without enthusiasm.

"What? Oh…oh, no. This is fine for me."

He raised his eyebrow but made no further comment. If she wanted to starve herself of the simple pleasures life afforded, let her do so. It would just make her more desperate for the ecstasy he could show her.

"What would you like to do today?" she asked. "You know, until—"

"Until?"

"Until tonight, when the vampires…wake up. You said they'd come back, right."

"Oh, I don't think we'll have to wait until tonight."

She blanched. "You don't?"

"No."

As if on cue, her phone began to ring. She started, sloshing milk across the table then scrambled out of her chair to grab it from the counter. When she had it in her hand, though, she just stared down at the screen, allowing it to continue trilling.

It stopped, eventually, but then, after a space of several seconds, began again.

"Are you going to answer?" he asked, amused.

"Well, I…there's no number. It's withheld."

Of course it was. Because vampires were secretive bastards even when there was absolutely no need. Silently, he held out his hand for the phone.

She looked at him, then down at the phone, then back to him again. Her apprehension morphed slowly into fear.

"You think it's *them*? But it's daytime!"

He simply waited, and eventually she took two steps forward and dropped it into his waiting hand. He slid his thumb up the screen and pressed the phone to his ear.

"Hello."

There was a pause. Whoever was on the other end had obviously not expected anyone but Daisy to answer. They might have realized that her wards had been strengthened considerably, but they hadn't sensed him or seen him, Abigor had made sure of that.

And that was the least of his little box of tricks.

"Who are you?" It was a man's voice, deep and strong, but the tone was cautious. Respectful, even. Abigor's lips twitched.

"My name is Abigor."

There was no need for secrecy. Better for them to know who they were dealing with. The name might not mean anything to the person on the phone, but Abigor was quite sure it would resonate with the master vampire in the seethe. Tobias Hunter, he reminded himself. Not a name he'd heard before, but it didn't mean he wouldn't be facing a worthy adversary. He rarely involved himself with vampires—because they were rarely stupid enough to get in his way.

"I would like to speak to the witch, please."

"Would you." he flicked his eyes up toward Daisy and saw she was standing frozen, watching him. Her ears wouldn't be able to pick up both sides of the conversation; a witch she might be, but she didn't have preternatural senses.

"Is she there?"

"She's here."

"…May I speak with her?"

"No."

"I see." There was a short pause as the vampire lackey on the other end of the phone reevaluated in the face of this rather enormous obstacle in his path. "I have something to discuss with her, something urgent."

"You may discuss it with me."

Another short pause. "Do you speak for her?"

"Yes." Abigor suspected that Daisy wouldn't like that idea at all, but she was deaf to the other side of the exchange, had no idea what was being said. Besides, she had summoned him to help.

"Very well. My master—"

"Hunter."

"Yes, my master, Tobias Hunter, would like Ms. Bennett to visit him at—"

"No."

The pause lasted longer this time. Then, "No? He has a very delicate matter to discuss with her, and he would prefer to do so in person."

"He can come here, then."

"*Here?*" Daisy squeaked from beside him.

The lackey down the line sounded equally astonished. "My master is the pre-eminent vampire in the region. He does not lower himself to—"

Abigor had heard enough of the man's spluttering.

"If he wants to speak to Daisy, he comes here. Tonight. Eight pm is acceptable to us."

He hung up the phone while the fool was still stammering at him and turned to Daisy, whose eyes were wide, mouth pressed together. He braced for the outraged female explosion he knew was coming.

"Are you crazy? I don't want vampires here, *in my house*. And I certainly don't want a *master vampire*! You're supposed to be protecting me, not inviting them over for drinks!"

"There is no obligation to provide refreshment." He fought not to smile as her indignation deepened.

"Oh, well, that's fine then, isn't it?"

"Daisy." He injected enough authority into his voice to have her clamping her lips shut, though he could see she was still internally fuming…which was just a cover for the fact that she was terrified. Standing up, he moved toward her and rested his hands on her shoulders, rubbing gently with his thumbs. She smelled of lemon and something sweet, fragrances that had wafted from the bathroom after the shower she'd refused to let him share with her this morning.

Tomorrow, he'd not be taking no for an answer, but he could be a patient hunter when the prey required it.

"You called me here to protect you. In order to do that, I need to meet with Hunter and explain that you are under my protection. All right?"

It took a moment, but then she nodded. Her eyebrows were still drawn forward over troubled eyes, however.

"What happens when you leave, though?"

"I will be making it clear to the vampire that my protection of you extends indefinitely."

"But you won't be here and—"

He slipped a finger under her chin and tilted her face up until she met his gaze. "If you need me, you will be able to reach me, and I will be here between one breath and the next. Yes?"

She chewed on her lip instead of answering.

"Yes?"

It took a while, but eventually she gave him a slow reluctant nod.

"Good girl. Now, come. The breakfast you provided was satisfying, but it wasn't as deliciously sweet as you. I want to taste you again."

Her mouth dropped open and her face flamed red, but she offered no resistance as he tugged her toward her bedroom.

The afternoon bled into evening into dusk, and then gradually night fell. Abigor passed the time in the most enjoyable way possible—wringing orgasm after orgasm from his little witch until she lay utterly spent on the bed.

When he slid off the mattress away from her—something every fibre of his body protested—she gave a little satisfied mewl and rolled over, snuggling into the covers.

"It's time to get up, little one," he said. He pulled the T-shirt back over his head and adjusted his cock in the jogging bottoms he'd kept on to ensure he held to his word and pushed for nothing more than drowning her in pleasure. His cock was throbbing, but it was a good pain. Mostly.

Like he said, he was a patient hunter.

"Tired," she mumbled. "Sleep."

"As you wish." He smiled at her huddled shape in the centre of the bed. "But I thought you would wish to be dressed when the vampire appears."

As predicted, she made an alarmed noise that was halfway between a squawk and a squeal, then tore past him. A moment later the bathroom door slammed and he heard the shower turned on. A pity, he liked her drenched in the scent of her arousal. Vampires had good noses, though. Hunter would still smell it. Along with Abigor's signature all over her house.

That was good, he decided. It sent the right message.

He gave his cock a slow stroke through the material of his pants, thinking of Daisy in the shower, running her hands all over her soap glistening body, then willed it down as he concentrated on the task at hand.

Vampires. They posed no threat to him—very little posed a threat to Abigor—but Daisy was another matter. He had a tendency to be overconfident, he knew, and a slip of concentration, a moment's inattention, and her neck could be snapped. Killing all the vampires in the city wouldn't undo that.

"Is it eight yet?" The words came to him muffled through the bathroom door.

He glanced at the clock on the wall. "Just after."

She squeaked, then shouted, "At least they're not here yet."

They were. They'd been here since dusk. Not Hunter, but someone quite powerful. Every so often he felt a little press at his wards. A nudge, a reminder that they were waiting. As soon as he dropped them, he'd no doubt Hunter would appear, materializing into existence right on the front doorstep.

Of course, it wasn't as impressive as what Abigor could do, moving from the demon realm to Earth in the blink of an eye, but it was a handy skill, nonetheless.

"Take your time," he told her. He gave a smirk as he imagined the master vampire checking his watch and scowling. All right, it wasn't the wisest thing to antagonize him before they'd even begun, but Abigor knew how to handle another apex predator. This was a power play. Abigor wouldn't be rushed, and Hunter couldn't force him. Best to make sure the vampire knew that.

The door opened with a blast of scent, though not, sadly, the same delicious feminine arousal with which she'd entered the bathroom.

"I'm ready," she said.

He turned to look at her and felt a very unfamiliar punch to his gut. She looked small, and vulnerable, and frightened. Her hair was pulled back into a high ponytail and she'd put on some make up—the first Abigor had seen her wearing—in a transparent attempt to shore up her confidence. It wasn't working, not when those big green eyes were full of apprehension.

"You summoned me to protect you," he reminded her. "And I will."

She nodded, but that nervous look didn't leave her face. Abigor pulled a deep breath in through his nose. He could feel protectiveness running through him, along with a healthy dose of possessiveness, and it wasn't because of the bargain he'd sworn with her. He was going to have to be careful not to annihilate this vamp just for looking at her wrong.

He took her hand and led her to the kitchen, dropping his wards at the same time. As predicted, a knock rang out on the door within seconds. He felt Daisy's fingers clench around his.

"They're here."

"They are."

"What...I...uh." She stopped dead and started twisting this way and that, eyes darting around the house. "Where are we going? We should meet them in the living room, not the kitchen. I can't have a master vampire at my kitchen table!"

"No," he said calmly.

"No? What do you mean no? Did you hear what I said? He's a *master vampire*."

"And I am a higher-level demon. You sat me at your kitchen table, didn't you?"

"Well, that's different! I was feeding you. I'm not intending to offer the vampires dinner!"

An image of the vampire behind Daisy as she sat on her chair, his teeth buried in his neck, eyes staring challengingly at Abigor, flashed into his mind and he felt the human form he'd adopted tremble as a red haze overtook him.

"You will not be feeding him," he agreed, voice tight.

"We should bring him into the living room," she repeated.

"No. The kitchen is better. Having the table between you will make you feel more comfortable." Having a table between them would mean fuck all if the vampire was stupid enough to attack, but Abigor had plans to do naughty, naughty things to his little witch on that living room sofa, and he didn't want her thinking about the vampire's visit while he did them.

"All right then." She conceded with a modicum of good grace, taking the chair when he folded her into it. "Wait, what am I doing? I have to answer the door."

He stopped her rising with a firm hand on her shoulder. "I will grant the vampire entry."

He expected more argument, but she subsided easily, looking up at him with those big eyes, teeth back to gnawing on her lip.

"What do you think he wants?"

"We'll find out."

It was a small place. He could still hear Daisy's elevated breathing when he reached the front door. Hunter was on the other side, he could feel the pulse of his power. He was strong, Abigor realized, but still, if he released his own energy, he'd vaporize the bloodsucker.

He pulled open the door and stared down the vampire who'd frightened Daisy so badly with his politely worded letter that she'd summoned a demon to protect her. He was exactly what Abigor was expecting: tall, thin, well-dressed and cultured looking. He stood like he had all the time in the world, an impressive feat given that he'd been left long enough that most people would have knocked several times and probably given up by now. Shrewd eyes took in Abigor, measuring him. If Hunter realized he was hugely outmatched, he didn't betray it by so much as a flicker of an eyebrow.

"You're Hunter," Abigor commented unnecessarily.

"I am. And you are Abigor."

"That's me."

Abigor's eyes flicked over Hunter's shoulder to the end of the short pathway, where three others stood, melding so well into the shadows that human eyes would skim right over them. He picked out the one he'd sensed before, the strong one who'd been shoving at his wards with increasing impoliteness. A woman, he saw. She was tall and lithe and haughty looking.

Exactly his type, but in this moment, she didn't appeal to him at all. Instead, his thoughts were behind him, with the curvy little witch waiting anxiously.

"You only," he said, slicing his gaze back to Hunter. "The rest stay back there."

The female didn't like that. She weaved toward her master and made an unhappy sound, but Hunter silenced her with a wave of his hand.

"That is acceptable."

He was brave, this bloodsucker. Abigor stood back and allowed him to slide past him. He closed the door on three pairs of unhappy vampire eyes and threw his wards up, just in case one of them got any ideas. It was always better to assume people might do something idiotic, because in his experience there was a lot of stupid out there.

"This way," he said. He led Hunter through to the kitchen where Daisy was waiting, standing beside her chair and wringing her hands. When she saw Hunter she blanched, tiny tremors shaking her frame.

It wasn't a conscious decision. One moment Abigor was walking side by side with the vampire, the next he'd rematerialized just in front of Daisy, blocking her from Hunter's view.

Hunter stopped dead, eyeing Abigor warily. His hands had lifted ever so slightly in front of him, indicating his lack of threat.

"You scare her," Abigor accused. "Which is hardly a surprise given that the last time she saw you, you'd kidnapped her."

"It isn't my intention to frighten her," the vampire said slowly. "I am looking for her help." He grimaced, flicked his gaze to Daisy and away again. "She was not hurt under my care."

Daisy gave an indignant squeak. "You locked me up! You kept me there for *days*!"

"But I didn't hurt you," Hunter repeated, his eyes on Daisy but his entire focus on Abigor still. Which was smart, because out of the two of them it was Abigor who was the one who'd be tearing him apart if he made so much as one false move.

"What is it you want?" Abigor asked darkly. He'd been the one to draw the vampire here, and even though he was utterly sure that he could annihilate Hunter if it came to it, he was very quickly having second thoughts about bringing him into Daisy's home.

Hunter grimaced, the expression a surprising tell. "Perhaps we could sit down? Discuss things as civilized beings."

There was a hint of censure there that Abigor didn't appreciate. He might be a demon, but he was a damn cultured one, a point he made by pasting on his most charming smile and gesturing to the sticks of furniture Daisy used as a dining set. They'd be changing that because damned if Abigor was seating his ass in such discomfort for every meal.

"Let's sit then," he said smoothly.

There was a chorus of scrapes as the three of them took seats, Daisy by his side and Hunter across the table from them.

"What is it you want?" he repeated.

Hunter's eyes darted between the two of them. "You speak for Ms. Bennett?"

No, and yes. She'd summoned him to protect her, but he wasn't just going to sit there and expose her to Hunter's negotiation skills, because he was willing to bet they were a hell of a lot more developed than Daisy's. He opened his mouth to say yes, he did, dare Hunter to dispute him, but Daisy spoke first.

"It's a good question." Her voice was low and level, Abigor couldn't determine a hint of tremor in it. Her hands were clasped tight in her lap, though, and were white-knuckled, nails digging into her palms. She swallowed audibly. "What do you want from me?"

"To hire your services."

"For what?" Daisy unclasped her hands, curling them into fists which she rested on each knee. Abigor watched her lean toward Hunter, her eyes bright and angry, little spots of red on her cheeks. "I know you've a witch in your employ. That note didn't just drop through my door of its own accord. What do you need me for?"

"I need a witch I can trust," Hunter replied.

"You don't trust the witch that works for you?" Abigor asked, raising an eyebrow. "Can't you read their every thought."

"She isn't one of my children," Hunter said stiffly, betraying the first hint of temper.

"Make her one, then."

This time Hunter actually snorted. "Clearly you don't know everything, demon. Witches do not make good vampires."

"I've known a few." Though, now that Abigor thought about it, they'd all been crazier than a box of frogs and homicidal to boot. Just up his street.

But then…as he looked to Daisy, the thought of her like that, cold and vicious and ruthless, eyes red and gleaming, yeah, it gave him a shudder.

"Why would you work with her if you don't trust her?" Daisy asked.

"Because witches don't grow on trees," Hunter replied. "And trustworthy ones are as rare as hen's teeth."

He was watching Daisy intently, avarice in his eyes. This was a job, Abigor realized, but it was more than that. Hunter wanted a new witch in his employ. Abigor's witch.

Fuck that.

"Why do you trust me?" Daisy asked. "You don't even know me."

"I am a very good judge of character," Hunter replied simply.

She liked that, Abigor could see. He gritted his teeth, unreasonably irritated.

"What's the job?" she asked.

"A protection spell. As before. It's on a property this time. You can do that, yes?"

"A building or a home?"

"Both. A shop on the lower floor, a home above. Does that make a difference?"

"Well, it's trickier," Daisy said, making a face. "Different wards because, you know, you probably don't want a werewolf able to come into your house, but that doesn't mean you don't want them spending money in your store, so you don't want to drive them away entirely…" she tailed off, thoughts whirling behind her eyes.

"You can do it, yes?"

The look Daisy gave him could have shattered glass, and Abigor grinned.

"I can do it." Her glare sharpened further. "You'll be paying me this time?"

"Of course."

Abigor cleared his throat. "And you'll be paying her for last time, too. Generously. For the spell and the inconvenience."

Inconvenience was a piss-poor word for the fact that Hunter had terrified Daisy so badly that she'd resorted to fishing in the cesspit that was Hell for someone to protect her, but she was holding her own here and he didn't want to take that away from her. Truth be told, he was impressed. Daisy had a core of steel he hadn't anticipated.

He liked it.

"Of course," Hunter agreed smoothly.

"Like you should have done already."

"That was…an oversight. One which will be corrected immediately."

"Oversight," Abigor snorted.

Daisy elbowed him in the side.

"How much?" she demanded.

The sum Hunter named meant nothing to Abigor. He didn't deal in cash, souls were so much more valuable. Daisy exhaled sharply, her face bleaching of color, so it must have been a decent amount. She recovered quickly though.

"I want that for the work I already did," she asserted. "And the same again for the new one."

"Agreed." Hunter replied without hesitation. "When can you do the job?"

Interesting…

"My schedule's pretty open," Daisy said, glancing at Abigor. "I'd need a little time to prepare, but I already have everything I need."

"Excellent." Hunter flashed his fangs in a wide grin. "How about tonight?"

Chapter Five

I was expecting the address Hunter had left me with to lead to a seedy part of town, though I don't know why since Hunter himself was well-dressed and sophisticated. I guess I just figured vampires would operate in the shadows, in narrow alleyways and places where victims walked about at all hours of the night. When I pulled up, though, it was to a recently regenerated part of town, a nicely cobble-stoned street lined with smart boutique shops. Abigor sat beside me, squashed uncomfortably in the passenger side of my little hatchback and twitching with impatience at my slow, careful driving.

I was a pretty cautious driver, but I was also doing it to wind him up, just a little bit.

I'd been here before, I realized, as I parked and killed the engine. Just window shopping, because I didn't have the spare cash to shop in fancy places like this, but I'd definitely been for a nose around the little gallery in front of me. The woman who ran it sold vibrant, colorful paintings and gorgeous glass pieces. And, apparently, had some serious links to vampires.

Racketeering, maybe?

I got out and Abigor was suddenly there, even though I hadn't heard the passenger door open or seen him walk around the car.

"I'm driving us back," he said.

"No, you aren't," I disagreed. "It took me ages to get the seat and the mirrors just right." I repressed a smile. "If you don't want to be driven, you can always poof back and meet me there."

He froze to utter stillness, fixing me with a look. "Poof?"

"You know." I gave a casual little wave of my hand, trying desperately to keep my amusement off my face. "When you pop in and out of existence. I thought that was a vampire thing, I never saw Orphon do it."

He drew himself up, affronted and the laughter threatened to slip free.

"I am no clod-headed minion. I am Abigor, the Grand Duke of Hell! I have powers beyond your comprehension." He clenched his jaw. "I do not *poof*."

Somewhere along the way I'd lost my fear of Abigor. It might have been his relaxed sensuality, or perhaps the way he'd protected me so diligently when Hunter had come to my house. Or it might have been the countless orgasms he'd given me yesterday and today. Either way, I was no longer scared he was going to eat me.

In fact, I was rather hopeful that he might.

"Well," I said, "If you want to meet me at home, you can. Since you hate my car."

"That is not a car, it's a torture device. A vicious one. And trust me when I say I'm in a position to know."

"It's a Nissan," I pointed out.

"Hmph." He waved the offer away. "I cannot protect you if I am not with you. And speaking of—" He nodded into the shop, where shadows were moving about under the dim lights. "Shall we?"

There was a vampire at the door. A woman. She was everything that I wasn't: tall, elegant and willowy. She glowered down at me, clearly unimpressed, her nose wrinkling slightly, but she didn't say any of the uncomplimentary things I could see were hovering on her lips. Probably because of the shadow looming over me. When her eyes flicked to him for a fraction of a second, they widened in fear. Wordlessly, she stepped aside.

Inside was like I remembered, all gleaming glass and canvasses liberally splashed with riotous color. The artist appreciator inside me sighed with pleasure, but the rest of me was much more sensible and focused on Hunter, waiting in the centre of the room, and the woman who stood with him.

Not a vampire. She was glowing with life, curves not quite as generous as mine, held in check by tight jeans and a pastel-purple long-sleeved shirt. I recognized her, I thought, and was pretty sure she was the store owner. She didn't notice me at first, too busy looking up at Hunter with what could only be described as a lovesick expression on her face.

Well, each to their own, I supposed. I'd spent the last two days being orgasmed to unconsciousness by a demon. I glanced up at him, and saw that he was watching Hunter and the woman closely, something like intrigue on his face.

"She owns this place," I whispered.

"And he owns her," he murmured back.

"What?"

He nodded toward the woman. "The marks on her neck, and I'd bet there are more on her wrists under that shirt. She's his concubine."

I spluttered. "There's no such thing as concubines, anymore. People don't *own* people."

Even as the words came out of my mouth, I knew they were nonsense. Slavery and trafficking went on all over the world—but not in a fancy schmancy boutique in the middle of my town!

"Underworld creatures are a bit backward sometimes," Abigor replied. "I assure you concubines are very much a thing."

"Do you have any?" The words were out before I could call them back.

He grinned wickedly. "I'm the Grand Duke of Hell. What do you think?"

I thought he probably had hundreds of them, and given that we'd only known each other for a couple of days, it was astonishing how much that hurt.

It's a bargain, I told myself. The things you and him have been up to, they're nothing more than fulfilling the terms. And he's here right now, fulfilling his side, so…

"Let's get this over with."

With my stupid fragile heart still reeling, I took a deep breath and plastered a confident expression across my face before approaching Hunter and the woman.

"Hi," I said, addressing her because, Abigor or not, the vampire still made me quake in my boots. "I love your store. I've been in before, just browsing, you know. It's gorgeous. Maybe when I've saved up enough—"

"Pick something," Abigor said in a low voice at my side.

"What?" I asked, turning to him.

"Pick something you like, and I will buy it for you."

"You don't need to buy it," the woman interrupted, before my eyes could even start sweeping the store as my brain struggled to work out why Abigor would make such an offer. "You're doing me a huge favor. Anything you want, you can have."

"Oh," I said, in a slightly strangled voice. "I couldn't do that."

"Yes, you can," she assured me.

"Ms. Bennett, this is Cat," Hunter broke in smoothly. "She is my consort."

"Your *consort*?" Abigor asked, clearly astonished.

"Yes." Hunter's curt response could have cut glass. I saw Cat put a small, restraining hand on his arm.

"It's Daisy," I told Cat.

"Daisy?" She raised an eyebrow ever so slightly.

"I know," I said mournfully, and she laughed. As an icebreaker, it worked. She stepped away from Hunter and he let her, though his body was positioned to jump in between Abigor and her at a moment's notice. There was a lot of testosterone in the room, but I was attempting to do the same as Cat and just ignore it.

"So how do we do this?" she asked. "What do you need?"

"If you could show me around?" I suggested. "I'll get a good look at the space, set some wards and then we'll do the protection spell."

"All right." She gave me a small smile. "Well, what you see is pretty much it for the shop floor. Come on and I'll show you the back and then we can go upstairs."

Cat showed me a crowded back room and then took me up a rear staircase to a small one-bed apartment. It was neat and tidy, decorated with little bits and pieces that were recognizably Cat's art, but it was basic. Not the luxurious living conditions I'd expect from a woman who was Hunter's *consort*. That word felt as weird in my mind as concubine. What was wrong with just plain old girlfriend?

"Thanks for doing this," Cat said to me in an undertone as I started drawing wards on her living-room window, Abigor and Hunter lingering in the doorway and eyeing each other like a couple of tomcats deciding whether to fight. "It was the only way to stop Tobias from installing me in the mansion of gloom or having a stooge sleep on my sofa."

"You're welcome," I whispered back. I glanced over at the vampire again, beyond curious now.

"You and him are a thing?"

Cat looked over toward him too, and the smile that unfurled across her face…yeah, she'd got the cream all right.

"We are," she said. Then she looked back to me. "I know, it's weird. I mean, he's a vampire. I didn't even know vampires were real. But look at him, the man's sex on a stick. And he's a really good guy, once you get to know him."

Right. I decided not to mention that her *good guy* had kidnapped me and held me captive in his *mansion of gloom*—which was a perfect description of the place. Instead, I thought about Abigor, studying him discreetly from the corner of my eye. He wasn't a good guy, not even close. The Grand Duke of Hell had a reputation for a reason…and yet. He'd been nothing but courteous and respectful—and very, *very* generous—to me. But that was nothing more than the terms of our bargain, and after I did this job, it'd be fulfilled.

He'd be leaving.

Before he did…perhaps there would be a chance to drag him into my bed one more time. If so, I intended to get my mouth on that hot, hot body and, if I was very lucky, my hands on his cock. You only live once, and I doubted I'd ever see him again after tonight.

Take the demon by the horns, Daisy.

I snorted and Abigor looked over toward me, our eyes locking for a fraction of a second. Could he tell what naughty, naughty thoughts were in my head? I hoped so.

It didn't take long to finish doing the wards, though the shared walls with the businesses on either side made it a little trickier than usual. The spell was harder, the energies I called on being unruly and uncooperative with so many vampires roaming about the place, stinking it up with their menacing air.

And yes, fine, I was aware that Abigor was watching me, and I felt the pressure of his intent and curious gaze. It's not easy to concentrate when your subconscious is screaming, *Don't muck it up, Daisy! He's watching!*

When I was done, we were escorted out of the building by the scary female vamp—after effusive thank yous from Cat—but Hunter met us on the pavement outside the shop.

"You have my thanks," he said formally, the hint of softness I'd seen when he was around Cat wiped clean away.

"And she'll also have your payment," Abigor replied.

"The money is already in her account," Hunter said coolly.

Yeah, things hadn't warmed any between those two.

I clutched the box holding four beautiful hand-painted, stemless wine goblets that Cat had pressed on me before we left and forced my face into a small smile.

"Thank you, I appreciate that." So would my landlord. "We're good now, right? You…uh…you'll leave me alone now? I mean, you won't have any more jobs for me?"

Because while the cash was extremely welcome, the vampires were just too scary for me, and I wouldn't have Abigor at my side next time.

"If you do not wish to accept future jobs, I will respect your wishes. But I hope you will reconsider, Ms. Bennett."

"I'll think about it," I promised.

I tried not to run to my car, but I got behind the wheel as quickly as possible, engaging the locks the moment Abigor had his door closed. It's impossible to peel out with any speed in an ageing Nissan hatchback, but I moved with all the gusto the car could muster, studiously ignoring the small smile on Abigor's lips.

"In a hurry to get home?" he asked quietly when I accelerated through a yellow light.

"No," I said, lifting my foot off the accelerator slightly. Then, "Do you have to leave straight away?"

There was a small pause where Abigor watched me closely and I stared deliberately out of the windscreen.

"Are you still afraid of the vampires? I do not think they will bother you further—Hunter seems a man of his word—but I can release someone to watch over you?"

"No," I said. "You don't need to do that."

I tried to keep my tone neutral, and failed miserably. I had half a second to hope that Abigor wouldn't notice before he chuckled quietly.

"So, it is me that you wish to keep?"

I choked. "I, uhm. No. I mean...I'm sure you have lots of important things to do."

"I do," he agreed. "But I have time to pleasure you one more time before I leave. Perhaps twice."

I gripped my steering wheel tightly and summoned all of my courage—which wasn't a lot.

"No," I said. "This time it's my turn to pleasure you."

Less than a beat of silence passed before Abigor responded in a voice redolent with sin. "I accept."

Chapter Six

My hands shook as I slotted the key into my front door. I opened it and shoved my way inside. I took a moment to kick off my shoes, then stalked through the house, straight to the bedroom. We needed to get right down to business or I was going to lose my nerve.

I didn't look behind me to see if Abigor was following. I knew he was, I could practically feel his breath hot on the back of my neck, that sexy, sinuous body stalking my footsteps.

The sight of my bed—neatly made but echoing with the ghosts of all the orgasms Abigor had given me on it—was my undoing. I ground to a halt and he folded his body around me, hands sliding around my side and his head dipping down until his mouth hovered over my ear.

"What's wrong, little witch?"

"I…nothing."

"You haven't changed your mind, I hope? I was very much looking forward to being pleasured by you."

My stomach—and other places—clenched at the deep timbre of his voice. My nipples peaked, hoping his hands might slip up and cup my breasts. Instead, he let go of me and brushed past, pulling his shirt over his head in one smooth, glorious movement before he crawled onto the bed like a big cat. He rolled onto his back, the rest of his clothes disappearing in an instant.

Handy trick, that.

I took a step forward and he stopped me with a small shake of his head.

"It would give me pleasure to see you undress for me."

Well, damn. I had promised to pleasure him, but I hadn't anticipated it involving me standing in the middle of the bedroom like I was under a spotlight, being watched as I bared myself to my skin.

"You could just poof them off," I suggested.

"I could," he agreed, "but I like to watch you."

Terrific.

I drew in a deep breath and grabbed the hem of my long-sleeved shirt, yanking it off much less gracefully than Abigor had. I fought against the instinct to round my shoulders, standing as tall as I could as I let it drop from my fingers. I left my bra where it was and slipped my jeans over my hips, grateful I'd chosen to wear my one set of matching underwear.

"Naked enough?" I asked, placing my hands on my hips and trying to project a confidence I didn't feel. I was eager to get over there and get my hands on the muscles I could finally see in all their glory, the cock that was resting against his thigh, growing more erect as he watched me.

"No," he said, shaking his head and grinning at me.

All right, then. I reached back and unhooked my bra and let it fall from my body, then I hooked my thumbs in my panties and bent forward slowly, making a show of slipping them down my legs.

When I stood back up, Abigor's cock was rock hard, bobbing slightly against his stomach. Because of me. The nerves in my stomach melted away as a strange, powerful feeling overtook me.

I walked to the bed with swaying steps, hopping up and going on my knees before him, my hands reaching for his thighs. He was almost hairless, his muscles tensed beneath my fingers. One of them twitched as I stroked my way higher, but I skimmed around his cock, sliding my palms over his stomach until I was resting against his glorious chest. His skin was warm under my hands, his molten eyes fixed on mine.

Holding his gaze until I had to close my eyes or risk going cross-eyed, I leaned down and pressed my mouth to his. His lips were soft against mine, the cavern of his mouth hot when I delved inside it. He licked at me, twisting round my tongue and drawing me down until my body was plastered against his, my hands clutching at his shoulders. When I pulled back, I was breathless.

"I thought I was in charge?" I said, the teasing nature of the complaint slightly diminished by my ragged breaths.

"You are," he said, releasing hands that had gravitated to my hips and lying back against the covers. "I am yours to do with as you wish."

He placed his hands behind his head and grinned at me, utterly at ease.

Right.

Mine to do with as I pleased.

I tried to dredge up some of the courage that had seen me face off the vampires and stroked my way across his chest, down his stomach. I was straddling the top of his thighs, his cock protruding out between us, thick and long and hard and ready to go. I licked my lips and thought about slipping back, taking him in my mouth, but if I was really honest with myself, what I wanted to do was just jump on.

Catching his gaze and holding it, I skimmed my hand over his cock and then lifted up, cupping my neck, sliding my fingers down until they caressed my breast. His eyes followed their tantalizingly slow movement, a small growl rumbling up his throat when I pinched my nipple.

Okay then, he liked that. Let's see what he thought of this.

Feeling brazen beyond my wildest imagining, I let my other hand glide between my legs. My fingers dipped lightly into my core, gathering up some of the slickness there. Oh yeah, I was definitely ready to just jump on.

Drawing the moment out for him and me, I split my labia, revealing pink and glistening flesh to his gaze, and started circling my clit. God, it felt good, the usual sensations from when I touched myself magnified a million by his eyes on me. He wasn't lounging relaxed against the bed anymore. The muscles in his arms were beautifully defined as he held them behind his head, his jaw clenched with the effort to keep them there.

He wanted to touch me.

I wanted him to touch me, too, but I was also revelling in the heady feeling of playing with myself for him, having his complete and undivided attention. For once I wasn't thinking about my thighs or about how my stomach wasn't flat and toned. I was watching a hell of a specimen of a man lie under me and fuck me with his eyes.

It was glorious.

"You know, it would be more interesting if we replaced your fingers with my tongue," he murmured.

"It would," I replied. "But..."

He froze, torso half curled up, hands reaching to tumble me onto my back—or slide me forward so that I was straddling his face. Yikes, there was a thought.

"But?"

"But I have other plans," I told him.

Done with tormenting the both of us, I lifted up and shifted forward a bit, grasping his cock with my hand and angling it a bit so that I could slide down in one delicious movement. My eyes rolled back into my head and I moaned softly, a sound that was drowned out by his snarled out, "Fuck, yes."

Fuck yes, indeed.

I open my eyes as his hands landed on my thighs, scalding hot against my skin. Goose bumps erupted over my body, sending a tingling rush all over me that coalesced at my core as I lifted up and sank lower.

I choked out a ragged sob, astonished to realize I was already teetering on the edge of orgasm. My inner muscles contracted around him, my clit pulsing, demanding I *do that again*. Now.

Abigor agreed, his hands moving from my thighs to my hips so that he could grip them tight, urgh me up, and down. Up, and down.

I tried to reproach him, remind him that this was my show, but all that came out of my mouth was, "Yes, yes! Oh God. More!"

I had my head thrown back as I chanted, my hips working as Abigor guided me in a rhythm, my orgasm just a hairsbreadth away, when I noticed that the fingers gripping me had sharpened to points, tiny pinpricks digging into my skin. At the same time, I felt something lashing around my ankle. I opened my eyes and looked down at Abigor.

He wasn't looking at me. His mouth was open in an expression of ecstasy and his head was tilted back into the bed—as far as it could roll with the sleek back horns that were curling over his skull. His skin had gone from a deep tan to a dark red that rippled to black at his collarbone and down the sides of his torso. He'd morphed into his true form, his glamour slipping away.

I had a moment to take this all in before eyes dark as the deepest part of the night snapped open and fixed on me. They were nothing like the eyes I'd become used to. They were utterly bottomless, and they drew me in completely. I lasted the space of three quick gasps before my orgasm tore through me, blinding me to everything except those eyes, robbing my senses of everything except the points we were connected.

Abigor took over then, holding me still as he thrust up beneath me. Every stroke rolled against my g-spot, prolonging the ecstasy until I was crying with the exquisiteness of it. I fell forward, my hands landing hard on his chest, which had swelled with thicker muscle, was so hot now it felt like it scorched my palms. He snarled and I felt something—a tail, I presumed— wrap around my ankle, then we were rolling, the world blurring until I was on my back, softness beneath me and hardness inside me as he thundered toward his own finish. All I could do was lie there, pinned like a butterfly, and revel in the waves still rushing over me.

When he came, it was with a growl and a tightening of his muscles, his forehead dropping down and pressing into mine, our eyes staring into each other's, as his rhythmic thrusts became harder, choppier.

"Little witch," he hissed. "*Fuck.*"

He stroked home two, three more times before stuttering to a halt, his whole body tensing before it melted down into mine.

I was still gazing into those incredible black eyes when he realized he'd dropped his glamour. His features tightened for an instant before the Abigor I'd come to know appeared before me. He was wearing an expression I'd never seen before though: uncertainty. Doubt.

"I'm sorry," he said. "I—"

"Bring it back," I said.

"What?" The worry morphed into confusion.

"The real you," I said. "Bring it back."

It took him a moment, but slowly the red stole over his skin again, the horns shimmering into existence on his head. The eyes that held mine bled black until it engulfed them.

"I like it," I said.

"Hmmm," he said, sounding like he didn't believe me.

I intended to say something else to convince him, but a yawn burst out instead.

"You've had a hard night, little witch," he murmured. He shifted to the side and took me with him, curling me into his body. "Sleep."

"Will you be here when I wake up?" I asked, my eyes already closing. Because our bargain was finished now, there was nothing else to keep him here.

"Sleep," he repeated.

I thought I felt a hint of power in the words, but before I could really think about it, I was gone.

When I woke up, I was alone. I had a moment to feel the crushing weight of disappointment before a loud thump had me jack-knifing in the bed. Shit. Fuck. Abigor was gone and, from the sounds of it, someone was breaking into my house.

I dragged on some clothes as quickly and quietly as I could, trying not to feel a pang as I stepped over Abigor's discarded T-shirt, and crept out of my room. It was still dark outside, I must have been asleep for only a short while. I hovered in my hallway, listening hard, trying to decide whether to just leg it—the front door was *right there*—or investigate. Another thump rang out while I was dithering and I realized that whoever it was, was in my basement.

My house was shit. I'd cobbled together the furniture from thrift stores and yard sales. It worked for me—I'd created a sort of nothing-matches-and-it's-totally-on-purpose-honest kind of style for myself…but every single thing of value that I owned was *in that basement.*

"Dammit." I tiptoed into the kitchen and grabbed the biggest knife I owned. It was actually the only knife I owned, and I used it for everything from levering open cans, since my electric can opener had died, and cutting bread. And now, apparently, butchering intruders.

I muttered a protection spell to myself as I approached the basement stairs. There was a dim, flickering light glowing down below. To add insult to injury, whoever was down there was using my spell candles, and those suckers were expensive. Growing rage propelling me down with a bit less caution, I reached the bottom tread just as whoever was down there cursed and revealed themselves.

"Abigor?" I rounded the wall to see him topless, back in his glamour, staring at my basement wall with a tube of my lipstick in his hand. He'd torn down the curtain hiding the ugly concrete, and covering the wall were a series of wards in a suspicious shade of plum. I set the knife down on the steps behind me and stared at him. "What are you doing?" I asked. "You nearly gave me a heart attack! I thought someone had broken in!"

He snorted. "If they had, you should have known I'd protect you."

"I thought you were gone."

That made him give up his perusal of my wall and turn around fully. "You thought I'd just left? Without saying goodbye?"

It was the hurt tone in his voice that really did it. Feeling suddenly like an utter asshole for the presumption I'd made, I gave a little shrug. "Our bargain was over. I thought…I thought you'd have to leave."

"And you thought I'd do that by sneaking off in the middle of the night?"

"Well…I…some people don't like goodbyes," I offered lamely.

"When I get you back in that bed, I am going to spank you until you beg me to stop," he murmured darkly.

Ooooooh boy. My hands wanted to cover my ass—though admittedly they wouldn't be up to the job all by themselves—at the same time as my girl parts tingled.

"What are you doing?" I asked desperately.

As a distraction, it worked. Abigor turned around to scowl at the wall. "Isn't it obvious? I am creating a portal."

"A portal?" I echoed.

"To make it easier for me to travel here to you."

"I see." I didn't. "You plan on returning here frequently, then?"

Did I sound as pathetically hopeful as I thought I did? Probably.

"I do." The look he turned on me was utterly wicked. "I imagine you'll need my attentions at least four times a week if I am to keep you satisfied."

I clutched at the wall as my knees went suddenly weak. Considering I hadn't had anyone satisfy me for months (and months) before his arrival, I thought that would do it.

"I...yes. That sounds acceptable."

"Although," he went on, "if I can be here nightly, all the better."

"Well, I...uh..." I swallowed. "I'll be here."

"Waiting for me," he murmured. "Good girl." He turned back to the portal site and a moment later exclaimed, "Aha!" I watched as he reached forward and rubbed out a ward, the lipstick leaving a lavender smear all over my wall. The ugly splodge didn't seem to deter him, he sketched out a new ward over the top and then stepped back just in time for the whole thing to flare.

"Shit!" I squeaked, though the effect was gone again in an instant.

"That's better," he said. "I'm usually excellent with spells, but it's been centuries since I've needed this one."

I tried not to show the blushy, squirmy, happy feeling that left me with, but from the slight smirk on Abigor's face, he knew anyway. He approached me and drew me to him, planting a soft kiss on my forehead then a deeper, more sensual one on my lips.

"I'm sorry," he said as he drew back, "but I do have to leave. I will be back, soon, but there are things that demand my attention."

"Of course," I replied, trying very hard not to pout and succeeding quite admirably, I thought.

"Don't pout," he said, tugging at my bottom lip with his forefinger and thumb. "Blink and I will have returned to you. I won't leave you unprotected, there will always be someone here with you when I am not. Orphon?" he suggested. "You know him."

"I, honestly, I don't need anyone. I'm sure I'll be fine."

"It is non-negotiable, Daisy."

I debated arguing for a whole half second, then I nodded.

"Orphon is good," I agreed.

"Then it is settled. Until I return, little witch." He leaned down and kissed me again, harder and longer, then pulled away entirely. He kept his eyes on me until he reached the basement wall and then gave me a quick wink as he disappeared straight through it.

I was alone for the space of a heartbeat, the empty space suddenly cold, then the wall blazed blindingly bright and the familiar sight of Orphon toppled through, his massive form collapsing in a heap on the floor.

"Orphon!" I exclaimed. "Are you all right?" I hurried over to him then paused just before my hand touched the meaty muscle of his shoulder. He wasn't bound in bargain to me right now and he could very easily rip that arm off. I snatched it back and he looked up at me, only there was no rage or violence in his eyes. They were the clearest I'd ever seen them.

His hand snaked out and latched onto my wrist. He was panting and gasping, the journey through the portal obviously painful, but he seemed determined to get a word out.

"What?" I asked him. "What is it?"

Big, terrifying, dangerous demon eyes looked tremulously up at me. "Pizza?" he warbled.

CHARLI MAC

HIS MATE SERIES
BOOK 5

HIS CLASSY MATE

Chapter One

I sat at the bar, my untouched drink in front of me, hands folded under my chin as I perused the establishment's clientele in the mirror behind the barman. There were two men to my left who had been shooting me covert glances for the past twenty minutes, but they'd also both consumed several drinks, if the glasses in front of them were any indication, and I didn't fancy beginning my night with a beer buzz.

There was a woman in the corner, shoulders curled in on herself as she took up a tiny circular table to herself, her drink as unattended as mine, but sadness radiated from her every pore. It wasn't something that would briefly transfer in the blood like alcohol or drugs did, but still, strong emotions clung to me like spiderwebs, and I had no desire to get any closer to her misery.

A group of frat boys crowded round a large table in the centre and any one of them would have been perfect, but they tended to travel in packs. Splitting one of them off wouldn't be easy, and I wasn't in the mood to work that hard for my breakfast.

I sighed, annoyed. I'd chosen this place because I'd expected easy pickings and yet—

I sat up straighter on my stool as a pair of older gentlemen rose slowly and stiffly from a table that had been hidden behind a large potted plant. They shook hands and one of them headed for the door, jacket slung over his arm in preparation for the chill outside. The other took a moment to slide his overcoat over his shoulders, putting his wallet, keys and phone in various pockets. By the time he was ready to go, his companion had disappeared. Perfect.

I slithered off my stool, ignoring the man on the seat beside me who, liquid courage acquired, looked finally set to make a move, and timed my exit to coincide with the older gentleman's.

"Please, after you," he said, catching my approach and giving me a small smile as he held the door wide open for me to pass through.

My returning smile was genuine, I loved manners in a man.

"Thank you," I replied, my voice pitched low and even, hitting that register that somehow caused brain cells to misfire, making people so much easier to manage. I didn't know the biology of how it worked, just that it did.

I stepped through the door then paused there, chewing on my lip and shifting from foot to high-heeled foot.

"Is everything all right?" he asked, picking up on my incredibly unsubtle gestures.

"Oh," I said, giving a small, hesitant smile. "I'm sure it's fine. It's just..." I trailed off.

"It's just?"

"Well." I made a face. "I heard those boys talking about me. Impolitely." I raised an eyebrow delicately and the old man's face folded over in a disapproving scowl as he caught my meaning. "I parked my car a little way away and I'm just nervous that they might—"

"I'll escort you," he cut in.

"You would?" I overdid it a little, throwing enough gratitude at him that he wouldn't notice that none of the boys had made any effort to follow me out.

Something that didn't dent my ego at all. Honestly.

"Of course." He offered me his arm and I took it, walking with him along the pavement past shut up shops and restaurants still doing a busy trade. The scents of cooking food didn't affect me, though hunger was a gnawing pain in my stomach. The low thump of the man's pulse, however, was making my mouth water.

We were just passing a small alleyway when I made my move. Tightening my grip on his arm, I stepped into the shadows, swinging him around so that his back collided with the damp brick wall. I thrust my face against his neck, taking a moment to breathe past the lingering scent of aftershave to the rich metallic warmth of his blood beneath the skin.

"What—"

Quiet. I thrust the word into his mind, and he obeyed immediately, the words cutting off to be replaced by shocked little gasps. I had enough experience to know that he wasn't the kind of man to be held for long by such a command, so I got straight down to business, latching on to his neck and letting my teeth slice through the skin. Hot, coppery blood flowed thickly into my mouth and I moaned. I swallowed it down, feeling my body absorb it until every nerve was singing. A warmth flushed through me, almost orgasmic, promising ecstasy if I would just take more. *Just a little bit more.*

Gasping, I wrenched back, breaking the connection. Slicking my tongue over the wound to seal it up, I stepped back and let him slither down the wall.

He toppled to the side, half-sitting, half-lying in a puddle of dirty water, his neat suit soaking up the filth. I felt bad about that, but I didn't dare reach for him.

I knew what would happen if I did.

"Tut, tut, tut."

I whirled around to see a figure standing at the entrance to the alleyway, the streetlights behind turning it into a silhouette. I knew who it was, though. I knew the lines of those shoulders, the curl of that thick, luxurious hair. The clean, cultured scent that came to me just a moment too late. I knew all these things intimately.

And hadn't that been a mistake.

"Julian," I murmured.

I stepped away from the man and approached him, bracing myself for another excruciating conversation since dematerializing would, I knew, just lead to an even less pleasant conversation at a later date.

"Evangeline," he replied, drawing out my name in that way that used to make me melt—and now made me shudder. He glanced down at the old man. "You aren't going to take him home and tuck him in?"

I rolled my eyes. "Amusing, Julian."

"He's old. Fragile. No one would have commented had he failed to survive the feeding…" He let his voice trail off, that small smile on his face that told me he was imagining it, taking and taking until the heart failed and life was gone. I kept my gaze fixed on his cold, calculating eyes so that I wouldn't imagine it too.

I'd done it, once. Stolen a life. It had been an accident—I'd been very young and far less controlled—but I remembered it. Exquisitely. And ohhh, had it been exquisite. There was no feeling quite like it, no ecstasy to compare. Once I felt it…I craved it. Frighteningly so, to the extent that I could have drowned in it, taking a life every day, multiple times a day, and still not been satisfied.

I made myself promise never to do it again.

That was nearly a hundred years ago and still, I hadn't forgotten the wonder, the rush, the exhilaration. Master was very strict about feeding— taking lives was forbidden—but I knew that Julian chose victims whose "accidental" demise could be easily explained away, spreading them out just enough to avoid suspicion. He wasn't the only one to do it, either. Vampires were not nuns.

But not me. Not again.

"He'll be fine," I said. His breathing was a little rattly and it was cold out, but I hadn't taken that much. I plastered a benign smile on my face. "What can I do for you?"

"Do I need a reason to seek you out?" he threw back.

Urgh. I didn't have the authority within the seethe to tell him yes, he damned well did. Almost any other vampire and I could have thrown on my most haughty look—which was pretty haughty—and demanded to know why they dared waste my time like this. But Julian and I, we were the same age, more or less, and had roughly the same power. Most importantly of all, we held the same amount of favor with Master.

Ok, I might just sneak that one, actually, but if I started causing drama over nothing, that would quickly change. Master did not appreciate drama.

"No," I ground out as politely as I could. "But I know you're busy. So, to what do I owe the pleasure?"

The final word almost choked me, but I got it out.

"I am busy," he agreed, "but I always have time for you."

He reached out and tucked an escaped tendril of hair back behind my ear, resting his hand on the curve of my neck, and I fought not to shudder.

"Have you thought any more about my proposal?"

Oh yes. I'd spent hours and hours thinking about ways to politely say no to it.

"Julian—"

The hand that was on my neck moved until he was able to press a finger to my lips, silencing me.

"Think a little longer," he told me, guessing, from my tone and the hint of a grimace on my face, just what I was going to say. "You and I would make a stunning partnership. There would be none in the seethe to challenge us." He paused for a fraction of a second. "Save the master, of course."

I bit my tongue against the two things I wanted to say to that. Firstly, Julian aside, there was no one else in the seethe to challenge me anyway. Not unless they banded together. But also...that little pause. It was deliberate, I was positive. What did he mean by it? Surely, he wasn't hinting, oh so subtly, that he had designs on challenging Master?

Julian had nowhere near the power of Master. Tobias Hunter was the ruler of the seethe for a reason, there wasn't a vampire in the whole region to challenge him. But then, if he and I banded together—

The thought was such a dangerous one, I wiped it from my mind even as it began to form.

"I am not looking for a mate," I told him gently.

That was a big fat lie. But I wasn't looking for a snake for a mate, and that's what Julian was.

"I suggest you reconsider," he said softly. Then he shifted closer, dropping his voice to a sensuous murmur. "I can't wait to have you under me again."

I held still, feeling the threat as well as the desire in Julian's words. I wasn't going to be able to fend him off much longer, I realized. He was running out of patience, and I needed to find a way to put his proposal to bed. Preferably not mine.

I opened my mouth, still not sure what I was going to say, when he made a face and stepped back, growling low in his throat.

"Again?"

"What is it?" I asked.

"I have to go," he told me. "The moron requires rescuing."

Oh dear. Though, it was enormously good timing from my perspective.

"Be kind," I said, but Julian dematerialized before I got the second word out. "Damn."

Poor Kevin. He tried hard, but calamity seemed to follow him everywhere, and since the master had started sending Julian to clean up every time things fell spectacularly apart on him—a duty Julian despised—he'd got worse. Terrified of failure, and the unhappy vampire that would arrive with it, he was even more of a disaster.

Heaving out a sigh—Kevin wasn't my problem, even if I did feel sorry for him—I turned back to the man in the alleyway behind me. He was sleeping, his head dropped down to rest on his chest at an angle that was going to give him a very stiff neck in the morning. He looked a little ashen, but he was fine. I could leave him there and he'd either wake in a few hours or, if he was lucky, some passer-by would notice him and realize he wasn't a homeless person, wake him up and help him back to the car.

I turned away and prepared to dematerialize—I had my own duties to attend to—but something held me back. I glanced at him once more. He was fine, he was, but something was tugging at me.

I thought of the look in Julian's eyes when he'd seen the man. The disdain, but also the opportunity. It had been a while since he'd "mistakenly" taken more than a victim could handle. He was off dealing with whatever catastrophe Kevin had created right now, but he could easily come back. Maybe the man would still be here, and maybe he wouldn't. But if he was…

Shit.

Thinking about the delicate silk of my shift dress, I reached down and hoisted him up. I immediately felt the damp of the puddle weeping into my side. Wonderful. I shifted my grip, getting underneath him. I could have carried him back to the restaurant without a problem, but there were still plenty of people milling about. No human woman could have managed it, so I couldn't either. I was reduced to hobbling along, the man dazed and semi-conscious with his arm around my shoulders, his weight awkward and uncomfortable.

A quick fumble in his jacket pockets produced the car keys, and when I aimed them hopefully at the car park, a fairly new, sleek sedan car lit up with flashing lights. I managed to get him folded into the passenger seat then slid in behind the wheel. He was so tall, I had to adjust the mirrors and seat positioning, which was a novel experience for me. I glanced over at him, asleep once more with his head tipped back against the rest. He was handsome, for an elderly man.

"You haven't got a hot son somewhere, have you?" I joked.

The only answer was a gentle snore.

Chapter Two

I started the car and flicked on the satnav, which very helpfully had Home programmed into it, so I didn't have to go rooting around in his clothes again for his ID. The car was a joy to drive, purring quietly but ready to explode forward at the lightest touch of my foot. Coasting through the light, late evening traffic, I felt a calm I'd not experienced in a long time.

I felt like I was just an ordinary person, going home.

Which was stupid, because when I'd been an ordinary person, cars like this hadn't existed, and I certainly hadn't been able to afford anything more extravagant than a bicycle to get about with.

He lived in a nice part of town. The garage opened automatically when I approached, and I pulled in. There was a blue truck parked in the second half of the driveway. I grimaced as I looked at it. It was covered in dirt, machinery lumped in the rear. I very much doubted it belonged to the man in the car beside me, which meant someone else might well be home. It didn't matter, I could probably dematerialize before—

The internal garage door opened just as I was shifting the car into park, spilling yellow light into the space and highlighting me behind the wheel. A man stood in the doorway, a younger version of the elderly man. I froze, like startled prey, thinking quickly.

I definitely couldn't dematerialize now. He'd seen me.

Okay, I'd just get his dad inside and then alter who I was guessing was the son's memories before I legged it. No problem.

Only...ever since I'd failed to properly modify the master's mate—Cat's—memories, I'd had a bit of a crisis of confidence over that little skill. Like a man whose cock fails to perform one night in the bedroom, I was afraid to try. Just in case it happened again.

"Dad?" he called, squinting through the windscreen, trying to make sense of what he was seeing.

Sighing—I should have left him in the alleyway, pneumonia or Julian be damned—I slid out of the car.

"Hello," I murmured, pitching my voice at a purr and smiling seductively.

The younger man blinked, then shook his head slightly. His eyes went back to his father before returning to me, narrowed with suspicion.

"What's going on? Who are you?"

"Is this your father?" I asked, wishing I'd taken a moment to get that ID after all so that I would at least know his name.

"Yeah, that's my dad. What's happened?"

The look he threw at me was far too shrewd. He wasn't at all mellowed by the power of my voice. Which was...very unusual.

Oh well, I could improvise.

"I'm glad you're here. I found him in the car park of a restaurant downtown. He seemed confused and I didn't think it was safe for him to drive. I offered to bring him home, but he fell asleep on the way. Perhaps you could help me get him inside?"

I gave him my most winning smile. He continued to stare at me, mistrust writ all over his face.

What the hell?

"Could you help me?"

I rounded the car and opened the passenger door. The man paused for a moment, then came slowly down the two steps before approaching me. I stepped back to give him plenty of space, still smiling innocently. He ducked his head down and looked in at his dad.

"Dad? You okay?" He reached in and gave his shoulder a gentle shake and I heard a mumbled groan in response.

I grimaced, glancing back out into the darkness. Freedom was right there. And I'd prefer to get away before the old man was conscious enough to start contradicting my story.

"Well," I said, "He's home now, and you're here. So, I should be going."

The younger man stood up and considered me. Now that he was up close, I could see that he was as tall as his dad. He had the same features, too, just tighter and slightly more tanned, his face undisturbed by lines. He was handsome.

Evangeline.

My name whispered in my head, the word coming with a hard tugging in my stomach, a compulsion to dematerialize at once and return to Master's side.

I needed to go.

"Thank you for bringing him back," he said, resting a sleekly muscled arm on the top of the car. There was still a little reticence there, a hint of wariness, but now that he'd seen that his father was—at a glance, anyway—

unmolested, he'd lost the stiff, aggressive stance. "How are you going to get home? Do you need a lift?"

"No," I said, shaking my head and taking a small step back. "No, I live nearby. I can walk."

"It's dark," he said, frowning. "Let me drive you."

"I'll be fine," I promised. The idea that there was anything out there in the night that might be a threat to me was pretty laughable, but I had to admit, the fact that he was concerned about me was a novelty I could definitely get used to. "Honestly. It's a very short walk. You should stay here." I gestured to the car. "Make sure your dad is okay."

Evangeline?

A hint of temper now, and the hard tug of compulsion that told me I really, really had to go. A younger vampire would've been forced to dematerialize on the spot, but I held it off. Just.

"If you're sure," he said, not looking happy about it. "Could you…would you text me, just so I know you got home okay?" He smiled impishly. "I don't even know your name."

"Evangeline," I said. Then I blinked, astonished at myself. What on earth did I tell him for?

"Pretty name," he commented. "Will you message me, then? My number's on the side of the truck there."

A yank on my senses that scraped at every nerve. Shit.

Sorry, Master, I thought, though I knew he wouldn't hear me. Not from this far away.

"All right," I said desperately. I looked to his vehicle and quickly memorized the name—Michael Evans, builder and contractor—and a telephone number. Then I waved and hurried quickly back down the driveway.

I dematerialized the instant I knew I was out of sight.

"Where have you been?"

Master's displeasure was so strong, it almost sent me to my knees. He stood in his study, the room opulent with rich colors which shimmered with the heat of his anger. I stared at him, my gaze skating across his eyes and coming to rest on a mouth pursed tight with unhappiness.

"I am sorry for my delay, Master. I was…cleaning up an incident."

"Incident?" The word came out clipped, and I winced.

"A feeding. I was concerned that he might perish if I didn't attend to him, and then there was a family member to deal with."

"You altered the memories of both?"

No. I should have, though. Would have, if I wasn't such a neurotic mess about my abilities right now.

"I dealt with it," I said.

Not a lie. There was no lying to Master. Even bending the truth like this was dicey. I held my thoughts as tight in as I could and waited, anxiety a hard knot in my chest where my racing heart should be.

"Hmmm." His mouth tightened ever so slightly, then he turned away from me, bursting into fluid motion. "I have something I need you to do."

"Of course, Master."

"You are aware of the collection point we have in Riddermarsh?"

I stilled, the wariness I'd started to lose returning full force.

"Riddermarsh is Julian's territory," I said carefully.

"I am aware."

Oh boy. What the hell was going on. I tried as hard as I could to keep my mind blank, but the suspicious little thought I'd had in the alleyway kept trying to sneak in. Master ruled the whole area, but it was split up into territories that higher level vampires were given charge over, and we were fiercely territorial. Most of the scuffles that went on—out of Master's sight, of course, though I was sure he knew about them—were about vying over the most prestigious "patches".

"Of course, Master. I apologize."

He waved away my words.

"I need you to go down and…inspect the premises."

I drew in a deep breath. Julian would not like that. And there would be no way to hide it from him. A collection point was one of the places Master stored bagged blood, where it could be retrieved as required—for very badly injured vampires who couldn't feed or, more recently, for the master himself because he would only drink from his consort Cat now, and she couldn't safely supply enough blood to meet all his needs. They were extremely secure, and constantly manned. While I could alter memories—I *could*, I told myself— Julian would know. That would be a bigger mark of my being there than scrawling my name across the wall in blood.

"What am I looking for, Master?"

"You will know."

Great. Helpfully specific. I kept that thought scrupulously off my face. Master wasn't fooled, though. He shot me a look, stripped clean of its usual wry humor.

"Yes, Master. When would you like me to go?"

Another look, this one exasperated. Right now, then.

I gave a nod of respect and farewell, then dematerialized.

Chapter Three

One moment she was there, the next she was gone. Michael blinked, staring at the spot at the end of the drive where the mysterious woman—Evangeline, a beautiful name for a beautiful woman—had been standing. He listened hard, but he didn't hear the distinctive clip of high heels on pavement, just the night's silence…and a heavy groan.

"Dad?" He turned his attention back to his father, who was rolling his head, eyes fluttering. "Come on, Dad. Let's get you inside."

It wasn't easy to manoeuvre the old man out of the car—he'd gotten his build from his dad after all—but he managed, then hoisted his dad's arm around his shoulder and limped inside with him.

Upstairs to the bedroom seemed like too big a challenge for both of them, so he opted for the wingback armchair in the rear living room. Michael helped his dad into it, then crouched down in front of him.

"Dad, can you hear me? Dad?"

Instead of answering, his father groaned, tilting his head back to rest against the brown leather of the chair.

"I'll get you a coffee, shall I?"

His dad muttered something unintelligible.

"What?"

"Tea." Then another string of mumbled sounds that Michael interpreted as, *Who drinks coffee at this time of night, idiot boy?*

He retreated to the kitchen and started heating up the kettle on the stove. There was a perfectly good microwave on the wall, but even insensible as he was, Dad would know the water hadn't been properly cosseted and he'd be back in here to do it again. Correctly, this time.

While he waited, he slurped at his own coffee, which was foul and made with freeze dried granules because Dad wouldn't keep a coffee maker in the house. His thoughts went back to the woman and he pulled out his phone to check it. Nothing. She'd said it was a short walk, and he'd managed to extract a promise from her to text when she got home, albeit reluctantly. It was a decent enough area, but still. A woman, walking on her own…

He should have insisted on escorting her, but what was he meant to do, just leave Dad sitting there passed out in the car? She'd been so skittish, he knew she'd have vanished the moment he went inside if he'd asked her to wait until he got Dad indoors.

"She'll be fine," he told himself. It didn't quell the unease in his stomach, though. She'd been tall but so fine-boned, willowy to the extreme. He could imagine her being overpowered easily, those dark eyes in that hauntingly beautiful face widening in fear. "Stop it, man."

"Michael?" The voice didn't have much strength behind it, but the thin rasp jolted him out of his thoughts. "Michael, are you there?"

"I'm here, Dad," he called. "Just getting your tea."

A minute later he had the cup—complete with saucer, of course—all prepped, and he grabbed a couple of the shortbread biscuits Dad liked so much as he made his way back to the living room.

"Here," he said, putting the cup and saucer down on the little table beside the armchair and pressing a biscuit into Dad's hand. "Eat that. Bit of sugar will do you good."

"Is there no sugar in the tea?" his dad asked.

"Two cubes," he replied, promptly. "But by the color of you, the shortbread won't do you any harm either."

"I've got to watch my figure," his dad replied, with a hint of his old vigor. "Make sure I stay irresistible to the ladies."

Michael snorted. Dad had met Mom at the age of fifteen and married her at sixteen. And they'd spent every day together till three years ago when she'd slipped away in the middle of the night, leaving them both heartbroken. Dad hadn't looked at another woman since, and he never would.

Which was why Michael was an eternal bachelor, he reckoned. If he couldn't have love like that, he wasn't interested. Soulmates, they'd been. Two parts of the same whole, and though Dad soldiered on as stoic as ever, Michael knew he was only half a man.

"Glad you're back with us. Have a bit too much sherry with your dinner, did you?" he asked jokingly, though there wasn't a whiff of alcohol on Dad's breath and Michael could count on one hand the number of times he'd ever seen his father drunk.

"I did not," Dad frowned. "I…I'm not sure what happened. I met with Stephen. We ate and then I bid him goodnight. I remember walking out to my car and—" He shook his head. "There was a young lady. But then, it's all fuzzy."

"Evangeline," Michael supplied. God, he couldn't get enough of saying that name, rolling it off his tongue. He took a moment to discreetly check his phone again, but there was still no message. "She drove you home. Did you…did you maybe take a funny turn?"

Dad stared at him for a moment, then drew himself up, utterly affronted. "A *funny turn*? Do you think I'm some senile old man?"

"Well, you are getting on a bit, Dad."

"I'm fine," he snapped.

"In that case, what happened tonight?"

Dad opened his mouth, but no words came out. He looked to Michael, and there was a hint of fear in his eyes. Something hard and uncomfortable dropped into Michael's gut right then. Dad was getting old, but he'd always seemed strong and unflappable, unstoppable. Until right this moment.

"I don't know," he said, in a small voice Michael had never heard from him before.

"Maybe call the doctor in the morning, yeah?" he suggested.

It took a moment, but Dad nodded.

His phone rang in his pocket and he snatched it out, hoping it was from her. Evangeline. It wasn't. He heaved a sigh as he recognized the number.

"Hang on, Dad. I gotta take this." He stepped away to the other side of the room and slid his thumb across the screen to accept the call. "Yeah?"

"Hey Michael, it's Grant. Sorry to bother you, I know it's late, but there's a job going. Simple board up, but get your name down on the file and you'll be likely to be offered the refurb. Could be good cash then. What do you say?"

Michael grimaced and looked over at Dad. He was sipping tea in between bites of the biscuit, and his color did look much better. And Michael could definitely do with the money.

"All right, message me the details, yeah?"

"Brilliant. Thanks, Michael. I'll owe you one."

"Just get me the refurb and we'll call it even."

"I'll do my best."

He hung up and returned to his father. The eyes that watched him approach were shrewd and sharp, much more like the dad he knew.

"I've got to go and do a board up job, Dad. Will you be okay here, do you think?"

Dad put the cup of tea and saucer down, brushed imaginary shortbread crumbs from his lap and stood. Michael pretended not to see the slight wobble as he did so.

"I am a fully grown adult, Michael. Of course, I will be all right. You go and do what it is you need to do. You don't need to worry about me."

He did, though, that was the problem. And after tonight's little episode, he was going to have to watch a lot more closely.

"Shall I help you get ready for bed before I go?"

His dad didn't dignify the question with an answer. He tilted his chin and stalked, back ramrod straight, through to the rear hall leading to the stairs.

"I'll call later on and check on you," Michael yelled.

"I shall be sleeping," came the muffled reply.

"I'll call in the morning then." Silence. "Stubborn old bugger," he muttered.

"Language!"

Michael snorted. The old man still had ears like a bat. Sneaking out when he'd been a teenager had been nigh on impossible.

He locked up the house and checked his phone as he climbed into the truck. As promised, Grant had sent over the details. It wasn't far, and better yet, it was on his way home.

And it wasn't like he had anything better to do with his night.

The premises were in a small industrial estate, tucked into a corner at the end of a row of units. It was dark and shadowy, the floodlights not reaching this far, but the owner had compensated by adding a host of motion detector lights and three of their own CCTV cameras. Not that it had helped any. The large window that took up most of the front had shattered, the thick wooden door splintered at the hinges until it gave way. Michael glanced at the alarm above the door that should have been blinking an angry red, but it was dark and silent. Odd.

Thinking that the front window might need more sheet-board to cover it than he had in the truck—and wouldn't that be a bitch if he had to drive back to the depot at this time of night, because that *would* be out of his way— he shouldered in through the door, a hefty flashlight gripped tightly in his hand, just in case whoever had done the damage was still around. Glass crunched under his feet and he whistled as he swept the torch beam around the room. There wasn't a piece of furniture not destroyed. What looked like a fairly nice desk had been reduced to firewood, and a swanky computer chair lay bent and broken under the window it had clearly been used to smash in.

The drywall hadn't escaped unmolested, either. Holes had been punched in at various spots, and the carpet beneath his feet had been slashed and torn.

Someone had really gone to town.

Adding up the possible cost of a refit and refurb in his head—Grant was right, this one could turn a tidy profit—he turned back to fetch the tools out of his truck, when a rustling sound made him freeze. He swung the torch round, braced for attack, but the room was as empty as before. There was a door, though, tucked discreetly into a back corner, that he hadn't noticed previously. It was an internal door, obviously leading to a back room rather than the alleyway behind the building. And it was closed.

Strange, that, when everything else had been so thoroughly wrecked.

Edging toward the door, he adjusted his grip on the flashlight. There was a gun in a lockbox under the driver's seat in the truck, but Michael didn't like to wield a weapon he wasn't going to use, and he'd never shot anything more dangerous than a Coke can.

He reached the door as quietly as possible, the detritus on the floor making a completely silent approach impossible, and wrapped his hand around the doorknob. A gentle twist told him it was locked, but this barrier was nothing like the solid wood front door. A hard wrench and a shoulder to it, and the thing would pop open. He took a breath, clutched his makeshift weapon in his fist, and burst into the back room.

The torch illuminated the scene in a blur as he moved. He caught a glimpse of refrigeration equipment—all empty, doors hanging open—and a workbench with machinery he didn't recognize, before the shifting beam fell on a figure, standing stock still and staring right at him.

"Fuck!" He almost dropped the torch when the face appeared in the dark, chalky white with dark, dark eyes. His shock intensified when he realized he recognized the person. "Evangeline?"

She was clutching a pile of papers in her hand—papers she'd apparently been looking through in the pitch dark—and she looked as astonished to see him there as he was to see her.

"Michael?" Hot on the heels of surprise came suspicion. "What are you doing here?"

"The insurance company sent me to secure the property." He hesitated, but he knew he had to ask. "What are you doing here?"

"My superior owns this property."

"I see." He took a step closer and couldn't miss the way she shifted to shield the papers she held from view. "And who would that be?"

"Hunter Enterprises."

"I'll have to call and verify that information."

"No, you won't." Her voice reverberated in his head like a gong. He had to shake himself, like a dog shaking water droplets from its coat.

"Sorry?"

"You don't need to confirm who I am, or why I am here."

"Yes, I do."

She frowned then, her head tilting slightly to the side and an expression of puzzlement sliding over her features. God, she was beautiful.

"Why?"

"It's a crime scene, isn't it?"

"Is it?" A curve of her lips that almost had him forgetting his name. "I don't see any police tape or flashing lights."

"It's not been reported? The security company won't pay out unless—"

She gave a casual wave of her hand, the expression on her face amused.

"The insurance company won't be involved."

"It was the insurance company who hired me."

"Was it?"

She raised a delicate eyebrow questioningly and Michael paused. He thought back to the conversation with Grant, tried to remember if his boss had actually said anything about it being an insurance job. Had he just assumed?

"It's going to cost a pretty penny," he warned her. "I'd suggest telling your superiors that they really ought to consider going through their insurance. And if they want to do that, they need to make a police report. I can wait, do the board up when the cops have had a chance to take a look around and get whatever evidence they might need?"

Why the hell had he said that? It could be hours before the police showed up to a dead crime scene—no point rushing if the perpetrators were long gone—and it was already late.

Because the woman in front of him would have to hang around too, that's why. And maybe he might get a chance to talk to her some more. Idiot.

Chapter Four

I tried to hold in my sigh as I stared at Michael. This night was not at all turning out the way I had imagined. I'd turned up to snoop at the collection point and found the place trashed. Just this unit. There wasn't so much as a broken window or line of graffiti on any of the other businesses. Hmmm. I'd been told on multiple occasions that I was a suspicious person—cynical bitch was the phrase used most often—but my sleuthy senses were tingling.

The destruction in the front room was epic: furniture smashed, walls punched in. But the scent heavy in the air was the reek of stress and anxiety, not the heat of anger. And the back room, where all the expensive equipment was, where the "intruder" could actually have hurt Master in his pocket, was stripped bare but otherwise untouched.

I smelled a rat.

I smelled a tip-off.

Julian must have realized that Master was suspicious enough to send someone out to have a little check and sent instructions for all tracks to be hidden. It'd been done in a rush, though. I might not have found anything incriminating, but the fact they'd felt the need to mock-up a break-in was telling in itself. Master would be very interested to hear my report.

Odd for Julian to be so ham-fisted. Nothing about this had his intelligent, methodical touch about it. But perhaps it was nothing more than time constraints and the need to rely on clod-headed humans to do his dirty work?

The human in front of me wasn't clod-headed. He was eyeing me with shrewd, calculating eyes. I needed to work harder to convince him that there was nothing to worry about, that he could just secure the front and disappear. Because, apparently, the suggestive power of my voice didn't work on him.

Yeah. This was turning out to be a great night.

"There's no need to involve the police," I said, smiling reassuringly. "What's most important to my superiors is getting the place up and running again as quickly as possible, and an investigation would only slow that down. Similarly with the insurance, we don't want to have to wait for them to authorize every little thing."

There, that sounded reasonable. I watched Michael's face carefully for his reaction. I'd been relying on my powers too much lately, it seemed. I was out of practise with plain, old-fashioned manipulation.

"It's going to cost you a lot more…" He lifted an arm to run fingers through his hair, looking dubious. He had good arms, the muscles shown off by a tight fitting T-shirt. Defined but not too bulky. Just the way I liked.

"Time is money," I reminded him. "We'd rather take the hit on the repairs and get things in motion."

"What is it you do here?"

Ah. I should have guessed that was coming.

"Storage?" I offered.

He glanced around deliberately, taking in the tight confines of the space.

"Small things," I added. I waved at the empty fridges. "Small things that need special handling."

The truth was, the fridges were the only things here that made sense. The microscopes and other little machines that I couldn't identify but had taken snaps of with my phone for later, along with the strange blank spaces on the slightly dusty counters where pieces had been removed…none of them should be here. This was a collection point, not a research lab.

At least, it wasn't supposed to be a research lab.

Master wasn't going to be happy if Julian was dabbling with things behind his back. Which was the understatement of the century. Unless…

Unless Master knew about it and it was me who was being tested?

My thoughts were whirling round and round in circles, and I didn't have time to deal with the man in front of me.

"Do you have what you need to secure the place?" I asked. A tiny raise of my eyebrow. "Or do I need to call someone else?"

Bitch move, but I could feel time tick, tick, ticking away. It worked too; his face set into an indignant glower.

"No, no. I can do it. I should have enough stuff in the truck to get you secure for now, hopefully," the last word was muttered, not for my ears, but of course I caught it. "Then…yeah. I guess if you aren't looking to go through your insurance, we can get you a quote for the refurb." A deeper scowl. "You'll want to get a couple of comparisons, since you're doing it yourself. I mean, we're good value for money and we do a good job, but still. It's the smart thing to do."

I bit my tongue against the smile that wanted to break free. He thought

I was some silly woman who didn't know what she was doing. Chivalrous of him to give me the advice, though. I liked chivalry. A lot.

"I'm sure you'll do a good job," I said. "You're already here, you've already seen the place. Like I said, speed is the main factor here. Just make the repairs and send us the bill."

"Are you sure? You really should—"

"It's decided," I said, cutting him off and throwing a bit of force into it. He swayed slightly then fixed me with eyes there were a little bit of respect, and quite a lot of heat.

"Yes, Ma'am," he quipped.

It was a flirt, I realized. I couldn't help myself; I had to flirt back.

"That's what I like in a man. Respect, and obedience."

He laughed, the sound rocketing around the small space, and reverberating somewhere deep in my chest. That was quite a laugh. Free, and happy. When had I last laughed like that?

Had I ever laughed like that?

I stepped toward him, drawn.

"I'll stay until you've got it all boarded up," I said.

"You don't need to."

"Yes, I do. Besides, I like to watch a man work."

What on earth was I thinking? This femme fatale thing wasn't me at all, but when the slow grin unfurled across his face—the grin of a man who's finally cottoned on that a woman might be interested in him—it was worth it.

"Yes, Ma'am."

My turn to laugh. And if it was a slightly hollow version of his, I pretended not to notice as I followed him through to the front room. I righted a heavy desk when he went out to gather tools from the truck and perched on it while he cleared up the glass and measured up the window for the board. He looked relieved when he came back from the truck a second time, hefting a wide piece of sheet board.

"You have enough for the job then?" I asked, legs swinging as I watched the muscles in his back and shoulders strain, moving a piece into position and then holding it there as he went at the edges with a nail gun.

"Just," he grunted.

"Oh good." I watched the sheet almost slip from his hand. "Do you need help?"

I'd meant it as a tease, even though I could have held the wood up and in position with a single finger in reality, and I was rewarded with a choked laugh.

"You just keep your pretty behind right where you are," he called. "I don't want you getting hurt."

"Well, bless your heart." I was zero per cent Southern, but I'd always wanted to say that. I even tried to put a little twang into it, though not very successfully if his snort was anything to go by.

"Sorry," he said. "That was an asshole thing to say. My mom would have smacked me round the head for it. Hard."

I tinkled a laugh, was about to say something back, when a cold, oily presence crept in behind me.

I was off the desk in a flash, positioned defensively in front of Michael. I wanted to crouch, extend my fangs and hiss…but that would have been a giveaway to the man both in front and behind me.

Instead, my voice was demure, carefully neutral, as I murmured, "Julian."

"Evangeline. What are you doing here?" His voice was the same deliberate calm, but the threat was easy to hear when you knew him as well as I did.

"Mr. Hunter sent me," I murmured. I was aware of Michael at my back, who couldn't fail to be trying to listen in. He'd probably have attended to his work and disappeared by now if I hadn't been here to distract him, and I wouldn't have Julian declare him collateral damage. "It seems we had a break-in."

"This isn't your territory."

I shrugged, as nonchalantly as I could manage. "He gave an instruction, I obeyed."

"I thought I was the obedient one." I'd been concentrating so much on Julian I'd somehow not heard Michael come in from where he'd been working on the outside of the window. He stopped at my shoulder and held out his hand. "Nice to meet you, I'm Michael Evans, the building contractor."

I watched, horrified, as Julian took the proffered hand and shook it, a polite smile on his face…and murder in his eyes.

"I am glad you could come out at such short notice," Julian murmured.

Michael shrugged. "Happens all the time. Damage is discovered and people want their property secured as quickly as possible." He grinned. "Looters seem to find vulnerable premises as quickly as flies find a dead body."

Julian purred a soft laugh but I couldn't force my face to stretch into a smile. Michael had no idea of the danger standing right in front of him, had no idea that at this moment Julian was imagining him as the corpse, flies buzzing around him. Then he made it even worse.

"Bit odd, though, the way they trashed this front room but barely damaged the back. Almost like they wanted to make it look like nothing but vandals when really they were after something specific."

Michael, shut up!

I screamed it in my head, but my telepathy was extremely limited. It only worked with touch, and inconsistently at that.

"I suggested to Evangeline that we really should bring in the police, but—"

"But I explained that that wasn't necessary," I cut in, smiling placatingly at Michael. "Like I said before, we just want to get up and running as quickly as possible." I looked meaningfully toward the window. "Which, hopefully we're almost done? For tonight, at least."

It was a dismissal, a crude one, and I felt bad about it, but I'd feel a lot worse if Michael talked himself onto Julian's *needs to be silenced* list.

"Of course," Michael said, much more stiffly than before. "I'm done. I'll be out of your hair then. Look for the quote in a couple of days."

"I will," I said, guilt tearing it me. I could sense his confusion over my abrupt change in demeanor, but I couldn't exactly explain to him.

"Right, then." Michael gave me a tight smile then nodded at Julian and turned on his heel. I watched Julian watching him. I could see the thought, right there in his eyes. *He needs to be dealt with.*

No, not on my watch.

"Michael?" I called. I waited until he'd turned around, his face a mask of polite disinterest. I froze, not having thought any further than intervening, but I found my feet taking me toward him, everything in me wanting the Michael who looked at me with unhidden interest back. "Would you like to have dinner with me?"

"What?" he looked as surprised as I was by my words, and I heard the disbelieving little huff of breath from Julian behind me.

"Dinner," I breathed. "With me."

I'd said it now and besides, I was really warming to the idea, the fact that I didn't eat anything notwithstanding.

"To talk about the job?" he asked, frowning slightly.

I laughed, forgetting for a millisecond the predator lingering behind me. "No, just dinner. A…a date."

"Oh." His frown deepened then, and I thought he was going to say no. "I…sure. Yes. I'd love to."

Three yeses in a row. That thawed the strange ice sitting in my stomach a little.

"Terrific. Shall I call you?"

"You do actually have my number then?" he asked, a hint of amusement coming into his eyes.

"Yes?" I said uncertainly. "Would you like me to recite it to you."

"You were supposed to text me," he reminded me. "You didn't."

"Oh." He was right. I hadn't. The meeting with Master had driven it right out of my mind. "I promise to be better this time. In fact, why don't I text you right now? Then you'll have my number, and you can call me."

What was I doing? Being an idiot for one, but also making the point to Julian, I hoped, that Michael was mine. I wasn't sure that would stop him if he had his mind really set, but perhaps it would at least give him pause.

Another little idea slipped into my mind, something that would really show him how serious I was, but I waited until I'd send Michael a quick little message of hello, then watched him check his phone to see that it had been received.

"You have a good memory," he commented.

"I do," I agreed. It was another little perk of being a vampire, an eidetic memory. Which was useful when Master was in a questioning mood and wanted every little insignificant detail of what had happened.

I had a feeling one of those moods might be occurring in the very near future.

"I'll call you," Michael said. "We'll set something up."

"Great." I took another step closer, until I was near enough to place my hand on his chest. I went up on my tiptoes, noting how he'd gone stock still beneath my palm, and placed a soft kiss on his mouth. It wasn't a toe-curler or anything, but as I moved my lips against his, I let one of my fangs graze his lower lip, flicking at the tiny wound I'd made and sealing it even as I took in the single bead of blood.

I felt it settle inside me as I stepped back, felt it pulse ever so slightly with the diminished echo of his heartbeat. He was part of me now, and I would be able to find him, if I needed to. It was also an age-old ritual, taking in the blood, a way vampires sealed servants to them. I knew Julian wouldn't have missed the tiny taint of blood on the air, knew he'd realize what I'd done.

When Michael left with another murmured goodbye and I turned back to Julian, his eyes were narrowed in thought, his mouth ever so slightly pursed. He wiped the expression clean an instant later, though.

"Playing with your food?" he asked, tone mocking.

"Claiming it as mine," I replied carefully.

"Hmmm." A quirk of his lips. "If that's what's holding you back from our mating, you needn't worry. I'll still allow you to have your toys."

I almost choked on the sheer arrogance of the comment.

"How very generous of you," I replied coolly.

"I am generous," he replied, "but my patience is not limitless."

Oh no, we were not having this conversation now.

"We should return to Master," I said quickly. "He'll be waiting for a report."

The slightest hesitance, something shifting behind his eyes, but then Julian gave a quick bow of his head and pasted a benign smile on his face. "Of course."

He disappeared with a tiny fission of power and I allowed him a moment's head start, waiting until I heard the rumble of Michael's truck starting up and then the low roar as it pulled away, before I, too, dematerialized.

Chapter Five

"I have no clue what any of this means." I sighed as I stared down at the reports that I'd painstakingly copied down from memory, the originals back in their hiding place in the strange laboratory. Just because I'd remembered what was on the pages didn't mean I understood what I was looking at. Medical stuff, as best as I could guess. Not something I normally turned my hand to.

Last night's report to Master had been brief, Julian taking centre stage as it was, of course, his territory. A break-in, he said, but the vandalism was a ruse. Well, that I agreed with. From there, though, it was all I could do to keep my incredulity off my face. The blood stores had been stolen, perhaps a new vampire or group of vampires in town? Or the werewolves, simply trying to play games, challenge Master's authority as the supreme supernatural creature in the city? Possibly even someone in the seethe, unhappy with their position and trying to cause trouble?

It was all utter nonsense, but I stood there beside him and said not a word nor betrayed my thoughts by so much as a flicker of an eyebrow. The only movement I made was a tiny shake of my head when Master's voice echoed in my mind: *You have answers for me yet, my Evangeline?*

"I will, of course, make sure those responsible for tonight are made to pay for the insult to you," Julian had purred, all charm and composure.

"Indeed," Master replied, his gaze fixed out the window and looking for all the world like he'd no interest in the conversation. I knew the truth was anything but.

I expect to know what he's up to—the full extent of it, Evangeline—and quickly.

Yes, Master.

Like I said, I wasn't much of a telepath, but this close to Master and projecting hard, I knew he'd catch the thought.

I was surprised Master didn't just execute Julian there and then; he knew Julian was lying to him. Julian couldn't utter a direct lie, not to our maker, but he was misdirecting, misleading and misrepresenting, and that was the same thing. I could only presume that Master wanted to know exactly what Julian had been up to, and whether the rot extended deeper into the seethe. And dead men—really dead men—didn't talk.

The sun had barely set and I hadn't even fed yet, but I was already at my desk in my snug little office in the turret of Master's deliberately over the top Gothic-style mansion. I liked it up here. It had a glorious view over the city, all the lights twinkling vibrantly now, but I could count the passage of time by watching them slowly fade as the humans took to bed. Best of all, it was tucked away up a narrow staircase, so I was rarely disturbed…

A knock preceded the door flying open as Kevin blundered his way in. He looked awful, his relative youth and utter lack of power meaning he rose latest of all of us. He also just…looked awful, though. Style and sophistication had passed Kevin by, and the little confidence he'd ever possessed had been eroded by being entombed with a bunch of cold, cruel and backstabbing vampires.

I felt sorry for him, but the slow to fade jolt of fear I'd felt, thinking it was Julian bursting in to catch me with papers I didn't want him to know I had yet, made my voice sharp.

"What was the point of knocking?" I demanded.

He paused, fixing slightly bleary eyes on me, expression utterly confused. "Huh?"

I gave him a look.

"I mean…pardon, Lady Evangeline?"

"Better. What was the point of knocking?"

He scratched at his head. "To let you know I was coming? Or…or to get permission to come in?"

I'd already lost the will to pursue this pointless reprimand, but I soldiered on. "And did you pause, even momentarily, after knocking to give me the option of denying you entry?"

"Uh…no?"

"No. in fact, you knocked *as you were opening the door*, so it was entirely redundant, wasn't it?"

"Re-dundant?"

I sighed, clamped down on my temper.

"Never mind, Kevin. What do you want?"

"Julian sent me."

I paused, revaluating. "He did?" Kevin nodded. "Why?"

"To help you." He hunched his shoulders slightly as he spoke, bracing for my response. I knew what he was expecting to hear. I'd heard it said to him, countless times. *Exactly what help do you think you would be?* I was thinking it, truth be told, but I couldn't find it in myself to toss it at him. It would be like kicking a puppy.

"Help with what?" I asked instead.

Kevin shrugged. "Something to do with fixing up a building? Julian said you had a contact. I've...uhm...I've got a little bit of experience with construction. He thought maybe I could be useful."

Julian had never once thought Kevin could be useful. In fact, he called him useless multiple times a day, every day. He thought he could be a spy, that's what. Not purposely, no one would send Kevin to do anything that required any level of slyness or subtlety. But Master had signed Kevin over to Julian, and Julian was a strong enough vampire to delve right into Kevin's mind and pull out his memories, examine them for himself. It hurt, was traumatizing for the person whose mind was being invaded, but Julian wouldn't care about anything like that.

What he'd sent me, in reality, was a walking, talking camcorder.

To refuse Julian's "generous" offer, though, would be a headache I didn't need. I'd just have to keep Kevin from reporting back to Julian until I was ready to report to Master.

I rubbed at my forehead. I felt slightly hungover, my stomach gnawing at me. I needed to eat.

"Kevin, there's some blood in the fridge there, warm it for me, would you?"

I'd turned my nose up at the little baggy of blood earlier when I'd realized I was hungry—it was the equivalent to the stale bun at the back of the pantry—but right now I didn't care if it tasted like it'd come from a rotting corpse. I needed something in my stomach.

Kevin surged forward clumsily, eager to be of assistance, and I went back to the papers in front of me, trying to do my best to ignore his presence.

"Blood reports?" his voice came from over my shoulder.

"What?" I turned round so quickly I startled him into sloshing blood over my beautiful, antique rug. The little color in his cheeks drained quickly, but I wasn't interested in the flooring right then. "You know what this is?"

I waved the sheets of paper under his nose.

"Well, yeah. Kinda. It looks a lot like the reports I bring back for Master when I take Cat to get her iron levels and things checked."

I snatched the blood out of his hand and had taken a gulp before I realized it was still cold. Yuck. In the same moment, I thrust the reports into his hands.

"What can you tell me about what it says?"

Kevin ran his eyes over the top page of papers, went so far as examining the second sheet, before he passed it back to me. "I don't know, I don't actually understand any of it."

"Oh." Disappointment crashed over me.

"Dr. Walker would though."

"Who?"

"Dr. Walker. The lady who does Cat's tests."

I stared at him, unable to believe assistance had come from such a source.

"Kevin," I said, "you've just been extremely helpful."

"I have?" he asked, pleasure lighting up his eyes.

I drained the rest of my breakfast. "You have. Let's go. We're going to see this Dr. Walker."

Dr. Walker, Kevin told me, had a spacious suite in the fancy new hospital by the highway, but she only stayed into the darkened hours on the nights she had an appointment with Cat, which wasn't tonight. He took me to her home instead, sticking meticulously to the speed limit and driving with a caution that told me having me in the car with him was making him nervous. I was dematerializing home, I decided. It would be easier on both of us.

Dr. Walker had a very nice house in a very nice neighborhood. There was a long, sweeping driveway, but Kevin pulled up on the curb beside a cute mailbox made to look like a bird house.

"You have an invitation inside?" I asked, unbuckling my seatbelt.

Kevin shook his head. "I just grabbed the reports from the mailbox."

Damn.

"Well," I said. "I'm sure I can persuade her. Master pays her well, she'll not want to lose such a lucrative little side deal."

We made our way up to the house and I pressed the doorbell. It rang out with a delicate little tinkle of chimes and I stood back to wait, taking in the pretty little flowerpots around the door and the welcome sign embellished with hummingbirds. I was expecting a feminine, genteel kind of lady from the appearance of the house, so I was somewhat shocked when the woman who yanked the door open and peered suspiciously out, had a bark like a bulldog and a scowl to match. She was small and skinny, like a scrawny bird. One with a vicious bite.

"What do you want?" she demanded.

"Dr. Walker?"

"Yes."

I gave her my most winning smile and watched her expression alter not one jot. "I'm Evangeline, I work for Tobias Hunter. I'm sorry to disturb you this evening, but I was hoping you might be able to perform a short consultation for me." I paused, then went on, "There will be a fee, of course."

That stopped her from shutting the door in my face.

"How much?"

I loved people who were motivated by money, they were so much easier to deal with.

"Triple what you receive for performing Catriona Jenkin's tests." And that was a healthy amount.

She stood back and opened the door wider, the glower quickly disappearing when I didn't immediately enter.

"Well, what are you waiting for? I don't conduct business on the doorstep."

"You will have to invite me in," I informed her politely.

That gave her pause for a moment, but the thought of all that cash decided her.

"Come in," she spat. "Will that do?"

"That's wonderful." I stepped inside with a smile, Kevin at my shoulder, and waited while she closed the door.

She led us a short way down the hall then pushed open a door and flicked on the light. Her study, I realized, as I stepped inside. It was messy, papers strewn over the expensive looking desk and medical books shoved haphazardly on the bookshelf. A filing cabinet in the corner had a drawer left open.

I could work for exactly thirty-seven seconds in this room before the disorder drove me insane.

"What's the consult?" she asked. "I don't have a lot of equipment here and I'm not going down to the hospital at this time of night."

"That won't be necessary," I soothed her. Then I got serious. "Before we begin, I would remind you of the arrangement you have with Mr. Hunter. It was made very clear to you how important confidentiality was."

She blanched for a moment before folding her face back into what I was beginning to realize was a habitual scowl. Master was very good at frightening people, and if he was entrusting this doctor with anything to do with Cat, I knew he'd have been excruciatingly specific about what might happen to her if she broke his trust.

"I know, I know. Keep my mouth shut, and I have."

"I'm glad. This particular piece of information goes no further than this room. You will not share what I share with you with any other members of the seethe, understood?"

A slightly sly gleam entered her eye. "Hiding things from your master, are you?"

"Forgive me," I said. "You may of course discuss it with Mr. Hunter...but no one else."

I threw as heavy a warning as I could at her and watched her nod, no smart comeback this time. Intelligent woman.

"Let's see it, then," she said, holding out her hand.

Wordlessly, I passed the papers over to her, followed her progress as she rounded the desk and dropped into her chair. I saw the professional take over as she drew in the information I'd meticulously written down.

"What is it you want to know?" she asked, her voice slightly mumbled as she turned a page, thoroughly enthralled.

"Those are blood test results," I began.

"Yes."

"Vampire blood test results."

"Yes."

That was a guess on my part, but it was also extremely damning evidence. Leaving information about our blood makeup around where it could be discovered? That was monumentally stupid, and Master would crucify Julian for it.

"Is there anything unusual about the results?" I asked cautiously.

"Well," Dr. Walker lifted her head and fixed me with a dryly amused look. "It's vampire blood. There's nothing usual about it."

"Is there anything unusual about the results, for vampire blood?" I persisted.

She took a moment to answer, going back through the pages.

"Not at first," she said. "But here." She tapped her finger midpoint on the third page. "From this point on the levels start to get all sorts of interesting."

"Define interesting."

"Increased levels of adrenaline and testosterone, but also, the make-up of the cells has altered slightly. It's almost like…like if you took a glass of milk and poured oil into it. It's not right. It smooths out in the later tests, but it never entirely goes away."

"So, someone mixed something into the blood? What?"

"I have no idea," the doctor replied tartly. "I'm a haematologist…for humans! You're lucky I recognized it as vamp blood."

Hmmm.

"Thank you," I said. "You've been incredibly helpful."

Well, quite helpful.

I moved to retrieve the papers and saw her hand tighten on the sheets ever so slightly. I gave her a look—she couldn't hope to win a tussle against me over them—and she handed them over reluctantly.

"The money will be deposited into your account tomorrow," I told her.

I didn't bother waiting for her to get up and see us out. I looked to Kevin, who had been standing silently against the wall all this time.

"Home," I said, then I dematerialized.

It took Kevin several seconds longer to pop up in the foyer of the mansion.

"What about the car?" he asked, somewhat green about the gills. Dematerializing was an acquired skill, and he'd only recently acquired it.

"It's unimportant," I said. "We need to talk to Master."

When I went to his study, however, he wasn't there. I could feel his energy trace, though, so I knew he wasn't far. There was a young vampire kneeling on the floor in the corner, a small pool of blood around her telling me she was kneeling on spikes, one of Master's favorite punishments for small misdemeanors.

"Where is Master?" I asked the woman. I didn't know her name, or her face when she lifted it to look at me, tears pooling in her eyes. She was too new, too unimportant. I gathered from the pain on her face that she hadn't built up much of a tolerance yet, this might even be her first offense.

"In his playroom," she gasped.

Shit.

If he was in his playroom, then he was in there with Cat. He'd likely be in there all night, and the instructions were crystal clear: he was not to be disturbed for *any* reason.

Damn, damn and double damn.

"Kevin," I said. "Make yourself scarce."

"What?" He looked slightly offended.

"For the rest of the night. Make yourself scarce. I don't want you going near Julian, understand?"

Something not unlike terror passed behind his eyes and I saw that he did indeed understand. He gave a small nod and popped out of the room. I sighed, wondering what I should do. If I was smart, I'd also avoid Julian. He couldn't pilfer through my memories like he could Kevin's, but I didn't want to tip him off about my discovery. I was still debating when my phone rang in my pocket, startling me.

I picked it out and stared at the screen. Michael. It wasn't the time or the place, the young vampire being punished pretending to stare at the floor but watching me covertly, but I answered anyway.

"Hello."

"Evangeline? Hi. It's Michael."

"Michael." His voice was warm and smooth down the phone, and it did odd things to me, soothing some of the anxiety I felt. "How are you?"

"I'm good, yeah. Listen, I've got that quote for you, and I know it's a bit late for dinner, but I thought maybe you might want to catch a drink and talk about it."

I found myself smiling down the phone.

"So, is this a business meeting or a date? Just so we're clear."

He took a moment to answer, and I heard him clear his throat quietly. My smile grew.

"A date?" he said, turning it up at the end to make a question. "I, uh, I mean. A date."

"You're sure?" I teased. "You don't want to change your mind?"

"No," he said, sounding more confident. "It's definitely a date."

"Then I accept."

It was something to do while I waited for Master to be available, I told myself, and it would get me out of the way of Julian. But also, I really, really wanted to.

And I couldn't remember the last time I'd really (really) wanted to do anything.

Chapter Six

"Is this place okay?" Michael was nervous, his palms sweating as he watched Evangeline walk toward where he lingered in front of the entrance to the bar. God, she was utterly breath-taking, far too good for the likes of him.

She was here, though, he reminded himself. She'd accepted the date.

"It is." Her smile was slightly amused, and it knocked the breath out of his chest. Christ sakes man, get it together. He couldn't remember being this nervous in a long time. Scratch that, ever.

"Have you been here before?"

"Just the once. Recently."

"On a date?" Smooth, Michael.

"To eat." A flash of perfect, sparkling white teeth, as if she was laughing at some private joke.

"Right. We can eat now, if you'd like. I just thought, well, it's quite late."

"I ate before I came," she informed him. "Just a drink would be lovely."

He held the door open for her and tried to keep his gaze respectfully on the back of her head and not her ass, shifting slightly as she walked in a sheath dress that skimmed her figure, or her legs, looking incredible in a pair of low spiked heels…and failing miserably. Everything about her was classy and understated, and sexy as hell.

He followed her in and scanned the place. It was busy, the only free seats he could see were the high stools at the bar. He grimaced. That didn't scream cosy or intimate.

"Over here?" Evangeline suggested. She led him to a small table he hadn't noticed, half hidden behind an enormous potted plant. That small, privately-amused smile was back on her face again, and he wondered for a horrible moment if it was directed at him.

"So," he said, draping his jacket over the back of his chair. "I don't think this place does table service. What can I get you to drink?"

"Wine," she said. "Red, please. A cabernet sauvignon if they have it."

"I'll ask," he promised.

It was strangely hard to leave her sitting there. Not that he thought she'd be in any danger—it was a nice place—but because he had the odd impression that she'd disappear if he so much as took his eyes off her. He tried to be subtle about it, but he couldn't stop from shooting her covert glances as he headed for the bar. At least until the damned plant hid her from view.

It took a while to be served, the barman trapped in an argument with a customer over the amount of head on his beer, and by the time it was Michael's turn to be served, the fancy name of the wine Evangeline wanted had slipped right out of his head.

"A Peroni," he told the barman, "and a red wine. Uh, the French sounding one."

The barman gave him a look. "Shiraz? Pinot noir? Merlot?"

Nope, that wasn't right. "Something to do with cabinets?"

The barman managed not to roll his eyes, but Michael was pretty sure it was a close-run thing.

"I gotcha," he said, selecting a bottle from the shelf and pouring a healthy glug of the blood red liquid into a delicate stemmed glass. The Peroni he plonked down with zero ceremony.

"Thanks," Michael grunted, sliding his card through the reader.

His heart was in his mouth as he returned to the table, half convinced he'd be returning to an empty chair, but there she was, looking too amazing to be real, those long legs crossed and tucked under the table, her gaze on her phone as she tapped her way across the screen.

"Your drink, my lady." He placed it down in front of her with exaggerated care and then slid into his own chair, taking a sip of Peroni.

"Thank you." She kept on typing for a moment, her fingers flying across the screen at a speed that didn't seem possible, then tucked the phone away in a hidden pocket in her dress. Leaning forward, she wrapped her slender fingers around the stem of her wineglass.

"So." She smiled at him warmly.

And his brain misfired.

"So," he repeated, mind casting desperately for something to say and coming up with nothing except how stunning she was. "I, uh, I did bring that quote if you want to look at it."

A quirk of her lips. "I told you, my superior simply wants it done. I'm sure the quote will be fine. I'd ask you when you could start, but I'm sure there are more interesting things we could talk about."

A coy smile, a slight tilt of her head that caused her silken sheen of hair to gleam in the light from the wall sconces.

"Tomorrow," he blurted. "I can get going on it tomorrow."

"Excellent." She paused, took a slow sip of wine. "How is your father? I hope he didn't suffer any more ill effects from the other night?"

"He's fine," Michael replied, waving away her concern. "He blistered my ears this morning when I suggested he call up the doctor, so I think he's back to his old self."

"I'm glad to hear it," she said. An impish grin. "Well, not the bit about your ears, but they seem to have survived without too much damage."

"I am worried about him," Michael admitted. "I mean, this is the first time anything like this has happened, but he's getting older and he lives alone since mom died."

"He's lucky he has you to look after him," she said.

Michael threw her a wry look. "Would you mind mentioning that to him?"

Her laugh was louder than he expected, a shock of sound that seemed to surprise her as much as him. She clapped her hand over her mouth, embarrassed.

"He's a good man," he went on, "and he was a great dad. But he can be a pain in the ass sometimes, you know? He hates that his body's breaking down on him, I think the thought his mind might do the same is terrifying."

"I can't imagine," Evangeline murmured, gaze on the depths of her drink.

"I don't know." He tried to intrude a bit of lightness into his tone, escape the sombreness they'd suddenly waded into. "The way my knee has been acting up lately, I'm starting to think I might be cresting that hill they're always talking about."

"You are not!" she chided, chuckling.

"I am," he argued jokingly. "You don't understand. Look at you, not a line on your face. Not a grey hair to be seen. You don't expect it, but it sneaks up on you."

She made a show of examining him. "I see no grey hairs."

"Just For Men," he quipped, and was rewarded with another one of those carefree, abandoned laughs.

"If you could stay young forever, would you?" she asked.

"In a heartbeat."

"No." A tiny line formed between her brows as she frowned. "Really think about it. You stop ageing, but no one else does. It would be fine for five, ten, fifteen years, but then…"

"But then everyone you knew would get old and die," he finished. "Yeah, that would suck."

She snorted. "It would. It would suck indeed." A pause. "Tell me about your work."

She was a good conversationalist, Evangeline. She seemed interested in everything he had to say, asking questions and laughing at all his attempts at humor. Subjects flowed into each other until he found he was sliding the dregs of his beer down his throat.

"Another?" he asked.

Evangeline made an apologetic face.

"I can't," she said. "I need to report to my superior about something."

"This late?"

"It really can't wait until tomorrow."

Slightly sceptical, wondering if she was giving him the brush off when they'd seemed to be getting on so well, he moved slightly woodenly as he stood up and dropped a couple of bills on the table for a tip. He'd intended to help her with her coat, but by the time he'd shrugged his jacket on, she was all buttoned up and ready to go. Michael blinked, feeling he'd missed something somehow, but she glossed over the moment by taking his arm and leading him away from the table, toward the exit.

"I enjoyed our drink," she told him. "You are good company, Michael Evans."

"Well thanks," he said, slightly mollified. "You're not so bad yourself."

She smiled at him, her arm wrapped tight around his. It certainty didn't feel like she'd suddenly gone off him. Maybe she really did have to report to her boss at—he checked his watch—close to midnight.

The night had cooled slightly when they went outside, Michael was sure that was why she leaned into him. It was nothing more than borrowing some of his warmth. An ex had told him he made a great wind shield.

"Where's your car?" he asked, eyes raking the parking lot. He imagined she drove something sleek and shiny, maybe an Audi SUV or a Mercedes sedan. Something classy...but fast.

"This way," she said, inclining with her head the direction they were travelling, which, by happy coincidence, was also the section of the car park where he'd left his truck. "This is your vehicle, isn't it?" she asked as they approached it.

"Bit of a giveaway," he replied dryly, "what with my name being on the side."

A low giggle he felt right down into his groin.

"I guess this is where I leave you then."

"No," he said, shaking his head, "I'll walk you to your car."

"There's no need." They'd reached his truck now and she shifted her weight so that he was leaning against its mud-spattered side and she was pressed the length of him. Which…was definitely not the worst feeling in the world.

She gazed up at him, the lights from the carpark sparkling in her dark eyes, and he couldn't think of anything except touching her.

"A goodnight kiss?" she suggested, arching one brow. She didn't give him much time to think about it, going up on her tiptoes and pressing her mouth against his. Fuck, the scent of her! It was delicate and flowery, but with an icy afterbite that was intoxicating. The fingers that gripped his biceps were strong, digging into the muscle and telling him she was enjoying the kiss just as much as he was. When she gave a soft moan, her tongue lapping out to meet his, his cock turned to solid rock inside his jeans. He tried to shift his hips back so she wouldn't notice, but there was not an inch of space between them, her body moulded to his. She made another soft, urgent little sound, rocking against him, so he figured she wasn't upset about it.

The kiss went on and on. He drowned in it, a voice in his head shouting at him to invite her back to his place so he could kiss her all over, but he was afraid to do anything to break the moment. Even though she was there, mouth hot on his and body pressed tight into him, he still couldn't shake the weird feeling that she might poof out of existence, vanish and leave his hands stinging and his cock pulsing at empty air.

God this feels amazing. The thought slid through his mind, although the voice wasn't his own. *Fuck, I could come just from this.*

Ok, he didn't disagree, but he definitely didn't think that. When the words fell silent in his head and were replaced with a blast of arousal that damned near sent him to his knees, however, he forgot everything but getting as close to Evangeline as he could. She helped, writhing against him and pressing tight into him, the truck at his back and—

When the metal behind him suddenly gave with a dull twang, he couldn't have cared less, but Evangeline jumped back as if she'd been electrocuted. She wiped a hand across her dampened lips, looking at him with horror.

"I'm so sorry! I don't know what I was thinking! I—"

"It's all right." He turned to inspect the side of the truck, saw the large indent where his weight had caved the metal in slightly. He laughed shaking his head. "Damn, I've never done that before. That's awesome."

"No, it isn't." Evangeline's voice was small and almost frightened. He turned back to her and saw something like panic in her eyes. "I'm so sorry!"

"Evangeline, it wasn't your fault!"

"I'll pay for it," she said, ignoring his words. "I really am sorry. Look, I've got to go."

She spun on her heel and hurried off, disappearing exactly as he'd feared.

"Evangeline!" He made to go after her, but his booted foot made contact with something on the ground and sent it skittering away, He looked down just in time to see Evangeline's phone spin under the next vehicle. "Dammit!"

He crouched down and retrieved it, and by the time he'd straightened up and was ready to rush after her, she was gone. Not a soul moved among the parked cars.

"Evangeline? Evangeline!" Nothing. No car lights came on, no vehicles reversed out of their slots. He jogged in the direction he'd seen her go, apprehension gripping his chest. Was she hiding in one of the cars, hoping he'd just go home? He couldn't understand why.

He didn't understand what had just happened at all.

He checked every car before he had to concede that she was gone. At that point, confusion morphed into worry. He couldn't even call her to make sure she was ok because he had her damned phone in his hand! He turned on the screen and was surprised to see it wasn't fingerprint coded or even password locked. That was one piece of good news. He opened her contacts and scrolled through until he found an entry for her superior, Tobias Hunter.

I'm just trying to return the phone, he told himself as he listened to it ring. I'm just doing the responsible thing.

It was answered quickly by a low male voice. "Good evening, Lady Evangeline."

"Is that Tobias Hunter?"

A pause. "Mr. Hunter is unavailable. To whom am I speaking?"

"Sorry, my name is Michael Evans. I'm the contractor for the property Mr. Hunter owns in Riddermarsh. Evangeline has left her phone with me accidentally and I'm trying to return it."

"I see." Another pause. "You may bring it to the house. Do you have the address?"

"No."

The man rhymed off an address at lightning speed then Michael was suddenly listening to the dial tone.

"Shit!" He jumped into his truck and started it up, quickly tapping the street into his satnav before he forgot it. It wasn't far, he saw, as the map started up. It wasn't an area he was familiar with, though he knew of it. The houses started at seven figures, some of them climbing even higher than that. Evangeline's boss was clearly loaded.

He felt the suspicion of a thousand winking security cameras as he wound his way through the neighborhood and toward the house. When the satnav helpfully told him he'd arrived, it was to find an impenetrable pair of locked gates. He drove up and stopped beside a small speaker set into the wall, rolling his window down.

"Hunter residence, how may I help you?" He thought it might be the same voice that had answered the phone when he'd rang from the restaurant, but he couldn't be sure.

"Hi. I called a little while ago. I'm returning Evangeline's phone."

"Ah, yes. Drive up to the house, please. You will be met at the front door."

"Thanks." Michael waited while the gates ghosted silently open then drove forward slowly, marvelling at the grounds and the quite frankly massive Gothic mansion that appeared, artistically lit up, as he rounded the driveway. He parked and climbed out of the truck, wondering if Evangeline would be the one to greet him as he made his way up the handful of steps to the imposing front doors.

She wasn't, but he did recognize the face when one half of the arch-shaped, solid oak double doors swung open. What was his name again? Michael had introduced himself, but he didn't think the man had had the courtesy to respond. He'd been cold, and aloof.

He was smiling now, however, a wide, delighted smile that revealed gleaming white teeth with oddly pointed incisors.

"Hello, Michael."

Chapter Seven

I opened my eyes as soon as the sun dipped below the horizon. I couldn't see it, but I felt it. An instant later, I felt the low whirring of my electric shutters rolling back, allowing light to flood into my room. It was so bright it hurt my eyes, but I basked in it. This was the closest I came to feeling the sun's rays on my skin again—something I longed for with the desperation of one who knows it can never, ever happen—and I took a moment every morning to touch the tiny slice of day I was allowed.

I knew I was lucky, most vampires, younger ones especially, couldn't bear any light that wasn't artificial.

When the sky outside had dimmed enough that the lights in my room clicked on, I rolled up and out of bed. My gaze immediately went to my bedside table where there was a piece of note paper, folded in half to hide its contents from my gaze. I stilled, senses ranging out instinctively, but whoever had left the note had gone. Good. I *hated* the fact that the humans working for Master could roam about the house freely while the vampires slept. I'd left very specific instructions that *no one* was allowed in my rooms while I was sleeping unless it was at Master's wishes…or a dire emergency. Vampires were extremely vulnerable when asleep; a bomb could go off over my head and I wouldn't notice, not even while it burned me alive.

Expecting the note to be from Master, I was surprised to see the fluid sprawl of Julian's hand across the paper. It said nothing: no greeting, no message. Just an address.

2487 Turnbull Drive, Jameshill

I knew all of Master's properties, including the ones looked after by other vampires. Whatever this place was, it definitely wasn't in the books.

"Dammit." I'd had plans to report straight to Master this morning—he hadn't reappeared all night, and eventually the dawning sun had forced my retreat—but I knew I was going to have to check this place out first.

Cautiously, because this was a clear move from Julian. I was very probably walking into a trap.

I didn't intend to walk in alone, though. If things really came to a head with Julian, I might need someone to get word back to Master. Dressing quickly in jeans and a long-sleeved shirt—it was difficult to fight in a dress—I headed through to the section of the house where Kevin slept.

I had a suite of rooms: a lounge, a luxurious bathroom and my bedroom, which was large enough to contain my grand four-poster. I liked a bit of drama. Being much lower on the totem pole, Kevin had a room in the attic, which was set up much like the servants' quarters in Victorian England. I walked into his room without knocking and saw him splayed out on the bed, still, eyes closed. I could see perfectly well, but I flicked on the light. It wouldn't rouse him—he'd wake when he woke, no matter the disturbance I made—and it made it easier for me to find a clean spot to sit while I waited. Kevin was a disorganized slob.

When I saw his eyelids starting to flutter, I shifted closer. I was leaning over him fully when he opened his eyes.

"Kevin."

He let out a frightened little squeak and I clapped my hand over his mouth. When I was sure he'd gotten over his shock, I pulled it away. I tried to be surreptitious about wiping my palm on my jeans before resuming my seat.

"My Lady Evangeline," he said, reaching for a blanket and covering himself, even though he was dressed decently enough in a T-shirt and shorts. Well, covered decently enough. The clothes had seen cleaner days. "What brings you to my room?"

"I need your help," I said. "With Julian."

Kevin swallowed visibly.

"I'm going to meet him tonight," I went on, aware of time tick tick ticking away. Julian knew when I rose. He'd be wondering why I hadn't arrived yet. "I need you to come with me, but stay out of the way. Be close, but make sure Julian doesn't know that you're close. Can you do that?"

"No!" Kevin replied, eyes wide and frightened.

I repressed my sigh. Kevin lacked confidence most of all, and the little he possessed crumpled when he felt others saw him as stupid, or useless. Which…pretty much the entire seethe did.

"Yes, you can, Kevin. Do this, and I'll be pleased with you."

"What does that mean?" Kevin asked.

This time it was a smile I had to repress. I had his interest now.

"You may ask me for a favor. Such as, whether I would speak to the master about having you work fully under me. Instead of Julian."

I had a feeling by the end of this night Kevin probably wouldn't have to worry about Julian anymore, but there were plenty of others within the seethe who would also make his life a misery.

"You would do that for me?" he asked, suspicion thick in his tone.

"I don't lie, Kevin." Annoyance and a growing sense of urgency pushed more power into the words than I meant, and Kevin flinched away from me.

"I'm sorry," he gasped. "I'm sorry, I didn't mean that."

I released the energy I was still holding, and Kevin's shoulders sank back to normal levels.

"Get dressed," I told him. "Then get yourself here." I passed him the note Julian had left me. "Remember, he mustn't know you are there."

Kevin nodded nervously.

"You can do this, Kevin," I reminded him, then I dematerialized.

Back in my room, I went to grab my phone out of last night's dress, cursing myself for having been too loopy from the approaching dawn to put it on charge. I needed to check where the address was in Jameshill. I could only materialize in places I knew, places I'd been. Hopefully Turnbull Drive wasn't too far from—

My phone wasn't in my dress. Nor was it on the chair I'd slung my dress over, or on the floor around it. I even got down on my knees and checked under the bed in case I'd kicked it in my disoriented state. Nope.

Oh, for the love of blood, had I left it at the restaurant? That was all I needed. Worse, had I left it with Michael after I'd clambered over him so hard, I dented his damned truck?

I'd not let myself think about that this morning—there were more serious games afoot—but I cringed to remember how I'd been so absorbed in the kiss that I'd forgotten my strength. I could have cracked Michael's ribs, it was sheer luck that the truck had given way before his body did, pulling me out of the pleasure haze I'd succumbed to. I was mortified, and I'd legged it. Not my finest moment.

Well, I'd have to suck it up and call him, after this thing with Julian, of course. I needed my phone back.

Aware I was taking far too long, I booted up my laptop and used that to search the address. At last, a bit of good news. The property was literally around the corner from a jewellery store I frequented fairly often. It had interesting, steam punk-style pieces and helpfully late hours. I tried to visualize the street itself, but I'd never had cause to go any further than the store car park. There was a handily shadowed corner where I could poof in and out.

Imagining that spot in my head, I dematerialized. When I appeared there, it was to be confronted with a young couple not three feet away. Thankfully, they were far too involved with each other to notice me—had Michael and I looked that passionate when we were kissing? I couldn't help the fleeting thought—and I was able to slip away.

It was a residential street, that was the first thing to register. The houses were older, but large and spaced well apart. Number 2487 was mid-way along and looked in no better or worse shape than any of its neighbors. I paused for a moment outside, debating the best route forward. Julian solved that by opening the front door and leaning against the jamb, smiling at me lazily.

"You came."

I took a moment to look at him before I answered. He looked as handsome as ever, dashingly dressed in a well-cut suit. But there was something about his face, his eyes. It looked like madness.

"Well," I said, trying to sound as light and carefree as possible, "how could I not when you left such an enigmatic note."

He grinned at me, eyes lighting up, then disappeared into the dark, leaving the empty doorway waiting for me.

All right, then.

I walked forward slowly, waiting for something to jump out and get me, but there was nothing but the slight creak of the wooden steps as I made my way up them, the ticking of a grandfather clock I could see standing sentry in the foyer.

The décor inside was old-fashioned, like the place had been caught in a 1950's time warp. I wondered if the house belonged to Julian, a little bolthole he kept for himself, or whether there was an old woman buried out back. Knowing Julian, odds were fifty-fifty.

I moved into a living room stuffed full of heavy furniture. I could hear Julian through the next doorway, which I could see led to a kitchen and dining room, but I held position here. What was he up to? I could hear him…*humming* to himself.

Julian did not hum.

"A toast?" he asked, appearing in the doorway without warning. That was unnerving. Vampires moved faster than the human eye could see, but I wasn't human.

He walked toward me, two small glasses of what smelled like red wine in his hand. Something was off about it, though. The scent wasn't quite right. I was too distracted by Julian, though, who was shifting and twitching like a junkie in need of a fix. He was either extremely excited about something—which I doubted was good for me—or on something. Which also didn't bode well. Drugs didn't work on us, and effects from drinking blood laden with substances lasted a very short time and came with a hell of a hangover. But I was reminded of all that odd equipment in the back room of the unit in Riddermarsh.

Was Julian developing drugs for vampires?

Master would never condone that, and I couldn't see how Julian thought he could hope to keep it under wraps. Master knew everything. One way or another.

"What are we toasting?" I asked as he passed me a glass.

"Partnership?" Julian asked. "The future?"

What?

A thousand questions hovered on my tongue, but I held them for a moment, taking a small sip of my wine as Julian downed his in one.

I tasted it. Immediately. As Julian must have known I would from the sly, excited way he was watching me. The glass dropped from my suddenly numb fingers, hitting the carpet with a dull thud and splashing over my shoes.

"What have you done with him?" The electric lights flickered about the room at the power in my voice, though Julian didn't so much as blink.

"He's safe, for now."

I felt rage swell up inside me, but I held it back. I could find Michael if I had to—I'd ingested his blood—but it might take me a while, and for all I knew Julian had someone standing over him, ready to snap his neck. I needed to play Julian's game for now.

"Is this the big reveal?" I asked, arching an eyebrow because it wouldn't do to let Julian think he had me. "Is this where I find out what you've been up to?"

"Perhaps," he replied, lips twitching in a smirk. "I'd love to know what you've found out on your own first." A wink, like we were co-conspirators. "You haven't told Master, that much I know, or I'd be dead. Which tells me you're curious." Another smirk. "Which tells me you want in."

He was utterly delusional.

"And Michael?"

A shrug. "I know you're loyal to Master. I thought you might need something to give you a little push."

"What makes you think he means anything to me?" I asked artlessly.

Julian looked down to my spilled wine and back up again. "Just a hunch. So, tell me. What do you know?"

"I know Master doesn't know anything about this place," I offered, though I wasn't actually sure about that. When Julian's grin widened, however, I knew my suspicions were correct. "And I know the blood bank at Riddermarsh was much more than just a blood bank."

"Oh really? What is it then?"

"You're doing something with the blood."

"Doing what?" His stare was a challenge, but I could see he was loving this.

I hesitated, then gave him my best guess. "You're creating a vampire drug, infusing the substance into the blood somehow."

Julian stared at me for a moment, then rocked his head back and laughed. It went on and on, the sound ricocheting so hard off the walls the windows rattled, and when it finally stopped, he wiped at his eyes as if there were tears in them. A moment later, all expression vanished from his face and he looked me dead in the eye.

"No."

"No?" I replied, trying not to show how rattled I was by this new, mercurial Julian.

"Come on." He took my hand in a gentle grip and tugged at me. "I'll show you."

I really didn't want to go anywhere with him—and I certainly didn't want to hold his hand like we were teenage sweethearts—but I let him tow me back out to the foyer and to a door hidden into the panelling under the stairs. It swung open to reveal steps to a basement, a dim light shining down below.

"After you," Julian said, releasing me so I could step into the tight, claustrophobic stairway.

Yay.

I could feel him behind me as I descended, the hairs on my nape prickling. His excitement was palpable...and extremely unnerving.

"Oh, come on!" Julian exclaimed before we'd even made it halfway down. "You have to smell it!"

I did smell it. What I didn't know was what the fuck it was doing down here.

"How did you get it?" I asked.

"I caught it!" Julian told me. I glanced back and saw that he had clapped together in front of his chest, his expression giddy. "Well, I caught a different one first, but the males are so volatile! That one killed itself, trying to break through the bars." He rolled his eyes. "Idiot. This one is a girl and it's much more biddable."

"I see."

This was bad. This was very bad. When I rounded the wall at the bottom of the steps and got my first look at the room, my gaze immediately sought out the werewolf. There she was, crouched in a damned silver cage and watching me with narrowed eyes.

Julian was keeping a *werewolf* in the basement.

And now I knew exactly what he was mixing in the blood.

I didn't have time to puzzle out the ramifications of that, because there was Michael, right beside her, chained at the wrist and ankle and attached to the wall. He was unconscious right now, head propped against the wall with some bruises on his neck and temple, but he'd retreated from the silver cage and the werewolf as far as the chains would allow, which wasn't very far. Looking at the girl's slender arms, naked and grimy from her dirt-floored home, I guessed she could still reach through the bars and savage him, if she wanted to.

I took it as a good sign that she hadn't.

She also hadn't changed, either, though I could see from the scraps of fabric in her cage that she probably had at one point.

I rotated slowly on the spot, ignoring my every instinct and putting the werewolf at my back, and stared at Julian. He looked just pleased as punch, and extremely dangerous. He appeared to vibrate as I looked at him, and I'd assumed it was excitement, but I was starting to think he might have shot himself up with some of the tainted blood. The doctor had said it increased levels of testosterone and adrenaline. I wasn't sure what that would do to a vamp, but it certainly wasn't making him sleepy.

"Why?" I asked quietly, trying to keep my judgement and my fear out of my voice.

"Advancement," Julian said, eyes lighting up with the fervor of the devout. "Do you know what happens to vampires when we ingest the blood of werewolves?"

"We puke." Vampires' stomachs were delicate. Human blood only. It was a somewhat limited diet, but given that human blood tasted like ambrosia, I'd never found cause to complain.

Julian huffed, annoyed by my answer. "Well, yes. We can't drink it directly—"

"Also, because it's supremely dangerous," I added. What with werewolves being as strong as we were and with very sharp claws.

A glare this time. I was winding him up, and I wasn't sure if that was a good idea or not. But I didn't have any other good ideas and I was focusing mostly on not letting him see how scared I was.

"I found a way to synthesize it with human blood," he said loudly, a warning for me to hush it…which I heeded.

"And what does it do?" I asked carefully.

He shifted away from where he'd been hovering at the bottom of the stairs, moving into the centre of the floor space and forcing me to choose between standing my ground and letting him closer to me, or backing up toward the werewolf.

I held, for now. I was fairly certain the most dangerous creature in the room was right in front of me.

"It makes us stronger," he said, voice reaching that low register that rattled right through me. Only Master could do that. Up till now, at any rate. "It makes us faster."

"Makes us smell a little funny?" I quipped. It was a joke, Julian smelled as good as ever.

He hissed at me, red flooding into his pupils and I knew I'd pushed him far enough.

"Don't you understand what I'm doing here?" he demanded. "I'm elevating us above all other creatures."

"Us?" I asked softly, "Or you? You haven't shared any of this with Master."

Julian spat on the floor. "He's a fool. He fawned over the werewolf alpha, over Kevin's idiocy, and he let that demon push him around."

"So, you plan to what? Use your new super-serum to usurp him?" I was kidding, but also not. Julian could never have taken Master in a fair fight, so he'd made it unfair. His odds of winning a fight between them were still extremely low in my opinion—Master was the master for a reason, and it wasn't just his strength—but then there was me. Julian had showed his hand and I wasn't stupid, I knew what that meant.

Join him or be silenced. Because a fight between Julian and me would have been too close to call, and I didn't have werewolf blood running through my veins.

Oh boy.

"You and I could be King and Queen of vampires," he told me, voice low and throbbing with emotion. "We wouldn't be the strongest pair in the region, we'd be the strongest vampires in the world. We'd—"

I flung myself at him, using the only advantage I had: surprise.

It worked, for a moment. I toppled him to the ground, teeth bared and aiming for his neck. There aren't a lot of ways to kill a vampire. Sunlight, obviously, and if I had something sharp and pointy to turn his heart to pulp with, that would work too. With just my fangs to play with, though, my best bet was tearing out his carotid arteries.

I had my hands tight around both wrists and I bore his arms to the ground, leaning in with my teeth, eyes fixed on that smooth, pale skin. I didn't make it there, however. With an enormous burst of strength, he flipped us, tearing my grip free. With his body pinning mine to the ground and both of my wrists somehow trapped in his one, he gripped my hair to still my head. I could have torn free—even if it meant ripping every hair from my head—but I stilled. He was holding back; he still wanted to talk.

"Evangeline," he panted. "We are kindred spirits, you and I. Let go of the blind devotion you hold for Master and *see*. See what we could be!"

All I could see was a madman above me. I licked my lips, thinking fast, and the werewolf chose that moment to launch herself at her cage, growling and snapping teeth. She'd changed in the scant few seconds we'd been fighting.

The burst of sound distracted Julian and he turned his head. I used the brief respite to shove at him, loosening his grip enough that I could slither free, get my feet beneath me. I skittered away a few steps, but I didn't try to run, or dematerialize. If I did that, Michael and the girl would die, and Julian would disappear. Instead, I crouched, measuring my opponent, my hands bent into claws and my fangs exposed. A quick glance around the basement told me there was nothing I could use as a weapon, except myself. And I'd already proven to be an inadequate one.

According to Einstein, the definition of insanity is doing the same thing over and over again and expecting different results. I thought that the exact moment I launched myself at Julian for the second time. He was ready for me, and I slammed into an immovable force which then pushed me backward until I was tight against the wall, Julian's face just inches from mine.

"Last chance, Evangeline. Don't throw this away. Think of what we could be. We're meant to be together and you know it."

"I'd rather fuck a dog," I hissed.

Something changed in Julian's face then. Anger and righteousness gave way to resignation and I knew I was about to die. I didn't surrender to it, pushing and twisting and wriggling for all I was worth, but it was no use. He was just so much stronger than me now. The inevitable was, well, inevitable.

I didn't see Kevin enter the basement. I didn't hear him sneaking up on us. I didn't even know he was there until I caught a glimpse of something shiny, slicing in from the right and cutting Julian's head clean off.

It hit the ground with a sickening thud, and a moment later his body toppled over to join it, falling at Kevin's feet who stood there, a pale-faced knight in shining armor with a sword, of all things, dangling from his right hand.

"Where the fuck did you get that?" I gasped.

"It was fixed to the wall over the mantlepiece," Kevin replied, sounding as astonished about what he'd just done as I was.

"Good job, Kevin," I muttered shakily. "Good job."

I stood up, panting, covered in Julian's blood, and saw Michael, conscious and wide-eyed, and staring right at me. Oops.

Chapter Eight

I pulled up outside Michael's house and killed the engine. He'd wanted to drive back himself, but since his hands wouldn't stop shaking, I'd insisted. Plus, I hadn't wanted to let him out of my sight. He wasn't the only one shocked by the events of the night.

We hadn't said a single word the whole drive here.

After Kevin beheaded Julian, I'd called for Master. He appeared in an instant, and he came alone. The werewolf girl had lost her shit then, but she'd allowed Master to talk her down enough that she changed back to human, and though she wouldn't let Master or me near her, she'd allowed Kevin to unlock the cage and he'd driven her back to the pack with a firm promise from Master that he'd be in touch with her alpha before the night was out.

That was going to be a tough conversation. From the tight press of Master's lips, he thought so, too.

Michael was another kettle of fish entirely. He was human, he was a nobody, and silencing him there and then was a more practical option than wiping his memory and hoping that it took. I knew Master, I knew how he thought. I knew that was the conclusion he'd come to.

"I'll deal with it," I told him quietly. Beseeched him, really.

Master looked at me for a long, long moment, then looked at Michael. I thought for a moment he was going to ignore me and do it anyway, but eventually he nodded.

"Get him out of here. Now."

I did, tearing Michael's chains free with my bare hands and all but carrying him out of the basement. By the time we reached the front door of the house, I knew Master would have flooded the scene of the crime with vamps, intending to find out every little titbit of what Julian had been up to.

I had a feeling Kevin and I might be in trouble later for not keeping Julian alive so that Master could turn his mind to unveiling its secrets, but I couldn't change that now.

When I'd taken Michael out of the house, when I'd driven him back to the mansion to collect his truck, and when I'd driven him home again, Michael had said not one word, except for a very brief exchange where he'd tried to insist he could drive himself. I had no idea what he was thinking. And I had no idea what I was going to do.

Silence him? I couldn't.

Wipe his memory? I wasn't one hundred per cent sure I could do that either, and I was ninety-nine per cent sure that I didn't want to.

So that left, what?

"So," Michael said suddenly.

"So," I replied.

"You're not human."

Okay, we were going to talk about this now. Here. In the car outside his house, the streetlight providing just enough light for him to read my face. I didn't need any such assistance to read his, but right now it was unhelpfully blank.

"No."

A pause. "What are you, then?"

"A vampire."

"A vampire? Like, a blood drinker?" He nodded once, just a brief jerk of his head. "That makes sense." Did it? "That girl, she's a werewolf?"

"Yeah." The technical term was shifter, but most vampires called them werewolves, just to piss them off.

"Right." He was taking all of this far too calmly. I looked down at his hands and saw they were clenched tight in his lap. My nose, also, told me that he was more stressed than he was pretending to be. "So, what happens now, then? Do you...I mean, I'm assuming most normal people don't know about vampires?"

"No, they do not."

"Does that mean you're going to have to shut me up?" A wry glance in my direction. "I'm assuming you're not going to take my word that I'll keep quiet about it."

"I'm not going to kill you," I told him.

He snorted, a brief release of tension.

"What, then? Are you going to turn me into a vampire?"

"Do you want to be a vampire?"

That got his attention. He turned to stare at me, astonished. My heart was in my mouth. I don't know what made me say that, but I could see it now. I wouldn't be the one to do it, only Master made vampires, but I thought he would turn Michael for me, if I asked.

I didn't know if I was relieved or disappointed when he shook his head.

"Then I guess this is where we part ways," I said. I was disappointed. Heart-wrenchingly so. "You won't remember me or anything that's happened since, well, since we first met. I'm afraid we'll have to get another contractor to do the work on the vandalized property."

He coughed an incredulous laugh. "Right."

"Shall we go inside?" I suggested. I wanted to get it over with. My eyes were burning and my throat was tight and I wanted to get the hell away from Michael so I could stop feeling like this.

"Wait." He stopped me from unbuckling my seatbelt with a hand over mine. "What if I don't want to forget? What if...don't vampires ever have friends? Or lovers?"

No. We didn't. There hadn't been a vampire with a human mate in all the time I'd been in the seethe...until Master took Cat as consort.

"I'm not sure," I said hesitantly.

He nodded, accepting that, then looked up at his house, a porch light glowing welcomingly by the front door. "Would you like to come in?" he asked. "For a drink?"

"I would." The words came out before I'd thought about them.

"All right then."

He climbed out of his side and I met him by the truck door, not bothering to conceal my speed. He blinked once, then smiled. "That's... wow."

"That's the least of my bag of tricks," I told him.

It was very, very strange to be taken by the hand and led up the path to his house. Brought inside and shown around the ground floor. Even the moment where he opened the kitchen door to show me inside and then caught a glimpse of the mess he'd left, dishes littering the sink and the counter, closing it quickly and ushering me back to have a seat on the couch.

"I'll bring you a drink," he promised. "Red wine? I think I can do that."

"That would great," I assured him.

Yeah, very, very strange. It was like being on a real date. It was like being human again after all this time. I suddenly knew exactly what Cat's appeal was to Master. It was the chance to touch life after being left outside in the cold.

When Michael returned with two glasses of wine, I knew that I wasn't going to wipe his memory, that I was going to plead my case with Master instead. And I had a funny feeling he might just be understanding.

"Did Julian hurt you?" I blurted as he sat down and handed me my drink. "I know he took some of your blood."

It was hard to force myself to take a sip, remembering the terror I'd felt, catching Michael's blood mixed in with the wine, but this tasted of nothing but grapes and alcohol. A Shiraz, I thought.

Michael tugged his shirt sleeve back to show me a shallow slice on his forearm. "Just this. It's fine."

"I'm sorry," I told him. "I'm sorry this happened to you. It's my fault. Julian realized I cared about you, so he used you to try and convince me to join him. You could have died tonight, for no reason other than you were unfortunate enough to meet me and—"

I'd been talking down to my glass, too ashamed to look at Michael, and I gave a start when his hand reached in and plucked the delicate goblet from my grip. When I glanced up, he'd shifted closer on the sofa, his expression sombre and serious.

"I didn't die," he said. "I was barely hurt. Was I shit scared? Yes. Would I undo what happened over the last twenty-four hours? Not if it meant never meeting you."

"It might be very dangerous to be my friend," I warned him.

He quirked his lips in a small grin. "How dangerous is it to be your lover?"

Not at all, because I'd annihilate anyone who dared threaten him. Even so, I smiled back. "Frightfully so."

"Lucky I'm a brave man then, isn't it?"

His lips were soft on mine when they kissed me. I held stock still, not quite believing this was happening after all the things Michael had witnessed over the last day, but as had happened in the car park outside the restaurant, my blood rose in me and I found myself drinking in his scent, pulling the kiss deeper. I didn't even realize I'd straddled him until I was leaning over him, clutching his hair and grinding my hips down against what I could already feel was an impressive erection.

His hands stroked around my sides to my back, then slid down to cup my ass, startling a squeak out of me when he took a firm hold and stood up with me in his arms.

"What are you doing?"

"Taking you to my bed."

He carried me through the living room and up the stairs, stumbling when I tucked my head to kiss and nibble my way up and down his neck.

"I won't bite," I breathed. "Not unless you ask me to."

He grunted then angled his neck, encouraging me to shift to the other side so that I could give it the same treatment.

I lost myself, drinking him in, tasting him, not realizing we'd reached our destination until Michael tumbled forward and dropped me onto the bed, pressing down on me, his mouth moving across my jaw and then to my collar bone.

"We need to be naked," I gasped, arching up against him and already imagining how incredible it would feel just to be skin to skin.

"Naked, right." He reared up and tugged off his shirt. I just tore at my clothes, ripping them from my body then reaching immediately for him. My hands were so eager they snapped his belt when I tried to unbuckle it, and I felt a seam give way when I tore at the buttons of his jeans. Michael moved back long enough to kick them off, along with his underwear, then he was back with me, hot in my hands as I caressed his chest and down over his stomach.

His cock bobbed slightly in my hands as I curled my fingers around it, and he hissed, closing his eyes in ecstasy, when I started sliding up and down, gripping then releasing, drawing the pleasure out. I'd leaned forward, preparing to take him in my mouth, when he stopped me with a thumb and forefinger on my chin.

"I want to explore you," he said.

He urged me back and went back to kissing me, licking at the hollow of my throat while a hand cupped my breast, moulded it for his tongue. I gasped, hips flexing, when he darted his tongue out to lash at my nipple, treating it a little roughly, just the way I liked. I reached up and gripped the other one, twisting and pulling at it, and Michael stopped what he was doing to watch me.

"Fuck, you're incredible," he rasped.

I beamed, overly pleased by the simple compliment.

He took my free hand and brought it up to the breast he'd wetted with his mouth. "Play with yourself," he instructed.

I did as he said, squeezing my breasts and rolling my nipples as he settled between my thighs and gave me a long, slow lick, running his tongue through my wetness. He dipped into my core then turned his attention to my clit, mirroring what I was doing with my nipples.

I moaned, writhing against him, my thighs pressing into the side of his head until I felt a sharp nip.

"I bite too," he said, looking up at me with eyes drenched in passion. "Now open your legs wide and keep them there."

I lifted an eyebrow at this more assertive Michael, but obeyed, widening my legs and fighting against the urge to close them when the pleasure coalescing in my clit became too much, when everything became too sensitive.

"Can't," I whimpered. *Whimpered.* "Need you in me."

"Can," he mumbled, not lifting his head from his work. "Come on Evangeline, come for me."

It was as if the words lit a fuse in me. I orgasmed spontaneously, hands abandoning my breasts to tangle in my hair and hold tight as I lifted my pelvis up to his flickering tongue.

"Yes," I gasped. "Yes, yes, *God* yes."

He made me ride it out, a hand on the inside of each thigh as a reminder to stay spread as he wrung every ripple of pleasure out of me. I'd no sooner collapsed on the bed than he was rising over me, putting a hand beneath one side to flip me onto my front. I scrambled to my knees and felt him fit himself at my entrance. I arched my back, shoving backward and impaling myself, loving the feeling of him splitting my flesh, the strangled groan he made as I enveloped him.

"That's it," he said. "Fuck me."

I intended to. I felt him lean over me and brace himself with one arm on the bed, then I rammed back into him, again and again, forcing him to strain to hold position. I was going to come for a second time, but I didn't want to do it alone.

"Are you with me?" I gasped. "Are you there?"

I could feel he was rock hard, swollen and throbbing.

"Jesus, yeah," he grunted. "God, what you do to me."

That was all I needed to hear. Dropping my head down, I moved faster, keeping him inside me, shifting in hard little thrusts. This orgasm, when it came, rippled around him, turning my inner muscles into a vice. I felt it when his own orgasm erupted, seed spurting into me. A hand on my back held me steady as he drew slowly in and out, luxuriating in me, our combined wetness making slick, obscene noises that only made me want to go another round.

When I felt his weight push down on me, I let him take me down to the mattress. He rolled us so that we were side by side, spooning, a hand softly stroking up and down my side.

"Wow," he murmured into my shoulder.

"Wow," I agreed.

I lay there as long as I could, but it wasn't long enough. I didn't want to leave, but I couldn't stay. It wasn't that I didn't trust Michael, but his blinds and curtains were not vampire-proof. I couldn't rest safely here.

"I'm sorry," I told him. "I have to go. It's going to be dawn soon."

His eyes were dark as they held mine. "Will you be back?"

"Tonight," I promised. "As soon as it's dark."

A tiny grin. "Then you can go."

I snorted at the presumption in his tone and rolled off the bed. I picked up the tattered remains of my clothes and grimaced. There was no way I could put these back on my body. Maybe if I materialized right in my bedroom, no one would see.

Knowing my luck, half the seethe would be there, waiting to greet me back and question me about all the drama.

Well, it looked like I'd be naked while they did so.

"Here." Michael handed me a folded-up bundle of fabric. A T-shirt, I realized, one of his. "I'd give you trousers but there's no way they'd fit you."

The T-shirt didn't either, falling to my knees like an over-sized nightie. It smelled like him, though, which made it better than a form-fitting designer dress in my eyes.

"I'll return at nightfall."

"You better. Don't make me hunt you down like a dog." His eyes crinkled with laughter.

I wrinkled my nose. "I'll have you know I'm a vampire, not some filthy werewolf."

"A beautiful, elegant, terrifyingly strong vampire," he agreed.

"And don't you forget it." I blew a kiss at him, then winked out of existence.

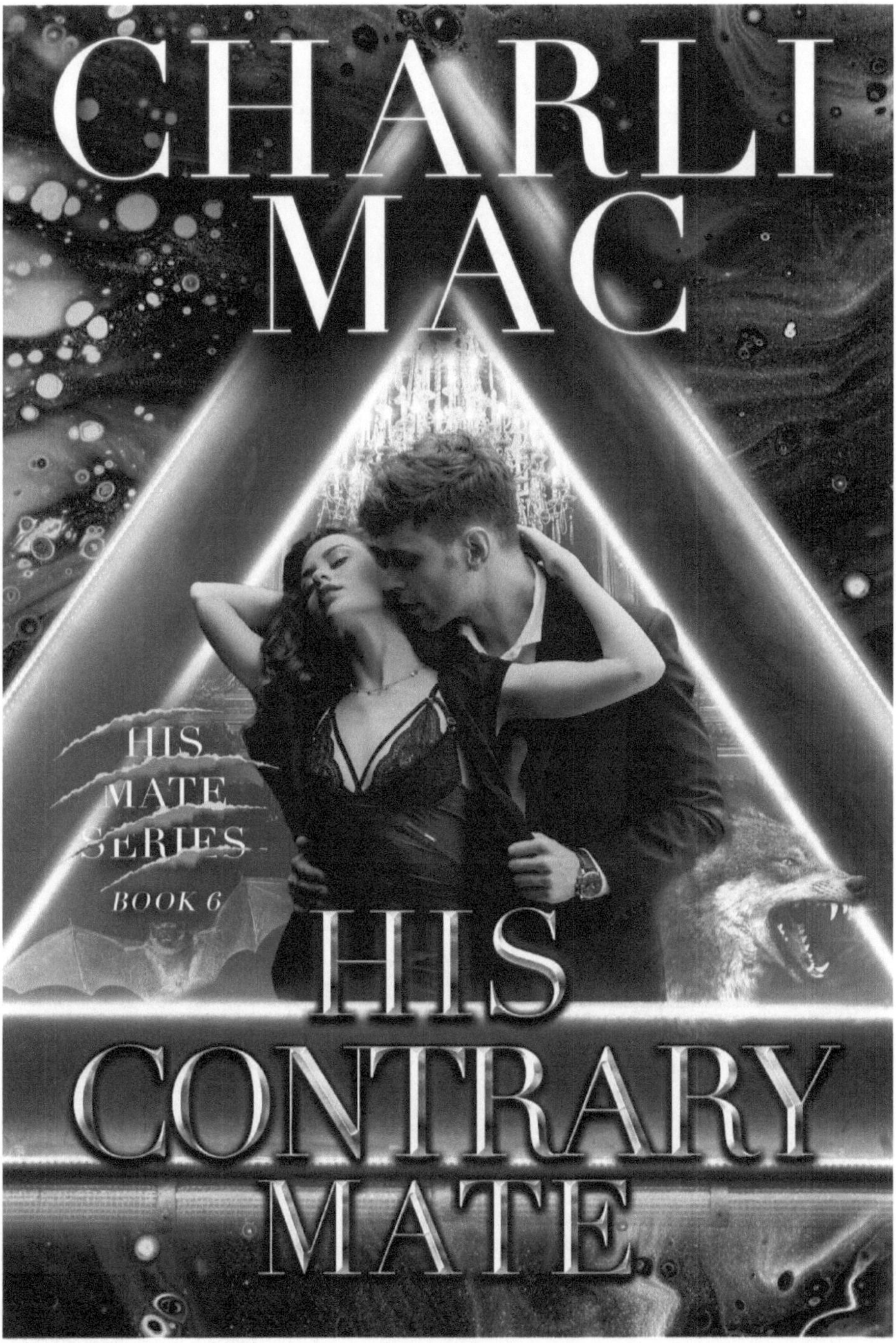
CHARLI
MAC
HIS
MATE
SERIES
BOOK 6
HIS
CONTRARY
MATE

Chapter One

The heat was going full blast in the car and still I couldn't stop shaking. There was a vampire sitting beside me in the driver's seat, but it wasn't his fault, even though he did have the ice-stink of the rest of them. Actually, I found him kind of calming. The careful way he drove, the slight hunch of his shoulders that told me he was scared of me even though I was a wreck right now. And the twenty-seven and counting apologies he'd stuttered—about my kidnapping, about the silver burns on my skin that were slowly fading, even the light he'd missed by a fraction of a second.

Kevin Wiltkins might be a vampire, but he was not the stuff of nightmares.

The creature of my nightmares was back in the house we'd just left, beheaded in the basement. By Kevin. He didn't look like the kind of person to take a sword and chop the head off an evil villain, what with his hands deliberately positioned at three o'clock and nine o'clock on the steering wheel and his foot on the accelerator keeping the speedometer two miles an hour under the limit, but he had. An unlikely hero, but a hero nonetheless.

"I hope you understand," he said, voice wobbling in the silence, "that Julian's actions weren't at all condoned by Mr. Hunter and were not an official act on the part of the seethe."

"You said that," I told him. Because he had, several times.

"I, well, yes. I just…" He swallowed audibly. "Hopefully Mr. Hunter will have contacted the pack by now, warned them of our arrival. And let them know you are safe, of course."

Ah, that made sense. He was obviously shitting a brick at the thought of going onto pack lands. Especially, to face a bunch of angry shifters who were going to be extremely anti-vampire right now.

"You don't have to take me up to the house," I said. "You can just drop me on the edge of our lands, I'll run in."

"I will return you to your alpha," he replied, both sounding absolutely resolute and totally freaking terrified at the thought.

"I don't think that's the best idea," I cautioned.

"Even so, I will do it."

"Your funeral," I quipped. I was impressed, though. He had balls, even if they were quaking right now.

"You can use my phone if you want to ring them now. I'm sorry I didn't think of it earlier." He fumbled in his pocket and held out a cell phone. I looked at it for a moment, then folded my arms across my chest.

"Nah, that's ok. Like you said, Hunter's going to ring."

A sideways glance, surprise cutting through the stoic I'm-going-to-die mask he'd been wearing ever since he was told to take me home.

"You don't want to call your family, let them know you're ok? They must be going out of their minds with worry for you."

They might, but I knew that wasn't going to manifest as cuddles and cups of cocoa. Da was going to lose his mind, and it would be my fault. My fault for being out where I shouldn't have been, my fault for not listening to him. My fault for not being a perfect, obedient little submissive who would be content under his rule and under his thumb.

I couldn't argue with any of that, but it was *not* my fault that I'd been kidnapped by a deranged vampire, and that fact would be lost amongst all the yelling.

"It's fine," I said quietly.

"All right." Kevin put the phone away, but I could tell I'd piqued his interest now. "The alpha will probably talk to your family—"

"The alpha *is* family," I cut in.

"Of course," he corrected. "You're all family."

"No. Well, mostly. But definitely in my case. I'm his daughter."

A car horn blared as Kevin took his eyes off the road to stare as me, slipping across the central reservation. He swerved back with the first curse word I'd heard from him, staring out the windscreen with wide eyes.

If I'd thought he was scared before, he was practically hyperventilating now.

"You're *Janna Walker?*"

"I am."

"Fuck!" The steering wheel cracked under the pressure of his white-knuckled grip.

"You could have asked my name at any point," I observed.

"Yes. No. I mean, you're right. I should have, and I didn't. It's just..." He shot me a look. "It's been a night."

I snorted incredulously. "Tell me about it."

Kevin turned to me, realizing what he'd said. He looked horrified. I couldn't help it, I burst out laughing, and a moment later he followed suit.

"Oh God," he said, wiping at imaginary sweat on his forehead. He did that a lot, I noticed. I had had very few dealings with vampires, but the ones I'd seen all had a serious Otherness going on. Except for the paleness and the ice-stink, Kevin could have been human. I didn't think he'd been a vampire very long.

"It's going to be all right," I told him jokingly, a smile still on my face.

"Is it?" he grimaced, but there was humor still in his eyes. "Please don't let them eat me."

"We don't eat vampires," I assured him. "You guys taste tough as boots."

A laugh that was more a strangled cry. "That's...reassuring, I suppose?"

"It shouldn't be," I deadpanned. "Just because we don't eat vamps doesn't mean we aren't good at killing them." I snapped my teeth playfully. I don't know why the hell I was feeling playful after the couple of days I'd had, but it was better than curling up in a ball and crying, so I was going with it. "Sure you don't just want to drop me at the end of the drive?"

"No," he said firmly, but quiet terror was back.

"I won't let them hurt you," I promised. "You saved me."

"Let's lead with that," he suggested, and I laughed.

The closer to the pack lands we got, however, the more curling up in a ball sounded appealing. There was going to be a lot of yelling, my mother was going to give me her best disappointed look, and for the next age everyone was going to mutter about how irresponsible Janna was and it really was time her father just put his foot down and got her mated. A couple of pups would settle her right down.

Fuck that.

I wasn't sure I wanted kids. I was very sure I didn't want to mate someone Da picked out for me. And I was positive I didn't want to prove right all those pack members who had been whispering since I hit maturity.

Except, no one seemed to care what I wanted.

"Turn here," I told Kevin, my voice dulled. I was just so sick of it. Truth be told, when Julian had found me, I'd been stewing over a milkshake in an all-night diner, trying to find the gumption just to run. If I'd thought I'd a good chance of getting away, I'd already have been gone...but to try and just be dragged back by the scruff of my neck? It would be just another Janna plea for attention.

Kevin's car wasn't built for the dirt road that led up to the main pack house, and it bounced and juddered as it hit every pothole along the mile and a half stretch.

"Can't vampires see in the dark?" I snapped, finally provoked.

"I can see perfectly," Kevin replied, just a hint of temper in his own voice. "Trust me I'm missing more than I'm hitting."

"I doubt that," I muttered. There was no way his vampire senses missed that, but he ignored it, hands tight on the wheel, taking me excruciatingly slowly toward my doom.

The main house blazed with light, every window lit up. My eyesight wasn't quite as good as Kevin's, but even a human could have seen that half the pack was crowding the driveway. Kevin mumbled something that was too low for me to hear, but he kept on going, coasting to a stop right in front of my father.

The headlights illuminated his tall stature and his well-muscled body, highlighted by the way his arms were tightly folded across his chest. It turned his face into patches of light and shadow, emphasizing the sharp cut of his jaw and the dark pits of his eyes. I didn't need to see his expression to know he was pissed. I could smell it, the testosterone reeking off him. Da was about to explode.

"All right," Kevin said. He glanced at me, eyes raking across my face, and seemed to steel himself. I watched him give a little nod. "All right."

He reached for the door handle, but a pack member was already there, on the other side of the door, ripping it open.

Shit.

I scrambled out as quickly as I could, but in the short time I was blind to what was happening, Kenny, Da's second, had Kevin in a hold that would snap the vampire's neck if Kenny applied any more pressure.

Kevin, to his credit, was standing stock still, his hands raised slightly in surrender. Submitting totally.

"Wait!" I yelped. "Don't hurt him!"

Kenny looked at me like I'd lost my mind. He wasn't the one to answer me, however. Da was.

"Janna, get inside."

Oh, hell no. If I disappeared, Kevin lost his only supporter. In the mood my father was in, he'd kill him and deal with the consequences later. I'd never seen him so angry, though it was carefully caged for the moment, and I'd seen him angry *a lot*.

"Da—"

"I said *inside*." My whole body convulsed fighting against the command. It physically hurt to ignore him, but I pulled on a hard ten years of teenage rebellion, straightening my spine and lifting my chin.

"No," I said. Someone gasped, horrified I'd deny the alpha. "Da, you can't hurt him. He saved my life."

"He what?" I winced at the curtness in his voice, but at least he was listening.

"He saved me," I said. "Didn't Tobias Hunter call you?"

"He did."

"Then you know."

Those angry eyes turned on me. I ducked my head, but held eye contact, just. "What do I know?"

"Kevin was the one to kill the vampire who kidnapped me."

"It was probably a ruse," someone muttered from the dark. I was concentrating too hard on Da, who only had to nod in Kenny's direction to end Kevin's life, to pay attention to who it was. "They wouldn't kill one of their own."

"He cut off his head," I replied angrily. "I don't think you can fake that."

"He did?" Da asked. He didn't sound impressed, more incredulous, his eyes skimming over Kevin's slender form disdainfully. That rankled with me. Kevin might not look like much, but he *had* saved me, and then he'd driven me here, right into the heart of the pack's territory, delivered me to the alpha himself. He had more balls that half the wolves gathered here.

"He did," I said.

"Get in the car." I blinked, thinking Da was talking to me, but when Kenny released Kevin, I realized he was talking to the vampire. "Get the hell out of here before I change my mind. And you can tell Hunter that we'll be having more conversations about this, conversations he will not enjoy."

Kevin was free to go, but he didn't move. He stood there, his gaze fixed on me. He was asking a question, I realized suddenly. Asking if I was OK, if it was safe to leave me here.

Emotion welled in my throat, my eyes suddenly burning. I gave a brief nod, blinking rapidly to make sure no tears would fall.

He climbed into the car at human speed, trying to show, I suppose, that he wasn't scared. A pointless exercise as we could all smell it. I listened to the sound of the engine start and then watched Kevin carefully manoeuvre the car in a tight circle, something none of the pack helped with as they stayed where they were, cramping the area.

No sooner had the taillights disappeared around the corner, than Da turned to me.

"Janna, inside."

Right. Of course. Time for the yelling.

Chapter Two

Three months later

It was raining, and he was early, so Kevin materialized right inside the treehouse hideaway. Janna hated it when he "poofed in right out of nowhere", but she wouldn't be there yet so—

"Hey." He jumped at the dull voice that called out from behind him.

Turning round, he saw Janna wedged into the corner, her knees drawn up. Her face was smudged and dirty, tear tracks tracing down her cheeks.

"What's wrong?" he asked.

It only took three paces to cross the space and crouch down in front of her. The treehouse had been a childhood playground of hers, tucked away in a back corner of the pack lands, and it was at most ten feet by ten feet. They'd had to do a bit of patchwork on the floor when they chose here to meet, but it was solidly built. Construction was pack business, after all.

"Nothing." She sniffed and wiped across her face, making it worse.

"Here." He produced a handkerchief and handed it to her, watched as she scrubbed at her cheeks. "You missed a bit."

"Where?"

"Everywhere." An attempt at a smile she didn't return. Taking the handkerchief back, he wetted it with water from the bottle resting by her feet and daubed at her forehead and chin, the streak of dirt by her left ear. "Want to tell me why you're crying and covered it dirt."

"You see me covered in dirt all the time," Janna said dryly.

That was true. Janna kept clothes here so she could run to the treehouse in wolf form, and she liked to splash her way through the stream and roll in the leaves. The tears, though, they were a first.

Kevin handed her the now filthy scrap of fabric back so that she could blow her nose.

"Come on, what happened?"

"Not in here," Janna said. "I need to breathe."

They ended up sitting outside the front entrance to the treehouse, on a large branch, staring out at the night with their legs swinging down. The enormous canopy of the tree kept most of the rain off them, but it had slowed down to a drizzle at any rate. Janna didn't talk for the longest time; she just sat, gazing at nothing, and sighing occasionally. Kevin didn't mind, though. Being with her was restful. She had the wolf's edginess, but she never looked at him with disdain or derision, like she was waiting for him to fail. She just…looked at him, which was a gift beyond measure.

"There will be some shifters coming to visit us from another pack soon," she said eventually.

"All right," Kevin said cautiously. "Is this something I should tell Master, or should I try to pretend I don't know?"

"Try?" Janna glanced at him.

"I can't lie," Kevin reminded her, "you know that. But I can try not to think about it."

Not something he was very good at—or good at, at all—but practise made perfect.

"It's all right," she said. "I doubt they'll leave the pack lands much, if at all. And Da will make sure they know to behave if they go into the city."

"No pissing on lamp posts, pick up their poop in the park?"

A wan smile. "Yeah. That sort of thing."

"So…this is bad, this visit? Is it like when the drunk uncle that no one likes comes to stay?"

"No, no, I like them. I just—" she gave a shrug and sniffed hard. "I don't like why they're coming."

All right…

"Why are they coming?"

"For me." That sounded ominous, but Kevin forced himself to wait, to let Janna explain in her own time. "Da says…well, everyone seems to think it, but now Da agrees with them…" She tailed off, drooped her head.

"Your father says?" Kevin prompted eventually.

When Janna spoke again, it was to the forest floor, more than twenty feet beneath their feet.

"He says it's time I took a mate. And he reckons…he reckons I need a fresh start. So, I'm going to go and be fostered with this other pack. I've to stay at least a year, but I know he's expecting that I won't be coming back. He wants me to find a mate there."

"He's sending you away," Kevin said, voice as dull as Janna's had been earlier.

"Yeah." A whisper of sound.

"How far?" Vampires could travel very quickly, materializing in spots across their journey, if they had references points, but it didn't matter if it was a hundred miles or a thousand. He didn't have permission to travel outside Master's territory. And he wouldn't get it, not to go and visit a shifter.

"Five hundred miles."

Kevin winced. That was far enough that Janna wouldn't be coming home often for visits, either.

"Did you tell him that you don't want to go?" He glanced at her. "You don't, do you?"

She shrugged. "No one likes me here anyway."

"I like you."

That raised a small, sad smile. "You know what I mean. No one in the pack. They all want rid of me, think I'm too much trouble. Spoilt little Janna. And that makes Da look weak, because he's Alpha and he should be controlling me." Her eyes narrowed. "Not that any of them would dare say it to Da."

"You mother will miss you, surely? Can you not appeal to her?"

She shook her head.

"Why not?"

"Mom would never question any of Da's decisions." A dry look. "She's a good mate." Janna sighed heavily and her shoulders sagged. "I'm going to miss you."

Kevin felt panic wrap itself around his heart and squeeze, hard.

"When are they coming?"

"Tomorrow."

So soon.

"Will you be able to come and see me, while they're here?"

Janna bit her lip, the big-eyed look she gave him answering his question even before she spoke.

"They'll be watching me like a hawk, like I might do a runner or something like that. There's no chance I'll be able to get away." She reached out and wrapped her warm fingers around his ice-cold hand. "We can talk on the phone."

"Until you get a mate. He won't allow you to talk to me." Kevin heard the bitterness in his voice, but he was helpless to prevent it. She was his only real friend in the world, and she was leaving him.

"No mate will tell me who I can or can't be friends with," Janna repudiated, a hint of the defiance he loved so much about her flaring in her eyes. Janna would never allow herself to be used and abused in the seethe the way he was. It wouldn't matter if she was the youngest or the weakest, she'd make them respect her.

And she made him want to try to do the same…not that he'd had the courage to start yet.

"I hope you're right," he said softly.

"I am," she said firmly. Hauling in a deep breath, she straightened her shoulder and climbed lithely to her feet. "Come on, we've still got tonight, and I've got something to show you."

Intrigued, Kevin followed Janna back into the treehouse. It was sparsely decorated, a little table with child-sized chairs tucked into a corner and a cot along one wall. On the wall opposite the entrance was a series of shelves for keeping little girl treasures. Janna went straight to those shelves and pulled something out from a small, handmade box. When she turned to Kevin, he saw she held two coils of rope in her hands, one black, the other a deep purple.

"What's this?"

"You wanted to try that Shibari thing. The Spiderman."

"Spider's web harness," Kevin corrected softly.

"Yeah. I…well, I didn't want you doing it with anyone but me. It's our thing, right? Or have you been mermaid's tailing every girl you know?"

"No," Kevin murmured. "Only you."

"Well then." She handed him the ropes and while he was untying the coil, whipped her shirt off over her head. She wasn't wearing any kind of bra.

"What are you doing?" Kevin asked, staring at her then yanking his gaze away as her hands went to the button of her jeans. "I can do it over your clothes!"

"It won't look the same," Janna told him. "I want it to be pretty. I'll keep my knickers on." She rolled her eyes. "Shifters see each other naked all the time. I don't change with my clothes on, you know?"

"I know," Kevin said, eyes darting everywhere but at Janna's pale, lithe body. "But I'm not a shifter, and I've never seen you naked."

"Well, first time for everything." A pause, filled with amusement. "You're going to have to look at me to do the rope tie, you know."

"Right. Yes. Of course." God, she was beautiful, standing there smirking at him, utterly unabashed. True to her word, she wore nothing but a small pair of flesh-colored undies.

Stepping close, he dropped the purple rope to the floor and slid the black around her neck, knotting it just below the hollow of her throat. She shivered as his fingers brushed her skin.

"Sorry," he said. "Cold hands are an occupational hazard for vampires."

"It's all right, I like it. Tickles."

Well, that was the first time Kevin had ever been told that. He tried to stop himself over-analysing the comment, winding the rope around Janna's middle before anchoring the tie between her legs and creating the cross ropes over her shoulders and hips.

"You know, a spider can create an entire web in thirty minutes," she commented, shifting her feet to emphasize her point.

Kevin smiled. "You can't rush perfection."

"Oh, so you're telling me spiders are slap-dash workers? I'll be sure to pass on your thoughts. Expect an eight-legged invasion of your coffin. You're not arachnophobic, are you?"

"You know I don't sleep in a coffin," Kevin said, shaking his head.

"Shhh, you're ruining my fantasy here."

He snorted. His favorite thing about Janna was the thing her alpha father was always complaining about: her free spirit. The joy in her. It was a relief to see it again, one last time.

That was a sobering thought. One last time. He tried to keep the idea that he was losing his one and only friend out of his head as he tied off the black rope and picked up the purple.

"Now we make it pretty," he told her. "So that it's fit for its wearer."

He wasn't smooth with lines, but Janna beamed at him.

"I like this," she said quietly as he painstakingly wove the purple rope in and out of the lines of black.

"Being tied up? I confess, I'm surprised at your interest. I didn't think Shifters liked being confined."

"Well, I'm not really confined, am I?" She waved her arms to emphasize her point.

"It's the deep pressure stimulation," Kevin told her, hands still moving fluidly, weaving the rope in and out, knotting anchors as he went. "It's calming. The rope compresses you and shifts your body from its sympathetic nervous system to your parasympathetic nervous system."

"What now?"

Kevin paused and looked up at Janna's bemused expression.

"It's like the rope is giving you a hug," he said.

"Oh. You could have just said that."

"I could have. But then I wouldn't have got to show off my useless knowledge."

"Of course." A soft chuckle. "I don't think it's that, though. I wouldn't let anyone else do this to me. I mean, I can move, but I can't shift. Not through rope like this. My wolf should be going nuts, she hates being vulnerable."

"Why do you think she isn't?" Kevin asked, head bent back down to his work, trying not to show just how much her words were affecting him.

"I trust you. *We* trust you. You're my friend. A *real* friend. You're the only person who doesn't look at me like I'm a disappointment, Kevin."

He laughed then, he couldn't help it. "Ditto, Janna."

She gave him a tiny grimace. "How are things in the seethe, anyway?"

"They're fine."

"Hmmm." A raised eyebrow that said she didn't believe him.

"No, really. Things are fine. Well, better. Evangeline requested me from Master, and no one messes with her so most of the other vamps pretty much leave me alone now."

They didn't dare do anything overt to him, because Evangeline would eviscerate them. Not because she cared, but because it would be an insult to her. And perhaps she cared a little. Still…

"It's much, much better now that Julian is gone."

Janna shivered.

"Sorry, I didn't mean to say his name."

"I'm not scared of him!" A toss of her head that pulled at the rope Kevin was knotting at her collar bone, disrupting the symmetry.

"Hold still!"

"Oops, sorry. I'm not, though. I'm not scared of him."

"Good. No point being scared of a ghost."

"I wasn't scared of him while he was alive, either!" she said, eyeing him warningly. "I had everything under control."

"Of course you did. You could have got out of that cage any time you wanted. You didn't need me to rescue you at all."

"That's right, I didn't!" She lifted her chin, gave him her most condescending look. "I simply wanted you to have your moment in the sun."

"Trying to kill me, are you?"

The haughty expression descended into giggles. Kevin smirked along with her and finished tying off the final knot, tucking the loose end away so it wouldn't ruin the look of the harness.

"How do I look?" Janna asked.

"Incredible," he told her honestly. "And the rope is nice too."

She rolled her eyes at him, amused, then she held up a finger excitedly. "Hang on! I've something else to complete the look! One second!"

She darted back to the wall of shelves and ferreted about in her little box. When she rushed back to him, she had something hidden in her hand.

"No spider's web is complete without..." She pressed her hand to her left breast and when she took it away, there was a dime store comedy spider dangling from the ropes, just under her right nipple. "Ta da!"

Kevin burst out laughing. It was less the spider and more the delighted look on her face.

"Perfect," he promised her. He took his phone out of his pocket. "Do you want to see how it looks?"

There was no mirror in the treehouse, so every time he tried a new tie with Janna, he took some snaps so that she could see it. If he spent hours upon hours looking at them again when he was alone, well, he didn't think Janna would begrudge him that. At least he'd have them to look at when she left to live with the other pack. When she was out of reach.

Used to the drill, Janna shifted her weight to one hip and propped her hands on her lower back. The move emphasized the curve of her waist and thrust out her breasts. Kevin had to take a breath, steady himself, before he could take the pictures. She did that so effortlessly, with no guile, moved from a state of almost childlike innocence to an incredibly sexy woman.

She blew Kevin's mind, but he had always known she wasn't for him.

"Here," he said, going to stand by her side so he could show her the screen. "What do you think?"

"It looks amazing!" Janna exclaimed.

Yeah, he thought. You do.

Taking the phone from him so that she could look more closely, Janna rested her head against his shoulder.

"I'm really going to miss this, Kevin," she said quietly. "I'm really going to miss you."

I'm going to miss you, too. The words echoed in Kevin's brain, and in the empty chambers of his heart. His throat was too choked with emotion to get them out of his mouth, though, so he wrapped a cold arm around her shoulders and let himself soak in her warmth.

Chapter Three

"Janna! They're approaching. Get out here!" Da's voice ricocheted around the main pack house, easily reaching my bedroom, especially since he stood in the hallway just two doors down.

"A moment," I called back.

"No. Now." The words came with an edge of command that scraped my nerves raw. I'd levered myself up off my bed before I could think to try and defy the order.

There was a mirror on the wall facing me, and I caught my reflection as I turned to go out and face my doom. I looked like shit, violet from several nights' poor sleep splodged under my eyes and my hair coming loose from a sloppy ponytail. Had I even brushed it before I tied it up this morning? I didn't think so. I was wearing my good leggings that shaped my butt perfectly, but I'd hidden it and the rest of my figure beneath an over-sized sweatshirt I'd pilfered off Kenny ages ago. As Da's second and a mated shifter, no one could really object to me wearing it, but it was a deliberate tactic, covering myself in a male's scent. I was not above being petty.

And Kenny was the only pack mate I wasn't currently mad at. He might not have argued against Da's decision, but at least he hadn't voiced support about it like the rest of them.

I stuffed my feet into sneakers and scuffed my way down the hall like a sulky teenager. Da had disappeared—no doubt to go out and greet our guests—but Mom was there waiting for me. She eyed my welcoming outfit with horror.

"You can't go out there looking like that!" she gasped. "What's the matter with you? Your father will be furious."

"Well, that'll make two of us then, won't it?" I snapped back.

Truth be told, I wasn't furious, I was hurt, but hell would freeze over before I'd admit to that.

Mom's mouth pinched up tight and I knew she was thinking about sending me back to my room to change into something more "appropriate"—and what *was* appropriate for the occasion? Naked with a *For Sale* sign round my neck?—but we both heard car doors opening and closing, greetings being exchanged. Too late. I gave her a satisfied little smile.

"It's your funeral," she muttered, manoeuvring me past her and giving me a little shove toward the front door. "You should be out there! Go!"

I went, trooping as slowly as I could with Mom breathing down my neck.

"Where is your lovely mate?" I heard a voice I recognized—James, the Boulder pack alpha—call. "And Janna?"

I didn't want to hear whatever cutting, caustic thing Da might come up with, so I hauled the door open and stepped out onto the front porch.

"I'm here," I said.

There were four wolf shifters from the other pack standing in front of the house, all males. I don't know why that was a shock to me, but it was. I'd been expecting Elle, the pack matriarch, and had been hoping for Kayla or Melissa, young females I'd played with last time we'd gone to visit. Instead, James stood there, looking exactly as I remembered him, big and strong and tanned and mostly unsmiling, and he'd brought with him his second, Matt, who *was* smiling at me, but he was doing it in a way that was not at all reassuring, bright blue eyes clearly looking me up and down despite the fact I'd done my best to hide the goods. Behind them were younger males whose faces I vaguely recognized, though they'd done a lot of growing up since I last saw them. Their names escaped me, but their dominance didn't, they were practically swelling with testosterone, so much so James looked back and snapped something at them.

Yeah, I was guessing this was their first time going onto another pack's land since adulthood, and they were bristling with aggression to hide their uncertainty.

Behind the four males was a new looking pick-up truck and slightly battered SUV. They'd come in two cars, probably expecting me to have a lot of shit to cart back with them.

Well, they'd got that right, at least. I planned to take every item of clothing, every pointless little trinket. I planned to be a massive pain in the ass so that, when my year was up, they would be only too happy to hand me back. It hadn't been Plan A, or even B or C, but it was the only thing I could come up with that might get me out of this—and stop Da from trying it again. I was braced for a long, unpleasant year, but I couldn't say I didn't have experience at being an asshole.

James wolf-whistled at me, following it up with a wink. "Well, look at you. You're all grown up! Come give me a hug, sweetheart."

I didn't want to. Shifters were tactile creatures and we hugged a lot. Like, a lot a lot. I almost raised a small smile thinking about how unnerved Kevin had been by that, how he'd stood stiff as a board the first time I'd spontaneously hugged him. And the time after that. He'd got over it eventually, I mused, or at least had just come to terms with how important it was to me and resigned himself to enduring it. But I did not want to hug James.

I didn't have any good reason not to though, and what, was I going to go a whole year without touch? I didn't think I could handle that, and the wolf inside me most definitely couldn't. She needed that visceral connection. Taking a deep breath and trying to hide my trepidation—easier said than done when your scent changes with every minute swell of emotion and shifters have super sensitive noses—I moved off the porch and covered the short space of gravelled driveway between us. I didn't have to do anything other than walk within arm's reach. As soon as I was within his personal circle, he reached out and snagged me, pulling me into his body and encircling me with arms that were warm but also utterly restraining.

Don't panic, I told my wolf. *We're safe.*

Da was right there, and James wasn't a bad man. For all Da could be overbearing and immovable, he was a good father, and he wouldn't be sending me away with someone he didn't have complete trust in. My wolf didn't care about that, though. She felt the tightness of the hold and worse, the heavy, oily feel of his dominance as he pressed it down on me. Da did that sometimes, he couldn't help it. But whereas that was comforting and reassuring, this was foreign and unwelcome. *Not my alpha!* The thought screamed loud in my head, coming from the both of us.

There was no hiding my reaction, though I tried to minimize it, staying still and quiet in his embrace, keeping my breathing even despite the fact I wanted to scream and struggle.

"You're a skittish one, aren't you?" James murmured, his mouth at my ear and his voice low enough that the sound wouldn't even travel as far as his second, Matt, standing right next to us. "I don't remember you being a shy girl."

I wasn't. No one who knew me at all would say I was shy. I was out-going, mischievous, strident. A brat, was the phrase used most often. Right now, all those parts of me were pulled tight into my core, like a fish hiding on the seabed, watchful and wary, as the much larger predator swam by overhead.

This predator wasn't going to drift off into the murky gloom, though. He'd already ensnared his prey.

"I was a precocious child," I replied. I dared to dart a glance up at his face, saw he was looking back down at me, his focus absolute. "Or so my mother tells me."

He laughed, squeezing me tighter, then let me go, resting a hand on the nape of my neck so I wouldn't go too far.

"You've all grown up now, though." Appreciation in his tone. I guessed the sweatshirt was a bust.

"That's not the general consensus if you ask around," I replied wryly.

A round of titters, from his pack and mine, then Mom stepped forward, no doubt mindful of what else I might say and not wanting James and his pack to drive off before she could get the suitcases in the car.

"Why don't you come in," she said. "We'll get you fed, and then we've organized one of the guest cabins for you. You can relax."

"I don't know that relaxing is on the cards," James said, letting go of me finally and taking a step toward Mom. "It was a long drive, cooped up in the truck."

"A run, then," Da suggested. "Janna can show you pack lands, point out the boundaries." A short pause. "It would be best to stick to them while you're here, unless you're accompanied. There's a strong vampire presence in the city. I've an understanding with the master, Hunter, but I won't lie, there have been tensions. Best you're with a pack member should you come across them."

"They've been here before," I said, trying to keep the mulishness out of my tone. "They know the boundaries. They don't need me to show them."

"Well, you can just entertain them with your sunny personality, then," Da replied. His tone brooked no argument.

Great. He was, literally, throwing me to the wolves, then.

"Food first," Mom said, taking James' arm and leading him inside. His packmates followed, one of the two I didn't know deliberately brushing against me as he passed, sniffing deeply. Ew. I gave him my best glower and saw him pause, aggression flaring as he registered my lack of submission or respect. I saw him make the decision to change that just as a low growl rumbled through the air around us. Da, putting his two cents in.

The shifter smirked at me, the knowledge that Da likely wouldn't be around next time clear in his eyes, then went in after his alpha.

"I'm not mating that one," I told Da, not caring that my voice was loud enough to carry.

He gave me an indulgent smile and tugged me into a hug of his own, his stubble catching in my hair as he rubbed his jaw against the top of my head.

"I told you, I'm not sending you away to find a mate."

Right.

"Mom is."

"Your mother only wants to see you settled. She wants the best for you, we both do."

"I want to stay here," I said, my head tucked into his chest and my voice small and childlike.

"I know you do," he told me, thumb rubbing soothing circles into my shoulder. "But I've made up my mind." He dropped a kiss on my temple. "Come inside and eat, Janna."

"I'm not hungry." I wanted to go to my treehouse and sulk. Though, actually, I didn't want to be there alone. But I couldn't invite Kevin over, not now.

Da squeezed me tight. "Fine, suit yourself. But you are going on a run with them, angel. If you try to sneak off to get out of it, I'll find you, I'll bring you back and I'll punish you. In front of everyone."

I winced, my head down so Da wouldn't see. Last time I'd pushed him too far he'd put me over his knee—*over his knee!*—and spanked me in front of everyone. That had been before I'd reached maturity, and it was almost unheard of to treat an adult female in the pack that way. But I wasn't just an adult female, I was his daughter, and I absolutely wouldn't put it past him.

"I'll be here," I intoned woodenly.

"Good girl." Another swift kiss and then he was gone too, leaving me alone in the driveway. I sniffed and wrapped my arms around myself, feeling cold and alone. I was cutting my nose off to spite my face, refusing to go inside for food, but the way my stomach was twisting with misery, I didn't think I could force down a mouthful anyway.

It was both forever and no time at all when they emerged from the pack house, bringing with them the scent of steak and the buttery garlic aroma of Mom's epic mashed potatoes. My insides grumbled—contrary bitch—but it was too late now. I unfolded from where I'd been sitting on the bottom step, arms wrapped around my knees.

"Ready to go?" I asked James. "Or did you change your mind? Would you like to see the cabin instead?"

James raised an amused eyebrow. "Want to show me where I'll be sleeping, Janna?"

Uhm, no. That wasn't what I meant at all. My reaction must have been pretty clear on my face, because he laughed.

"We could use the exercise after the feast Fran laid on." A wink. "You can show me the cabin later."

Oh, that'd be a big no. "Mom likes to take guests on back," I said. "Then she can point out all the fancy frippery she bought to decorate it."

Da wouldn't let Mom put more than the most basic frills on the pack house, so she'd gone to town on the guest cabin.

"Shame," James said. The look he threw me said he knew what I was doing. I tried to give him my most winning smile back, what I managed was more of a guilty-looking grimace.

"I hear there's a run happening," a warm voice broke in. I turned with relief to see Kenny rounding the pack house. He was topless, with his hair a tousled mess on top of his head. He looked like he'd just rolled out of bed. When I caught the strong scent of his mate on him as he came closer, I realized that was exactly where he'd been.

"Janna is going to take us around the pack boundaries," James said. There was no invite for Kenny to join us.

Luckily for me, Kenny was Da's second, and he didn't need one.

"Terrific. I could do with some exercise." He came and stood shoulder to shoulder with me, arms folded across his chest. I could smell sweat as well as sex on him; he'd been exercising all damned afternoon, I reckoned.

There was a reason Kenny was my favorite pack member. He could have been rolling around in bed with his mate still. Instead, he was here, holding my hand on my first outing with my new pack. Making sure they behaved themselves. I felt my throat tighten and swallowed it back. Kenny knew, though. He swayed ever so slightly so that our shoulders bumped. Touch. Support. Love.

There was a stand-off for a quick moment as James debated objecting and just as quickly decided against it. He gave a carefree little shrug then tugged his shirt up and off.

"Let's get moving, then."

Right. I tried not to stare as we all divested ourselves of our clothes. If it had been my pack, it wouldn't really have even registered that we were naked, it was such a common occurrence. But this wasn't my pack, and no matter what Da said, I knew some of these shifters had ideas about mating me. Besides, they were damned well looking at me every chance they got.

Muscles, they all had muscles. And tanned skin. And scars. Hairy chests and lean hips, long lines. It was a veritable smorgasbord of deliciousness and I wasn't interested in any of it. I shucked my clothes as quickly as possible and dissolved into my wolf shape.

I was the only one who did.

The rest stood and gawped at me, Kenny still at my shoulder like a bodyguard. James ambled over, cock swinging right at eye height—and it was an impressive cock, to be fair—before crouching down right in front of me.

"I forgot what a pretty little wolf you are," he said, a hand sliding into my fur and gripping my ruff.

I gave the barest hint of a growl—pretty? little?—and he laughed and let go. He stood up only to shrink down again as the shifter inside overtook him. That was clearly the sign the rest of his pack had been waiting for, because they changed in tandem. A moment later, Kenny followed suit.

I led the run, deliberately choosing a route that would be harder for the bigger males to follow—pretty little wolf, indeed!—with tight curves and fallen trees, narrow gapes between rock formations. James kept up with me well, but I could hear pants and unhappy snarls from the rest. A time or two, I looked back and saw Kenny, shoulder bumping one of the younger males right off the track, his tongue lolling mischievously and his eyes alight with humor. I laughed then, the sound coming out a choked cough, and upped the ante, trying to see if I could lose James.

I couldn't. What he lacked in manoeuvrability and agility, he made up for with speed and brute strength, ramming obstacles out of his path. He was a four-legged bulldozer and no matter how hard I tried, I couldn't shake him. I actually started to enjoy the challenge, delighting in the small moments where I'd lose him for a handful of paces. He always caught back up, though, and fast.

By the time I flew back out onto the road and started heading up the driveway, we'd left the rest of them far behind. I was panting hard when I stopped at the neatly folded pile of clothes I'd left in a tangle on the bottom step. Mom had been out, collecting everyone's belongings and laying them out for us. And oh look, she'd placed mine right next to James'.

I changed back into my human shape, a sheen of sweat on my skin and goose bumps breaking out in the cool evening air, and then darted into my clothes.

"That was fun," James commented as he dressed, much more casually.

"It was," I agreed.

Much to my surprise, I had enjoyed myself. When the rest turned up a minute or so later and Mom emerged to take them back to the guest quarters, I even managed a genuine smile of goodbye. Maybe it would be all right. Maybe I could earn James' respect and we could be friends. Maybe I might even like it there, a fresh start, like Da said.

My optimism lasted all the way through dinner, which was a quiet affair with just me, Mom and Da. Mom had made three enormous cherry pies while we'd been out running, and after we demolished one of them—it was hungry work, changing—she instructed me to head on back to the guest cabin with the other two. I went without complaint and without trepidation, almost looking forward to seeing James again.

Right up until I was a hundred feet from the front door.

"So, what do you think?" The low voice of Matt stopped me in my tracks. They were outside, sitting in the sky chairs in the little porch. The wind was helpful, carrying his voice to me, and keeping my scent from them.

I could have, maybe should have, kept on going, but something made me pause. I had the feeling they were talking about me, and I wanted to hear what James had to say. I wanted...all right, I wanted to hear some praise. That he was impressed with me, that I'd done well today, pushed him on the run.

That wasn't what I got.

"I think she's a hot little piece. She'll make a good mate once she learns to curb that tongue."

"Andrew likes her." Andrew was one of the other wolves, I'd discovered. Andrew and Craig. I had known them in childhood, their names bringing back memories of gangly boys. They weren't boys anymore.

"Andrew might get a bite. Once she's good and tamed. And once I've whelped a couple on her."

I...what? Tamed? Whelped? My numb fingers dropped the pies to the floor. They landed with a soft splat. If James or Matt had been listening, they'd have heard the sound. They weren't listening though, they were too busy discussing how they were going to bring me to heel.

"Logan will expect to be told that you want to mate her," Matt was saying. "He'll expect you to ask for his blessing."

James snorted. "Once she's on my land, adopted into my pack, she's mine to control. Logan understands how these things go. How do you think he landed Fran? It wasn't with roses and a grovelling request to her father." I frowned, perturbed by that. Da had told me himself that he'd stolen Mom, but he'd done it with a wink and a smile that had made me think they'd been young lovers who'd run away together, and Mom, Mom had never said anything. James made it sound...sinister. I wanted to reject his words, but it was just him and his second in this conversation, as far as he knew. Why would he lie?

"Things have changed since then," Matt hedged.

I could hear the smile in James' voice as he spoke. "Not that much. Janna's going to be my mate, and she'll be a good, obedient little bitch. Just you wait and see."

I didn't wait to hear Matt's response, if he had one. I backed slowly away, barely breathing, terrified now that I'd give myself away and draw their attention.

Be his mate? After listening to that? Not a fucking chance.

Chapter Four

"What is it, Kevin?"

Kevin stood in front of Evangeline's desk, watching as her fingers danced across the keyboard. She was beautiful, even for a vampire, with her fine features and her tall lithe figure, but she was also incredibly powerful. Now that Julian was gone, she was the clear second in the seethe. Not only was she stronger than anyone else, and by a margin, but she was also Master's favorite.

And since the scene in the basement, she'd adopted Kevin as her secretary-cum-dogsbody. That had rocketed him up the hierarchy in the seethe, made him privy to all sorts of interesting things he shouldn't be important enough to know, but it had also painted a big target on his back.

"I—" he stared at the top of Evangeline's head as she bent to read something on the screen, his brow furrowing in confusion. "You called me here, My Lady."

"Yes, I did." She flicked her eyes up to his and he forced himself not to step back. She could squash him like a bug under her foot, without thought, but unlike the rest of the seethe, she'd never been cruel.

Of course, that could be a cruelty of its own, making him think he had an ally and then crushing him, but he doubted it. Unlike most vampires, Evangeline had integrity and honor. She still had kindness in her.

"Well then, I…uh. I don't understand."

"What's wrong with you?" she demanded. "You've been moping about like a discarded puppy for the last few days." Ouch. It was hard to deny, though. "So, what is it? What's wrong?"

There was no way he could tell Evangeline the truth, but he also wouldn't—and very probably couldn't—lie to her.

"Would you teach me how to defend myself?" he asked.

It obviously wasn't what Evangeline had been expecting, because she blinked, surprised, before her eyes narrowed.

"Who has been bothering you in the seethe?"

He did take a step back that time, he couldn't help it. Her words rang with power. She was angry, he realized. Likely not at the thought that anyone was bothering him, but that they would do so knowing he was hers. Her runner, her lackey, hers to kick if she felt like it—no one else's.

"All of them?" Kevin offered with a small smile. "It's not…it's not as bad as it was, but I can feel it. A tension. They know I don't deserve my position with you."

"Don't you?" Evangeline asked, one eyebrow lifting delicately. "You executed one of the most powerful members of the seethe. Anyone else will think twice before challenging you."

Yes, Kevin had a feeling that was the only reason no one had tried to come at him. Yet. Although…

"I snuck up behind him and cut off his head when he wasn't looking," he reminded her.

Evangeline smiled, a cat's smile. "They don't have to know that."

Kevin just stared at her, no mean feat when it involved holding eye-contact. Eventually she rolled her eyes and sighed.

"All right, we'll look at some training for you. You'll feel better if you've got some moves you can pull out of the bag and—" she paused, frowning, the expression causing the tiniest line to appear on her brow. "Why would the alpha of the shifter pack want to see you?"

Ice drenched Kevin's veins.

"What?"

"The alpha of the shifter pack. He's here and he's furious, he's demanding to see you. Master is not happy." Her eyes lost the faraway look they'd had as she listened to Master, and the stare she fixed on Kevin was laser focused. "What have you done?"

"The shifter wolf we found in the cage in Julian's basement?" he said immediately, not even contemplating trying to hide the truth this time. "We're friends."

"Just friends?" Evangeline asked sharply.

"Just friends."

"All right." She nodded thoughtfully. "Why would he be here?"

"I have no idea," Kevin told her honestly. "Unless he found out about our friendship."

"I don't think it's that," Evangeline murmured, her expression distracted in a way that made Kevin think she was listening to Master again. She stood abruptly, her chair making a sharp screech against hardwood floor. "Let's go and find out."

The shifter alpha was pacing. As they descended the stairs toward the spacious foyer, Kevin took in the scene over Evangeline's shoulder. Master was standing in front of the ornate grandfather clock, arms folded and expression serene as he watched the alpha—Logan, Kevin reminded himself—wear out a track in his expensive slate floor. Several other vampires were watching from discreet vantage points on stairs or in shadowed alcoves, and no wonder; it was quite the spectacle. He radiated aggression, his hair dishevelled and jacket buttoned wrongly. His eyes were glowing, and as he paced, he kept flexing his jaw, bringing deadly-looking teeth flashing into view.

Master spotted Evangeline descending, gifting her with an indulgent smile designed to tell the alpha that he wasn't flustered at all by the shifter's display. When his eyes flicked to Kevin, a pace behind, Kevin was hit with a blast of displeasure that almost sent him to his knees. He kept his feet just, and made to present himself before Master, ready to genuflect or, perhaps more wisely, fling himself at Master's feet and beg forgiveness—even though he wasn't quite sure what he would be asking forgiveness for.

He didn't make it there. Logan caught sight of him as he reached the bottom of the steps and the next moment the alpha was up in his face, clawed hands tearing shreds into his T-shirt and the skin of his shoulders' underneath.

"Where is she?" he demanded.

He could only be talking about one person.

"Janna?" Kevin asked. This time the ice in his veins froze and he felt as if he couldn't move. "What's happened?"

"I know about you two," Logan went on, ignoring Kevin's question. "I know all about your little secret meet ups. Where is she? If you think you can hide her from me, you're wrong. I'll tear this place apart looking for her if I have to."

Kevin opened his mouth, but nothing came out. Instead, someone quietly cleared their throat behind Logan. Master.

"Let him go." It was said calmly, reasonably, but with command. Kevin registered the fire in Logan's eyes and thought he was going to ignore Master, the alpha looked like he wanted to rip Kevin to shreds with his bare hands, see if he was hiding her somewhere in his vital organs, but eventually, after a long moment, he released Kevin, shoving at him so Kevin toppled back and landed heavily on the stairs, his elbows and back making painful contact with the corners of the treads.

He picked himself up and tried to look unaffected, but Logan had rattled his bones with that one, casual push.

"Kevin, come to me." It was an order, one Kevin was helpless to disobey. Not that he wanted to, with a rabid shifter alpha in the entranceway. Between one blink and the next, he stood in front of Master, head bent respectfully. "Look at me." Invisible strings jerked his head up. "Do you know where the girl is?"

"No, Master."

"He's lying," Logan growled.

"He cannot lie to me," Master replied mildly. "Kevin, do you know where she might have gone?"

Kevin dared to flick his gaze to Logan. "I might if I knew what happened."

"Nothing happened!" The alpha's hands balled into fists. "She went out on a simple errand and never came back. We have scoured the pack lands and she's not there. She didn't take a vehicle, and her scent trail disappears at the roadside."

"Kevin?" Master prompted. He could feel the disquiet of Kevin's thoughts.

"You invited another pack down to foster her," Kevin said, unable to keep the accusation out of his voice. "You were sending her away."

If Logan was surprised that Kevin knew that, he didn't show it. Master didn't show any reaction either, but his voice whispered through Kevin's mind. *We will discuss later why you knew a second pack was coming to the area and didn't inform me.*

Shit.

"It was the best thing for her!" Logan argued. "And she agreed to it!"

"Clearly not," Kevin bit back.

He expected a wave of aggression in response, but instead the alpha seemed to deflate. The eyes, so full of rage and fire a moment ago, shone with desperation.

"Can you think of anywhere she might have gone?"

Kevin could do one better than that. "I'll help you find her," he swore. "On the condition that you agree she doesn't have to go anywhere she doesn't want to."

He realized what he'd done a moment after he said it, turning back to Master nervously.

"Oh, don't worry about me," Master said caustically. "I'm just in charge of this seethe."

"I—" Kevin didn't even get out the rest of his plea for forgiveness. Master dismissed him with his eyes, looking over his head.

"If we help you in this task, it will resolve the tensions between us?"

"If you find my daughter, there will be no more hostility between us," Logan swore.

"Very well, then. I give you Kevin to assist you."

"Thank you, Master," Kevin breathed.

"Hmmm." Fuck. There was likely to be an exceedingly unpleasant conversation with Master in Kevin's future, but right now all he cared about was finding Janna.

"Let's go," he said, but Logan was already on the move. Kevin followed him out the door and down the steps to where a car was waiting. There was another shifter leaning on the bonnet, looking just as twitchy as his alpha.

When he caught site of Kevin, however, that agitation morphed into surprise and then anger. "You!"

Kevin stopped dead, not wanting to get any closer to the finger now pointing in his direction like a gun. He glanced at the face of the shifter attached to the finger and tried to decide if he'd ever met him before. Maybe?

"What is it?" Logan asked impatiently.

"Him! That's the vampire who was stealing from the construction site! He's the one I fought over the damned copper coil, the one that flung me into the traffic and left me for dead."

The memory came back as the shifter was speaking. Kevin could see it happening behind his eyes, feel the panic as the shifter held on for grim death.

"I'm sorry," he said. The same thing he'd said back then.

"Sorry? You—"

"Can it," Logan snapped. "He's going to help us find Janna, and you ended up with a mate because of that night. Now get in the car, Gregor."

Gregor looked unimpressed, glaring daggers at Kevin, but he folded himself into the passenger seat as Logan took the wheel, leaving Kevin to crawl into the back. Yeah, no thanks.

"Have you got any ideas?" Logan demanded, hand on the driver's side door, ready to slam it closed.

"Yes. Pack lands first."

Logan cursed. "I told you, we went over the pack lands with a toothcomb. She's not there."

"Just trust me," Kevin urged. "You know the old treehouse—"

"She hasn't used that for years!" Gregor growled from within the car. Logan silenced him with a wave of his hand, eyes sharp on Kevin.

"That's where you two were meeting, is it?"

"Yes," Kevin replied, no hint of apology in his tone. "I'll meet you there."

Not waiting for the alpha's agreement, he dematerialized.

Someone had been in here, he realized, as soon as the air in the treehouse settled around him. There was a scent he didn't recognize. Someone had checked the space, but they'd only been looking for Janna, nothing else.

If she'd had the presence of mind to leave him any kind of clue, it would be here. Although…she hadn't called or messaged him. Kevin didn't want to admit it, even to himself, but that hurt. A lot.

Of course, a cell phone was trackable, if you knew how, so maybe she hadn't taken it with her.

The first place he went to was the corner by the pallet, where she left her spare pile of clothes. All gone, the little wooden box empty bar a scrap of tissue that must have fallen out of a pocket. So, she'd at least had the presence of mind to take some things with her, hadn't bolted in a blind panic, that was reassuring. He checked the shelves, noting that she'd also emptied out the little Tupperware box where she kept snacks, although admittedly he couldn't be sure that had happened tonight. The small stack of bills she'd started stashing away for the motorcycle her mother didn't want her to have was also gone.

But there was no note—to Kevin or anyone else—and there was no clue where she might have gone.

"I told you," an unhappy voice ground out behind him, "She's not here. You think we wouldn't check this place?"

He turned to see the shifter he'd fought with at the construction site, Gregor, glowering at him from the entrance to the treehouse. He had a sheen of sweat on his face; he'd obviously run, and hard, from the car and through the pack lands, to get here this fast, and he didn't look happy about that fact.

Well, Kevin hadn't been going to waste time driving when he could travel in the blink of an eye; Janna was missing.

"She *was* here, though," Kevin told him, the same edge in his voice. "Her spare clothes are gone, and so is the food and money she kept in here."

"Why was she keeping food and money here?" Gregor asked, scowling.

"Snacks because she was always hungry." Kevin's dry reply was met with a huff of reluctant amusement. "And money because she was saving up for something her mother didn't approve of."

"What?" Gregor asked.

Kevin pressed his mouth together. He wasn't going to give away Janna's secrets unless he had to.

"You seem to know her pretty well," Gregor commented, eyes narrowing in suspicion.

"She's my friend," Kevin replied with absolute sincerity.

They locked eyes and Kevin felt Gregor's dislike and mistrust, but he could also sense the beginnings of respect for the fact that Kevin would walk—well, materialize—without hesitation into the heart of the wolves' den like this.

In all honesty, Kevin would walk through fire for Janna. If she really needed it, he'd walk into the sun.

"Any idea where she'd go, then?"

To me, Kevin thought. But she hadn't, had she?

She'd said before that there was no point running, that her family would find her. And she'd left with almost nothing. She wasn't stupid, but she was obviously desperate. It was a knife in Kevin's gut that she hadn't felt she could turn to him.

Out of ideas, he grabbed out his phone and opened up the local news. It was a one in a million chance, but maybe someone had noticed a wolf roaming the suburbs or—

"I've found her."

"What?"

Kevin didn't respond immediately, his eyes raking over the scant information in the news report.

"Vampire! What do you mean, you've found her?" Instead of replying, he crossed the space of the treehouse, putting himself uncomfortably within mauling range, and showed his screen to the shifter. "Trucker attacked by young woman and left for dead," he read. Gregor frowned. "You think that's her."

"I do," Kevin said. There was a little more detail in the story, a description that fit Janna, a location that wasn't all that far away, but it was a slim lead at best. Still, though, Kevin had a feeling, a sense of rightness, and he couldn't ignore it. "I'll meet you there."

"No, you won't. We can go toge—"

He dematerialized before Gregor could finish his sentence. Let the shifter know what it was to be slow for once. He needed to get to Janna.

Chapter Five

There was too much salt on my fries. I stared down at them, limp and soggy on my plate, and wondered if I could manage to choke them down if I smothered them with enough ketchup. Doubtful. I was going to have to pay for them, though, so I didn't want to waste them. It wasn't like this place was an expensive restaurant—they wouldn't have served me over-salted fries if it was—but I was mindful of the limited stash of dollars in my pocket. I needed to use them sparingly if they were going to last.

I snorted—who was I kidding? There was no way this idiotic attempt was going to last long enough for me to run out of money. The sound drew the attention of the waitress wiping down the rows of empty tables. It was late and there were hardly any other customers, just an old couple and a few solitary men who I presumed owned the big rigs parked outside. She gave me a look, one that was part curious, part *I know your story*.

I was willing to bet all of the money in my pocket, and my gross fries, that she didn't.

Well, you see, my dad wants to ship me off to live with another pack of wolves. Not *wolves* wolves, the shifter kind. That's right, lady. Men that can turn into wolves. Anyway, I was going to go, but then I heard them talking about me, and the leader of the group thinks I'm going to be his little lap dog. Fuck him and have his offspring and then sit about like a good, obedient little mate. Can you believe that?

Looking around at the dingy interior of the diner, where desperation seemed to have soaked into the very walls, I thought it might not actually be the craziest story she'd ever heard. I stuffed a fry into my mouth. Yeah, gross.

"You okay, hon?" she asked me, pausing in her cleaning.

"Me? Sure." I gave her my best attempt at a reassuring smile.

"You here all by yourself? It's late."

"I'm just passing through," I said. "I'm driving up to see my aunt, thought I should refuel."

I waved a soggy fry at her to emphasize my point, hoping she wouldn't probe any further because I was very unpractised at lying. There was no point trying usually, shifter noses being what they were. That, and I had a terrible poker face. I tried my best to look innocent and genuine. I don't think I fooled the waitress, but she apparently didn't care enough to probe any further.

"Just you be careful then, lovely. We can get some rough types in here. You watch yourself when you head back out into the carpark."

I tried not to laugh. Any of those rough types would get quite the surprise if they tried anything with me. It was nice of the woman to warn me, though.

"Thank you, I will."

She nodded and disappeared into the kitchen with her washcloth, leaving me alone with the dregs of my meal. I'd eaten enough—more than enough, I could feel the grease and salt seeping into my body—but I wasn't ready to leave quite yet.

Because I had no idea where I was going to go.

There was no aunt to take me in. No other pack I could shelter with. I'd run in a panic, taking advantage of a moment alone and pausing only long enough to gather the most pathetic of provisions, and now that I'd stopped, it was sinking in just how stupid I'd been. I could keep running and wait for Da to catch up with me, or I could return home with my tail between my legs and take the dressing down of a lifetime.

And then, after the dust settled, I'd be sent off to live with my new foster pack.

Tears stung my eyes as frustration and helplessness overwhelmed me. I didn't even have my phone. It had been in my room on charge, because Da didn't allow cell phones at the dinner table, and I hadn't wanted to risk going back to the pack house, worried I might not be able to sneak back out again, especially as panicked and agitated as I'd been. Any shifter within fifty feet would have smelled it.

If I had my phone, I would have called Kevin.

I should have gone to him in the first place. I'd wanted to. But as comfortable as I was with him, I couldn't bring myself to go to that creepy mansion that was crawling with vampires. Now, sitting alone in a nasty diner attached to a run-down truck stop, I was regretting that cowardice. Hard. Maybe it wasn't too late, though.

I checked my watch and winced. It was after 3am. Dawn was a little later this time of year, but I'd run to the diner on foot. If I wanted to try and get to the seethe mansion before Kevin...did the sleeping vampire thing...I'd have to move.

I didn't know what Kevin could do to help me, but I knew he'd try his best. Maybe I'd end up going home eventually, but not right now. Not yet.

I shoved my plate away and slid out of my booth, leaving enough money on the table to cover the meal and a small tip. Gathering my tired muscles, I readied myself for a change and a long, tiring run. It only dimly registered that one of the truckers got up to leave at the same time as me, following me out the door.

The dark was thick in the car park. There were no streetlights out on the highway and the truck stop owner had only stuck floodlights up on the building. It wasn't a problem for me—I could see perfectly in the dark—but I thought the trucker might have a trickier time making it to his vehicle without breaking an ankle in one of the myriad potholes strewn across the parking area.

It should never have happened. I was thinking about finding a spot to change, mapping out a route to the seethe mansion in my head. I was thinking about what I was going to say to Kevin when I got there, and what the master of the seethe might have to say about my sudden appearance. Thoughts upon thoughts whirling round my head. Even so, I should have picked up the sound of the footsteps stalking me, should have caught the beer stink on his breath long before I felt his meaty hand wrapping round my arm.

"Hey," he wheezed, tugging me round the face him, "where are you off to?"

I wasn't afraid, though I did object to the waft of fetid breath he blew in my face.

"Home," I told him. "It's late."

"It is late," he agreed. "It's bedtime. Want to join me?"

"No," I said firmly. "Let go."

I tugged at my arm, but he had a firm grip and I didn't manage to dislodge him. I didn't tangle with humans often and he was stronger than I imagined. He had a large belly protruding over his jeans, but the muscles in his arms were thick, tattoos peeking out beneath the sleeve of his T-shirt.

"Don't be like that," he crooned. "You and I could have a good time."

"I said no," I replied, punctuating my words with another yank, but his grip only tightened, fingers bruising me.

"Shhh," he murmured, "just shhh. You'll enjoy it." He pulled at me, until I fell against his body, and then suddenly those arms were wrapped tight around me and there was a hot mouth on my neck, licking at me.

I'd held back before—because the number one rule about being around humans was never appear anything other than human—but trapped in his embrace, I forgot all about that. My wolf was snapping and snarling inside me, demanding to be let out. I managed to avoid changing, but I couldn't prevent the burst of strength that erupted out of me.

The next thing I knew, I was free and the man was on the floor several feet away, staring at me and clutching his arm. To say it was broken was the understatement of the century. I'd snapped both the radius and humerus, possibly in more than one place. He opened and closed his mouth a couple of times, obviously speechless, but that didn't last long.

"What the hell are you?" he howled. "Fucking freak! You've destroyed my damn arm. You're not normal! What are you?"

"I—" I gaped at him, horror struck. I'd never hurt anyone before, not like this, and the fact that he deserved it didn't lessen the awfulness of what I'd done. "I'm sorry," I stuttered.

"Sorry? Sorry!" He spat at me. "Freak. Freak!"

"Shhh!" I flapped my hands at him uselessly, too agitated to get any closer but nervous of the noise he was making. If he kept this up—

"What's going on? Hal, what's happened? Are you all right?" Too late. The waitress from the diner was in the doorway, peering out into the dark, another trucker at her back. "Hal?"

"Her!" Hal spat, pointing a finger at me. "There's something wrong with her! Was only trying to be friendly and the bitch broke my arm. She's one of them things, I tell you! Mitch, get the shotgun. The special one. It's in my cab."

"What?" The waitress took a step out into the parking area, the trucker, Mitch, I presumed, hot on her heels, and I panicked.

I turned and shot across the car park, bolting across the road and into the thick copse of trees on the other side. I heard shouts of "Hey!" and "Stop!" behind me, but I ignored them, pushing on harder. My breath came in gasps that were really little sobs.

How the hell did that happen?

How did I become the bad guy when he'd been all over me, ignoring me when I said no, touching me without permission? I could still feel his saliva on my skin, and I swiped at my neck, rubbing it away with the sleeve of my sweatshirt as I ran. They'd looked at me like I was a monster, and oh God, if they called the police there might be CCTV in the diner, footage of my face.

The car park was too dark for any security cameras to have caught what had happened, but I'd shattered the trucker's arm and there wasn't a mark on me. His word against mine.

And what did he mean, I was one of them things?

Shit, shit, *shit*.

It wasn't fair. None of it. Everyone in the pack getting on at me because I wasn't like them, Da trying to send me away with a bunch of wolves who wanted to do the same thing, put me in a box, and fuck me too. And everyone staring at me with horror when it had been the loathsome Hal putting his hands all over me. *None of it!*

I was crying in earnest now, tears blinding me to branches that whipped in my face and thorny bushes that tore at my clothes. Even nature was against me! I blundered on, unable to see where I was going, my only thought was of getting away—from everything.

When the ground gave way beneath my feet, at first I didn't understand what was happening. My arms windmilled as I dropped, fingers scrabbling at dirt walls that tore my nails. I opened my mouth to let out a panicked scream, but I hit the ground, hard, before it could come out of my throat. I did scream then, because pain shot up my leg. What had happened? The fall shouldn't have been enough to break bones, not for a shifter. The hole I'd fallen into wasn't deep, but it was enough to dim the light so that even I struggled to see. I reached down and felt around my ankle, felt the hot wetness of my own blood, and the coldness of metal.

A bear trap. It had sprung when I'd landed on it and fastened its teeth deep into my lower leg.

Bastard. Tears sprung in my eyes, my throat tight with emotion, as I felt around the trap, slicing my fingertips on the razor-sharp teeth. Everything that had happened tonight, and now this!

I tried to pull the sides of the trap apart, but it was difficult with everything slick with my own blood. I felt strangely sluggish too, and the wound was burning wicked hot. I tried to change; it wouldn't help me get out of the trap, I needed fingers and opposable thumbs for that, but it was an instinctive reaction to being hurt and ensnared.

I couldn't.

Panic set in then, an adrenaline rush of fear as I realized why I didn't have the strength to pull the teeth apart, why my leg was throbbing with devil's fire. Silver. The trap was made of silver.

And who would do that to trap a bear?

No one.

If you wanted to trap a shifter, though, it would be very effective. A pit wouldn't hold us, and an ordinary bear trap would rend flesh and skin, but then all you'd be dealing with was a very pissed off shifter. Not smart. Add in silver, though? It incapacitated us, weakened us. I looked up at the top of the hole, not ten feet above my head, and knew I couldn't make it. Not like this.

I was as useless as a rabbit, well and truly caught in a snare.

Maybe Hal and Mitch and the waitress were combing the woods right now, "special" shotgun in hand—and I could guess what that meant now— and maybe they weren't. I wasn't sure it mattered either way, because I couldn't get out and no one who'd help me knew where I was. If I wasn't caught and shot, I'd just bleed out…or starve.

Bubbling, I tried once more to free myself, but my efforts were more pathetic than before, the poisoning effects of the silver stealing into every muscle and robbing them of strength. When my fingers slid off the slick edge one more time, I gave up. Curling into a ball, my back tight against the cold, unyielding wall of the pit, I hugged my damaged leg into my body as best I could, and I cried.

Chapter Six

Kevin materialized several miles from the diner, emerging into existence in the middle of an industrial estate. It was the closest he could get—he couldn't materialize anywhere he hadn't been, he needed to be able to visualize the space—but it still left a long way to run.

Thankfully, vampires were fast.

He took off into the night, the heavy soles of his boots slapping down hard against the concrete. There wasn't much traffic on the road, but he made no effort to hide himself from the few vehicles that drove past. If they saw him at all, he'd be no more than a blur. By the time they blinked and looked twice, he'd be gone.

The diner was perched just beyond the edge of civilization, giving truckers and late-night travellers a place to stop and rest and refuel without having to navigate the tangled snarl of the city. It was grubby and run down, but apparently truckers weren't fussy because there were still a handful of big rigs parked in the dirt carpark. There was also an ambulance, lights flashing, and a police car parked by the front door.

Kevin slowed, taking in the scene. The front door of the diner had been propped open, allowing light to spill out and supplement the lights dotted haphazardly around the building. From what Kevin could see through the windows, there was no one taking advantage of the 24-hour hot meals advertised by the ugly red neon sign. Instead, everyone seemed to have gathered around the rear of the ambulance: two police officers, a woman wringing her hands on her apron who Kevin presumed was the waitress, and a middle-aged man in a stained chef's jacket. Shifting through the shadows, Kevin moved until he could see inside the ambulance itself, where a man was arguing belligerently with a paramedic, who was trying to splint a seriously mangled arm.

He didn't need vampire senses to hear what was said: everyone was shouting at the top of their voices.

"I tell you, I'm fine! I need to get out there!" The trucker struggled—and failed—to get his considerable weight up off the gurney with one hand.

"Hal, please. Listen to the medic!" That was from the waitress.

"Sir, you need to sit down and let the paramedic take care of you." Police officer number one.

"We've units on the way. They'll bring out the dogs and then we'll be able to find the person who attacked you." Police officer number two. "But you need to calm down."

"You don't understand, she's not just a girl!"

"Hal!" The waitress again, almost in tears.

The chef, Kevin noticed, was simply enjoying the show.

"Sir, if you don't calm down, I'll instruct the medic to sedate you." Police officer number one, his hand drifting down to rest on the weapon holstered at his side.

"I need to get out there! Mitch and Cole are all alone, they need back up!"

"Against one little girl?" Police officer number two's face screwed up in derision.

"You don't understand," Hal howled. "You don't understand what we're dealing with! She's not just a girl!"

Police officer number two looked to the medic. "Sedate him."

Kevin turned his back on them as Hal started to fight with renewed vigor, grunting and yelling into the night. Kevin didn't pay any attention to what he was saying, he'd heard enough.

Janna had been here. Not only did she fit the description—and not only was she very capable of turning the trucker's arm into a noodle—but he could smell her, just a vague hint of her scent on the air. He wasn't a tracker, not like the shifters, but if what Hal had said, two men had gone after her, so he wasn't going to wait for Gregor to show up with the cavalry. Not when she might need his help.

It was easy to find the point where Janna had crossed the road and disappeared into the trees and bushes on the other side. There were snapped branches and a single shining strand of her hair caught on a twig. Plus, there were her footprints, bold as day...and two other sets marring the mud around them. Kevin felt all of his senses sharpen, a lethal hunting instinct he'd never experienced before surge into life as he looked at those boot tracks. One of them overlapped Janna's much more delicate tread, squashing it into oblivion.

The ambulance's headlights shone right on the entry point, but nobody saw Kevin slip down the embankment. He knew how to use the shadows to his advantage, and he did it now without thought, his every thought focussed on finding Janna, eliminating the two men who were after her. Killing humans was strictly prohibited within the seethe, but Master had given Kevin to the pack to assist in this task. Had told him to help. Breaking the necks of the two men who would dare to threaten Janna was helping.

And Kevin would take any punishment that came his way in recompense, willingly.

It was a simple trail to follow, even for an inexperienced hunter. Janna had crashed through the undergrowth, leaving a clear path of footprints and more snapped and trampled plants. All the footprints were human, though, she hadn't stopped to change. Either she hadn't dared to take the time to do so, or she'd been too panicked, too upset, to think straight. Both of these possibilities reaffirmed Kevin's decision to murder the men after her.

With the dark no obstacle and her route through the trees so obvious, he was able to move fast. He hadn't gone all that far, perhaps a mile passing in the blink of an eye, before his sharp hearing caught the murmur of voices. Kevin crouched down, eyes flicking about the scene and taking everything in.

There were the two men. He couldn't see Janna, but they were standing over something, looking down. They both had shotguns in hand, held loosely but ready to aim at a moment's notice. Frustrated at his limited view, Kevin launched himself silently into a tree, climbing high up into the branches until he was able to discern what they were looking at. A pit, little more than a metre wide but obviously quite deep because Kevin couldn't see what was at the bottom of it.

He could guess, though. Janna.

They'd trapped her, and given that she wasn't screaming obscenities or snarling with all the fury of her wolf, he could only surmise that she couldn't. They'd incapacitated her somehow. Hurt her.

Blind fury overtook Kevin then. They had his...*his*—he knew the word hovering on the tip of his tongue, but he also knew it wasn't his to use— caught in a trap like an animal, and they'd wounded her so she couldn't fight back.

So, he would fight for her.

Running lithely along the tree branch, he dropped down onto the closest hunter. Strong hands went around the man's neck and he was dead before they both hit the floor. The second man had time to turn to Kevin, lift his shotgun to aim, shock and surprise writ all over his face, but his reactions were a mile too slow.

Kevin was on him before he could think to pull the trigger, fingers digging into the man's shoulders like claws, teeth latching onto his neck. He didn't drink—he wouldn't take any part of this man into himself—but used his razor-sharp incisors to tear at his flesh, ripping open the arteries in his neck, then thrusting the man away from him. He fell with his comrade, hands around his throat to try and stop the bleeding, his body twitching like a fish out of water.

Kevin didn't stand to witness his end. He spun away to stare down into the pit, and what he saw made his long silent heart squeeze hard in his chest. Janna lay at the bottom on a bed of dirt, curled up in a tight ball, her flesh pale. Blood saturated the jeans of one leg, the gleaming metal of a bear trap cutting deep into her ankle.

Her eyes were closed, her body lifeless.

A small step forward allowed Kevin to drop into the pit, land beside Janna's body. His hands reached out, searching for a pulse, feeling the unnatural coolness of her skin. She was alive, though. This close he could feel the sluggish beat of her heart, it's rhythm calling to him.

"You're safe," he murmured. "If you can hear me, Janna, you're safe. I'm here, and I'm going to get you out. Let's start with this, shall we?"

He reached for the bear trap, intending to rip the offending thing free from her leg, but pain shot up his fingertips as soon as he touched it, and he hissed. Silver. Fucking silver. The bane of vampires and shifters alike.

He was glad twice over that he'd killed the hunters, because they obviously had known what it was they were after. Master could not be angry at him for eliminating threats. He made a mental note to deal with the trucker back at the diner, too, the one who had frightened Janna so much she'd run right into this trap.

Bracing himself against the pain, Kevin reached for the teeth of the bear trap and slowly, gently, began easing it apart. It felt like acid against his fingertips, but he ignored the sensation. If it was hurting him, how much was it hurting Janna? Despite how careful he tried to be, he knew he was inflicting more agony on her. She roused and started trying to pull away, semi-conscious.

"No, Janna, hold still. It's all right, it's okay. I've got you. Just…let me get you free of this. It'll be better in a moment, I promise."

"Kevin?" The word was mumbled, almost indecipherable, but it was music to Kevin's ears.

"Yes, it's me. I found you. I'm going to take this off and then we'll get out of here, all right?"

It wasn't easy to get the trap off her, his every effort causing Janna to give little moans of pain, but finally Kevin was able to wrest it free. He tossed it aside and tore at the material of her jeans, baring her lower leg to assess the damage. Shit. Kevin hauled in a breath through his teeth. It was deep and she'd reacted to the silver, her leg all puffy and angry looking. It wasn't bleeding much, but judging by the stains saturating both legs of her jeans, she'd already gifted far too much blood to the trap's teeth. Bereft of anything to bind the wound with, Kevin ripped his shirt sleeve off at the shoulder and tied it tightly around Janna's ankle. It had to have hurt, he bound it tightly, but this time she didn't so much as stir.

He needed to get her out of here.

Sliding his arms beneath her shoulders and under her knees, he thanked the stars for his vampire strength as he vaulted out of the pit in one smooth movement. He looked for a moment at the bodies of the two truckers. What to do with them? He refused to put Janna down, even for a moment. He supposed he could kick them into the pit, but it wouldn't take more than a rudimentary search for them to be discovered. It was too much to hope that their injuries might be ascribed to the fall. Not when he'd ripped one of their throats out. Perhaps he could come back and—

Movement out of the corner of his eye had him whirling, Janna cradled tight against his chest. He tensed, preparing to run with her, but then he caught the hint of a scent on the breeze.

Shifter.

A moment later his eyes caught up and he saw Gregor emerging from the shadows, along with a couple of other wolves Kevin didn't recognize.

Gregor's stance was wary, his eyes flicking over the corpses on the ground the returning to Janna.

"You've got her?" His eyes narrowed. "She's hurt?"

He started moving forward with more purpose and Kevin drew back instinctively, his thoughts only on protecting his...Janna. Protecting Janna.

Gregor paused too, the tightness around his eyes revealing his caution as he took in Kevin's tight grip on Janna. He was worried, Kevin realized, afraid he might hurt her before the shifter could cross the space and take her from Kevin.

He would never hurt her.

And he wasn't letting them take her, either.

"She fell into the pit," Kevin said, working to form words against the snarls and hisses building up in his throat. "There was a bear trap at the bottom, waiting to be sprung. It was made of silver."

That stopped them in their tracks.

"Silver?" Gregor asked. "You're sure."

Kevin gave him a look and the shifter had the decency to look sheepish. When he turned his gaze to the dead truckers, however, his eyes were hard and angry.

"We need to clear the scene," he said. "Move the bodies, get rid of any evidence. We need to make sure there's not so much as a drop of Janna's blood left here for anyone to find."

"You do that," Kevin replied. "I'm taking Janna somewhere safe. She's freezing, and her ankle needs to be looked at."

"You're not taking her anywhere," Gregor growled. "She's coming back to the pack; we'll look after her."

"Like you looked after her this time?" Kevin shot back. One of the shifters in the background growled menacingly, but Kevin kept his eyes on Gregor. He was the real threat here.

"Vampire, hand her over."

"Your alpha asked for my help. I'm helping."

"You have helped, you found her. Now it's time to give her back."

Gregor took a step, his hand outstretched, and Kevin did something he'd never even attempted before, didn't know that he even could. He dematerialized, and he took Janna with him. All he heard was a harsh, grated out, "Motherfu—" from Gregor before the world went white.

When he rematerialized, it was in the foyer of the seethe mansion. It was blessedly empty, but it wouldn't stay that way for long. Sunset was less than an hour away, and the younger, weaker vampires—vampires like him—would already be feeling it's approaching presence, would be drawn home to seek shelter.

He should tell Master. He would, just as soon as he had Janna safely ensconced in his room. He headed beyond the main staircase to the back steps, but a low voice calling his name stopped him in his tracks.

"My Lady," he said quietly, respectfully. He turned around slowly and saw Evangeline standing in the middle of the foyer, eyeing him thoughtfully.

"That is the missing shifter girl," she said. "The one Julian kidnapped." A twitch of her lips. "She does have a penchant for trouble, doesn't she?"

Kevin bit back the angry retort that rose to his lips. Evangeline could annihilate him with minimal effort, but she was also his only ally in the seethe.

"How did you get her here?" she asked.

"I dematerialized with her," Kevin said.

That surprised her. He saw her eyes widen, then she took in the protective way he held Janna, the way he stood, half up on his toes, ready to run with her if he had to, and a small smile graced her face. "I see. It's like that."

"Like what?" Kevin asked, frowning, but Evangeline simply shook her head.

"Have you informed Master that she is here?"

"No."

"Does her alpha know that you have…taken her?"

"No."

Evangeline pursed her lips, but she looked more amused than anything else. "Go," she said. "I will inform the master. Get her safely into your room, and deal with her injury. I smell silver, and shifters are even more susceptible to that than vampires."

Unwilling to look a gift horse in the mouth, Kevin gave her a quick nod of gratitude. "I will," he said. "Thank you, My Lady."

Less than a minute later, he was in his room, lying her out on his bed. He stood back and looked at her. She was pale and filthy, evidence of her traumatic night written all over her skin, but she was here now, and Kevin would look after her.

With slightly trembling hands, he reached to undo the bandage on her ankle. The pull of the rising sun chose that moment to stop asking and start demanding, however. Against his will, Kevin's eyes closed.

Chapter Seven

My ankle hurt. That was the first thought that registered, before I'd even opened my eyes. Correction, it hurt *a lot*. I could feel it throbbing and burning, pulling me out of sleep. The second thing to register was that I was trapped. A cool steel band wrapped around my upper arms and chest, pinning me in position. That same coolness continued down the length of my back.

Kevin.

Not trapped, not pinned, I was being held.

I relaxed and opened my eyes, took in the lightless room. A human would have been totally blind and even I was having trouble seeing more than shadows. I could make out a vague lamp shape on the bedside table, which had to be aesthetic as I was pretty sure Kevin didn't need light to see. Well, I did. It took a moment—Kevin's arms resisted my efforts to shift them—but I managed to wriggle a hand free so that I could lean across and switch it on.

There, that was better.

Kevin didn't stir at all, but I'd expected that. He'd told me that vampires slept the sleep of, well, the dead. That once he dropped, he was out until the sun dipped below the horizon, no matter what happened. No matter if the building went on fire, or if a crazy vamp hunter snuck into his room and tried to stake him through the heart. Scary thought.

I took a moment to take in my surroundings. Da had been in the seethe mansion, had described it as gaudy and over the top. Luxurious to the point of bragging. Kevin's room was nothing like that. It was furnished plainly, with a desk and set of drawers along with the bed, which was a twin. One wall held shelves stacked neatly with books, and there were slightly dog-eared posters of bands who didn't look like they'd performed this century hung up on the walls. It was a bit of a sad room and it made my heart ache for him. I knew he had a tough time in the seethe, and it seemed like he didn't even have a haven to retreat to. My room in the pack house was…well, it was a mess. But it was my mess, filled with my things, and it was somewhere I could go and hide when the entire pack was getting on at me, which was often.

Feeling a rush of sympathy and tenderness toward Kevin, I twisted round until I could face him. His face in repose was utterly unremarkable. Pale, with pointed features, no one would call him handsome. But he was, when he made that impish little grin that made a dimple appear in his right cheek, or when his eyes darkened with anger or frustration. Would they do that when they were filled with passion? The thought made my pelvis give a little twitch.

He was tall enough, but he wasn't broad like the shifters I was used to hanging out with, his physique lithe and lean rather than packed with muscle, but that didn't mean he wasn't strong. Or brave. My memories of what had happened after I'd fallen into the damn pit last night were vague, but I remembered Kevin's scent in my nose, his soothing voice breaking through my pain-filled haze. I didn't remember getting here, had no recollection of travelling, but I wasn't unhappy with the situation. I would much rather be here with Kevin than at the pack house.

And I…really meant that.

My hand had been reaching out to stroke the line of Kevin's brow, but it halted as that thought took hold. I'd rather be here, with Kevin. I'd rather stay in a house full of *vampires* than go home and be among my fellow shifters, because Kevin was here.

I knew what that meant, but it took me another moment to find the courage to voice the word in my head. Mate. The wolf inside me had chosen Kevin as its mate. That shouldn't be possible—other shifters were mates, occasionally humans could be mates. Not vampires.

Da was going to lose his ever-loving mind.

I snorted, imagining his apoplectic face, but in reality, I wasn't really bothered. There would be nothing Da could do, or Mom, or any of them. With a true mating—and that was what this was—the shifter side made the choice and the human half simply had to go along with it. Sometimes that made for a disaster, but it almost always worked out in the end. This wasn't a disaster—I was delighted, a wide, goofy grin plastered all over my face.

I didn't have to worry about the other pack anymore, or deal with my mother's disappointment, Da's frustration.

Kevin was my mate. My best friend was going to be mine.

I wanted to wake him up, share the news with him. He'd be happy about it, I knew he would…well, once he got over the shock of the whole idea, but he remained immobile as stone, his chest still and breathless. I poked him in the side, impatient, but it had no impact. I got the same response when I reached up and blew into his ear. Sighing, I settled back down and closed my eyes, nestling against him. My ankle was still there, still pulsing pain at me, but it had dimmed in the face of my startling revelation. I had a mate. One who made me smile, who looked for ways to make me laugh. One who would walk into a shifter's den for me, face down my alpha Da. Yeah, I'd be proud to stand beside Kevin.

I didn't mean to fall asleep, but the next thing I knew, the comforting wall of marble that I'd been pressed against was sliding away. I gave a little mewl of unhappiness and tried to reach for it, but I was too slow; it slithered out of my grasp. By the time I'd blinked my eyes open, Kevin had shifted away from me as far as the bed would allow. I sat up and he tried to move a little further, almost toppling off the mattress.

"Are you all right?" I asked. I was fighting against the hurt I was starting to feel, my rational brain taking in the guilty look on his face and the way that, although he was as far from me as he could get, his body was turned toward me and leaning slightly in my direction.

"I'm sorry," He croaked.

"Sorry?"

"For…" He gestured toward the bed, the depressed covers where we'd been sleeping. "I didn't mean to do that. It must have happened when I fell into sleep. I hope—" he swallowed. "I hope I didn't hurt you. Or…it must have been uncomfortable, trapped lying there beside me all night. I, well, I'm sorry. I really am, so sorry. I—"

"Stop apologizing!" The words came more snappishly than I'd intended, whipping through the room, but they had the desired effect. Kevin's mouth was still open, but the words stopped. "My bad," I muttered, embarrassed. "But you say sorry too much."

Kevin gave me a small, sheepish smile. "Like this is news to you. *My apologies* and *I'm sorry* make up at least twenty-five per cent of my vocabulary."

"Well, you shouldn't," I told him.

"I'm almost bottom of the seethe," Kevin reminded me. "It behooves me to remain subservient and respectful."

"You know I don't know what behooves means," I told him, rolling my eyes.

"It means if I mind my p's and q's, I find myself upsetting fewer seethe members. And since almost everyone in the seethe is stronger and more powerful than me, that seems a smart move."

"Does that bother you?" I asked quietly.

"It is not fun, being near the bottom of the ladder," he admitted. "But I'm not sitting on the lowest rung anymore, which is something, and as time goes on, I'll gain strength. How much isn't clear, every vampire plateaus, but Master believes I have potential yet."

"I see."

"Anyway," he smiled at me almost bashfully. "I am sorry to have inadvertently kept you captive all night."

"I'm not," I said. "I liked it."

The bashfulness increased tenfold. If Kevin could have blushed, his face would have been on fire. I liked that.

"Your ankle," he said, a blatant change of subject. "Let me look at it."

My ankle. I winced as I extended it toward him, getting my first real look at my blood-stained and torn jeans, and what looked like the sleeve of one of Kevin's shirts employed as a temporary bandage. He was as gentle as possible, nimble fingers picking at the knot and then slowly unravelling the fabric, but my breathing sped up, my fingers digging into claws on the bed, as the clotted blood acted like glue, the wound pulling as Kevin eased the makeshift dressing free.

"Ow," I whined.

"I know," Kevin murmured. "I'm sorry. I tried to do as little damage as possible getting the trap off you, but I think you'd already tried yourself, and you must have been panicking. There's quite a lot of torn flesh, and it's going to heal human slow." I felt his fingers prodding and pressing. "No broken bones, though."

"I'll take your word for it," I said through gritted teeth, my gaze fixed on the top of his head as he bent over me. "It feels bad enough, I don't want to see."

"Wimp," he said, laughing softly. "Give me one moment."

Before I could reply, he'd poofed out of existence, leaving me alone in the room. In a vampire mansion where the seethe was just beginning to wake. I looked to the door, apprehension starting to grip my stomach and—

Kevin was back, sat on the bed right where he'd been.

I shrieked, then clapped my hand over my mouth.

"Sorry," I said. "You startled me."

"Clearly." He threw me an amused look. "You say sorry too much."

"I do not," I retorted. "I don't say sorry enough, ask my mother."

"No, thank you." He ripped open a sealed pouch and drew out what looked like a wet wipe. "This might sting," he said, "but I want to make sure there's no dirt left in there."

"All right," I said. I wasn't likely to get an infection, not with the shifter blood running through my veins, but it was sweet watching him fuss over me. Although…I started feeling a lot less warm and fuzzy toward him as the sting of the alcohol registered.

I hissed, the sound on the verge of turning into a growl, and he crooned sympathetically. "Almost done," he promised.

"I need to tell Da about the pit," I mused, trying to keep my thoughts away from the burning pain of my lower leg. "And Hal."

"Who?" Kevin's head jerked up.

"A trucker at the diner. He called me a freak, said I was *one of them things*." I used my fingers to create quotation marks. A horrible thought occurred to me as I reviewed the memory. "He wasn't alone, he had a friend. Mitch or something."

"He had two friends," Kevin corrected me. "At least, there were two of them standing there, over the pit they'd trapped you in."

"There were?" I asked, my voice dropping down into a whisper. "What happened to them?"

Kevin waited to answer until he'd finished cleaning my wound and was ready to rebind it.

"They're dead," he said quietly, nimble fingers wrapping the fresh bandage around my ankle. "I killed them."

"You did?" I asked, astonished.

When Kevin looked up at me, his eyes were molten fire. "They dug that pit, baited it with a silver trap, to catch a shifter. They were going to hurt you."

"You're my mate!"

Chapter Eight

Oops. I hadn't meant to blurt it out like that, but the dark intensity of Kevin's protectiveness of me just…melted my brain.

"I'm…what?" His brow crinkled in confusion.

"You're my mate," I repeated.

"Janna, I can't be your mate." The look he gave me was heart-breaking. "I'm a vampire. Vampires and shifters aren't compatible."

"Well, looks like someone forgot to tell my wolf that," I told him, "because she's picked you."

He finished tying the bandage, checked the tightness, then very deliberately pulled his hands back.

"Janna—"

"Don't tell me I don't know what I know," I said mulishly.

"How do you know?" he asked.

"I just do. I feel it."

He licked his lips, his posture tense. "Since when?"

"Since I woke up this morning."

He didn't like that, a frown folding over his face. "I can help you with your alpha. Talk to him with you. You don't have to—"

"You think I'm pretending you're my mate so I can get out of going off with the other wolf pack?" I gasped. My voice was shrill and harsh.

"Aren't you?" he threw back. His expression was open and understanding, which was the only reason I didn't kill him. Instead, I leaned forward and shoved him, hard.

"No!"

"No?" he asked, his tone completely different. "You think…you really think I'm your mate."

"I know you are," I said hotly.

I was mad now, indignant, but he cut right through when a look of utter delight unfurled over his features.

"I'm your mate?"

"That's what I said, isn't it?" I was holding onto my pique by the skin of my fingers, and I lost grip on it entirely when he leaned forward to hug me then stopped himself, eyes going to my damaged ankle. Fuck that. I got my legs under me—*God,* that hurt—and burrowed myself into his side.

"You're sure?" he mumbled into my hair. "You're absolutely sure?"

I pulled back enough so that I could look into his eyes, our faces just inches apart. "I am sure," I said. "Positive. Certain. Utterly convinced. Completely without doubt."

He looked lost for words. "Fuck, Janna!"

"Yes," I said. "We should."

Well, that shocked him out of his little daze. His eyes sharpened on me with laser-focus.

"Come again?" he asked.

"I haven't come once yet," I said, shooting for humor to hide the fact that I was actually pretty nervous.

"Janna," he said warningly.

"Kevin," I threw back.

His was more impressive, which impressed me. He was a worthy mate, my wolf and I were in no doubt about that, but I hadn't had much opportunity to see that he could do manly growly. I liked it.

"You want to—" he trailed off, back to looking uncomfortable.

"Fuck?" I supplied helpfully.

"Be intimate," he finished, giving me that slightly stern look again. Oooh. I might have been anxious, but I was also ramped up, the wolf inside me, having decided on a mate, wanting to get to the claiming and fast.

"If be intimate means fuck, then yes."

"Did your father ever spank you?" Kevin asked, rolling his eyes at me.

Everything in me went still at that. "Do you want to?"

"I never thought I was the spanking kind, but I might be reconsidering." His hand went to my thigh, stroking down toward my damaged ankle. "You're hurt," he reminded me.

"It's fine."

"I don't want to hurt you more."

"You won't," I promised.

"Hmmm," he reached out and stroked a strand away from my face, the backs of his fingers tickling my cheek. Those fingers trailed down to the curve between my neck and shoulders, leaving little sparks in their wake. It was blissful.

"I'm a virgin," I blurted. Well, shit. I was just chucking things out all over the place today.

Kevin took it in his stride, though. He ran his hand down my arm until he could take my hand. "Then we should take things slow," he told me.

"We can go slow," I agreed. "We can take hours if you want to."

"Janna, that isn't what I meant."

"But it's what I meant." I grinned at him winningly. Then I got a little more serious. "Kevin, maybe vampires do it the human way, dating and shit, but we shifters are a little simpler. Find a mate, mate a mate. I found you, which only leaves…"

He didn't look convinced. "I don't want to rush you."

"You're not. I chose you. I trust you, and I want you." I couldn't put it more simply that than. "And my wolf is getting antsy, so if you keep stalling, you might find yourself getting pounced."

I wasn't kidding. My body was primed to get to business, my breasts feeling sensitive and between my legs hot and slick. Just his simple hold on my hand, thumb stroking the soft skin of my inner wrist, was setting my nerve endings alight.

A devilish light came into his eyes. "Pounced, huh?"

I wasn't quite sure what happened next, whether I did indeed pounce or whether he moved with those lightning-fast reflexes, but the next thing I knew, he was leaning back against the wall on the bed, and I was straddling him. My ankle gave a sharp twinge, but I ignored it. Now that Kevin was getting with the programme, I didn't want to give him any reason to stop. His hands were moving on me, shifting from my waist up my sides, then dropping down to stop just short of my ass. There was just one problem.

"We're wearing too many clothes," I protested.

"No, we aren't," he disagreed. "We're taking things slow. First, I want to kiss you."

Oh. All right, then.

I bent down eagerly. Truth be told, I didn't have any more experience with kissing than I did with fucking, but I figured mouth to mouth was a good place to start. Kevin halted me with a hand on my jaw, though, arresting my progress and then drawing me in slowly, capturing my bottom lip and sucking on it lightly, then changing the angle so he could kiss me deeper, his tongue sliding in to tease the top of mine before retreating again. Drawing back, changing the angle, going deep once more.

When he finally pulled back, I was breathless. I clung to him, slightly dizzy.

"That was a good first kiss," I informed him.

A quick grin that revealed just a flash of those razor-sharp incisors that I hadn't felt at all when he'd been kissing me. "Wait until I kiss you other places."

He punctuated his statement by cupping my right breast and swiping his thumb over my nipple. I gasped as lightning shot down toward my clit, ground against him without even realizing I was doing it.

"You like that idea," he murmured.

"I do."

"Then let's divest you of some of these clothes."

He slipped my shirt off over my head, throwing it onto the floor while I attacked my bra clasp. I chucked my bra on top, catching sight of the mud and grass stains that dotted the creamy-white fabric. That probably covered my face. And my hair, what did that look like?

I was just about to get myself into a full-blown tizzy when Kevin leaned down and drew my nipple into his mouth, lathing it with his tongue then nipping it with his teeth.

Fuck my hair.

I gripped his shoulders, arching my back slightly, giving a satisfied little moan when his left hand crept up and covered my neglected breast, fingers plucking and rolling. I tilted my head back, my breath speeding up, hips rocking against his crotch. I could feel him there, hard against me. I was affecting him as much as he was me.

He teased me for what felt like an age, alternating between breasts with his mouth, then abandoning them to his fingers while he kissed his way up to my neck, my jaw, taking my mouth and taunting my tongue with quick little flicks before working his way back down. I was putty in his hands, a needy mess, my fingers like claws, kneading at his chest and shoulders, tugging at his shirt in frustration until I felt it rip.

"More," I demanded. My hands went down to his waist, fumbling at the clasp of his trousers. I didn't get far, his hands capturing mine almost immediately.

"Slow," he reminded me.

"This is too slow," I complained. "I want—"

I ground hard against him to show exactly what I did want, and he gave a little shudder. Hands grabbed my waist and then I was on my back on the bed, Kevin looming over me, eyes burning into mine.

"Behave and I'll reward you," he said.

Hmmm. I definitely wanted to be rewarded. I gave him my best *I'm a good girl* look, and he chuckled, shaking his head in amusement. I didn't mind that he was laughing at me, though, because his fingers were already unsnapping my jeans, slipping them down my legs along with my underwear. Getting the torn jean leg over my ankle was a little dicey, but then I was naked, spread out beneath him. He ran his hands up and down the outside of my legs then placed them on either side of his hips. He reached up and tugged his shirt off, revealing pale skin and tight muscles. His chest was hairless, but there was a little trail running down from his belly button and disappearing into his trousers.

I wanted to follow that trail, see what treasure lay at its end, but Kevin distracted me, placing a soft kiss on the inside on my knee then swirling his tongue there. He licked and kissed his way to my centre, settling between my thighs. I watched him, excited and just a little apprehensive. When he spread my pussy with his fingers, though, and licked right up the centre of me, that apprehension melted away, replaced by a serious desire for him to do that again, now.

"More," I demanded, tilting my pelvis up toward him.

Contrary vampire that he was, he ignored me, moving to the other knee and giving it the same treatment, making his way back to my core even more slowly this time.

"More?" he asked, putting his fingers where his tongue had been and sliding it through my wetness before finding my clit and circling it with aching gentleness. "Here?"

"Uhuh," I panted, reduced to wriggling now as I strove to get a firmer touch. "There."

"Your wish is my command."

He took his finger away and pressed the flat of his tongue against my clit, rubbing against it with hard pressure that had me arching at my back and grabbing my breasts, my fingers pinching at my nipples.

"Like that," I gasped. "Just like that."

He chuckled, shifted to circling with his tongue then lashing at me.

"Oooh, no, I've changed my mind, this is better. Maybe. Both, do both."

I sounded like a babbling idiot, but every lick, every swipe of his tongue was like a whip of flame against my nerve endings.

He did as I asked, playing with my clit, teasing it, while his finger circled my hole, spreading my wetness around. Slowly, agonizingly slowly, he started sinking that finger in and out. To the first knuckle, and retreat. A little more, and retreat. All the way in, the tip of his finger pressing lightly on my g-spot and making the pleasure in my clit spiral. Then out again.

Gently, gently, he pressed forward with two fingers.

"It's ok," I panted. "You don't have to go so slow. I have...a toy that I use."

I'd snuck into town and bought myself a dildo, one of those lifelike ones. It didn't do anything fancy like vibrate—because shifter hearing—but it did the job. I had to admit, it didn't do the job anywhere near as well as just two of Kevin's fingers, sliding back and forth, scissoring to stretch me and then crooking to play against my g-spot.

"You deserve time and patience," Kevin told me, shifting his head to nuzzle my thigh. "You deserve gentleness."

"Do I deserve to come?" I asked, half plea, half pointed.

He smirked at me, fingers sliding out to go back to my clit.

"I don't know, do you?" He ran the tips of both fingers, slick with me, around and around in tight circles, then he shocked me breathless by spanking my pussy one, two, three times.

I felt the sting briefly, then my clit bloomed in reaction, throbbing and twitching. Demanding. Kevin bent his head once more, fixing his mouth over it and sucking hard, and at the same time, thrusting two fingers back inside me with much less gentleness that he'd used before.

I screamed.

The orgasm ripped through me with such force that I arched like a bow, every muscle tense. It was too much, and I tried to jerk away, but Kevin held me fast, making me ride it out, stroking me through the aftershocks with the flat of his tongue. When he finally released me, pulling back and kissing my lower stomach, I collapsed onto the bed like a limp noodle.

"I...wow."

The grin on his face was obscenely smug, but he'd earned it.

"A moment," he murmured, then he used that crazy vampire speed to lever himself up off the bed and strip out of his trousers and boxers. He was back with me on the bed, crawling up between my thighs, before I'd had the chance to lever myself up onto one elbow.

"You're very fast," I commented.

"I'm motivated."

I was, too. Finally, I was getting to see his cock, and it also didn't disappoint. Erect and ready, it seemed almost to be reaching toward me. It was pale as the rest of him, except the head, which was a deep red, the slit at the top shining slightly.

I stretched out a hand, looking forward to seeing what it would feel like in my hand, seeing whether I could make him moan and twitch and shudder like he had me, but he grabbed at my fingers and pressed me back down, nestling both our hands on the covers up by my head. I frowned at him, confused and a little hurt.

"You don't want me to touch you?" I asked.

"Yes," he promised, "Oh God, yes. But if you put your hand on me right now, I'll detonate." A pause while he gazed into my eyes, holding me captive with his intensity. "And I want to claim my mate."

Ooooh. Ok, then.

"Next time?"

"Next time you can play as much as you want, I swear it."

I expected him to get on with it, to slide into me, but he held himself above me, our hands clasped together, his other hand pressed to my cheek, and he kissed me. Softly, gently, then deeper. He drew my tongue into his mouth and duelled with it, then pressed back. He filled my senses, our breaths mingling, my every thought focused on the kiss.

When his hand took hold of my thigh and hitched it wide so that he could press into me, I accepted him willingly. I was hot and wet and ready, and he glided in right to the hilt. He held me there for a moment, our pelvises pressed tightly together, and allowed me to get used to the feeling of being filled by him, being so connected to him. Then, finally, he began to move.

In and out, grinding against me, building a rhythm. Every thrust pressed on my g-spot, every grind pressed against my clit. The whole time he kept his lips pressed to mine, the kisses becoming clumsy and more desperate as his speed picked up and we raced toward climax. I was right there, on the precipice, the pleasure building and building in intensity.

"Oh fuck!" I gasped, yanking my head away for a moment to breathe. "I'm going to come again!"

"Come for me," Kevin murmured, dropping light kisses along my jaw, sliding his tongue into my ear. "Come around my cock, let me feel you squeezing me."

Oh, bloody hell. Dirty talk.

It was too much. I felt my orgasm catch and then explode, ripping through me like a fireball. Kevin captured my mouth as it hit, stopping me from crying out, forcing me to contain it within me. Every pump of his hips, every thrust of his cock, kept it rolling on and on. My nails dug into Kevin's hand where we were clasped together, my other hand grabbing at his hip, clinging on as he started moving faster, spearing into me with short, sharp jabs, his rhythm lost as he found his own release. He stopped kissing me, burying his face into my neck as he jerked and trembled. Then he collapsed, dropping his full weight onto me. It was comforting, and his coolness was a balm to my overheated skin.

"I wondered if you were going to bite me at the end," I murmured, hand stroking up and down his back. When his mouth had pressed against my neck, I had almost expected it. Because…vampire.

"Vampires can't digest shifter blood," he told me.

"I can't digest cheesecake," I replied. "Doesn't stop me from eating it."

He chucked, the release of breath ticklish against my clavicle, then lifted up to look at me.

"I would never have done that without talking with you about it beforehand," he promised me. "It is a very intimate act with my kind, and I would love to share that with you one day, but only if you're comfortable."

"All right," I agreed, because while I was curious, I also had a healthy respect for the veins in my neck and I had to admit the whole piercing them with razor sharp teeth idea was kind of scary.

"Come here," Kevin said, and he rearranged us so that he was lying on the bed and I was draped halfway across his body, my head tucked into his chest.

We lay that way for a long time afterward, a tangle of limbs on the single bed. Every so often Kevin's grip would tighten on me inexplicably, then I'd feel him purposefully loosen his muscles, one by one.

"Are you all right?" I asked, after the third of fourth time.

"I…yeah. Sorry." He loosened his hold immediately. "I just…I can't believe this is happening. I can't believe that you're mine."

Warmth suffused my entire body at his words. I lifted my head up so that I look at his face. The eyes that stared back at me were nothing short of adoring.

No one had ever looked at me like that my entire life.

"You better get used to it," I said. "Mates are forever, you're stuck with me."

"It might be short-lived," he told me. I felt my blood run cold in my veins until I saw the humor in his eyes. "I still have to ask your father for your hand. I imagine it's a little trickier when the father is an alpha shifter."

"You don't have to do that," I said. "We're mated, there's nothing he can do."

"Still," Kevin replied. "I will ask. I would like his permission. His approval, even."

"Good luck getting that," I muttered. "I've never managed it."

Kevin chuckled softly and leaned over to kiss the tip of my nose.

"I have won you," he said. "I dare aim for anything now."

Well, that was romantic.

"All right," I said, "But there's no rush. It's traditional for newly mated couples to elope for a honeymoon for two, three, four…years."

"Are you ashamed to take me to your pack as your mate?" Kevin asked, his face troubled.

"No," I replied, shaking my head emphatically. "No, that's not it. I'm just not in any rush to go back and have to deal with everything." I waved my hand in a circle in the air, *everything* encompassing the other pack, my running away. The truckers, the pit. And mating a vampire. It was quite the list, and all achieved in the last twenty-four hours.

"The sooner we confront it, the sooner it is over," Kevin countered.

He slid his arm out from underneath me and climbed off the bed, turning to reach out a hand to assist me. I sat up, but that was as far as I went. I folded my arms across my chest, tucking my hands out of the way.

"Uh uh. I don't want any part of this foolishness."

Unfortunately, Kevin's vampire strength was easily a match for mine. He reached out and snagged my wrist, pulling me off the bed and toward my doom.

Epilogue

The whole glade was strung with fairy lights, illuminating the scene for the few who didn't have preternatural eyesight. Autumn had fully taken hold and the ground was a carpet of leaves in brown, russet and gold, and peeking through the half-stripped branches of the trees was a glorious full moon.

Callum stood in front of his assigned seat, just off the central aisle, about four rows back from where an alter had been created out of an arbor that Fran had festooned with so many flowers, the pretty wrought iron framework had all but disappeared. He was uncomfortable as fuck, shoe-horned into a black suit, a tie choking his neck.

"Why the fuck are we here again?" he hissed to Gregor, who was standing beside him and also dressed up like an idiot.

"I'm here because I was told I had to be," Gregor muttered back, throwing an unhappy glance down at his mate, Bea, standing on his other side, her hand curled around his bicep, an expression of delight on her face.

"This is ridiculous," Callum went on. "We're shifters. We mate, we don't get *married*."

Gregor shrugged. "It's what Janna wants. Was important to her vamp or some shit, I don't know."

A vampire. A freaking *vampire*, that's who stood up by the alter, waiting for his bride, his Master by his side. Callum still couldn't believe Logan was allowing it. When the music started and they all sat down, the stick furniture creaking unhappily under Callum's weight, he turned to catch sight of his packmate, gliding toward her husband-to-be in a tight-fitting cream dress that exposed her throat but accentuated all of her curves. The look on her face was utterly radiant, the smile she aimed at the vamp, at Kevin, beatific. Callum couldn't help it, he glanced down at Anna, who had the same woman-at-weddings expression on her face that Bea was sporting, and looked at her slightly rounded stomach, barely noticeable under the flowing gown she was wearing. He'd no idea if it was a boy of a girl, but if he had a daughter and she ever looked at a man like that, he'd…well he'd kill him. But if that didn't work, he'd have to give his blessing, like Logan had done.

Even if it was to a damned bloodsucker.

The ceremony was mercifully short, and they didn't make Callum stand up to sing or any shit like that, which was a blessing. The actual blessing, performed by a beautiful, elegant looking vampire Bea whispered to them was called Evangeline, made Anna cry, and then it was the vows. Callum couldn't hear a word the male said, Kevin tucking his head and fumbling over a bit of paper, but whatever it was, it made Janna beam. Her own responses were simple, spoken clearly in a low voice, swearing to love and honor her husband.

"I notice she's not promising to obey," he whispered to Gregor, earning him a sharp jab in the ribs from Anna.

A moment later, it was the big kiss, Kevin surprising the hell out of Callum by dramatically grabbing his mate-bride and draping her over his arm, planting a kiss on the exposed column of her neck. She laughed, the sound ringing out across the clearing, and then wrapped a foot around his ankle, spinning him and taking him to the ground, dirt and leaves and all in her fancy dress, and kissing the hell out of him.

Afterward, the happy couple were surrounded by well-wishers...and Fran, who picked bits of leaf out of Janna's hair and brushed dirt from the clothes of both the bride and groom, her face somehow managing to convey disapproval and satisfaction in the same expression. Callum took the opportunity to sidle up to Logan, who'd just finished a brief conversation with the master, Hunter, and was momentarily standing alone.

"So, she's off your hands," he said to his alpha.

"Something like that," Logan replied, his eyes on Janna, who was batting Fran away as her mother tried to adjust the front of her dress.

"Never imagined her mating a vampire."

"I never imagined you mating a human," Logan shot back.

"Anna changed," Callum replied defensively.

"Bea didn't, is she any less a mate?"

Callum didn't have anything to say back to that. He wouldn't say anything against Bea, and not just because Gregor would rearrange his teeth for him if he did.

"Still," he muttered, "a vampire!"

Logan just shrugged with the look of a man who had accepted his fate. "He makes her happy, that's all I wanted. And you know," a flash of a grin. "Vampires can be useful. I just had a very interesting chat with Hunter about some contracts he's got coming up. This could be a lucrative partnership."

"Times are changing," Callum mused. Then his gaze narrowed on an odd-looking couple, a cheerful, rounded little woman and a man who looked like he should be lazing in a chaise while concubines saw to his every need. "Is that…a demon?"

"That is a demon," Logan agreed, somehow not sounding horrified by the very idea. "Like you said, times are changing."

About the Author

Charli Mac writes Erotic Romance, often with a Fantasy or Science-Fiction twist. Originally from Scotland – yes, she still has the accent – she now lives in sunny Colorado where she dreams of meeting a hot Alpha werewolf hiking in the Rocky mountains. No, it hasn't happened yet. She also likes running and wine and cake.

Website: www.charlimacwrites.com

Twitter: @charlimac2

More Great Books
From Deep Desires Press

Prey
Britt Collins

Most people learn after the first mistake, two at the most. It took Lucas Ford three and now it might cost him his life.

Mistake number 1:

At eighteen years old he saw the unthinkable, a vampire. She told him her name is Victoria. He followed her through the woods and enviously watched as she drank from another. He fell in love.

Mistake number 2:

He told other people what he saw. From that moment on Lucas was labeled as crazy. After years of therapy and joining the army he was cured and beautiful, exotic Victoria—and his love for her—it all became a fading dream.

Mistake number 3:

He let twenty years pass, thinking she was a figment of his imagination. Now she's here and very real and needs his help.

Vampires are under attack by a new kind of predator. They are no longer at the top of the food chain. Lucas is determined to find this twisted executioner before Victoria becomes the latest victim.

He's more than willing to lose his life for her.

Wolf Heart
Dorian Flynn

It's been years since Elias has seen his childhood rival and friend Julian. The last time they were together, Elias kissed him, sending Julian running away. And by morning, he was gone. Since then, Elias has kept his secret close to his chest, hoping Julian would do the same.

But Julian is back now, and simultaneously a string of mysterious animal attacks have struck the town, rousing superstitions about a Beast that swept through before Elias was even born. A Beast that was only stopped by Elias's grandmother.

Elias may have been keeping his own secret, but as he and Julian reconnect, what secrets will he discover about Julian's family...or his own?

www.ingramcontent.com/pod-product-compliance
Lightning Source LLC
Chambersburg PA
CBHW020538020726
47494CB00006B/1824